DIFFICULT

BRIANNE GILLEN

This is a work of fiction. Names, characters, places, and incidents either are the product of the author's imagination or are used fictitiously. Any resemblance to actual persons, living or dead, events, or locales is entirely coincidental.

Difficult: Phoenix Pictures, Book 1

Copyright © 2021 by Brianne Gillen

All rights reserved. No part of this book may be reproduced in any form or by any electronic or mechanical means, including information storage and retrieval systems, without written permission from the author, except for the use of brief quotations in a book review.

Edited by: Three Point Author Services LLC

Cover Design by: www.DaybedBooks.com

Print ISBN: 978-1-7372403-0-3

E-book ISBN: 978-1-7372403-1-0

Published by Brianne Gillen

www.briannegillen.com

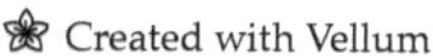 Created with Vellum

*To my mom, Lynn,
who showed me how to be a storyteller.
I love you. I miss you.
And I am so incredibly proud to be your daughter.*

The Latest from Hollywood!
—November 1937
Quite the racket emerging from Neptune Pictures lately! Rumor has it the brunette stunner they were counting on to be their new Siren has turned out to be quite the Sea-Witch instead. Despite the whispers of her already being a diva on day one, we graciously gave her the benefit of the doubt. But it seems we were too merciful. Word comes from the set of her new picture—only her second, if you can believe it!—that she unleashed what could only be called a Temper Tsunami on everyone present. We have no idea what could have caused such an eruption, but really, is there ever an excuse for that kind of behavior? Looks like studio head Arthur Ronson might be regretting his decision to sign this troublesome beauty already...

Hollywood Happenings
—June 1940
Big change-up in Contract-land today! The fine folks at Neptune Pictures are finally unburdening themselves of their resident Difficile Dish, passing her contract across town to Parkmoor Studios. Talk of her outrageous behavior on set has become the stuff of Tinseltown legend, so it's likely for the best that she's moving on. We will admit, her talent is undeniable. Perhaps her new studio will have better luck taming this Shirley Temper into more of a Norma Sheer-Dream. Let's raise a glass to Parkmoor— they've certainly got their work cut out for them!

Chapter One

Hollywood, California
1947

*L*ois Ashford perched on her leaning board, in an effort not to wrinkle her costume, while she scanned the pages of *Variety* for any hint of the news she'd been awaiting practically since her arrival in Hollywood. She didn't know quite why she tormented herself day after day with the same fruitless search, but it had become a ritual. As frustrating as it was, she still harbored her faint hope, buried deep, that someday she would be vindicated, that karma would eventually catch up to that bastard Ronson and he'd be forced out of his beloved Neptune Pictures. Preferably in the most humiliating scandal Hollywood had ever known.

Today was apparently not that day.

Lois forcefully flipped another page while she waited to be called for her next take. As the crew worked to reposition the camera for the next angle, John Whittacre, the director, eyed Lois warily, as if waiting for her to explode at any minute.

Here we go again.

There were only a few days left of shooting on this picture, and Lois had been expending more effort than usual to behave. Despite that, every time there was a pause, or a reset, or even if someone sneezed—literally sneezed—Whittacre's whole body tensed up and he started to look like some poor paralyzed rabbit, eyes darting frantically.

Lois rolled her eyes. Hard.

Her reserves of good behavior were running out, and fast.

She'd been in this business for nearly a decade, had made more than enough films to know how the process worked. Each shoot required multiple takes, from multiple camera angles, with loads of equipment that needed to be moved in between. It meant a fair amount of lounging time for her as an actor. But these men were professionals. They worked hard and knew what they were doing. Did Whittacre honestly think she couldn't recognize that, and would object to a perfectly normal part of the process? She wasn't a monster.

Except that she was—according to anyone who "mattered," which amounted to far too many people in this business.

One of the studio pages—the real miracle workers who kept the studios from imploding—tentatively approached Lois's corner of the soundstage.

"Um, Miss Ashford?" the young man in the maroon jacket breathed.

She looked up, arching a perfectly groomed eyebrow.

The page swallowed audibly. "Right. Um. I have a message for you. From Mr. Bartholomew." He looked positively terrified.

To be fair, Lois could—and often did—throw quite an impressive diva tantrum. If the gossip rags were to be believed—and judging by her charming director's nervous face over the last several weeks, they were—she was unrivaled in this town.

Not that she had ever intended to be this way.

But ten years ago, fresh off the train to Hollywood, Lois had been hired at her first studio, Neptune Pictures. It had felt too good to be true…because it was. She'd been stopped in her tracks practically before she could even prove herself.

All because she had said one word, one of the simplest, clearest words anyone could ever say. So simple and universal that it's the same in multiple languages.

No.

That one word had derailed everything.

Not that she wouldn't say it again. She had absolutely no regrets about saying it. It was exactly the right thing to do, and there was no way in hell her dream would mean anything to her if she had compromised in order to achieve it. But that only made her situation even more frustrating, since everyone who had seen her screen tests could see she had something special. In no time at all, what she had thought was a simple "no" had been transformed into another word—an unmistakable label, never to be shaken off.

Difficult.

Lois's fury was incandescent. But that fury had nowhere to go —she was stuck, under contract, and completely powerless to change anything. All because of one jackass studio executive.

So she had made a decision, done what little she could to wrest back just a bit of control. If they were so determined to label her as difficult, Lois Ashford might as well make the most of it, define the kind of diva she would be. And at the very least, she gained an outlet for all that pent-up rage.

Over the years, she had turned in some of her finest performances when the cameras weren't rolling, if she did say so herself.

She realized that an almost painfully awkward silence was ensuing with the page, and thought it best to finally intervene.

"Are you going to tell me the message?"

"Oh. Right. Yes. Of course." The poor man really was quite flustered. "He asked to see you in his office as soon as you're finished on set." He blinked furiously. "Please. Thank you."

He turned to flee the scene, and Lois took pity on him.

"Young man?"

He whipped around, eyes wide.

She flashed a dazzling smile, rarely seen around these parts. "Thank you for the message."

"Oh!" His cheeks blushed a deeper crimson than his jacket. "Of course. You're welcome, Miss Ashford." He gave her a small smile and hurried away.

Lois chuckled to herself as she turned back to her magazine. But then the young page's words sunk in.

What does Barty want? If he's summoned me from set, it's either really good, or really bad...

She inwardly snorted. When had it *ever* been something really good?

With filming wrapping up, she was due to find out her next role any day now. And she had her eye on a juicy one. Hence the good behavior of late. It was damn time she finally got her due.

As her thoughts swirled, Lois glanced up and found the director looking in her direction once again. This time, there was something more than simple trepidation in his gaze, but it took her a minute to put her finger on it. Then it dawned—disappointment. He actually looked disappointed. What did he expect? Had he actually wanted to see her rip that poor page's head off, as if she were some sideshow, here for his entertainment?

Growing awareness of the sudden and potent frost radiating toward him caused Whittacre's gaze to snap back up.

"Is there a problem, Mr. Whittacre?" Lois asked venomously.

He blanched. "No. No problem at all, Miss Ashford." He at least acted somewhat abashed. "We'll be ready for you shortly."

"Excellent."

A COUPLE OF HOURS LATER, the day's takes finished and her costume hung back up in its place, Lois made her way toward Joe Bartholomew's office. As if by magic, another page had shown up at her trailer the minute they wrapped, offering her a ride to the meeting, but she turned it down, preferring to walk. After so many hours under the hot lights, she wanted some fresh air on her face. And it would give her a few extra minutes to think.

She mentally crossed her fingers. The studio was readying to adapt one of the most popular novels of the past year, an intense drama called *Rue the Day*, and the leading female part was exactly the type of role she'd always wanted to play. The type of role she never got…because of her notoriety.

As reluctant as she was to admit it, she desperately wanted this one. Not only for the acting challenge, but because of the leverage it would give her when her contract came up for renewal.

Her nerves warred with a sense of cautious optimism. It had actually been a while since the last time she'd been "summoned" —and she'd underestimated how much relief that would bring. She'd rather been enjoying the reprieve of late, as her long reign as the studio's biggest problem had recently been toppled by all-around golden boy Nick Bradley.

The handsome matinee idol had come to the studio direct from Broadway several years earlier, quickly made a name for himself as a reliable dramatic moneymaker, and easily achieved the highly coveted reputation of being a man female audiences wanted and male audiences wanted to be. And as if that wasn't enough, he had then enlisted in the Army and come back from the war an actual hero.

Needless to say, Lois had never been cast in a film with him. No way would the studio risk ticking off one of their best and brightest by pairing him with the Difficult One.

Then he had gone and ruined it all.

The fool had gotten himself arrested for an incident involving marijuana. Lois had been stunned, along with all of Hollywood, when she picked up the paper one morning and saw the story splashed across the front page. The studio had bailed him out and clamped a lid on the press, though not quickly enough. God knew how they had actually done it, but the charges were dropped and Bradley had gone into a hiding of sorts.

But the damage had been done. Almost a month later, the columns still buzzed about the golden boy-war hero's fall from grace. Lois shook her head, thinking of the story she'd seen only this morning in *Variety*.

To be honest, Lois had some questions herself. After years on the blacklist with no way off, she couldn't comprehend how an actor who actually had power and a robust career could behave so carelessly. Was he really nothing more than a pretty face, too stupid to know how not to get caught? Or did some truth exist to what everyone said about war being hell, and he simply couldn't help himself? From everything she'd heard, he was one of the rare nice ones in this business. She supposed it was impossible to ever know what existed behind someone else's scenes.

But one thing she did know—her boundless gratitude to Nick Bradley for stealing the negative attention. It couldn't last forever, but she'd enjoy it while it lasted.

Lois arrived at Bartholomew's office and found his long-suffering secretary at her desk, looking frazzled as usual.

"Hello, Jenny," she greeted her. "It seems my presence has been requested."

Jenny gave her a sympathetic look. Lois had always liked the woman.

"I'm afraid so," Jenny said. "You're the first one here, but you can go on in."

First one? Oh, great, what does that *mean?*

Lois knocked quickly but didn't hesitate before opening the door. "Well, Barty? You rang?" She leaned on the doorknob and tried to look as bored as possible.

Barty remained seated, waving her to sit in front of his desk. "I did," he replied. "Come in, Miss Ashford."

When he didn't immediately say more, Lois lowered herself into the chair, weighing her options for a moment before plunging in. "So, I'm assuming this meeting has something to do with my next assignment?"

"It does."

"Let me guess, you're giving me the Jules Marshall adaptation." *What the hell, might as well own that conceit. Diva, and all that.* "I would be perfect for it, after all."

As she watched Bartholomew visibly swallow, she knew. Should have known. Anger bubbled up in the pit of her stomach, more at herself than anyone. *This is what happens when you let hope in, damn it.*

"While you would be great for it, Miss Ashford," Bartholomew began, "I'm afraid the studio's decided to go in another direction for that role. We have something else in mind for you instead."

Lois crossed her arms over her chest and spoke through gritted teeth. "I've kept a lid on it, Barty. There hasn't been one single incident on this film."

"I know." He looked at her pleadingly. "I *know*. It's just that… they've given it to Robertson to helm and…he wants someone else."

"He's brand-new to this studio!" *Shit.* She hadn't expected to raise her voice so soon into this meeting.

"Yes, he is. But he brings with him a lot of clout. And…"

"And he's heard all about me." At Bartholomew's nod, she seethed. "Wonderful. Just wonderful."

"Your reputation precedes you, and you know it. One picture where you behave isn't exactly going to make up for everything that's gone before it." He took a breath. "And with your contract up soon…"

Her head snapped up. "And with my contract up soon, I could use a film like this under my belt. You know that, Barty."

"I do, which is why—"

A knock interrupted him, followed by the slow, cautious whine of the door's hinges.

"Ah, come in. I've been expecting you," Barty greeted the new visitor.

Lois firmly clamped a lid back on her control as she turned to see what more she'd have to endure—and her eyes went wide.

It was the reefer-happy golden boy himself, Nick Bradley.

Surprise flitted across his features, but he recovered quickly and strode toward her.

"Miss Ashford, a pleasure to finally meet you," Nick said, offering his hand.

"Mr. Bradley," she replied, accepting his handshake. Despite her years of practice, it was a massive challenge to hide her own surprise. Along with a few other unexpected reactions.

His handshake was warm and firm, not one of those limp-fish attempts that most men seemed to think women deserved. And quite an intriguing storm roiled in his eyes, several emotions seemingly fighting for dominance—defiance, wariness, confidence, embarrassment, and—*was it possible?*—respect.

And dear god, he was handsome up close. She'd seen all the tricks used in this business, so she knew how rare it was for the real thing to live up to the projected image. But in this case, the screen did not actually do him justice. Chiseled jaw, brown hair with just a hint of auburn sparked by the late afternoon sun coming in the window, tiny flecks of gold and green trying to break through the blue sea of his eyes.

Damn. Pull yourself together, Ashford. Never *with coworkers, remember?*

Over the years, she'd developed an impressive and ever-evolving list of Rules for Being Difficult, and that one in particular consistently resided right at the top. Nothing good ever came of trusting the men in this business. No matter how blindingly good-looking they might be. *Especially* then.

She blinked and gathered herself up to her full height.

"Please, have a seat, Mr. Bradley," Bartholomew said, with impeccable timing for once.

Her control had already slipped once with Barty, and she needed to keep her wits about her, be prepared for whatever was coming next. Not go all mushy just because Nick Bradley happened to be more handsome up close than she would have expected. And seemed to actually look at her without fear or disdain. He had "too good to be true" written all over him.

As they settled into their seats, Bartholomew cleared his throat, almost nervously. "So, I'm sure you're wondering why I've asked you both here this afternoon."

That fresh tone of hesitancy coloring his voice made Lois instantly more wary. *What was he about to say before Nick came in?* She risked a glance at Nick, and suddenly everything clicked into place. His newfound reputation. Her summons, and the "something else" they had for her. Bartholomew's reluctance.

She looked back to the producer, eyes narrowing.

"Oh, I think I might be able to venture a guess," she seethed sweetly. "I'm not getting the Marshall film in part because you finally want to pair the two of us on-screen, don't you?"

"Well, yes," Bartholomew said, "as a matter of fact, we do. We think the timing is just right actually."

Lois couldn't help rolling her eyes. They were getting quite the exercise today. She looked at Nick again, and a flush of anger began at the tips of her ears.

"Yes, I suppose the timing is quite perfect, isn't it? Your golden boy has had such a spectacular fuck-up that naturally the best punishment you can devise to put him in his place is to partner him with the studio's resident bitch and box office poison. Do I have it correct?"

Chapter Two

Tinseltown Trappings
It's been a whole month since a certain dreamboat traded in his wholesome hero act for the chance to misbehave, and we're still not over the transformation! From the way his studio's been keeping him under lock & key, it seems they're not either. But rumor has it they're finally ready to let Dreamy & Dangerous out of the dog house… Or are they?

*N*ick Bradley knew Bartholomew had been at the studio for years, had probably seen and heard everything, so the redness quickly rising up the producer's throat surprised him. Nick had to hand it to Lois, she didn't mince words. He'd had an inkling about the reason for this meeting, but hadn't been completely certain until he'd walked in to see her sitting there, all poise and confident veneer.

He felt badly about dragging her into his mess, especially with the studio so willing to use her as some kind of pawn in his punishment. Because that was clearly what they were doing. Did they think she wouldn't see through their plan and make a fuss, or did they simply not care? Nick guessed it was the latter.

Lois Ashford was a force of nature, as anyone who'd seen even one of her pictures could attest. And he had seen plenty more than just one. As a matter of fact, the film where she played a turn-of-the-century casino maven, he'd seen three times—not that he was likely to admit that to her. Knowing what he knew of the studio system and what it could do to people, he'd always wondered just how much of her reputation as a diva she'd really earned. So many times at studio parties over the years, he'd wanted to approach her, see for himself what she was like, but the whispers, the rumors, the warnings always swirled. A star of his "caliber" couldn't be seen fraternizing with the studio pariah. And so he'd kept his distance.

Until today, when he'd been practically knocked off his feet the minute he faced her.

Despite the surprise she couldn't quite conceal upon seeing him, Lois had taken his hand and looked at him unflinchingly—and analytically—and a jolt ran up his arm and right into his soul. He'd been prepared for her beauty, well-acquainted with how stunning she was—glossy jet-black hair that fell in sculpted waves around her face and shoulders, the curves of her body accentuated by her regal posture and bearing. She really did look like she had been made for the cinema.

No, what had completely and utterly leveled him were her eyes. A dark emerald green, unlike any he'd ever seen. He had the impression those eyes would see right through to the core of him if he let her look long enough. It both intoxicated and terrified him at the same time.

But he couldn't spend time thinking too hard about either feeling, because Bartholomew had completely botched the reveal of the studio's plan. Lois's scorn filled the room in palpable waves. Incredibly justified waves. A part of him rather hoped he'd get to see her unleash one of her infamous diva episodes right then and there.

"Really, Miss Ashford," Bartholomew finally managed, simultaneously strangled and evasive, "that kind of language is hardly ladylike."

Even from several feet away, Nick could feel the anger vibrating off of her. He felt angry himself on her behalf. *That* was what Bartholomew chose to seize on?

Nick couldn't manage to control the snort that escaped him. "Oh, please. There's hardly a soul on this lot who deigns to view Miss Ashford as a lady, so why on earth should she be expected to act like one? Who are any of us to stop her from making a sailor blush if she so chooses?"

Lois stared at him with what looked like disbelief, as if her guard momentarily dropped along with her jaw.

Oh, god, I actually said that aloud, didn't I?

"Really, Mr. Bradley," Bartholomew said. "I hardly think you're in a position—"

Lois recovered quickly and interrupted. "I wasn't aware I needed permission of any kind, Mr. Bradley," she replied, a growing hint of amusement warring with the coldness in her eyes. "But thank you, nonetheless."

"My apologies," Nick smirked, eyes still on Lois. "I meant no offense… And you're quite welcome."

And now I'm flirting with her? Geez, this is off to a great start. Get it together.

Bartholomew cleared his throat, and the green iced over again as Lois turned back to him.

"May we please get back to the matter at hand?" Bartholomew asked.

"Right, the meting out of Mr. Bradley's punishment," she said acidly.

Bartholomew leveled an exasperated glance at her, and she actually softened slightly.

"Look, Barty," she began, "I know you've had my back more than most around here, but please don't treat me like an idiot. Don't deny that this is exactly the studio's intention. Bradley's bad publicity isn't fading as fast as you all want it to, and you need it to look like you're doing something about it. Sticking him in a stinker with me will take some of the pressure off." She paused. "Am I wrong?"

Nick watched Bartholomew deflate slightly as the man sighed. "I told them you'd see right through it," he let out. "I never said it was a stinker, by the way."

"You didn't have to." The muscles in her jaw twitched before she muttered, "I'm getting passed over for *Rue the Day* for *this*." The amount of venom she injected into that last word was enough to make a ghost pale.

Nick looked between them, guilt brewing under his ribs. After the arrest, he'd known the studio would shunt him off into some low-budget comedy, had counted on it actually. What he hadn't counted on was their involving Lois Ashford.

He was growing increasingly intrigued by the opportunity to work with her, now that they'd finally met. But the studio definitely used her ill, and he hated being the cause of it. She had tremendous talent, and clearly wore quite a thick mask to guard herself, but there was no missing the bitterness behind her eyes. To which he now contributed.

Nick leaned forward in his chair, drawing on his own acting experience to project a confidence he didn't quite feel. "Mr. Bartholomew, I am fully aware of the situation I've put you and everyone else at the studio in, and I'm prepared to do what I need to do. But is it really necessary to put Miss Ashford in this position? She has nothing to do with my…mistakes."

"That eager to work with me, are you?" Lois retorted drily.

"Of course not!" Nick countered quickly. As her eyebrow quirked up, he caught his misspeak. "I mean… That is… Of course I am eager to work with you… I—" Nick couldn't believe how much worse he'd just managed to make this, until he looked more closely at her face.

That glint of amusement came back in her eyes and a smile threatened the downturned corners of her mouth.

Huh. Interesting.

"Interesting." Nick jolted, until he realized it was Bartholomew, and not him, who had spoken his thoughts aloud this time.

"I beg your pardon?" Lois asked, before gesturing to Bartholomew's face. "And what exactly is that look about?"

Now that Nick stepped away from his own thoughts, he noticed the producer did have a funny look, as if he had some brilliant idea he wasn't willing to admit. That didn't bode well.

Bartholomew made an effort to tone down his expression. "It's nothing. And I'm not giving you a look."

Lois looked as skeptical as Nick felt, but for some reason didn't press the issue.

"Regardless of how either of you feels about this, it is happening," Bartholomew said, back in control mode. "As soon as Miss Ashford's current picture wraps, you'll begin work together."

"And if I refuse?" Lois asked.

"Do I really need to bring up your contract again? You'll do—"

"Whatever the studio tells me to. Right." She crossed her arms and leaned back.

Bartholomew looked back and forth at the two actors. "You may not see it, but I do have a great deal of respect for the both of you."

When Lois opened her mouth, likely ready with a retort, the producer continued, "Don't look at me like that. You said it yourself just a moment ago—I have your back. And I am sorry about *Rue the Day*. Truly. But this is what the studio wants. In spite of my better instincts, I've taken risks and gone to bat for the two of you with the higher-ups. Neither one of you is in a position to argue about much of anything right now, but I think you might just have a chance to pull off a win if you play this right." Nick idly wondered if Bartholomew's idea of a win matched his own. Or Lois's.

The man finished his entreaty with a placating gesture. "Show everyone you can play nice, work together. It could go a long way toward pulling *both* of you out of purgatory."

Bartholomew looked pointedly at Lois, and Nick could see her weighing her options. For himself, there weren't really any options to weigh. He knew he needed this, not just to get him out of his current predicament, but, with any luck, to start to fix all that had led up to it. He had taken quite a huge gamble with his actions, and he had no way of knowing yet if they'd pay off the way he hoped.

And if he could somehow help Lois improve her reputation as well, that would be a bonus. While fully aware that the prospect of alleviating his own guilt at involving her in his problems appealed to him, he did genuinely want to help her as well. A scant few minutes in her company confirmed that there was far more to her than anyone gave her credit for.

Lost in thought, it took a moment for him to realize she had turned her gaze to him. He looked up, right into her eyes. She regarded him speculatively, then seemed to come to a decision.

Turning back to Bartholomew, Lois said, "Do you really think this could be good for both of us, or are you just saying whatever it takes to keep me from exploding in your office?"

"As much as I'd like to protect my fine collection of bric-a-brac," he replied with a smirk, "I really do think you could use a win, Lois. It might not be the leverage you want, but it is something."

"All right, fine." She turned to Nick with an almost breath-taking ferocity. "But if we're doing this, you are not wasting my time, do you understand? I trust you will take this seriously."

"Of course," Nick responded, suddenly desperate to reassure her.

"I mean it. No funny business… Or funny cigarettes."

Nick placed his hand over his heart. "You have my word."

Lois nodded briefly. A current of understanding pulsed between them, filling Nick with a renewed—and rather heady—sense of purpose.

"Wonderful," Bartholomew interjected. "Now get out of here, the both of you. I have work to do. I'll be in touch when we've found you a director… God help him, whoever he is."

Lois gave him a sarcastic salute and stood. Nick followed her out of the office. Just as they crossed the threshold, Bartholomew bellowed to Jenny and she scurried in, leaving the two of them alone in the reception area.

Lois calculatingly ignored him as she started toward the door, but Nick couldn't let her go without a word.

"Miss Ashford?"

She turned.

"There's something I'd like to say," he began. "I owe you an apology."

"Whatever for? You haven't done anything to me."

"Maybe not. But the studio has, because of me, and it was unfair of them to put you in this position. I assure you, despite what they seem to think, working with you does not, in any way, feel like a punishment to me. As a matter of fact, I am very much looking forward to our collaboration."

"Oh." She sounded faintly surprised. "Well, thank you. I appreciate your saying that."

"It's only the truth."

"Thank you, again, for the defense of my profanity in there," she said. "I didn't need it, of course."

"Of course."

"But I suppose it was…refreshing to have some support for once. So thanks."

Nick nodded, and they smiled at each other. Lois opened her mouth as if to ask something, but then stopped herself.

He knew what she wanted to ask. It hovered over every conversation he had. He couldn't complain, as he'd brought it on himself. He wasn't sure it bothered him this time, though.

"Go ahead," he sighed theatrically. "I know you're dying to ask."

"Not true."

He cocked his head to the side and simply looked at her.

She laughed. "Okay, fine, yes, I am dying to ask." Then she astounded him yet again by saying, "But I'm not going to. It's none of my business."

Nick smiled wryly. "I'm afraid I've just made it your business. But thanks for your discretion just the same. I did have my reasons..."

He looked at her, and it occurred to him that of all people at this studio, Lois Ashford might just understand him. He had a suddenly overwhelming urge to tell her everything.

What are you thinking? You've only just met her. She's liable to bite your head off.

They still had an entire movie to film. And while his gut told him he could trust her, he also wanted her to trust him. On the off chance he was wrong, and she didn't understand, he'd be creating a huge mess before even one frame was shot. He couldn't afford to alienate her.

"You know, you're very unexpected, Mr. Bradley," Lois mused. She shook her head as if to clear it, and then her mask settled back in place. "Well, I'm off to a costume fitting. Until next time..."

"It's been a pleasure, Miss Ashford."

She turned and left. As Nick watched her walk down the hall, a warmth he couldn't quite explain started to build in his chest. It felt almost like hope.

Chapter Three

It seems we have an update for you, dear patient reader! You may recall our recent reporting on the possibly-clearing (and deceptively sweet-smelling!) smoke surrounding the Dangerous Dreamboat. Well, do we have a scoop for you! His studio may be letting him back to work, but wait till you hear who with... Let's just say he might be dipping into the funny stuff now more than ever after spending a day with her on set. And the script! We've obtained a glance at the first few scenes, and hoo-boy, it's a doozy! Kudos to Parkmoor for putting our erstwhile hero in his place—we didn't think you had it in you!

*L*ois paced around the cavernous accessory room of the studio's costume department, oblivious to the stunning array of shoes, fake jewels, hats, stoles, and various other bits used to adorn the ladies who graced the screen. The room normally served as her favorite place on the lot to escape and unwind. Most of the time, there was something unusually comforting about being surrounded by all that silent, inanimate beauty, but today even her favorites were doing nothing to calm the whirlwind going on in her mind.

"You know, if you don't land somewhere soon, I'm going to have to put you to work." Natalie "Nate" Reynolds, the studio's head costume designer—and Lois's dearest friend—stepped back and assessed the mannequin she attempted to accessorize. One of her arms was loaded up with jewelry, and a large pile of discarded baubles sat on the chair next to her.

"I like that one," Lois replied absently, gesturing in her general direction. She started to sit, but Nate shooed her away in the nick of time.

"It'd be much easier to believe you if you hadn't just almost impaled yourself on my handiwork."

"Huh?" Lois looked down at the chair seat filled with jewelry. "Oh. Sorry."

Nate stared at her for a moment. "Wow, you're on another planet, aren't you? Come, sit." She took Lois's arm and led her to a small couch on the other side of the room.

"You're working. Don't mind me."

"I can take a break. Besides, I'd like to keep my job. As much as they seem to not like you, I'm sure the bosses wouldn't be thrilled if a doctor had to be called to pluck paste jewels out of your caboose."

Lois laughed in spite of herself. "You never know, they might see it as a blessing. The doc might find whatever else has been stuck up there all these years."

"I did lose track of a necklace after your first picture here." Nate narrowed her eyes with mock accusation. "Is *that* where you've been hiding it all this time?"

"I'll never tell."

They both laughed. Leave it to Nate to brighten her mood. She had always seen through Lois's walls, practically from the day they'd met, and it was one of the many reasons they were such good friends. It wasn't just the accessories that made this place her oasis.

"So," Nate said, growing more serious, "spill it. What's got you so rattled this time?"

Lois looked at her, surprised. "Do I really have to go through it all again?"

"Of course not." Nate waved her free hand. "But this is hardly the first time the studio's done something boneheaded—and underhanded—to you. It's asinine, but hardly surprising." She paused, seeming to choose her words carefully. "It's your reaction that's different this time."

"Mine?"

"Yes. I'm used to seeing you react—you vent, you rave, you try on my costumes. We have a drink, and then you let it go and move on." Nate looked at her with concern. "You did all that, but you're still stewing. You've gone all inside yourself, which is new for you."

Lois started to protest, then stopped. Nate was right. This one did feel different. And she wasn't sure she wanted to admit why.

Understanding dawned on Nate's face. "Wait a minute... Is this because of your new co-star?"

"Of course not!" Lois exclaimed. "I mean, not entirely. Not like that. It's just..." She buried her face in her hands and groaned.

"You liked not being the studio's biggest problem for a while."

Lois leaned back into the couch. "So much, you have no idea. I was actually starting to feel like I could see the end of the tunnel, like I might actually get my first choice for my next role." She grimaced. "But apparently my being 'difficult' has become part of the fabric of the studio. I'm like the grippe; eventually everyone here catches me. Only now they've started to intentionally use me to infect others."

"That's not..." Nate began, but stopped herself. "Huh. As much as I hate to admit it, that's pretty accurate. Sorry, sweetie."

She grunted in response. Was it too much to ask for things to go her way for once, just once? Ever since she could remember, she had wanted to act. The theatre had captivated her as a little girl, but by the time she was a teenager, the silver screen had sprinkled its fairy dust in her eyes. All through school, she put in extra work taking acting classes every afternoon and weekend, and it had paid off. All her teachers said she had natural talent, and that combined with her looks, she'd be a sure thing in Hollywood. So at twenty, she'd hopped on that train, determined to make her dreams come true.

Those dreams had done nothing but bite her in the ass ever since.

And now, on top of it all, her traitorous mind—or maybe not so much her mind, if she was being honest—appeared determined to focus on some dreamboat with a drug problem. *Except it didn't seem like he had a problem...* This was ridiculous. Completely, utterly ridiculous.

Lois stood and started pacing again. "You know, he was actually the first person—besides you—to look at me with respect in I don't even know how long. He was so damn direct. Unafraid."

"And he liked your sailor-like tendencies." Nate smirked.

"Exactly! Not that I needed defending, mind you..."

"Which he did acknowledge."

"He did," Lois said. "Which makes it even weirder. What is his angle?" She sighed. "Or is it that I'm so pathetically unused to chivalry that I can't make sense of it when it actually shows up?"

"Believe me, it's not you who's pathetic," Nate reassured her. "I'm still not over that dynamo you dated a couple years ago."

"Ooh, the one who bragged about how much he was looking forward to—how did he put it—'taming Hollywood's brightest shrew?'"

Nate sneered along with her. "I still can't believe he had the balls to admit that to your face."

"Believe me, his balls were nothing to write home about." Lois chuckled. "It really is a shame I let him get away."

"Such a shame." Nate waved a dismissive hand. "But enough about the pricks. You know, I've only worked with Bradley a couple times, but I always did like him."

Lois stopped pacing and turned on her friend. "That's another thing—you've been holding out on me!"

"Me? What?"

"All the times we speculated about his arrest, and you never once let on just how handsome he is up close!"

"Well, it's kind of a given in this business, isn't it? The majority of the men I dress are good-looking. But considering I have to see them in their skivvies before that happens, I'd never be able to do my job if I let myself get distracted by it. Unless, of course, Cary Grant walks in—then all bets are off." Nate paused, then raised her eyebrows wickedly. "You're usually immune too. I had no idea you'd find that information so valuable, what with your rules and all."

"I don't!"

Nate snorted her skepticism.

"It's true," Lois insisted. "It's just that when a man is that obscenely good-looking, a woman needs to be warned."

"So she can be prepared."

"Exactly."

"Duly noted."

Lois looked up to find her friend smiling slyly at her. "Oh, shut up."

Nate laughed. "In all seriousness, though, what's always struck me, more than his looks, is the kind of guy he seems to be. I see it all pass through my doors, and I can always peg the asses within minutes. And usually the better the looks, the bigger the assery. I never saw that with him."

"You were more surprised than I was when he got arrested."

"Still no details about that, huh?"

Lois shook her head. "It's really killing you that there's a piece of studio gossip you don't know, isn't it?"

"It's in my job description to know everything about everyone around here at all times. My honor may prevent me from sharing any of it, but it is essential that I know it none-theless." Nate looked pointedly at Lois. "But getting back to *your* problem—it seems like you got the same impression I did about Nick."

"I did. I'm not quite sure what I was expecting, but there's definitely more there than he's letting on." Which she most certainly did not need to spend time figuring out at the moment. And yet...

Lois thought back to the meeting. Nick had done nothing but surprise her from the minute he walked into the office. Yes, he was remarkably handsome, but it was so much more than that. The respect and admiration in his eyes, his defense of her language, the way he'd actually stood up to Bartholomew, not wanting to drag her into his mess. Hell, he'd actually *apologized* to her on their way out. She had no idea what it all meant.

Nate waved her hand in front of Lois's face. "Yoo-hoo! I lost you again. What's going on in there?"

"Sorry, just thinking." Lois refocused her eyes on her friend. "He seemed genuinely sorry for bringing me into all this."

"Further proof that I'm right about him," Nate observed.

Lois smiled. "So that's what this is really about, huh? You being right?"

"Absolutely," Nate replied, winking.

Lois laughed, then sat back down and exhaled.

"What?" Nate asked.

"I'm not even entirely sure. I hate not knowing what to make of all this."

Nate placed her hand over Lois's. "So stop trying. For once, maybe you should just let go and see what happens. This movie could end up being a really good thing for you."

Lois tilted her head skeptically.

"It actually could," Nate said, more firmly, "and I think, deep down, you know it."

"That's part of what I'm afraid of." Lois shouldn't trust it, not after what had just happened with the other film. But... "I have this feeling, like...I don't know...like I'm on a speeding train and I have no idea if I'll be able to hang on, or if I even want to."

Or if I want to more than I can even say. And where does that leave me?

———

A WEEK LATER, Lois sat in her dressing room during her lunch break. The final days of her current picture were keeping her busier than she'd expected, which provided a welcome distraction from the never-ending swirl of thoughts about her next one—and her costar. She hadn't seen Nick since their first meeting, and it disturbed her immensely how much she continued to wonder about him. As hard as she tried, she was doing a lousy job convincing herself that it was all to do with anticipation about the film and nothing more. She absolutely *could not* go down that path.

This business was fraught enough. She didn't need any further dating-related burdens adding to her already massive uphill climb. The very first date she'd turned down in this town—and with good reason—had launched a disaster of epic proportions, so much so that she worried she'd never be free of the ramifications. And anyone she'd attempted to date in the years since had led to nothing but disappointment. The small-balled wonder hell-bent on "taming" her might have been the most blatant, but he sure wasn't the only one who had seemed to think their careers would skyrocket if they could subdue the studio's favorite witch. And the ones who didn't mind her reputation didn't exactly make a secret of how let down they felt when the real thing lacked the fireworks they'd expected.

It was enough to make a woman want to lock up her heart, throw away the key, and rely entirely on herself for everything.

Which is precisely what Lois had done.

She'd gotten quite good at it, as a matter of fact. Maybe when she finally achieved the success she wanted with her career, she'd think about trying again. But until then, her rule would stay firmly in place. At the studio, no dalliances. Films only.

And her new film with Nick was definitely proceeding. Earlier that morning, a page had delivered a copy of the script for the new project. Lois had wanted to dive into it immediately, but on-set duties called instead. Now she finally settled in her armchair, with her sandwich in one hand and the script in the other.

She regretted her anticipation almost as soon as she opened it.

She didn't expect the best thing she'd ever read; that was a given. But this… She shuddered. *Some scripts are a slow burn, you know that. Maybe it'll get better.* She kept going, morbidly curious.

More than halfway through her reading, a knock sounded at her door.

"Come in," Lois called absently.

So absorbed was she in the travesty on her lap that she barely registered when Nick opened the door and poked his head inside.

"Hi, there," he greeted her. "Mind if I join you?"

"Oh, hello," Lois looked up, pulled out of the script by his tentative smile.

Seriously, what business does he have being so stinking adorable? That's what is really criminal about him.

Stop. It.

Lois shook her head and pasted on an answering smile. "Please, have a seat." She gestured to the room's other chair, realizing too late she still held her forgotten sandwich. A stray piece of lettuce drifted to the floor.

Without missing a beat, Nick picked up the leaf on his way to the chair. "Judging by the look on your face when I came in…and your poor neglected sandwich…"—he held up the lettuce before tossing it in the wastebasket—"I'm guessing that's our divine script you're reading."

"Have you read it?"

"I have," he replied. "Every single page."

"It doesn't magically get good at the end, does it?" she asked bleakly.

Nick looked at her apologetically. "I really wish I could lie to you, but no. No, it does not."

"I was afraid of that," Lois replied. "I suppose I wasn't really expecting it to. I mean, that title alone."

"Right? *Teacups in July*? What does that even mean?" Nick asked incredulously.

"Not a clue!" she said. "And you've actually finished it. If you still don't know…"

"And you can't stop reading, right? I mean, the further I got, the worse it was, but somehow I just couldn't help myself from turning page after page after page…"

"As the train cars keep piling into each other…"

"The smoke gets thicker, the flames get higher, and yet…"

Lois met the devilish gleam in his eyes.

"You still keep turning the pages," they said together, laughing.

Have I ever laughed in this room?

Lois leaned forward in her chair. "Honestly, though, I'm not making too much of this, am I?"

She almost snapped right back up, completely unable to fathom where the question came from. She never showed anything but imperious confidence to most of her coworkers.

"Oh, no, it really is that bad," Nick reassured her. "I have to say, I'm pretty surprised. Roger's last script was fantastic."

"He's got one foot out the door. At least two other studios have been courting him, but his contract here's not up yet. They've been desperately trying to hold onto him, but I doubt it can last much longer. And judging by this"—Lois held up the script—"Roger's finally given up and decided to disgust the bosses into letting him go."

"If this doesn't work, I imagine nothing will," Nick said. He met her eyes with a disconcerting mix of determination and defiance. "So, do you think we can make something of it?"

"Of this?" Lois asked. "Do you actually want to try?"

Nick looked surprised. "Well, sure. Don't you?"

"I…" Lois began, but found herself at a loss for words. She took a moment to gather her thoughts before answering. "I truly hadn't thought about it. I mean, isn't this the kind of project we're supposed to phone in? You know, play our parts, put on a good front, hopefully get some decent publicity, and move on."

Nick considered her for a moment. He seemed to be assessing her, trying to figure her out while he chose his next words.

"I suppose that's what everyone expects us to do," he said slowly. The spark in his eyes grew. "But wouldn't it be a lot more fun if we did something else?"

Yet again, Lois had no idea what to make of this strange creature in front of her, so genuinely unlike anyone she'd ever met. He intrigued her—which would lead to nothing but disaster. But somehow louder than the alarm bells beginning in her head, Nate's words echoed through her mind. Maybe she should just see what happened—professionally, of course. It wasn't as if she had all that much to lose, right?

Just everything.

All these years of causing drama were getting to her. She needed to calm down.

"Okay, assuming we did decide to try to shatter their expectations," she asked, "how exactly do you suggest we do that? This isn't Shakespeare, remember?"

"Of course not," he responded, "but I can't help but feel like there's gotta be *something* there we can work with, you know?"

He actually looked enthusiastic. Such a foreign emotion to Lois. And yet she felt a small sliver of it rubbing off on her. *What the hell?* She looked back to the script in her hand.

Flipping it open to a random page, her attention caught on the dialogue. She couldn't help grimacing.

"It's almost like it's trying to be a comedy," she said.

"I know!" Nick paused. "It's just missing…"

"Anything funny," Lois deadpanned.

Nick chuckled.

"It almost…" Lois stopped, thinking.

"What?"

"I mean…if it was a screwball comedy, some of the dialogue

might work. Only problem is, it's not."

Nick stood up suddenly. "That's it!"

Lois frowned in a desperate attempt to quell the backflips her stomach began doing in response to the sudden—and glorious—wattage of his smile. "What's it?"

He knelt in front of her, a ball of contagious energy. "A screwball. We'll make it a screwball."

She dug her nails into the chair arms, fighting her body's annoyingly clear response to his proximity. *Focus on the script; focus on the script.* "But it's not written to be," Lois protested.

Nick shrugged. "So what? I doubt it matters all that much."

"But…does anyone at this studio even still want to make screwball comedies? I can't remember when Parkmoor last turned out a truly good one."

The shiny haze emanating from Nick dulled a bit at that, and Lois wanted to kick herself for protesting too much. But then he shook his head and shot to his feet, his glow back and brighter than ever.

"If expectations are so low, who's gonna care what we make? And you said it yourself, we could make the dialogue work." He started to pace around the room, and Lois felt her own enthusiasm grow with each step he took. "You're absolutely right. With the right delivery, the right action…" He looked down at her, eyes blazing, the most electric blue she'd seen yet. "That's how we make this into something good."

Her excitement rose, almost enough to propel her to join him in standing. Almost. Despite his contagious exuberance, all her years in this damn business kept her rooted to the spot. "I really hate to burst your bubble, but there's only so much polish you can add to a turd like this."

Nick sat back down, more serious now, and again she wished she could take her reasonable words back.

"We don't actually have to fool anyone into thinking we've made a masterpiece," he offered, "just give them something better than they're prepared for. Believe me, no one's more aware than I am of how little they expect of us with this." He met her eyes, taking her aback with the intensity there. "But you heard Bartholomew. This could honestly turn things around if we do it right. And maybe, just maybe, we can show them all what we're capable of."

He was so earnest, so passionate. "This really is much more than just some punishment for you, isn't it?" she asked.

"It is," he said.

She believed him.

Damn it, why does he have to make it so difficult to be pessimistic?

And so she gave in. "All right then. Let's make the screwiest of balls anyone's ever seen."

The bark of his laughter echoed around the small dressing room, flooding her with warmth.

"Excellent," he proclaimed as he got up and headed for the door. "I'll let you finish reading, and then we can start planning."

"Oh, wait!" Lois called out. "Aren't you forgetting something important?"

At his blank look, she continued, "A director?"

"Oh, that." He waved his hand dismissively.

"Yes, that. Whoever they rope into this is probably going to have a pretty large say in how we play it, you know."

"Maybe for most movies," he replied with a smirk. "They've already thrown their worst script at us, so what makes you think the guy they find to helm this iceberg is going to want to do anything more than... What was it you called it? Phone it in? They may think this is a punishment, but they have no idea the freedom they've foisted on us."

"Wow, that's almost diabolical in its logic." She let her grin spread. "Who do you think you are? Me?"

"Great minds do think alike, or so I've heard." Nick winked. "Enjoy the rest of that sandwich, partner."

Lois stared at the door for a long while after he left. No one had ever called her "partner" before, least of all in this town. *Shit.*

It felt rather lovely.

Chapter Four

Hollywood Happenings
An exciting (and perplexing) announcement from Parkmoor
Studios! Powerhouse producer Leo Orwell is turning the biz into
a family affair, with his nephew set to make his directing debut.
We've yet to lay eyes on the newbie, but if he's anything like his
uncle, we'll bet he'll be taking Hollywood by storm in no time.
The only thing we can't figure out—what in the world are they
thinking over there, putting a bright up-and-comer in charge of
the new vehicle starring…their two most Notorious Ne'er-do-
wells? Only time will tell, we guess…

*J*ust as Nick had predicted, Bartholomew did indeed find them a director it would be easy to override, though not quite in the way he'd predicted.

Several days after visiting Lois's dressing room, Nick still buzzed with the excitement that their new partnership had sparked in him. Despite her current filming schedule, they had managed to meet for lunch every day to talk over the script, and it was going beautifully so far, giving him something new to look forward to every day. While Lois had been correct about the script —it indeed proved to be an incredibly hard turd to polish—they at least found some ways to improve it. She had fantastic ideas, and while neither of them had ever actually done a screwball comedy before, he felt largely optimistic that they might be able to pull it off.

After one particularly good brainstorming lunch, he had been so focused on his and Lois's work that when Bartholomew called them to his office, Nick had genuinely forgotten all about their director.

Strolling into Bartholomew's reception area, Nick found Lois already there, chatting with Jenny. As he watched her in relaxed conversation, it took tremendous effort to keep his suddenly moony thoughts off his face.

"Oh, hello, Mr. Bradley," Jenny said, rising from her chair. "I'll tell Mr. Bartholomew you're both here."

As she poked her head into the office, Nick turned to Lois. "So, any idea who we're getting?"

"I was just trying to get the dirt from Jenny," she replied. "Seems he's some newbie. She doesn't know much about him."

"Huh. Wonder what he's like?"

Before she could answer, Jenny returned. "Okay, you can go in." As they passed her, she added in a whisper, "Good luck."

Nick looked at Lois warily, and she simply rolled her eyes. He closed the door behind them after following her into the office.

"Miss Ashford, Mr. Bradley, please come in," Bartholomew greeted them. "Allow me to introduce your director, Mr. Merrill Hornsby."

Nick almost didn't see the man at first. But when he looked toward Bartholomew's spacious couch, he spotted a nervous-looking young man who appeared to be actively trying to blend into the cushions. He startled at the mention of his name and belatedly got up, making his way in their direction with all the speed of a snail.

"Good god," Lois muttered under her breath, before extending her hand. "Mr. Hornsby, a pleasure."

At the sound of her voice, Hornsby jumped about a foot and let out what could only be described as a nervous giggle. "Oh, well, um, yes, hello," he stammered. It took him a minute to realize her hand was still extended, and he took it gingerly before dropping it again almost immediately.

The poor man was so skittish, it was almost comical. Nick had trouble schooling his face. He hoped he wasn't staring—not that Hornsby would even notice if he was.

Lois didn't appear to be having much luck in the same department, assuming she was even trying. At this point, Nick had seen her don haughty and imperious expressions on several occasions —not directed at him, however, which provided him a rather pleasant puzzle to sort out—but right now she stared at Hornsby with open disbelief.

Nick decided to intervene before things got even more awkward. He put on his most charming smile and offered his own hand to the man.

"Mr. Hornsby, I look forward to working with you."

Hornsby looked almost as startled as he had with Lois. He cleared his throat and took Nick's hand. "Mr. Bradley."

Nick noticed a slight trembling in the other man's hand before he let go. If he was this timid, how in the world did he expect to make it as a director? Nick had worked with a range of directors, both in film and in his earlier days in the theatre, and just about the only thing they all had in common was their ability to command a room when they needed to—which was often.

"Let's all have a seat, shall we?" Bartholomew said, gesturing toward his lounge area.

See, that's *how you command a room.*

Lois caught Nick's eye and smirked, clearly thinking the same thing.

She turned her attention back to their director and asked

sweetly, "So, Mr. Hornsby, do I understand that this will be your first time directing a picture?"

"Yes, that's correct," he responded.

"Fascinating." She leaned forward in her seat and placed her chin in her hand. "And so, what have you been doing up till now?"

"Oh, I graduated college just last June." Hornsby lunged for his glass of water and downed a huge gulp. Nick suspected this was the most he'd talked in a long time.

"My goodness," Lois drawled. Under her breath, so only Nick could hear, she added, "Quite the Wee Willie Winkie, isn't he?"

A laugh exploded out of Nick, which he quickly turned into a coughing fit. Lois took the pitcher of water on the table and held it up to him, all innocence.

"Do you need some water, Nick?"

"No, I'm fine, thank you," he replied with a last clear of this throat. He narrowed his eyes at her and she smiled back, an absolutely devilish gleam in her eyes.

Quite unexpectedly, Nick felt like he'd had the wind knocked out of him for real this time. Those eyes. He found himself suddenly picturing her giving him that same look in his bed.

Jesus, where the hell did that come from?

He glanced away quickly, hoping his lascivious thoughts hadn't reached his eyes. He tried to return his focus to the meeting.

Lois was thoroughly enjoying herself, but thankfully Hornsby seemed oblivious to anything but his own nerves. Bartholomew, however, was anything but oblivious.

He glared at Lois pointedly before taking back control of the conversation. "Mr. Hornsby may be new to our business, but his family is not. I believe you know his uncle, Leo Orwell?"

"Oh, sure," Nick responded.

"Yes, of course," Lois said, turning to look at him, again clearly reflecting his sentiments.

Leo Orwell was one of the studio's most prolific producers,

with a tremendous amount of clout. And they were willing to let his nephew work with the riffraff?

A sudden high-pitched noise drew their attention back to the corner of the couch. As Hornsby pulled a handkerchief from his pocket, Nick realized it had been a sneeze.

This certainly was going to be an interesting ride.

HAVING THE AFTERNOON TO HIMSELF, Nick wound his cranberry-colored Cadillac Series 62 over the hills on Barham Boulevard. He chuckled as he drove, still amused by the meeting with Bartholomew and Hornsby.

As he navigated the road, however, he began to regret thinking back over their meeting, instead of focusing entirely on his driving. His thoughts refused to linger on their mousy director, gravitating back toward Lois. As a matter of fact, the more time he spent with her, the more often he found his mind wandering in her direction. He couldn't remember the last time he'd felt such an attraction.

Sure, she was beautiful, but it wasn't just that. Her intelligence, and the way she observed absolutely everything around her, captivated him. And she was so witty too—she made him laugh at the most unexpected times. For so long he had felt buried under a hill of pressure, and the way that laughing with her magically eased that pressure astounded him.

At the same time, Lois inspired an altogether different kind of pressure, one he felt most acutely as he remembered that moment over the water pitcher in Bartholomew's office.

Nick shifted in his seat as much as he could while still helming the car. He rolled down his window, letting the breeze wash over his flushed face.

He had to figure out a way to maintain control over his attraction if he had any hope of getting through this picture. There was no way he could get involved with Lois Ashford. If he mangled their ability to work together by acting like one of those creeps who couldn't keep from coming on to his costar, it would ruin everything they worked toward. And then she might actually kill him.

Luckily his destination neared, saving him from having to think any further on the subject.

The heavenly scent of the best baked goods he'd ever tasted made its way through the open window a full block before he reached the narrow parking lot adjacent to Mom's Bakery. Once inside, he took a moment and inhaled deeply, peace descending on him along with the promise of a sugar coma.

"You are so dramatic."

Nick opened his eyes to find Max Mitchell, the bakery's proprietor—and his best friend since childhood—smirking at him from behind the counter.

"Then I guess I picked the right profession, didn't I?"

"You did," Max replied. "But do you really have to do that routine *every* time you come in here? Aren't you embarrassed?"

"You've known me long enough to know how little shame I have."

Max considered that. "Very true."

Nick chuckled as he crossed the room. "And it is a testament to how good you are. That smell really does get me every time."

Max rolled his eyes and gestured around the small shop, where the few tables were empty. "Relax. At least save the exuberance for when I have customers."

"You know I never bullshit you when it comes to your talents." Nick put his hand over his heart and grinned wickedly. "But rest assured, I'll lay it on thicker as soon as someone comes in."

"Just not too thick," Max growled good-naturedly. "You know this is my slow season, with the school around the corner out for summer. I can't have you chewing so much scenery, you scare away the customers I do have."

"I keep telling you, movie stars are good for advertising."

"Even the ones in hot water with the feds?" Max teased.

Nick flipped him the bird and Max snickered.

A thought occurred to Nick. "You know, in this case it might be just what you need."

"How do you figure?" Max asked skeptically.

"Well, it's not exactly a secret what I was caught doing… And given what you sell, it really would be a ringing endorsement. Think of all the new business you'd get. You could keep the shop open longer every day."

"Oh, yeah, that's exactly what I need. By that logic, I'd have to stay open into the wee hours, and then I'd really have no life."

"I'm just saying," Nick countered, raising his hands. "It's something to think about."

"I'll take it under advisement," Max said. He poured two cups of coffee and gestured to one of the tables.

"What, all I get is coffee?" Nick pouted.

"Again with the dramatics. Geez, you're impossible." He gestured broadly at the glass counter. "Whaddya want?"

Nick smiled. Needling Max was one of his favorite pastimes. And when it got him pastries in the bargain? Even better.

He perused the display, noticing some unusual twisted danishes. "Are those new?"

Max dropped his mock annoyance and perked up. "Oh, yeah! I've been experimenting with that chocolate hazelnut paste Rob sent from Italy. It's been turning out great. Want one?"

"Sure."

Nick grabbed the coffee mugs as Max plated up the pastries.

When they sat, Max's expression sobered. "All jokes aside, how are things? You doing okay?"

"Sure, I'm fine," Nick replied.

Max leveled him with a look, prompting Nick to glue his attention to his coffee cup. If he'd been talking to anyone but Max, he would have tried for his most charming movie-star smile.

"I've known you forever, Nicky. We've been through it. You don't have to pretend with me."

"I'm not pretending." He stopped Max from protesting, realizing that he truly wasn't. "I swear, I really am good. I've got this all under control."

Max regarded him carefully for a long moment. "You do seem pretty confident." He lowered his voice, even though he knew better than Nick that the shop was empty. "So is your crazy plan actually working?"

"Yeah, it seems to be." Nick took a bite of the danish, the chocolate and hazelnut gooeyness overtaking all else. "Wow. That is fantastic."

"Told ya." Max toasted him with his coffee cup. "So when do you start filming?"

"Pretty soon." Nick filled him in on everything that had happened in the last week, from his script doctoring sessions with Lois to Hornsby the Haunted.

"Come on," Max said through his laughter, "he couldn't possibly be that pathetic."

"Oh, no, he really is. I have no idea what they were thinking giving him to us."

Max considered this. "Maybe his family doesn't think he can hack it, and they're hoping you'll scare him right out of the business."

"That I can believe." Nick shrugged. "But at least he's not likely to give us much trouble when we try to do the screwball stuff."

"Yeah, a pushover's just as good as one who doesn't give a crap."

Despite his agreement, Nick couldn't help wincing at Max's choice of words. "I feel kinda bad calling him a pushover. I mean, he is one, but still. He's so young. You can't help but be sorry for him." He laughed. "You should have seen him every time Lois tried to talk to him. The poor guy never stood a chance."

"I'll bet."

Nick bristled at the hint behind Max's words.

"What the hell is that tone?"

"Nothing." Max eyed him over the rim of his coffee cup. "Nothing at all."

Nick crossed his arms and stared him down. "Spit it out."

Smirking, Max continued, "You should see yourself every time you mention Lois. Doesn't look like you stand much of a chance yourself."

"Don't be ridiculous. She's just my costar." Nick made a point of concentrating on his pastry, hoping Max wouldn't notice the embarrassing flush he could feel creeping up his neck.

No such luck.

Max threw his head back and laughed. "My god, you've got it bad!"

Nick opened his mouth to deny it, but then stopped. What was the point? He was drawn to her, and Max knew him better than anyone. He never had been able to hide anything from him.

"Okay, fine, yes. She's beautiful. And fascinating. But she's hardly the first actress I've been attracted to, and I never mix business with pleasure. I'm not about to start now."

As if any other women could even hold a candle to Lois.

Fuck it all, I really need to get a hold of myself.

"Fair enough." Max leaned forward. "So, is she really not the diva everyone makes her out to be?"

Nick once again turned over all the time spent in her presence in the last several days—the witty retorts, the laughter that always seemed to take her by surprise. "No," he replied. "I mean, I've seen her lob a few zingers, but…no. She's definitely no monster. Any time she's gotten upset, it's been totally warranted."

"Ever directed at you?"

"Aside from that first meeting with Bartholomew, never. I seem to make her laugh." Nick realized he probably sounded like an obnoxious ass, but he couldn't help marveling at the fact that Lois Ashford smiled as much as she did around him.

That warm feeling evaporated the minute he refocused on his friend's face.

"Oh, really?" Max had the balls to look like he was gloating.

"Shut up."

Max put up his hands in surrender.

"I'm serious, Max. There's so much riding on this. I can't afford to screw it up."

To his credit, Max dropped the amusement and looked apologetic. "I know, buddy. But it sounds like you might really have an ally in Lois. You think it's for real?"

Nick took a moment to let the lightness that continued to come from their little team of two fizz through him. *Damn, it feels good having a partner in her.* "I do," he finally replied. "I get the impression she's gotten nothing but trouble from the studio. Hell, they tried to use her as a weapon against me."

"That had to hurt."

"No doubt." Nick thought again of the pain in her eyes at that first meeting. "There's so much more there than anyone gives her credit for. I've gotta make sure this movie is good for her too, not just me."

"If anyone can do it, it's you," Max reassured him.

"I hope so."

Max looked at him thoughtfully. He opened his mouth to speak, but then closed it again.

"What?"

"It's…" Max hesitated, choosing his words carefully. "Just do me a favor, okay? Try not to get lost in all this. I know how much you've got at stake, but…don't forget to enjoy yourself while you're at it. You're a good guy, Nick. I want to see you take some happiness where you find it."

"When did you turn into such a philosopher?"

The bell above the door chimed as a mother entered with two small children.

Max stood to return to work, throwing his crumpled napkin at Nick as he passed. "I always have been, dumbass."

Nick laughed. "Hey, Max." As Max turned back, Nick said simply, "Thanks."

Max nodded and went to his customers. Nick reclined in his

chair, grateful that his back faced the counter so he'd be less likely to be recognized.

He had expected to escape for a little while, but Lois had managed to follow him even here. He was afraid that Max was right—he really didn't stand a chance when it came to her.

Equally as frightening was how little that bothered him.

Chapter Five

Tinseltown Trappings

*Batten down the hatches, dames and gents! We hear production
begins tomorrow—that's right, tomorrow!—on the new
stinker…ahem, pardon us…picture, from the silver screen's most
Dastardly Duo. Will it be just the penance Parkmoor is hoping
for? Will the smoke from the explosions (among other things) be
visible beyond the hills of Hollywood? Watch this space!*

*L*ois sat in front of the mirror in her dressing room, confused by the butterflies currently having quite the soiree in her stomach. The first day on any film was always a bit of a crapshoot, but she'd made enough movies at this point to not be fazed by much of anything. As she prepared to start this new comedy with Nick, she found herself feeling something completely foreign.

Lois was nervous. And at the same time genuinely…*excited*.

She reached for the bottle of Coke in front of her, hoping it would settle her a bit. As she sipped—through a straw, of course, as her makeup had already been done—she looked over the script pages for the day's scenes.

The prep work had gone surprisingly well. The script was still nowhere near perfect, but she felt pretty confident about the ideas she and Nick had come up with.

Working with him was a novel experience. He actually listened when she talked, and took her ideas seriously. More often than not, he seemed sincerely impressed by her. It was so refreshing. She'd become thoroughly accustomed to even her more positive work experiences going to hell in some way, and she kept pinching herself to make sure this one was still real.

It's too bad I can't pinch him.

Lois *really* wished she could keep a lid on thoughts like that. They'd get her nowhere. This was business. No entanglements with costars, period. And the more she thought about what Nick had said that day in her dressing room, the more she let herself hope he'd been right. This picture might just start to lift her out of her career purgatory. Nothing was more important than that.

She needed to focus.

There was a knock on her door. "Come in," she called.

Nate poked her head around the door.

"Hey, have —" Nate began.

"You're early," Lois interrupted. "I don't have to be in costume for at least another hour. They're starting with one of Nick's scenes."

"I know; that's why I'm here," Nate replied. "I need to double-check his costume before he starts, but I can't find him anywhere. You haven't seen him, have you?"

"No, I haven't." *That's weird.* "But I've been holed up in here all morning. Jackie just finished my hair and makeup."

Lois got up and headed for the door, still in her robe.

"I assume you checked his dressing room?" she asked as she followed Nate out.

"First place I looked. No answer."

Panic singed any of Lois's remaining butterflies. "He better not be pulling any crap on me."

"You said he's been really committed to this, right?" Nate asked. "I doubt he would. Would he?"

"I have no idea." *I should've known this was too good to be true.* No, that wasn't fair. She didn't know where Nick had disappeared to, but he was the first person to take her seriously in ages. She owed him the same courtesy.

As she neared the sound stage door, she turned back to Nate. "Is anyone else looking for him yet?"

Nate shook her head. "I don't think so. I poked my head in here first to check on the schedule and they were still setting up lights, so I knew I had some time. You were my next stop after his dressing room."

That was good. Maybe he was checking on things himself, or doing prep in a corner somewhere. And even if there was some kind of problem, they had time to fix it.

Lois and Nate entered the sound stage, taking in the scene. People bustled everywhere. To an untrained eye, it might look like chaos, but the crew members had everything down to a science and were working efficiently.

Merrill Hornsby sat in the middle of it all, looking to the wide world like he was about to be swallowed whole by his director's chair. Lois shook her head, still trying to figure that one out. Such an odd choice. The poor guy didn't seem capable of putting up any kind of fight, which reassured her they'd be able to get their ideas past him, but it depended on the camera operator and other assistants. He'd clearly have to use them as his mouthpieces, and Lois crossed her fingers that they cared little enough about the project—or had enough of a care for her and Nick—to let them do what they wanted.

But none of it would matter if Nick went AWOL.

"There." Nate nudged her and nodded her head toward the only quiet corner of the room, where a shadow paced back and forth on the wall behind a scenery flat. Lois exhaled. *Ok, still fixable then.*

The women wove their way through the crew. Thankfully, it was so busy that no one gave them more than a passing nod or quick hello.

As they reached the edge of the flat, Nick turned, mid-pace, his tuxedo tails swirling behind him.

"Hey there," Lois greeted him cautiously.

He swallowed convulsively. "They're ready for me, aren't they?"

God, he looked positively green.

This was not good.

Nate jumped in. "No, just me, I'm afraid. Wanted to do a quick costume check." She shot Lois a glance before continuing. "You okay there, hon?"

"Me? Oh, yeah, great. Never better." Nick laughed nervously and resumed pacing.

Nate opened her mouth to speak, clearly ready to tap into the amateur psychology that she deployed as easily—and often—as her tape measure.

Lois stopped her with a hand on her arm. "Let me."

"Yeah?"

"Yeah." She tipped her head toward the room behind them. "Keep an eye out."

"Got it." Nate took one more look at Nick, then stepped around to the other side of the flat.

Nick nearly rammed into Lois on his latest lap, and she grabbed his arm and dragged him further into the corner and away from any prying eyes. Through his coat, she could feel the tension vibrating in his muscles.

"What the hell is going on with you?" Lois hissed.

He met her eyes, and she was struck by the sheer terror in his.

"I don't know if I can do this," he whispered.

Her panic roared back with a vengeance. "Are you kidding

me? What happened to the guy I've been having lunch with every day for weeks?"

"I don't know, maybe aliens took him and replaced him with me?"

Lois glared at him. "Oh my god, are you high right now?"

She hated to ask, but it felt necessary.

That seemed to jerk him out of his blind panic, which she supposed was a good sign.

"What? Of course not! What the hell?"

"I'm sorry, but can you really blame me for asking?"

Nick sighed heavily. "No, I can't." He locked eyes with her. "But I promised you that wouldn't happen, and I meant it."

Lois doubted he could look at her with such intensity if he wasn't completely sober. And it certainly felt intense. A shiver started at the crown of her head and rippled its way down her back.

She had to get back to the matter at hand.

"So what, then? Why are you such a mess?"

Nick dropped his eyes and turned away, running a hand through his hair. "I just... I mean..." His shoulders slumped and the air seemed to deflate out of him. "What if I'm terrible?"

All things considered, it wasn't such an unusual question. Any actor who had never asked it really couldn't consider themselves an actor. This profession came with a constant balancing act between unfettered ego and crushing self-doubt.

But there was something in his voice, such utter fear and vulnerability. Lois felt something squeezing inside her chest. She suddenly wanted to wrap her arms around him and hold on tight.

A shout and the sound of clanking metal echoed not far from them, pulling her out of her reverie and reminding her what needed to be accomplished.

She settled for a light hand on Nick's arm.

"Nick."

He turned his head halfway.

"Your acting cannot possibly be more terrible than our script."

He laughed softly and faced her. "You sure about that?"

"As a matter of fact, I am. And I am always right."

Nick crossed his arms. "Oh really?"

"Yes, really. You should know that by now." Lois paused. "Seriously, though, why are you so worried about this? I thought you loved all the ideas we came up with."

"I do," he said. "They're great ideas. But what if I can't deliver on them?" The fear was creeping back into his eyes, and he began to pace again. "What was I thinking? I've never done comedy before, and I just jump right in to a screwball?"

Lois took a deep breath. The situation clearly needed far more than a light touch.

Luckily, she specialized in heavy-handed.

"Will you shut up?"

Nick's head whipped up. "Excuse me?"

"You heard me. You need to snap the hell out of this, and fast. Need I remind you, this was *your* bright idea? I was all ready to half-ass this and get it over with, but then you blew into my dressing room, all earnest and charming and 'Let's make a screw-ball comedy!' And here we are."

She gestured to the other side of the flat. "There is an entire crew out there waiting on you, not to mention a director who's probably been waiting his entire short life for the chance to whisper 'Action' in your general direction."

That got her a smile.

"You've been to war, for Chrissake. *Comedy* scares you?"

"When you put it that way, it does sound pretty pathetic," Nick groaned.

"Do you play an instrument?" she asked.

Confusion replaced his smile. "Excuse me?"

"An instrument. A musical instrument. Do you?"

"Piano, I guess," Nick replied. "Took lessons for years as a kid."

"You any good at it?"

"I haven't played in a while, but I'm not bad."

"There you go then."

Nick's eyebrows scrunched into a *V*. "I'm not following."

Lois smiled. "Ages ago in acting class, my favorite teacher shared a fabulous piece of wisdom. He was talking about how comedy can be so much harder than drama."

"Oh, great," Nick muttered.

"Will you let me finish?" she asked, skewering him with one of her best withering glares.

Nick held up his hands. "Sorry. Please continue."

"Thank you. As I was saying, he told us that comedy actually has a lot in common with music. It all comes down to timing. Hitting the right notes, the right beats, at just the right time. He said that comedians often make wonderful musicians." She paused for maximum dramatic effect. "And vice versa."

Nick considered that for a moment, and relief actually began to spread across his face. "So since I can manage the piano…"

"Yep. You'll manage the comedy."

He nodded.

"And besides," Lois added, "you know how little is expected of us. If you do fuck it up, it's not like anyone's going to be all that surprised anyway."

Nick laughed. "Gee, thanks."

"Brutal honesty is my strong suit."

"I gather that."

Lois held his gaze, aiming for a different honesty now. A slightly scarier one. "I meant what I said. I think you'll be fine. More than fine. And I'm nervous too."

"Really?"

"Sure." She pointed a finger at his chest. "And if you tell anyone I said that, I will throw the mother of all diva fits, so you've been warned."

"Said what?" he asked, all mock innocence.

"Smart man." Lois sobered. "Listen, if you really think you can't do this, just say the word and we can go back to my original plan and phone this in. It's not likely to worsen my reputation around here.

"But if it's only fear holding you back," she continued, "or your run-of-the-mill actor insecurity, you need to leave it here, behind this scenery. You managed to convince me that we might be able to do something interesting with this, which is a pretty big accomplishment. And now I want to see it through."

"Are you actually admitting that I softened your defenses?"

"Don't let it go to your head. We still have a whole picture to make."

"And we did agree to have fun, didn't we?"

"We did."

"Okay then." Nick squared his shoulders. He held out his hand. "Ready."

Lois took his hand and they shook. She tried to ignore the jolt that shot up her arm at his simple touch.

Focus. Professional. No jolting.

Still holding her hand, Nick spoke, his voice a low, velvet baritone. "Thank you, Lois."

She swallowed. "You're welcome, Nick."

They emerged from behind the flat to find Nate, standing sentry.

"All better?" she asked.

"I suppose you heard all that, didn't you?" Nick seemed slightly embarrassed.

"I hear only what you want me to, and make no judgments." Nate held up three fingers. "Designer's honor."

One of the assistants came toward them and called out, "We're almost ready for you, Mr. Bradley."

"Thanks, Luke." Under his breath to Lois, Nick added, "Okay. Let's go screw the hell out of this ball."

He walked away, leaving Lois trying desperately to control her blush.

If Nate noticed, she let it go without remark. She did, however, ask, "Did Lois Ashford just give a successful pep talk?"

"Oh, go fix Nick's tuxedo."

Nate laughed and followed Nick.

Lois was equally surprised by her success. But she supposed it was a good omen—if she could break Nick out of his panic, this comedy thing should be a piece of cake.

A SHORT WHILE LATER, Lois stood on the periphery of the crew as Nick got ready for the first take. She had planned to go back to her dressing room, but curiosity got the better of her. She honestly didn't have any doubt about Nick's performance. It was their director's she really wanted to see.

She watched as Nick exuberantly approached Hornsby, and heard him tell the director that he had a few ideas he wanted to try for the scene.

Distance and Hornsby's barely audible voice prevented her from hearing his response. But judging by Nick's face, he didn't get any pushback, which boded well.

Nick strolled onto the set. He was smooth—no one watching him would have the slightest clue he'd just had a meltdown in the corner. Lois wondered if she'd completely vanquished it, or if he was just skilled at stuffing it down. Not that it mattered either way, as long as he got the job done.

It'd be kinda nice to know I can have that effect on someone, though.

At that moment, someone put a clapboard in front of Nick, and he peeked over it, met her eye, and winked.

Her insides promptly resembled the ice cream in the bottom of a cone.

Before she could even react, a booming voice from the direction of the camera distracted her.

"Picture's up!"

It couldn't be. Could it?

Of course not. It was only Jerry, the loudest directing assistant at the studio. *Smart move, pairing him with Might-less Mouse.* It was the only way they'd get anything filmed at all.

Jerry called "Action!" and Nick snapped into character. Lois couldn't blame him for being nervous. He was the only actor in this particular scene, and it was the very first thing they were committing to film. He would set the tone for the entire shoot.

And what a tone it was.

He was mesmerizing. As written, the scene depicted a simple one-sided telephone conversation. But Nick had come up with the added layer of moving through the set during the monologue, while getting increasingly caught up in the phone cord. As he delivered the last line, he executed a final pratfall that left him sprawled on the floor.

It was all funny enough on its own, but Nick took it to yet another level by picking up his head and ad-libbing one last line —one he hadn't shared with Lois in their prep sessions.

Oh, he's good.

Jerry yelled "Cut!" just in time, because Lois couldn't contain the laughter that exploded out of her.

The crew assembled had been quietly—and professionally— stifling their chuckles, but as soon as they heard one laugh, they let loose with their own mirth, before realizing the original source and turning en masse to stare at Lois.

What was their problem? They acted as if they'd never seen her laugh before.

Oh, right. They haven't.

Lois straightened, slipping her imperious mask back in place. "Well. A good first take, Mr. Bradley. Admirable work. Keep it up. I'll be getting into costume now if anyone needs me."

She tried to ignore the smug grin spreading across Nick's face as she turned and swept as dramatically as she could off the soundstage.

Chapter Six

Tinseltown Trappings
Well, what do you know, kids? If the rumors are to be believed
(and we admit, we're having a little trouble with that ourselves),
it seems the goings-on over at Parkmoor are actually...pretty
smooth sailing. Everyone's not-so-favorite Diva and Doper are
not delivering the due disaster we've been waiting for. In addition
to word that the picture might not be so terrible after all, we're
even hearing stories that the mood on set is decidedly...pleasant.
Color us intrigued!

At the edge of the set, Nick started to run a hand through his disheveled hair but caught himself just in time. He glanced surreptitiously at Jackie, the hairstylist, hoping she hadn't noticed that he'd almost destroyed her handiwork. Today's scenes took place after another that involved a lot of physicality, and Jackie had taken great pains to arrange his hair in just the right amount of disarray to replicate what had previously occurred naturally.

He exhaled his relief to find that Jackie was so absorbed in adjusting Lois's coif that she was oblivious to him. Unfortunately, Lois had noticed and her eyes gleamed with mischief. She opened her mouth as if to speak, and Nick clapped his hand over his heart and gave her his best "Et tu, Brute" stare.

She chuckled, which did get Jackie's attention.

"Miss Ashford, please. You must stand still."

"Of course," Lois replied. "My apologies."

"And you," Jackie aimed over her shoulder. "Stop distracting her."

"Who, me?" Nick tried for innocence, but doubted she bought it.

"Yes, you. And don't touch your hair!"

Nick's hand stopped halfway to his head. *How does she do that?* She hadn't even been looking at him. Lois's lips pressed together tightly as she tried valiantly not to laugh again.

He was causing nothing but trouble, so Nick turned and walked a few steps away, smiling to himself.

The more they worked on this film, the more Nick reveled in his newly unearthed talent—making Lois laugh. He was so proud of it, he was thinking of adding it to his résumé.

Her smile sure is breathtaking.

He released a gust of air. He most definitely did not need any distractions right now. But he honestly couldn't remember the last time he'd had this much fun at work.

Nick looked up to find Hornsby staring—no, actually, glaring—at him from across the room, before the director's eyes shifted to Lois.

That was unusual.

So far, Hornsby had been working out very well. Every time Nick or Lois made a suggestion, he didn't bat an eye. They'd been filming for a few days now, with pretty satisfying results. A lot of the crew seemed impressed too, especially the ones who had seen the script ahead of time.

So what was Hornsby's problem?

The guy was so quiet, it was hard to tell what went through

his mind—besides fear. Nick figured he'd be happy with their progress. True, they were technically overstepping, and doing most of his job for him. But it meant the director barely needed to peek out from his shell. And he'd be the one to get all the credit if the end result was a bigger success than anyone anticipated. Hell, if it was a success at all.

Nick didn't have time to think much more about it, as the moment came for another take. They did a few more before a break was called, in order to give the crew time to shift to another part of the set.

He and Lois had almost made it to the soundstage door when Hornsby caught up to them.

"Mr. Bradley, Miss Ashford?" he asked quietly. "May I have a word?"

"Sure," Nick responded, as Lois nodded.

They waited as Hornsby paused. He looked around before gesturing toward the door.

"Perhaps, not here?"

"My dressing room okay?" Nick asked.

Hornsby nodded jerkily and headed for the trailer. As they followed, Nick and Lois exchanged a look, wondering the same thing. Lois shrugged.

Once inside, Nick motioned Lois toward his chair, while he perched on the counter. Hornsby immediately began pacing.

Nick guessed whatever was on the director's mind had something to do with the strange glare he'd witnessed earlier, but he remained in the dark as to what could be rattling the man so much.

After a few moments of waiting, Lois looked at Nick.

"Should I—" she began to whisper.

At that moment, Hornsby whirled toward them. He opened his mouth, then stopped and resumed pacing.

It was the most emotion they'd ever seen from him. Nick wished he'd just get to the point. He couldn't figure out what the problem was, and that worried him.

Lois glanced at him again, then took matters into her own hands, clearly as frustrated as he was.

"Mr. Hornsby, is something wrong?"

He stopped, facing away from them. After squaring his shoulders, he finally turned toward them.

"Just what exactly do you two think you're doing in there?"

"Last I checked, I thought we were making a movie," Lois replied cheekily.

"Oh, no, don't be cute," Hornsby fired back. "You think I don't see what you're trying to pull? What I want to know is why."

Nick was honestly confused.

Lois looked similarly baffled.

When neither of them responded, Hornsby threw up his hands in exasperation. "What, now you don't have anything to say?"

"If we knew what you're talking about, we might," Lois said. "Care to enlighten us?"

A touch of guilt flared in Nick. Was Hornsby actually upset they were speaking up and adding to the script? He knew they hadn't really taken into account that he might have feelings on the subject, but he had yet to raise any objections.

Nick supposed a little damage control couldn't hurt.

"Look, if you're upset about our ideas, we didn't mean to overstep. We figured they'd improve the picture."

"Exactly!" Hornsby exploded, startling them both. "You're *improving* the picture. Why?"

Nick and Lois stared at him, then each other. Then him again.

Nick held up his hand, incredulous. "Hold on. *That's* what you're upset about?" Of all the possible reasons for Hornsby's anger…

"This isn't how this is supposed to go," Hornsby complained. "You're ruining everything!"

"Now you've really lost me," Lois interjected.

"Me too," Nick added. "Do you…not want to make a good movie?"

"No!"

Hornsby flopped into a chair, seeming to actually deflate right before their eyes.

Nick looked to Lois. She wasn't even trying to conceal her shock.

He took a deep breath and waded in. "Maybe you could explain a little?"

Hornsby raised his head dejectedly. He glanced back and forth between them. "You're... I mean... You actually *care* about this movie."

"You don't have to sound so surprised," Lois muttered.

"I'm not!" At Lois's scowl, he backtracked. "Okay, fine, I am. But it's just that this isn't at all the way I planned it."

Nick's annoyance mounted. He knew what low opinions everyone had of him at the moment, but it still rankled. He didn't enjoy being used so freely as a pawn in other people's plans. Especially when he still didn't know quite what those plans were.

He crossed his arms. "Would you mind telling us what exactly you were hoping to accomplish, that we're so thoroughly ruining?"

Lois looked up at him in surprise. *What, she doesn't have a monopoly on sarcasm, does she?*

"I suppose I should," Hornsby replied, sounding apologetic. "You see, I came in expecting this to be quite a disaster. That's why I took it on. The last thing in the world I want to be is a director."

"But your uncle got you a job doing just that. Doesn't that usually happen for men who want it?" Lois asked.

"In most cases." Hornsby smiled shyly. "But it's really my mother and my aunt who pushed me into it. For as long as I can remember, Mom's wanted me to follow in my uncle's footsteps. She never shuts up about it. Says it's a family legacy or some-thing. She does nothing but scoff when I try to venture an opinion about my own career."

"I hesitate to ask," Lois ventured, "but what is it you want to do?"

"I'm a historian." Hornsby perked up. "I'd love to study and record film history, as a matter of fact. It's not like I'm straying that far from the family business. If she'd just listen long enough, she might see that…"

"So did she put your uncle up to hiring you?" Nick felt sorry for the guy, but he didn't want to get too far off track.

"She got my aunt to start hounding Uncle Leo and they've just been impossible." He smirked. "So he and I hatched a plan of our own."

Nick was finally beginning to understand. He laughed ruefully. "You set yourself up for failure."

"And when she sees that the big, bad harpy and the pot-head were too much for you, your mother would let you flee Hollywood with your tail between your legs?" Lois added.

Hornsby nodded.

She shook her head. "I can't tell whether to be impressed or highly insulted."

"Oh, please don't be insulted," Hornsby pleaded. "I mean, not that I'd blame you. But your reputation…well…"

"It does precede me everywhere."

Nick's anger flared back up again, this time on Lois's behalf. How she remained so stoic—so offhand—about the reputation in question astounded him.

"Uncle Leo said neither of you would want to do this film, so I'd have an easy time of it," Hornsby responded. "Just let you go through the motions, get it over with, and then I'd be free."

Lois turned to Nick, "I told you so" written all over her face.

"Just because you were right, doesn't mean I wasn't just as right to subvert those expectations," he countered.

"Fair enough."

Hornsby looked up. "Subvert expectations? So you are trying. But that brings it back to my question—why? If no one else cares, why do you?"

"That's it exactly," Nick answered. "It's because they don't care. No one thinks we can do this, which will make it that much sweeter when we do."

Nick paused. He'd been so focused on Hornsby's story that the truth underlying the outburst hadn't fully sunken in until now.

"Wait a minute. You're upset because we're not terrible."

"Nick, have you just been pretending to participate in this conversation?" Lois asked. "That's exactly what he's been saying this whole time."

"Very funny. Don't you realize what this means?" At Lois's blank stare, he continued. "It's working. He's terrified because we're good. Because this isn't a failure. *We're* not failures."

Lois smiled and stage-whispered, "Haven't I been telling you that?"

Of course she had. But they'd been so imbedded in their little bubble. Yes, it had seemed to be going well, but it felt good to have someone with outside eyes confirm it.

"Um, excuse me?" Hornsby interrupted his thoughts. "I can't direct a success!"

"No offense, but I think I liked you better when you were the Cowardly Lion," Lois retorted.

"None taken," he replied. "Timidity really gets you out of a lot. Pretty useful." He paused. "So, are we in agreement? Can we go back to making a flop?"

"No!" Nick and Lois exclaimed in unison.

Nick preferred the Cowardly Lion too. But the new Hornsby had another thing coming if he thought Nick couldn't be just as stubborn.

"I understand why you want this to fail," Nick said. "But you have to consider where we're coming from. We have a lot riding on this. We can't make a failure."

"You said it yourself," Lois added. "Everyone expects the worst of us. But they might just take notice if we deliver something else. You certainly did." She gestured to Nick. "And I've actually let this one get my hopes up. I can't turn back now."

"Thanks…I think," Nick responded.

So she was admitting that he gave her hope now? Okay, then.

Not that any of it would matter if they couldn't manage to get Hornsby on their side.

"You're both so very different than I thought you'd be," Hornsby admitted wondrously.

Nick saw the young man's resolve cracking and kept going. "You should know better than anyone what it's like to be judged." He turned on his most charming smile. "I mean, I judged you pretty harshly, and look how wrong I was."

Picking up on his lead, Lois also smiled. "As was I. And you can imagine how much I hate to be wrong."

"You two are proving very difficult not to like," Hornsby said with a frown. "But you don't understand what my family is like. I have to be able to get out of this."

"Just look at the progress you're making already," Lois pointed out. "You're standing up to two of the scariest people on the lot. If you can do that, surely you can do the same with your own mother."

"True," he laughed. "But if I somehow end up being a success at this, I'll be proving her right. I can't have that!"

They were losing the battle again. Nick needed to do something, fast.

"Listen, Merrill," Nick began, "what do you say we make a deal?"

He looked at Lois, and she nodded her approval.

"We've only just begun this process, right?" Nick asked.

"Right."

"So, that leaves us plenty of time to figure a way out of this for you."

"It does?"

"Of course," Lois jumped in. "You let us keep going the way we've been, and we promise we'll help you find the perfect solution to your problem."

"Yeah, you see what we've done with this script," Nick added.

"Especially given how it started out." He gestured between himself and Lois. "We come up with good ideas."

Hornsby smiled reluctantly. "You do." He took a deep breath. "I can really trust you?"

Nick and Lois glanced at each other triumphantly.

"Absolutely," Lois answered.

"You have our word," Nick promised.

"Okay, then."

They all shook hands, and Nick breathed an exhausted sigh of relief.

THE NEXT DAY, Nick stood at the edge of the on-lot tennis court, shorts on and racket in hand, waiting for his turn to play. The studio was hosting a mostly private match between some of its stars, to "continue to foster a sense of community among our little professional family"—or so they claimed on the invitations. Given recent events, Nick honestly didn't know why he'd been included on the roster, but he supposed he ought to be grateful.

His thoughts still lingered on the curve Hornsby had thrown them. They'd managed to dodge a bullet—for now. But he could still change his mind. They needed to make sure to keep him on their side.

"Nice shorts," a silky, now-familiar voice called from behind him.

He had a comeback ready as he turned, but it evaporated as soon as he saw her. He swore his heart actually stopped for a minute.

There was Lois, dressed casually, yet even more stunning than usual. Between her sailor-style pants and platform shoes, her legs looked like they went on for days. A wide scarf held her hair back from her face, its ends trailing down over her shoulder. She peered at him over the rim of her white round sunglasses.

God, she's like some nautical goddess.

Her dark red lips smirked at him as she clearly waited for a response.

His brain lurched back to life a beat behind his heart, but he still couldn't remember what he had been planning to say.

He settled for, "I wasn't expecting to see you here."

He cringed inside. *Suave, Bradley.*

Lois shrugged and pushed her sunglasses back up her nose. "Didn't have much else going on today, so I thought I'd come see what the fuss was about. And it is a nice day." She gestured down at his racket. "Played yet?"

"No, I should be up soon."

"You any good?"

"Are you kidding? I'm fantastic."

Lois laughed. "Humble, too, I see."

Nick joined in her laughter. "I am an actor, after all."

He looked over at the crowd of spectators and sobered a bit. He really shouldn't have been surprised, but it hit him in the gut every time.

"Maybe I oughta try to lose," he continued. "Might not go over too well if I win. The way everyone keeps looking over here, like..." He trailed off.

"Like we're plotting the best way to do away with them without getting caught?" She pulled her sunglasses down again and winked. "Why do you think I wore these sunglasses?"

Nick chuckled half-heartedly. How in the world had she managed to deal with this kind of hostile scrutiny for so long?

As if reading his mind, Lois added quietly, "I forget sometimes how new you are to Hollywood purgatory."

He met her vibrant eyes and saw plenty of sympathy, but thankfully not even a hint of pity.

"It doesn't ever get easier, does it?"

She took a breath and let it out slowly, taking in the crowd before turning back to him. "It does not. But you find ways to make it your own." She lifted one shoulder. "It's the only way to survive."

Despite the multitude of eyes watching them, Nick suddenly felt as if they were all alone. It was a welcome feeling, but unsettling nonetheless.

Lois understood his experience exactly, because she'd been there for so long. Everyone was so quick to dismiss her, to write her off as impossible, that they failed to see anything beyond the surface. He wasn't arrogant enough to assume he saw everything that was there himself, but he could at least recognize that the depths existed.

A wave of applause burst from the stands as the current match neared its end, pulling them from the moment.

Disappointed, Nick watched Lois focus her attention on the players currently lobbing the ball back and forth.

"So who knew Hornsby had a spine after all?" she asked suddenly.

So maybe not all her attention.

"I know," he replied, unable to keep from smiling. "I was worried we wouldn't win him over."

"Me too. Think we can keep him convinced?"

"I hope so. We just have to make him trust us." He heaved a sigh. "And get him out of ever directing another picture."

"Well, if we can make *Teatime for Junie* funny, I suppose we can do just about anything."

Nick snorted. "You mean, *Teacups in July*?"

Lois turned to him, surprised. "Of course. Isn't that what I said?"

Now he laughed fully. "You called it *Teatime for Junie.*"

She covered her mouth. "Oh god, I did, didn't I? But you can hardly blame me! It is one of the stupidest titles ever written!"

"No argument there." He paused, remembering something else from their talk with Hornsby. "'The harpy and the pot-head,' huh?"

Despite her emerging blush, Lois raised her chin defiantly. "Didn't you know? That's our next project. I was thinking we could serialize it. Just think"—she swept her hand wide—"*The*

Harpy and the Pot-head Take Manhattan… The Harpy and the Pot-head Go to Washington… The Harpy and the Pot-head Ride Again. There's no end to the possibilities."

"Blondie and Dagwood'll be shaking in their shoes."

"Damn straight."

They both grinned.

It'll be such a letdown when this picture is finished.

Where did that come from? They still had plenty left to shoot, and it wasn't as if they'd never see each other again when it was over. *Right?*

Nick very much wanted to keep seeing her. For a long, long time.

Oh, shit.

"Uh-oh, what is that about?" Lois asked, her gaze fixed on the stands again.

"Someone aiming a dart gun at us? Or a spitball straw?" Nick joked.

She rolled her eyes. "Maybe at you. They wouldn't dare aim for me." She lowered her voice. "No, it's Joe Bartholomew. He's looking at us like the cat that just swallowed the canary. What's his deal?"

"Maybe he's pleased with us," he shrugged.

"Pleased. With us?" Lois leveled him with a highly doubtful glance.

"I'm an optimist, remember?" He looked more carefully at the producer. He was looking rather pleased, but Lois was right. It somehow didn't inspire confidence. Even when Bartholomew turned his attention back to the match, the uneasy feeling remained.

"You don't think he's talked to Hornsby, do you?" Nick wondered.

"I doubt it. He couldn't have changed his mind that fast." Lois folded her arms across her chest. "But Barty's up to something. I don't like it."

Before Nick could reply, one of the organizers called out to him. "Bradley, you're up next!"

"It'll have to be a problem for another day," Nick told her. "Duty calls."

"Probably inappropriate to say 'break a leg' in this situation, isn't it?"

"Yeah, probably. But thank you for the sentiment just the same."

Feeling the need to lighten the mood, Nick bowed with a flourish of his tennis racket. "Madam."

"You really are such a show-off."

Despite the jab, she was smiling and there was color in her cheeks that hadn't come from a makeup brush.

Success.

Chapter Seven

Redemption for a Fallen Angel?
Seems Hollywood's newest bad boy is not only taking his punish-
ment like a man but spinning it into gold. Word from the set of
his new picture with a certain raven-haired diva is that it's going
more swimmingly than anyone expected. We might not have
believed it if we hadn't witnessed the scene at Parkmoor Studios'
annual tennis soiree ourselves. Not only was the handsome misfit
athlete spotted getting some pre-match encouragement from his
costar, but the beauty was actually seen laughing as well! Could
the studio's new kindred spirits be getting ready to cause some
trouble together?

*L*ois spent the next couple of days trying—and largely failing—to keep herself distracted from her own thoughts. She wished she'd never gone to that stupid tennis match. She couldn't stop stewing over Barty. There was nothing specific to put her finger on, but she knew he had something planned. And that usually didn't bode well for her.

She did have moments when she could turn off the worry, but

even in those moments her mind lingered at the tennis match. More specifically, on Nick playing tennis. In those tennis shorts. That showed off every lean, powerful muscle in those athletic legs of his.

Not that she was shallow or superficial. She appreciated lots of things about him—his smile, the way he seemed to sense when she needed a laugh, the way he tried valiantly to make the best of things no matter the situation.

But those leg muscles. They were *fine*.

She was in *so* much trouble.

A throat cleared gently, tearing her away from the vision of Nick's legs and their tennis skills playing out in her head.

Lois looked up from her largely ignored macaroni to find a page waiting next to her commissary table.

"A note for you, Miss Ashford," he said, handing her a folded slip of paper.

"Thank you."

As soon as he left, she opened the note. It was from Jenny, Bartholomew's secretary, requesting her presence in his office this afternoon.

"Damn. I knew it," she muttered under her breath.

LOIS WALKED into Bartholomew's waiting area to find Nick already there, with his legs fully covered this time, thank goodness. She didn't need any distractions.

"Do I even need to say, 'I told you so?'"

"You do not." He leaned in conspiratorially. "Any idea what's up?"

"None whatsoever."

Before Jenny had a chance to stand up, the door to Bartholomew's office opened and the man himself stepped out.

"Miss Ashford, Mr. Bradley, please come in," he said.

He actually had the nerve to grin at them.

What the hell is happening?

Once they settled in his office, Bartholomew braced his elbows on his desk and steepled his hands.

"So, believe it or not, I'm hearing good things coming from your soundstage."

"Are you now?" Lois asked with false politeness.

"I am. And not just from there. Have either of you seen Hedda Hopper's column from yesterday?"

Nick shook his head. "I've been trying to avoid the papers lately."

Bartholomew looked expectantly at Lois.

"You know I don't bother with that drivel," she replied.

"Well, you should sometimes; it might surprise you." He picked up a newspaper and handed it across the desk to them. "Go ahead, read it."

Nick took the paper and held it between their two chairs so they could read together.

Looks like the same old drivel to me.

Upon finishing, Lois rolled her eyes. Nick didn't seem too thrilled either. Bartholomew, on the other hand, looked obnoxiously smug.

"What did I tell you?" he said. "You're playing nice, and it's starting to pay off."

"Pay off?" Lois retorted. "How is this paying off? We're still the 'diva' and the 'bad boy,' aren't we? Or did I read something else?"

"That's what I saw," Nick agreed. "I believe the word 'trouble' was used."

"I think you're both missing the bigger picture," Bartholomew countered. "Your film is getting noticed. And so is your behavior." He pointed at Lois. "You were seen enjoying yourself."

"And Hedda's surprise was so very endearing. Remind me to send her a fruit basket."

He waved his hand dismissively. "The whole point of the gossips is thinly veiled snark, we all know that. No doubt that's why you avoid the 'drivel.' But you also know they're a necessary evil. This works in your favor, believe me."

Bartholomew took a swig of coffee before continuing. "Even before this, things were looking good. I'm sure I don't need to tell you what everyone thinks of your script, but you've somehow managed to generate some good buzz for *Teatime in Summer* anyway."

"*Teacups in July*," Lois interrupted.

"What?"

"*Teacups in July*. You really should try to get the name of the picture right, Barty."

Nick snickered next to her. "Since when do you defend—let alone *know*—our title?"

She smiled wickedly back at him. "It's *our* title. We can get it wrong all we like, but others need to respect it."

"Aw, see? I knew you liked it."

"May I continue?" Bartholomew asked. He looked as if he was torn between exasperation and—was it possible?—amusement.

"Go ahead," Lois replied.

Bartholomew hesitated for a moment, assessing the two of them, before nodding.

Uh-oh. Here it comes.

"Hedda's not the only one who noticed you at the tournament, you know. I was watching you two. I have been ever since our first meeting. I had the beginnings of an idea then, and I think it's an even better idea now."

She exchanged a questioning glance with Nick.

"What exactly are you talking about?" Nick asked. "Or do I even want to know?"

"Keep in mind, I haven't gone to anyone else here about this yet," Bartholomew began. "I felt I owed it to the two of you to run it by you first."

Dread pooled in Lois's stomach.

"Spit it out, Barty," she commanded, wanting to get it over with. The sooner she knew what they were dealing with, the sooner she could start planning what kind of fight she'd need to put up.

Bartholomew took a deep breath. "I think the two of you should get married."

What?

MARRIED?

Lois wanted to respond, come up with some witty retort, but her brain was frozen. Every thought arrested, skipping like a record needle.

Nick laughed. "Good one. What's your idea, really?"

He thought Bartholomew was joking. *How quaint.*

"I'm serious, Bradley. I think a marriage between the two of you would be just the ticket."

Lois was still unable to find words, let alone use them. After all this time, she had learned to be quick with a solution, an answer. She prided herself on staying one step ahead of everyone most of the time. She usually expected the worst, so she was always prepared. But this… She honestly had no idea what to do with this.

She couldn't even remember how to throw a tantrum.

And if *anything* deserved a tantrum…

Nick looked to Lois, then back at Bartholomew, eyes like saucers, finally registering the bewilderment she felt.

"Wait, you…you can't possibly be serious," he said. "Married? Us?"

He doesn't have to protest that much, does he?

Seeming to read her thoughts, he flushed. "Not that Miss Ashford isn't lovely. You are, truly."

He moved to touch her arm, but stopped himself when he saw her face.

Smart man.

He continued, "But you can't actually think this is a good idea, can you? I mean, we really hardly know each other. We've never even been on a date!"

"Plenty of real Hollywood marriages have been founded on

far less," Bartholomew answered. "And of course I'm not even suggesting a real one."

Lois wished she could shoot laser beams out of her eyes.

Nick turned back to the producer, his usual geniality slipping away.

"Oh, come on. Publicity relationships are a terrible idea. They're completely unfair to everyone involved. The public gets completely snowed, and it means we're always on, no matter what. We pretend for a living, but we shouldn't have to take that work home with us. Good press can't possibly be worth the cost."

How does he manage to look earnest and angry at the same time?

Lois took a deep breath. "He's right."

"It's not nearly as big a deal as you're making it out to be." Bartholomew held up his hand before they could interrupt. "Just hear me out. It'll be a few dates, a public wedding, and then a handful of appearances. Your private lives will still mostly be your own."

Neither of them spoke, simply stared him down.

He took a breath before continuing. "I really think you should consider it. You see how you're still being described in the columns. It's better, but there's so much room for improvement; you said it yourselves. This could push you into positive territory. You know I think you both could use a win."

"That's exactly what you said this picture was supposed to be," Lois pointed out.

"Yes. And look how well it's going so far! It's working beautifully."

"So then why do we need to do this?" Nick asked.

"Because one picture might not be enough. You need to start thinking about what more you can do, build on the momentum. Bradley, you're damn lucky the studio hasn't made this worse for you."

Nick's face flushed with chagrin. And anger.

As Bartholomew exhaled, Lois could sense the boom about to be lowered.

"I hate to even bring this up, but I might as well tell you. You both have contracts up for renewal in the not-so-distant future."

"You can't be serious!" Lois was incredulous. "Last I checked, our contracts do not give the studio the right to bind us in an arranged marriage."

"That is technically true. If you decide not to do this, no one's going to force you. But your contracts do give the studio control over your publicity. And make no mistake, this would be good publicity."

"You said you hadn't run this by anyone yet," Nick said. "Is this really coming from you, or the higher-ups?"

"From me, I assure you," Bartholomew responded. "But they'll all have seen Hopper's column. It won't be long until someone else comes up with it. Isn't it better to get out ahead of it, let me help you do this in a way that gives you a little more control?"

"Control?" Lois asked acidly. "You just threatened us with our contracts."

"That wasn't a threat, it was a warning." He leaned forward over his desk. "I won't lie to you. Given both of your reputations right now, how likely do you think it is that this studio will want to keep you on longer than they have to? A spate of good publicity will go a long way in your favor."

Lois and Nick both sat in silence. She wanted very much to scream over how ridiculous the situation was. But as much as she hated to admit it, Bartholomew's words were starting to penetrate the haze of her fury.

She loathed her unearned reputation, and the ease with which the studio used her as a pawn while treating her like a leper. But she honestly didn't know what would happen if she no longer had a contract. Sure, plenty of actors were starting to work successfully as free agents, but none of them had her track record. Would anyone even hire her if they didn't have to?

Bartholomew spoke again. "You don't have to make a decision

right this minute. I'll give you a few days to think it over. But I strongly suggest you consider it."

Lois looked at Nick. His expression was unreadable, but she had a strange suspicion he might actually be tempted to say yes.

To her surprise, so was she. *What in the ever-loving fuck is wrong with me?*

"WOW."

"Yep."

"I mean…just…wow."

Nate sat next to Lois on a raised platform in the accessory room later that afternoon. Her friend wasn't usually at this much of a loss for words.

Damn.

"I know," Lois said. She rested her chin on her arms, which were folded over her knees.

"So are you gonna do it?" Nate wondered.

"I have no idea."

"How'd you leave it with Nick? What does he want to do?"

"Don't know that either."

They hadn't really left it any which way. They'd just left.

After Bartholomew had dismissed them, they'd filed out of his office as if sleepwalking. Lois regretted the way they'd left Jenny, whose farewell had gone completely ignored by both of them. They had barely said goodbye to each other.

"Can I venture an opinion?" Nate asked cautiously.

"I was actually hoping you would."

"Well…I know I haven't had time to think about it much, but my gut reaction—you know, besides shock—is…that maybe…it's *not* the most terrible idea?"

Lois looked up at her and quirked her lips into a half-smile, half-grimace. "Same."

"Huh." Nate studied her closely for a moment. "And that's the problem, isn't it?"

"It should be so simple. It's crazy. End of story. I mean, given all the stellar things that have happened to me over the years courtesy of men, the last thing I need is a fucking husband."

"You don't even *date* guys from work."

"Exactly! So why I am having such a hard time coming up with reasons to say no?"

"Because it would be all for show?" Nate hesitated. "And because the husband would be Nick?"

Shit, shit, shit.

A soft knock sounded.

"Yes?" Nate called.

The door opened, and Nick peered in, almost shy, holding a small pink bakery box.

"Thought I might find you here," he said. He gestured into the room. "May I?"

"Sure," Lois answered.

Nate stood. "You two have a lot to discuss, so that's my cue."

She stopped as she passed Nick and noticed the box.

"Is that food?"

He perked up. *Poor, oblivious man.*

"Yes. A buddy of mine makes the best chocolate cheesecake on the planet." He smiled sheepishly at Lois. "It felt highly necessary to bring some."

Hard to say no indeed.

It should not be so. Damn. Hard.

"Aw, how sweet," Nate crooned. "But no."

"Oh, come on," Lois protested.

Nate crossed her arms. "May I remind you, you are on *my* turf."

"Chocolate cheesecake, Nate." Lois batted her eyelashes and gave her best pout. "After the day I've had…"

Nate rolled her eyes and groaned dramatically. "You know how much I love you. If you called and told me you'd murdered someone, I would pick up a shovel and help you ditch the body, no questions asked." She pointed at her. "But know this—if I find so much as one teeny, tiny speck of chocolate anywhere in here, you are dead to me."

Even though she'd mostly been talking to Lois, Nick held up his hand. "Scout's honor."

"I'm watching you."

As Nate turned to leave, he called out to her. "Oh, I forgot to bring a knife so we could share this. Any chance I could borrow a pair of your fabric scissors?"

Nate gave him a stare that would make Lois, at her most extreme, look like Shirley Temple.

"My shovel is always ready, and I have absolutely no problem disposing of *your* body, Reefer Boy."

She closed the door behind her and Lois laughed ruefully. "Wow, you have a death wish. Her fabric scissors, really?"

Nick grinned wickedly. "Couldn't resist." He paused, and the grin faded. "I'm gonna end up wearing something horribly humiliating in my next picture, aren't I?"

"You can count on it."

"I wasn't lying about not having a knife," he said, reaching into his jacket pocket. "But I did bring two forks, if you don't mind sharing?"

Lois gestured to the space next to her, and he moved to sit.

"Do you always carry forks with you?"

Nick chuckled as he handed her one. "Nah, I just swiped these from the commissary." At her look, he held up his hand. "Don't worry, I plan to return them as soon as we're finished. I may have an arrest record, but I'm no thief."

"Don't let Bartholomew hear you say that. He'll make that the title of your memoirs and hire you a ghost writer tomorrow."

"God, he would, wouldn't he?" Nick took a deep breath. "Lois, I do hope you know, all my objections back there had nothing to do with you, and everything to do with the situation."

"I know, Nick."

Lois took a bite of cheesecake, and promptly forgot everything that had ever bothered her.

"Oh my god. You weren't exaggerating."

Nick grinned. "Right?"

"Is your friend a magician? This is…" Lois had another mouthful while thinking. "There really are no adequate words. This is absolute heaven." She looked up at him in awe. "How did you know this was *exactly* what I needed right now?"

"It always works for me, so I took a chance it'd be mutual."

Nick held her gaze for a few moments, and the air vacated her lungs in a whoosh.

Marriage to him really wouldn't be so bad, would it?

And that was *exactly* why she needed to say no. She'd had to carve out far too many pieces of herself over the years. The prospect of making room for this, only to carve it out as well, would take energy she wasn't sure she had.

No, marriage to Nick Bradley, phony or not, was a distraction she didn't need. But she was coming to realize, to her abject horror, it was a distraction she might actually *want*. All the protections she'd erected for herself turned stubbornly, frustratingly elusive around this man.

She heaved a sigh and looked down at her fork.

"So," she ventured.

"So."

"I suppose we should talk about this, huh?"

"I guess we should," he replied.

The silence lingered between them for what felt like forever. What was there to say, really?

Like Nick, she had always hated the idea of fake publicity relationships. They were phony and ridiculous. And she firmly believed in doing things on her own. Relying on anyone else only led to disappointment. But that contract renewal loomed, and it might just take something as crazy as this to secure the professional future she wanted.

For that reason—and another she was terrified to examine too carefully—she thought this might be one risk worth trying, in spite of her nagging reservations.

Nick finally broke the silence. Barely.

"Marriage."

Lois looked up, expecting him to say more. He laughed.

"Sorry, I guess I'm still pretty speechless about it. Did you see this coming, at all?"

"I did not."

"Which must really be saying something. You seem like you'd be prepared for any and all crap they might throw your way."

Lois huffed a laugh. "I've always thought so." She paused. "I really don't know why I'm surprised. Given my reputation, I should've expected they'd try a publicity marriage sooner or later. Maybe they could never find any takers. It took someone with an arrest record to come along and save the day."

"Well, if that's the case, my arrest record and I are deeply humbled and honored to be the first."

"Why, thank you."

Nick propped his chin on his hand and watched her, assessing. "You know, you were quieter than I would have expected in that meeting. What are you really thinking about all this?"

The directness of his question surprised—and impressed—her. Despite being an actor, she was unused to being seen, really seen. And here sat someone who seemed to see a great deal.

After years of hiding and masking her feelings, it truly was nice to have someone new she didn't have to censor herself around.

"Can I be honest? As bizarre and unexpected as this is, I'm actually having trouble finding reasons *not* to go through with it. Which makes no sense, because…there are reasons. Plenty of them. I'm just not finding them overly compelling."

Suddenly it was too much to be sitting so close to him, his heat coming through his shirtsleeve, mere inches from her arm. How was she supposed to cope with a whole marriage when she could barely handle this proximity? She stood and took a few steps, keeping her back to him.

"You probably think that sounds crazy, don't you?" she asked.

"I might…if I didn't agree."

Lois whirled around to face him. His expression was such a perfect mix of sheepish and hopeful that she could barely stand it.

Why is he so damn endearing, all the time?

"You do?"

Nick nodded. "I can't believe it, but I do. I've spent the last hour feeling completely unhinged about it."

"Me too!"

Their shared laughter echoed through the room.

"I mean, it's ridiculous. I hate publicity relationships. They're a part of everything that's wrong with our business. And…well…" He trailed off, rubbing the back of his neck, almost embarrassed.

"What is it?"

"It's just… This might sound sappy, but…I've always thought that marriage…" He blushed. "It should be real, you know?"

"I know," she said quietly, the slight hitch in her voice surprising even to her own ears.

Nick shook his head and looked up at her. "But even with all that, I'm having more success convincing myself to agree to it. And we are already at an advantage."

"How so?"

"We're going into it as friends. Much easier to fake a marriage with someone you get along with, no?" His cheeks flushed again. "That is…I don't want to presume; I know we haven't known each other long, but I do consider you my friend…"

"Relax, Nick." Her smile came naturally. "I consider you a friend, too."

And she did. It was still so novel to her, having a friend here at the studio besides Nate. But it was true. In a short time, they had indeed forged a friendship, one she had come to value.

Fuck. There goes another crack in my wall.

"So there we are. Friends." Nick's throat moved as he swallowed. "And as much as I hate to admit it, Bartholomew had a point about the good press. Hopper's column was infuriating, but it was an improvement."

"It was," she agreed grudgingly. "As underhanded as it was, he wasn't wrong about the contract thing, either." She blew out a frustrated breath.

All afternoon, one particular doubt had been hovering on the periphery of her thoughts, and Nick's mention of the gossip column caused it to finally crystallize. While she debated with herself about whether or not to voice it, Nick spoke up in that uncanny way he had.

"What's wrong?"

How does he do *that?*

Lois turned away from him. "It's probably nothing, really."

Just be honest. If anyone will understand, it's him.

"It's only," she began, "if we do this, I need to make sure things continue to improve. For both of us."

"Both of us? Sure. Why wouldn't they?"

"Because I've been here before. Not exactly here, but close enough. So often I've thought I was finally getting out of this ditch, only to get pushed right back down."

"If anyone stands to gain more out of this, it's you. There were drugs and police involved with me, remember?"

She turned back to face him, not bothering to hide her frustration. "But you're a man. And everyone loves a good redemption arc. Tame the shrew, and you've got it made."

Nick stood and came toward her. "The shrew? Is that really how you see yourself in this?"

"Of course not. But do you honestly think that's not how everyone else does?"

"I—" He stopped, passing his hand across his chin. "I suppose it'd be pretty naive of me to think so, wouldn't it?" He shook his head. "Does it help any to know that it's not at all how I see you?"

"A little."

"Good."

"But Nick, you're one person. My role was defined a long time ago. And not by me. And here I am, about to maybe, finally have a shot at changing it." She hesitated. "But what if I just end up exchanging it for something else, something still not my own?"

He looked at her determinedly. "We make a good team, don't we?"

"We do." It still felt so unusual, but she couldn't deny it.

"Then that's exactly how we'll make this work. As a team. On our own terms." Nick's eyes lit with an idea, and he looked around the room. "Is there any paper in here?"

"It's an accessory closet. I doubt it. Why do you need paper?"

"To write down our terms." He waved his hand. "Never mind, we'll just commit them to memory."

"Our terms?"

"Yes. If we decide to get fake-married, we go in with our eyes open, and we get exactly what we want out of it. This has to work for both of us, or it's not worth it."

He really was a marvel once he got a plan going in his head. His attitude once again had her reaching for that tricky, elusive bastard. Hope.

Can I really believe it this time? Can we really make this happen? For both of us?

"Presuming we did do this, how exactly would it work, then?" Lois asked slowly. "It would be temporary, yes?"

Something flashed in Nick's eyes that she couldn't quite put her finger on, there and gone in an instant.

"Right," he replied. "What do you think, a year?"

"A year could work. Six months might not be as believable."

"True. So a year. That'll cover the premiere and all the publicity for our film, too. Should be a nice chunk of time for everyone to get used to seeing us in a good light."

"And I don't know about you, but that timeframe includes my contract renewal."

"It's close to mine too. Good thinking."

A new detail occurred to Lois, one that filled her with an unexpected surge of anticipation. And—*what the hell?*—shyness.

"We'll have to decide where to live."

Nick met her eyes, the air around them suddenly charged.

"Where to live? Oh. Yeah. I suppose we have to keep up the illusion by living together, don't we?"

"Uh-huh," she managed.

"As nice as it is, my apartment is pretty small, actually."

Her mind flooded with images of sharing a small space with Nick. Navigating around each other in the kitchen, preparing breakfast. Curling up on a sofa, listening to the radio. Nick emerging from a shower, a towel barely covering his...

With that, this room, always so spacious, seemed entirely too crowded.

Lois tried to stem the furious blush spreading over her skin.

Control. Must get control.

"I have a decent-sized bungalow," she offered, "if you don't mind moving in with me. Or I suppose we could look for something entirely new?"

Nick watched her curiously. *Oh god, was he reading her thoughts again?*

"I don't mind. I'm sure your place will be perfect." He paused, looking unsure for a moment before continuing. "And Lois, you have my word. I assure you, I will be a complete and utter gentleman at all times. You never need to worry that I'll take advantage of our situation. Our marriage will remain a ruse behind closed doors."

The most alarming mix of feelings rioted through her at his words. On the one hand, immense relief suffused her, even though it had—unusually—never even occurred to her that he might be anything but a gentleman. The expectation that men would take advantage had become such a daily, ingrained part of her life, it fueled her anger almost subconsciously at this point. And while she could tell Nick was attracted to her, he had always given the impression that he wasn't like so many of the others, that he *was* actually a gentleman. Seeing as they were about to start spending a lot of time under the same roof, that confirmation felt nice.

But then there was the other hand. That image of Nick fresh from the shower hovered in her mind. And imaginary Lois couldn't resist the urge to rip off that towel and convince him *not* to be a gentleman.

Shit.

She remembered that she hadn't responded yet, and needed to.

"Thank you." She looked up into those deep blue eyes. "I really do appreciate that."

Nick held her gaze. "And no one's going to call you a shrew on my watch, either. I promise."

Lois laughed heartily at his sincerity. "And what will you do if they do? Pistols at dawn?"

He shrugged. "If I have to. I am serious, though. The minute this starts looking like it's not your redemption story as well as mine, we fix it, whatever we need to do, even end it. Deal?"

It astonished her just how much of her reserve had slipped away. Yes, she might regret it later, but…she really did want to give this fake marriage thing a go. With Nick.

"Deal." Lois bit her lip. "Are we really doing this, then?"

"Yeah, I guess we are." Nick regarded her with a lopsided smile. "You okay with that?"

"Somehow I am. You?"

"Somehow I am too."

He seemed suddenly aware of their surroundings, and cocked an eyebrow, grinning. He stepped over to a case on the counter and started perusing its contents. After finding something he liked, he turned back to her.

He held up an ostentatious ring with a paste emerald in its center. "Better make this semi-official."

Lois stared at him incredulously as he dropped to one knee.

"Lois Ashford, will you do me the great honor of fake-marrying me?"

Her breath caught in her throat. *Fake. It's just fake. Don't do this to yourself.*

"Yes, Nick Bradley, I will," she answered as he slipped the ring on her finger.

He then proceeded to give her a wolfish, comically flirtatious wink, and Lois threw her head back and laughed, relieved that he'd broken the spell.

This marriage might be a farce, but it would at least be fun.

Chapter Eight

Tinseltown Trappings

Grab your hankies, folks! It seems wedding bells are about to ring, and you'll never guess who's doing the ringing! We don't know what's in the water over at Parkmoor, but a little discipline seems to be going a long way—and it's even causing romance to bloom! After their recent spate of cavorting and canoodling, Hollywood's most Notorious Duo is actually making an honest pair of each other. We've learned the ceremony is happening in a mere matter of hours, and you can be sure we're on our way to find out all the details, just for you, dear reader!

Nick paced around the lobby of the Beverly Hills courthouse, trying in vain to contain his energy. He'd barely gotten any sleep the night before, but he didn't feel tired. He was a bundle of nerves, and he didn't know why.

Okay, he did know why.

But he shouldn't be nervous. This was what they agreed to. Everything had been going swimmingly so far. Exactly according to plan.

The gossips had been fascinated by his and Lois's "whirl-wind courtship" which consisted of exactly four very public, studio-orchestrated dates—two nightclub outings, one concert at the Hollywood Bowl, and a movie premiere. On the surface, it was all lovey-dovey praise, but Nick could sense a darker expectation lurking below, as if they waited impatiently to see what mischief the couple could cause together. The fact that their dates had been so normal almost seemed to disappoint the columnists.

He supposed that should be a good sign, but it still unnerved him.

How has Lois dealt with this crap for so long?

He had no idea what they'd make of a hasty wedding. But Bartholomew had assured them that the publicity department would tip off one of the papers, so he wouldn't have to wait long to find out.

He had never spent a lot of time picturing his wedding day, but he had certainly not expected this.

And he very definitely hadn't expected to be such a nervous wreck.

"Are you ever going to sit down?" Max asked from his seat against the wall. "You're driving me nuts."

"Shouldn't she be here by now?"

"You insisted on getting here an hour early, remember? It's barely been twenty minutes." Max leaned forward in his seat. "What is with you?"

"Sorry, I guess I just want to get this over with."

"Just what every bride wants to hear on her wedding day," a honeyed female voice drawled behind him.

Nick whirled around, ready to apologize, but the words died in his throat.

She was beautiful. As usual.

Lois had dressed perfectly for a courthouse wedding. She wore an ivory day dress in what looked like silk, with that extra fabric at the waist—a peplum, was it?—that was so popular lately. Her hat had a tiny veil that hovered jauntily over one eye, and wrist-length gloves completed the picture of the blushing bride.

But she was anything but blushing. Even looking as "traditional" as she did, she had an edge to her, a sexiness that practically knocked him on his ass.

"You look lovely," he managed.

"Thanks." She smirked as she leaned in to add conspiratorially, "You have no idea how close I came to wearing red."

Nick laughed, his nerves suddenly much calmer. "They would've had a field day with that."

"No doubt. Oh, to have seen their faces." Lois sighed. "But they've been dying for us to make a mistake. It would've played right into their hands."

"Well, as I said, you do look lovely anyway. And I didn't mean—"

"I know, I was only teasing. I'd rather not do this in front of photographers either." She looked around the lobby. "Any sign of them yet, or are we too early?"

"I haven't seen anyone yet, but I'm sure Bartholomew will have them for lunch if no one shows."

"That's for sure."

Nate, who had arrived with Lois, cleared her throat. "So, does the rest of the wedding party get to meet, or do we have to stand here awkwardly for a while?"

"You read my mind," Max responded, extending his hand. "Max Mitchell, best man."

"Natalie Reynolds, matron of honor, but you can call me Nate. A pleasure."

"The pleasure is mine, I assure you." Max looked between her and Nick. "So Nate…and Nick." He turned to Lois with a wry grin. "That's not going to be confusing or anything." He moved to shake her hand as she laughed. "And you must be the bride."

"Guilty as charged." Lois winced and glanced at Nick. "Sorry, too soon to make courtroom jokes?"

Max laughed. "Oh, I've been making them from the minute he got picked up. Pile 'em on."

"Whatever did I do to deserve such a great friend?" Nick fired back.

"So how do you two know each other?" Nate asked.

"We grew up together," Nick answered. "Lived on the same block as kids, and never really got rid of each other."

"Of course not. I keep him in a near-constant supply of sugar. I run a bakery in Burbank."

"So *you're* the reason we're here!" Nate exclaimed.

At Max's confused expression, Lois gestured vaguely toward Nick. "I'm really only marrying him for your cheesecake."

"Wow, he actually shared my cheesecake? You must be special."

All at once, heat crept up Nick's neck. He needed to regain control of the situation—and get Max to shut up—before the blush breached the barricade of his shirt collar.

Luckily, he was saved by Bartholomew's booming voice.

"Hello, everyone! Beautiful day for a wedding, isn't it?"

"Just swell." Lois had plastered on her brightest, falsest smile. "Shouldn't you have a dozen photographers nipping at your heels?"

"They'll be here soon. I wanted to make sure you two actually showed up first."

"You doubted us? Barty, you wound me."

The producer held up his hands. "Can you blame me?" He paused to take in the two of them, and Nick was surprised to see a hint of sincere concern in the man's face. "I really am glad you're here. I won't steer you wrong, you know."

Nick glanced at Lois, who seemed to be making a herculean effort not to roll her eyes.

"Oh, I almost forgot, I brought this for you," Bartholomew said, offering his hand to Lois. Nick hadn't noticed before, but he held a small cluster of violets and pansies. "Every bride needs a bouquet, right?"

Lois took the little posy. "I love pansies. Did you know that?"

He waved his hand dismissively. "My wife grows them, and when I was leaving this morning, I remembered you mentioned it in an interview once. Thought you should have some."

Lois looked dumbfounded. "Barty, you mean to tell me you made this yourself? That's...so thoughtful."

"Don't spread it around; no one'll take me seriously anymore." He winked. "All right, where are those reporters?"

Bartholomew turned and brisked through the lobby.

"I'm so confused," Lois murmured. "Is it possible he actually means it?"

"Maybe you just overwhelmed him with your charm and gratitude," Nick teased.

Lois nudged his arm. "Shut up."

He watched her smile down at her flowers, and was thoroughly charmed himself. He felt a strange sense of jealousy. There had been nothing romantic in Bartholomew's gesture. But Nick wanted tremendously to be able to put a smile like that on her face.

A sudden and surprising jolt of anger followed. Lois clearly wasn't used to being on the receiving end of such a simple kindness as a bouquet of flowers, and it made Nick want to lash out, find everyone who had ever made her feel less than, and pummel them senseless.

And then fill her house—our house now—with a whole field's worth of pansies. Forever.

Forever? Where the hell had that come from? This was a temporary—and fake—arrangement. Nothing more. He needed to remember that.

"Bradley, come here."

He broke out of his reverie at Nate's voice. "Hmm?"

She beckoned him over. "Your tie needs fixing."

Nick made his way to her and she began fussing over him. "Thanks."

"Don't thank me, I'm just doing my job."

"I didn't realize you were on the clock today." He smiled at her.

"I'm always on the clock when it comes to my friends." She pierced him with a grave glare, and her hands tightened on his tie.

Nick swallowed convulsively. He'd kept his promise, hadn't touched her fabric scissors.

"I need to say something," she continued, quietly enough that only he could hear her. "Lois is my dearest friend, and I have watched her deal with endless crap that she does not deserve. I've always thought you were a decent guy, and I know this marriage isn't real, but I'm telling you right now—if you do anything at all to hurt her, in even the tiniest way, I will make your life a living hell. Do I make myself clear?"

"Clear as a bell."

She finally released her grip on his tie. "Good."

"You don't need to worry. I would never want to hurt Lois." He looked over at his bride-to-be, chatting with Max. "She's... well...most definitely not deserving of crap." He turned back to Nate. "And she won't get it from me."

"Okay then." Nate reached up and started to re-straighten the tie she'd thoroughly scrunched.

Nick leaned in. "She's also very lucky to have a friend like you."

"Yes, she is." Nate smiled through a slight blush. "Thanks, Reefer Boy."

"I'm never gonna lose that nickname with you, am I?"

"Nope." She winked as she headed back to Lois and Max.

THE CEREMONY WAS quick and efficient. When they were called before the judge, Nick took Lois's hands, comforted by the slight tremble he found there. She hid it well, but her nerves clearly lurked below the surface, just as his did. As phony as this marriage was, he couldn't escape the solemnity of standing in front of witnesses, reciting vows, slipping a ring on Lois's finger.

It almost felt real.

Which was ridiculous. Wasn't it?

"You may now kiss the bride."

Oh, shit.

Nick had been so focused on the ceremony, on getting everything right, that he'd forgotten the end of a typical wedding. They'd have to kiss now.

Not that he didn't want to. Looking down into Lois's piercing green gaze reminded him once again how much he did, in fact, want to kiss her.

Which was exactly the problem.

On closer inspection, he noticed a hint of uncertainty in her eyes. If he didn't know better, he might think she was having the same internal debate he was. Which would certainly be an interesting development.

Part of Nick wanted to give her a peck on the cheek and be done with it, deal with all this nonsense in his head at a later date. A much later date. Maybe never.

But no such luck. Bartholomew's photographer had shown up, and presumably, word would have spread so that more would await them out front when they left. But this one's presence mattered most. This was the picture that really counted, that would best sell their story. Their kiss had to be convincing.

It really isn't such a big deal. You're actors, right? Just a kiss, then move on.

Lois quirked her eyebrow and smirked at him, issuing a challenge.

He couldn't help the soft chuckle that escaped him, and so he leaned in.

The minute their lips touched, he lost all capacity for thought. Her mouth felt soft, warm. They held there, both tentative for about a second, as if to give each other an out if they wanted it.

Neither one of them took the out.

Her lips parted just a fraction, and it ignited a fire throughout his whole body. He let go of her hands and moved his to her waist, as her fingers slid up his arms to grasp his shoulders. Slow and languid, they continued to match each other, nip for nip, for what was probably a highly inappropriate amount of time for a wedding kiss.

Nick would have been content to continue exploring her lips all afternoon, but the pop of a flashbulb brought him back to reality, reminding him that this was all for show.

At least it was supposed to be.

They moved to break the kiss at the same time. Lois looked up at him, and for the briefest of moments, she looked just as dazed as he felt. Recovering quickly, though, she turned to their small, assembled group with a dazzling smile. He followed suit.

Lois held up her bouquet. "Shall we go celebrate?"

"Yes, let's." Nick gestured their friends toward the door, and noticed Max giving him the eye.

Great, he'll be impossible later.

Nick knew his insides might never stop feeling like molten lava, but god, what had that kiss *looked* like?

He decided to ignore it and move on. "Dinner's on me!"

The group laughed, and they turned to thank the judge before leaving. When they got outside, to Bartholomew's delight, they found a handful of reporters waiting for them on the courthouse steps. They stopped to play along, posing for pictures and answering a few invasive questions.

Throughout it all, Lois couldn't have been more gracious. Nick watched her give the reporters exactly what she knew they wanted. He thought it must be killing her not to roll her eyes right in their faces—it certainly was one hell of an effort for him—but she never faltered for a moment. His new wife was something else.

Wife. Wow.

At that moment, Max returned from retrieving their car, which he and Nate had managed to conveniently transform at some point. Nick had no idea when they'd found the time, but he'd have to remember to thank them later. A giant "Just Married" splattered across the back, along with plenty of crepe paper streamers. They'd even completed the picture with a few tin cans trailing behind.

Needless to say, the reporters ate it up. They inhaled the artfully crafted portrait of wedded bliss on display.

Max rounded the car and tossed the keys to Nick.

"Thanks." He nodded at the car. "Nice touch."

"It was all Nate. She snagged me while we were waiting for the judge, and we ducked out to fix it up."

As if conjured, Nate popped up at his side. "Let it be known, it's not just people I can outfit."

"I will shout it from the rooftops," Nick responded.

"Go rescue your bride from the wolves. We'll see you at the restaurant."

Nick started toward Lois before remembering that he and Max had driven together, but his friend was already hitting Nate up for a ride. He worried a little at the thought of those two swapping stories, but forgot to care as soon as Lois spotted him and smiled.

He stepped up next to her and slid his arm around her waist. *Just looking the part for the reporters. That's all.*

Nick leaned in and said quietly, "Ready to get out of here?"

"*So* ready," she whispered back.

He raised his voice to the small crowd of reporters. "Sorry to break up the party, folks, but we've got a wedding dinner to get to!"

A chorus of questions pelted them as they moved to the car.

"Where are you celebrating?"

"Who else will be there?"

"It'll be a wild party, right?"

Lois teased them flirtatiously as Nick opened the door for her.

"Oh, come on, you know we have to keep some things to ourselves."

Just before climbing in behind the wheel, Nick called out a hearty, sincere—or so they thought—farewell. "Thank you all for coming! It's made this day even more special!"

He started the engine, and Lois expertly blew them all a parting kiss as he pulled away from the curb.

Chapter Nine

Hollywood Happenings
Pardon us, we're a bit misty. After a positively dizzying
courtship, Nick Bradley and Lois Ashford have tied the knot! We
admit, we were a little surprised (and more than a little skeptical)
at the news, but boy, do these two crazy kids seem to be in love!
After sharing quite the zealous kiss at the Beverly Hills Court-
house, Bradley whisked his new bride away for a private celebra-
tion dinner—as private as one can be at Chasen's, of course! We
wish the newlyweds all the best. If anything can be certain, we at
least know these two will produce some gorgeous, albeit mischie-
vous, children!

As Nick turned onto Doheny Drive, Lois sank back into the car seat, relaxing for the first time all day.

"My face actually hurts. Do you think smiling that much can damage your cheek muscles?" She worked her jaw, trying to ease the ache that had settled there.

"My mom always used the threat that my face would freeze, but it was usually when I'd make dastardly mugs. I think you're probably safe with smiling." He flashed her one of his own before continuing. "Although if they decide to make smiling an Olympic sport, your performance today would surely put you in the running for a medal."

Lois laughed, and then immediately winced. "Ow. Don't make me laugh. It hurts too much."

"Sorry. I will endeavor to be more serious." He exaggerated a scowl.

They exchanged a glance, then sighed together. Which made them chuckle all over again.

"They really seemed to buy it, didn't they?"

"They did." Nick huffed a small laugh. "That kiss you blew them at the end was a stroke of genius."

"You liked that, huh?" It had occurred to her on a whim, and she decided to act on it. She was nothing if not a committed actor.

"The car looks fantastic, by the way," she added. "Was that your idea?"

"I wish I could take the credit, but apparently it was all Nate, with a little help from Max."

"Ah, that makes sense." Leave it to Nate. She left no stone unturned.

Nick absently rubbed his jaw. "I hate to say it, but I'm almost surprised how well it all went down. Was it just me, or did they actually seem like they were rooting for us?"

"It wasn't you. That was so weird. I've never seen reporters look at me like that, with…" She trailed off, unable to find the right word.

"Approval?"

"Yes, that's it!" The impact crashed down on her. The little group outside the courthouse had acted like they were in their corner. True, they needed to play nice to get their story, but it still felt extraordinarily strange to her.

She glanced over at Nick with a rueful smile. "That's a new one for me."

"Hopefully one you'll have to get used to."

Lois watched her new husband as he navigated the road.

Husband. Wow.

Even though it was all an act, this was going to take some getting used to.

The late afternoon sunlight filtering in through the windshield cast a golden light on Nick's jaw, bringing into focus the shallow cleft in his chin. He really was handsome. Lois let her gaze travel up to those full lips of his, and her stomach did a somersault as she remembered their kiss.

She'd had quite the internal battle in the moments leading up to it. Part of her—a bigger part than she cared to admit—had been afraid to kiss him. She had learned to be fearless in her acting roles, and this should be just another role. But she couldn't escape the fact that she wanted to know what his lips would feel like on hers. And that made it much more difficult to keep herself distant from the role, which could only lead to trouble. This production would have a closing night. She could not let herself get too attached.

But there was no way they could have avoided the kiss. It was their wedding, after all. So she had leaned in and rewarded her curiosity.

And boy, what a reward.

He was a very good kisser.

So much trouble.

Having to get through a whole year of this? That would be beyond hard. She needed to shore up her will power, fast. It was all for publicity. She took a breath, trying to think more seriously. Trying to think, period.

Yes, he was handsome. And a good kisser. And he made her laugh and feel seen. But what did she really know about him? She had no idea what his story involved, where he'd come from, besides the basic facts that everyone knew. She didn't know what had happened with that arrest, either.

There was absolutely a story there.

Every interaction they'd had didn't exactly scream drug addiction, or even careless frivolity. Lois was dying to know what led him to it. He came across as such a planner, and so passionate about his career.

She glanced over at him again, assessing. So much to uncover.

Will a year be enough, I wonder?

She turned back to the view out the car window, groaning internally. She most certainly did *not* need to get caught up in figuring this man out.

What she needed to do was keep her eye on the goal. Her career. The whole reason she had agreed to get into this car with "Just Married!" emblazoned on the back of it. If she could only get rid of her damn label, she might finally have a chance at the serious career she'd always wanted.

She wanted to accomplish so many things. Acting had been her passion for so long, and she yearned to sink her teeth into some truly meaty roles. But over time, her dreams had grown to include more than just performing. There was so much more she wanted to do, things she didn't dare tell anyone else, lest they take it as a joke, or try to tell her she couldn't. But maybe, just maybe, if they took her more seriously, she could branch out. Try something bigger, like producing. Directing, even.

You could tell Nick.

Lois nearly jolted in her seat at the thought. Where had that come from? She hadn't even told Nate about some of her plans. It didn't make sense to be tempted to tell Nick. Except that some-how, it made perfect sense. If she could trust anyone to listen—and not just listen, but *understand*—it would be Nick.

Oh, boy.

At that moment, Nick pulled the car to a stop outside of Chasen's.

Before the valet could rush up to open the door, he looked over at her with a small smile. "Ready for round two?"

Lois met his eye and steeled herself—for their wedding dinner, and for whatever this marriage was going to bring.

"Ready as I'll ever be."

THE DINNER WENT AS WELL as the wedding had, perhaps even better, considering that most of their nerves had worn off. Like the ceremony, they kept the dinner intimate. Nate and Max accompanied them, and of course Bartholomew, whose wife also joined. Lois had met Carol Bartholomew a few times over the years at studio events, and always found her company pleasant. Carol was part of the reason she gave Bartholomew more benefit of the doubt than most of the other producers. Lois liked to think of herself as a pretty good judge of character, and if this woman had been married to him for as long as she had, he couldn't be all that bad.

A couple of photographers greeted them outside when they arrived—tipped off, of course—but had respectfully not followed them in. Lois expected that their little group would share a few drinks, a nice meal, and then be on their way. She was completely unprepared for the steady stream of well-wishers who stopped at their table. Word of their wedding had spread faster than wildfire. She thought it might be a Hollywood record.

She didn't know if it was Bartholomew's presence, the excuse to have another drink, or just the general happy haze that weddings seemed to inspire. But people who typically avoided her like the plague—and had started doing the same to Nick since his scandal—gushed and sighed and toasted them. Lois found their joy surprisingly infectious. Before long, the poor waiters struggled to keep up as patrons bounced between tables. Their celebration had taken over the whole restaurant.

It was the first Hollywood party she'd ever truly enjoyed.

One of the best things about it was observing Nate and Max's behavior. While they participated in the revelry, they also flanked her and Nick in a state of constant vigilance. The pair very subtly tensed every time someone new came up to congratulate the happy couple, as if they were ready to spring into defensive action in the face of anyone being insensitive or insincere with their friends. Lois doubted they had planned it, which made it even more comical. And also incredibly endearing. She knew Nate was a phenomenal friend, and it gladdened her to see that Nick had someone on his side as well.

She had only known Max for an afternoon, but she already liked him immensely. She could see why he and Nick were so close. He was charming, and had no problem needling Nick on any number of subjects. When dessert arrived, he kept everyone entertained with a running critique of every bite, assessing what the Chasen's chef had done right and wrong, and of course assuring everyone he could have done better.

Which, given his skill with cheesecake, Lois believed whole-heartedly.

At one point, she and Nate were on their way back from the ladies' room, marveling at how much the day was exceeding their expectations, when Nick approached them.

He slipped his arm behind her, his hand resting on the small of her back. She leaned into his side without a second thought. It felt so completely natural, effortless. A moment passed before she realized that it hadn't even occurred to her to think of this as an act for all those watching them.

Wonder if he's acting, or if he's feeling it too?

Before she could dwell on it for too long, Nick turned his attention to Nate.

"So, Nate, your husband couldn't make it today? His name's Walter, right?"

Nate got that odd expression she always wore when the subject of her marriage came up. Despite their long friendship, it was the lone area where Nate remained completely unreachable. Lois knew to leave well enough alone, but it didn't stop her from wondering.

"Yes, Walter," Nate replied. "That's him." After a pause, she gave Nick an awkward smile and belatedly answered his other question. "And no, he couldn't make it. Traveling. As usual. He's a baseball scout; it keeps him pretty busy."

Nick perked up at the mention of baseball. "Oh, wow. No kidding? Max's cousin works with the Dodgers in Brooklyn. I wonder if they've crossed paths?"

Nate paled slightly. "Maybe. But I doubt it. Baseball's a big operation. It's not like everyone knows everyone or anything." She swallowed visibly. "Anyone want another drink? I'm going to get another drink."

She raised her glass and bolted away from them.

Nick turned to Lois, completely perplexed. "Did I say something wrong?"

Lois gave him a reassuring smile. "It's not you, don't worry. Walter's…a bit of a sore spot. I think it's all the traveling."

He quirked an eyebrow. "He does that much of it?"

"As long as Nate and I have known each other—and it's been a while—I've never once met her husband."

"Never?"

"Afraid not. Every important event, he's absent. He's absent for the unimportant ones too. He's just never there." Lois sighed and looked up at Nick. "Between you and me, I kinda wish she'd kick him to the curb. She's the best, you know? And she deserves a hell of a lot better than some guy who can't be bothered to show up for anything. I mean, there can't possibly be that many baseball players to scout, can there?"

She stopped herself before she got too agitated and started drawing attention. "Sorry, it's just—"

"She's your friend and you care about her."

"Exactly." She smiled, feeling sheepish, yet comforted.

What is this effect he has on me?

Needing to keep her walls up, she pointed her finger in his face and added, "But I mean it—if you ever tell her I said that, there will be consequences. You won't like them."

The corner of Nick's mouth twitched, and a wicked gleam lit his eyes for a second. He opened his mouth to respond, but then stopped as if thinking better of it. Lois thought she detected a slight blush spreading across his cheeks.

He suppressed his smile and solemnly put his hand over his heart. "I assure you, it stays between us. And I won't bring Walter up with Nate again either."

"Thank you."

They returned to the party, and Lois felt reassured by his promise. But she couldn't stop thinking about that blush. She had the distinct impression that he had been going to come back at her with something flirty. How terrible was it that she felt disappointed he didn't?

But she couldn't focus on that, so she let her ego take over. It told her that she affected him in much the same way he did her, and she was inclined to believe it. Her ego came in handy as an actor, and since it was a healthy one, she trusted its usual accuracy.

He might be attracted right back, and it would be a big mistake to act on it in any way, but it at least comforted her to know they were rowing upstream in the same boat.

LOIS AND NICK arrived back at her—*their*—house later than they'd expected, full of mirth and still a little tipsy. As soon as Nick closed the front door, they locked eyes and simultaneously let out heavy exhales of relief.

"We did it," he breathed. "We actually did it."

"Yeah." Lois couldn't contain her incredulous laugh. "Can you believe that party?"

Nick pushed off the door and came toward her with excitement. "I know! That was fantastic! I don't think I've ever felt such a rush."

She knew she probably shouldn't, but said it anyway. "Really? Never?"

"Never."

It took him a moment to notice her skeptical look, so she mimed smoking a joint with a grin.

"Very funny." He rolled his eyes as he stepped even closer to her. "Really. Never."

His face was now within inches of hers.

"You were extraordinary with everyone," he said.

"You weren't so bad yourself," she managed.

All the air in the room had been replaced with pure electricity.

He raised his arm, his hand hovering to trace the air next to her face. "Does your face still hurt from all the smiling?"

"Not from the smiling, no."

It hurts like hell from the effort it's taking not to kiss you right now.

"Maybe all that alcohol helped." His eyes seemed to have zeroed in on her lips, as if he knew exactly what she was thinking. Thought it himself.

"Alcohol. Right."

She took in his lips, so close to her own now. At this distance, she noticed just how full they were. She remembered the feel of them on hers earlier. The wonderful things he'd done with them. She wondered what he would do, how they would feel, if no one was watching. If he wasn't holding back.

He chose that moment to bite his lower lip, and her knees nearly gave out.

Jesus Christ.

She wanted to climb him like a tree and never come down.

Their eyes met again, and a question hovered in the electricity between them.

Do we dare?

Before they could answer, a small cry came from somewhere below, and they jumped apart.

A pair of gray eyes peered up at them from amidst a ball of orange fluff.

"Cat," Nick whispered, stunned. "I forgot you have a cat."

"So did I," Lois muttered, her heart pounding.

She looked at Nick and they both burst into nervous laughter.

"Right, well," Nick started. "I guess I should..." He gestured toward the stairs.

"Yeah, it's been an eventful day, hasn't it? I'm exhausted."

"Me too."

She gestured to the cat. "I should feed her before I turn in."

"Of course." He hesitated for a moment before reaching out to touch her arm lightly. "Good night."

"Night."

She watched him walk away, her arm tingling where his hand had skimmed it. He turned before he started up the stairs, offering her a small smile and a wave. She could see his chest moving rapidly, breathing as hard as she was.

As soon as Nick was gone, the cat mewed again.

"Oh shut up, I hear you," she crooned as she stooped to pick her up. "You have some timing, you know that, Lady M?"

The cat just stared at her.

It was a good thing she had interrupted them. Wasn't it?

Chapter Ten

Hollywood Happenings
No honeymoon for the Wicked! It seems Tinseltown's newest
newlyweds haven't been given a chance for a proper wedding
trip, as they were spotted back at the studio only a couple of days
after their romantic ceremony, to continue work on their picture.
We don't know if it's their Director who's the stern taskmaster, or
if the edict came from higher up the food chain, but we do feel for
the lovebirds. But those movies we all love don't make them-
selves, and so the camera's reels must keep turning!

Nick woke up the next morning feeling groggy and disoriented. Not because Lois's guest room wasn't comfortable—it might even be more comfortable than his bedroom in his old apartment. Slightly impersonal and bland, but comfortable. But he hadn't slept well at all. After the roller coaster of a day, and all the toasts at the dinner, he had fully expected to drop into a deep and wonderful sleep.

Then the incident in the living room had happened.

No matter how hard he'd tried, he couldn't get it out of his mind. He'd tossed, he'd turned, he'd tried counting sheep—*had that ever actually worked for anyone?*—and when he finally did drift off, it was only to fall into restless dreams. Of her.

He sat up and rubbed the sleep from his eyes before glancing down at the way the sheet tented in his lap. His cock was obviously still focused on last night, too.

Nick flopped back onto the pillow with a groan.

He'd almost kissed Lois. What had he been *thinking*?

He hadn't been thinking. That was the problem. He'd promised her. He'd given his word to behave as a gentleman. And couldn't even last a minute as soon as they were alone together.

But the way she looked, like she wanted to devour me.

It didn't matter. He should've been more careful, should've held back. He and the mess over his arrest were largely responsible for her involvement in this situation in the first place. Not only that—while he didn't know her full story, he knew enough to see that too many people took advantage, went back on their word all the time with her. Men especially, he suspected.

He wanted her to know she could trust him. Simply wanted her to feel safe. She deserved that.

And if they were going to live together for the next year, it would be so much better for both of them if some strange cloud didn't hang over them.

He had to apologize. Immediately.

But first he needed a shower. A very, very cold one.

After shaving and dressing, Nick made his way downstairs. He could hear noises coming from the kitchen. Good, she was already up. Lois's cat waited for him at the bottom of the stairs. He reached down to scratch her ginger head as he passed by.

"Thanks, kitten," he whispered. "You saved us just in time last night."

But did she, really?

Nick shook his head to clear the thought. No, today was a fresh start. No more almost-kisses. They were friends, roommates, fake spouses. Nothing more.

He stopped in the doorway to the kitchen.

There stood Lois, intently flipping through *Variety* while she poured herself a cup of coffee. She was dressed more casually than he'd ever seen her, in a summery green and white jumpsuit that cinched in at the waist. Sleeveless, with wide white lace straps that showed off her lightly toned arms. She had a scarf tied around her head, keeping her hair off her neck. As she looked up, he noticed that the green in the jumpsuit matched the shade of her eyes exactly.

Nick forgot how to breathe.

But really, how necessary is breathing anyway?

This new beginning was off with a great leap.

"Good morning," she greeted him. "I made a big pot of coffee. Help yourself."

"Thanks, I could definitely use some." He stopped in front of her cabinets. "Mug?"

"Oh, right. Left hand side, right above the coffee maker."

"Very logical."

Very logical? Smooth, Bradley, real smooth.

Nick grabbed a mug and poured. Maybe his brain just wasn't awake yet. He took a sip, willing the magic elixir to give him the jumpstart he needed.

Lois had taken her paper and moved to sit at the kitchen table, and Nick noticed the plate in front of her, loaded with fruit and toast, as well as the soft-boiled egg in its little cup. Following his gaze, Lois looked up apologetically.

"I'm sorry, I would've made enough for two, but I wasn't sure what you usually do for breakfast."

"No, don't worry about it," he jumped in. "I like scrambled eggs, mostly." He gestured toward the refrigerator. "May I?"

"Yes, please, help yourself. It's your house now, too."

They smiled awkwardly at each other for a moment. Nick felt a sudden emptiness that had nothing do with his hunger. Despite the unusual circumstances that had surrounded them from the minute they met, he and Lois had always managed to have such an easy, instant friendship. Where had that gone?

You almost-kissed it away, moron.

He reached in and grabbed a couple of eggs, steeling his nerves.

"Lois, I—"

"Nick, look—"

They laughed as they talked over each other.

"Sorry, may I go first?" Nick asked.

"Sure, please," she responded.

He took a deep breath. *Here goes nothing.*

"Lois, I want to apologize for last night. You must think me a total cad, the way I approached you like that. I told you I'd be a gentleman, and then I went and—"

"Nick, stop. Don't forget, I was there too. There was mutual approaching." She smirked at him ruefully, and he couldn't help but smile back.

"Fair enough. I'd just hate for things to be awkward between us."

"I know. It's the last thing I want, too." She took a breath and looked him square in the eye. "Let's start fresh, shall we? Friends, no awkwardness."

"Friends. No awkwardness." He held up his coffee mug and toasted her.

When she returned the toast, a sense of relief settled over him. It didn't exactly erase what had happened—he doubted he'd be able to forget for a long time—but it was at least a solid first step. They resided on the same page. A team again.

And committed to *not* kissing, or almost-kissing, each other.

Nick picked up the eggs again and then stopped, looking around the kitchen.

Lois chuckled softly. "Bowls above the sink, frying pan under the counter. Whisk in the drawer on the right."

He grinned as he collected the items. "I'm a quick study. Give me a week, tops, and I'll know where everything is."

"Oh, really? Can I test you?"

"Do your worst, lady." He paused for a moment, remembering the cat. "By the way, I keep forgetting to ask. You introduced your cat as Lady M. What's the M stand for?"

She stared at him over her coffee cup. "Oh, come on. And you claim to have a theatre background?"

Recognition flared, and he couldn't believe he hadn't realized it sooner. "The Scottish queen, of course." He considered it for a moment before teasing her. "Isn't that asking for trouble?"

She narrowed her eyes at him. "Watch it, Bradley. I'll have you know, Lady Macbeth is a highly misunderstood and misjudged character. Everyone is always far too quick to vilify her."

"Well, she did encourage her husband to commit murder. A lot of murder."

"Yeah, but *he* actually did most of it. And treated her like some crazy harpy when her conscience caught up with her. Meanwhile, he was allowed to whine and hedge and go completely nuts himself, consequences be damned."

"His head was on a spike by the end of the play. I'd call that a pretty clear consequence."

"It was only what he deserved." Lois winked at him.

The lady in question sauntered into the kitchen and leapt onto the chair next to Lois, on the alert for scraps.

Nick gestured at the cat. "So do I need to sleep with one eye open?"

Lois reached over and rubbed Lady M behind the ears. "Nah, you're safe. Her plan to insert herself in my life may have been diabolically clever, but she's not murderous. Are you, Lady?"

The cat took in Lois's attention for another moment or two, before growing bored. She hit the ground and came around the counter to Nick's feet, looking up at him with a comically hopeful expression.

"Hey, she likes me."

"Don't take it personally; she'll go to anyone if food's involved. She had no luck with me, so now she's trying you."

Nick picked up a bite of his just-finished eggs with his hand. "It's a good thing for her, then, that I'm not above a little bribery."

He extended the food to her and she took it, before rubbing up against his leg affectionately.

Lois rolled her eyes. "I wish the two of you every happiness."

THE REST of their first full day as a "married" couple passed pleasantly, and uneventfully. Both of them had lived alone for a while, so sharing a home was going to take some getting used to. He lost track of how many times they nearly ran into each other. But Nick was determined to figure out his way around the house, with minimal disruptions to Lois. By the time he headed up to bed, he had achieved at least a measure of success on that front.

And most importantly, they had fallen back into being comfortable around each other.

Mostly.

A few times throughout the day, Nick caught sight of Lois across the room and remembered how her closeness had felt the night before. How much he had wanted to close that small distance and kiss her, let go and lean in to the feelings that had erupted when he'd kissed her at the wedding.

Or he flashed back to some small moment from the ceremony or their dinner. The feel of her hand in his. The way she smiled at Nate, brimming with affection, and was so quick to defend her. How well she had gotten along with his own best friend. He could see them all having many a dinner together, laughing into the evening.

Lady Macbeth was proving to be his greatest ally. She had an uncanny sense of timing, entering his personal space at exactly the right moments, just when he needed the distraction from his thoughts of Lois.

He would definitely need to keep her well-fed.

Luckily, Nick and Lois were still deep in the middle of their film, so no one expected them to take off on a honeymoon. Bartholomew had arranged one day off for them, since the tableau of them jumping right back into work the day after their wedding might have raised suspicions. But it was just one day, and Nick was eager to get back to the studio and have somewhere else to focus his attention.

They returned to the lot to a congratulatory reception, though far more subdued than what they had encountered at Chasen's. No doubt because most of the people on the lot knew better. Publicity marriages were a common enough occurrence.

Nick did get the oddest reaction from their film's crew, though. Several of the men lower down on the moviemaking food chain—from an outside perspective of course; Nick knew just how essential they were—gave him careful looks throughout the day. As if they were evaluating him, almost warning him. In just the way a big brother would. It impressed the hell out of him. He wondered if Lois had any idea she had a group of knights ready to come to her defense should she need them.

He hoped she did.

The other reaction that surprised him—surprised both of them, actually—was that of their director. When the two of them walked onto the set, Merrill Hornsby's head snapped up, and they both stopped in their tracks at the cloud of hostility wafting toward them.

"Did you mention the wedding to Hornsby?" Lois asked.

"No, did you?"

"No. Were we supposed to?"

"I figured Bartholomew took care of it. We did have the last two days off, after all."

"Then why is he looking at us like that?" Lois's lip curled. "Oh, for crap's sake, were we supposed to invite him to the wedding?"

"It never even occurred to me. Oh, no, here he comes."

Hornsby stopped in front of them and swallowed visibly. "May I—" He cleared his throat. "May I have a word?"

He turned and shuffled off to the corner. Nick exchanged a worried look with Lois before they followed him behind a scenery flat.

The minute they were alone—of a sort—the mousy director's face transformed completely.

He was downright gleeful.

"Thank you."

Their worry was replaced with utter confusion.

"I beg your pardon?" Lois asked.

"You didn't invite me to the wedding. There wasn't one single person who told me about it. Or about production shutting down for two days. I showed up, and no one was here!"

This man confounded Nick every time he opened his mouth.

"And that's a good thing?" he asked. If anyone had left him out like that, it would have pissed him off no end.

"Of course! Don't you see?" Hornsby looked back and forth between them. "I'm inconsequential. So inconsequential that I didn't know my own movie shut down around me."

Lois's face cleared at the same time light dawned on Nick.

"The kind of thing that would never happen to a brilliant director," she said.

"Exactly!" The non-brilliant director clasped his hands together. "You know how worried I've been about this picture being good. But all anyone cares about is you two!"

Nick clapped him on the shoulder. "This will make quite the story for your mother, won't it?"

"The very best," Hornsby sighed. Determination lit his eyes. "I plan on milking this for all it's worth."

Lois laughed. "I have no doubt you'll sell it beautifully."

"But if you need some extra coaching in the acting department…" Nick added.

"You know where to find us," she finished.

Hornsby's face softened with genuine warmth. "Thank you. So much." He started around the flat, before turning back to whisper, "See you on set."

———

NICK STARED PENSIVELY out the windshield as he drove them home that evening. They'd gotten some good work in, and it was a huge relief to have Hornsby still on their side. But something the man had said in passing still needled him.

"I thought our scenes went great today," Lois said as she watched the cars go by.

Still lost in thought, Nick mumbled his agreement.

She turned her gaze to him. "What's up with you?"

"Oh, nothing. Just thinking about something Hornsby said."

Lois perked up. "Can you believe it? How great was that? I sure wasn't expecting that reaction." She paused, noticing that he wasn't with her. "Don't you think it's great?"

"I do. Yeah. It's a relief, that's for sure."

"But…"

Nick sighed. "It's stupid."

Lois turned in her seat to better face him. "I'll bet it's not. Spill."

Nick smiled at her tenacity. She never let him off the hook. Which he very much appreciated.

"He said all anyone cares about is the two of us. I'm afraid that's true."

"But isn't that a good thing? It gives him cause to be happy."

"It does, but…" He trailed off, searching for the right words to make her understand. "What if that's the only reason for the buzz around this film? What if it has nothing to do with it actually being good, and everything to do with us being a sideshow?"

"Nick," she said softly. "You've always known we're a sideshow. That's the whole rationale behind their wanting us to get married."

"I know." He took a breath. "I know. It's probably just my actor's insecurity, but I want all this sideshow to lead somewhere, you know? I want people to think we're funny."

"I can't speak for my own performance, but I've been

watching you, acting with you. And Nick, you are funny. People will see that. They're already seeing it."

He wanted to believe her, more than anything.

"I guess so. I know I'm not exactly Orson Welles, but I want to be taken seriously. But, you know, as a funny guy."

He glanced away from the road and saw her leveling a stern expression at him.

"So be the Orson Welles of comedy. Make them take you seriously. How do you think he got to be *Orson Welles*?" When Nick didn't answer, Lois continued. "He walked into the room and said, 'I'm here, I have ideas, and this is how we're doing this.' And now, he could fart the damn alphabet and everyone would applaud and say, 'We must give him all the awards.'"

"I've seen some of his early theatre work. Farting the alphabet would probably have made a bit more sense."

Lois swatted his arm. "I mean it. You can make them take you every bit as seriously as Orson Welles." The corner of her mouth quirked up wryly. "And you and Orson both have that one undeniable thing that all but guarantees success, no matter the circumstances. It's nauseating, but true."

She looked deliberately at the general vicinity of his crotch. He was about to protest, but then thought better of it. She had a point, after all.

"I'm sorry to say, I think you're right."

"Of course I'm right." Lois crossed her arms and slouched back in her seat.

"If it makes you feel any better, having one is highly overrated."

That startled a laugh out of her. "Is it really?"

"Oh, absolutely. It—" He became suddenly aware that he was having a conversation about his cock with the woman responsible for most of its activity in the last few days. As if sensing it was being talked about—or realizing its proximity to Lois—the offending party started to show signs of life.

Why is it so impossible to be a gentleman around her?

Nick shifted uncomfortably. "I'll spare you the details, but take my word for it. Highly overrated."

Hear that? Settle down.

Lois gave him a quizzical smirk. "All right, then."

Nick managed to push all jokes—and south-of-his-belt thoughts—aside, and let Lois's earlier, more serious words wash over him. She was right once again. He had to stop focusing on the worries and doubts, and concentrate on the work. He could do this. *They* could do this. Were doing this.

It was what she always managed to do, but it felt like magic each and every time. She knew exactly the right thing to say to pull him out of his fog and give him a much-needed boost of confidence.

"Thanks, Lois."

Picking up on the shift in his tone, she smiled at him. "You bet."

As he neared the house and pulled into the driveway, her earlier phrasing popped back into his head.

"So how exactly does one *fart* the alphabet? I've heard of belching it, but farting?"

"Oh, shut up." She threw an incredulous look over her shoulder as she got out of the car. "Seriously? That's your big takeaway from all this?"

Climbing out himself, he pushed further. "Or wait, is it like breaking a leg?"

Her laughter exploded, a sweet melody to his ears. "Yes, Nick, that's exactly it. Forget break a leg, or merde. Fart the alphabet from now on."

He grinned like a fool as he watched her go up the walkway.

Chapter Eleven

Despite some growing pains in their first few days of living together, it didn't take long for Lois and Nick to fall into a comfortable rhythm. Lois enjoyed having his company on the ride to and from the studio—when she wasn't reminded of his anatomy, that was. She certainly hadn't meant to bring it up. But her attempt to reassure him had reminded her of the ever-present frustration that came from all that eluded her simply because she lacked a penis. Not that she wanted one—she'd definitely concede that point to Nick.

Despite not wanting to sport one herself, she did acknowledge and appreciate the finer things they were capable of. And she was more than curious about Nick's capabilities.

Which is exactly why she *didn't* need her attention drawn there.

Her only comfort came from seeing that Nick was even more uncomfortable with the subject than she was. It was really rather adorable the way he'd caught himself and then tried to get out of talking about it.

Stop thinking of his adorableness. And his anatomy.

They'd managed to navigate their way around that almost-kiss and get back to their easy friendship. She needed to keep it that way. It was better for both of them.

On the whole, he was a pretty great person to live with. A bit on the fastidious side, but not to the point of being annoying. At least he wasn't a slob. And he actually knew his way around a kitchen.

Lois had to admit to a little apprehension in that regard. Yes, their marriage was fake, but it had occurred to her to wonder if he'd still be expecting her to play certain domestic roles anyway. She had a maid who came in a few times a week, so cleaning wouldn't be a problem. But while she enjoyed cooking for herself, she liked doing it on her own terms—and ordering in or making do when she didn't feel up to the effort. If he was expecting her to have a hot meal waiting every night, he'd be out on his ass faster than he could blink, studio expectations be damned.

Luckily, her worries amounted to nothing. Nick never said a word about it, and regularly—astoundingly—volunteered to make dinner himself. He was good, too. It had taken tremendous effort to pick her jaw up off the floor the night he'd made lasagna —an actual, entirely-from-scratch lasagna. He'd make some woman a fantastic husband for real someday.

She stubbornly ignored the stab of jealousy that invaded her mind at that thought.

Her maid became a bone of contention, for unexpected reasons. It never even crossed Lois's mind to mention her to Nick before he moved in. Because there had been so much going on in preparation for the wedding, and in moving his things over to the house, she had given Betty the week off. She called to check in the night before she was due to return, and Nick wasn't thrilled.

Lois supposed it could technically be considered their first fight.

Nick worried about the image they were carefully crafting. If someone was cleaning the house, there would be no way to hide the fact that they were sleeping in separate bedrooms. Well, unless they cleaned their bedrooms themselves before Betty arrived. And that wasn't going to happen.

She was highly insulted on Betty's behalf. The older woman had worked for her for a few years, and she trusted her enormously. Betty had become a motherly figure, a bit of a stand-in for Lois's own mother, whom she visited far less than either of them liked.

After several rounds back and forth with Nick, Lois finally prevailed, and Betty arrived early the next morning, before they left for work.

She still chuckled every time she thought of Betty and Nick's first meeting.

They were finishing coffee in the kitchen when Betty let herself in the back door. After Lois introduced them, Nick straightened his tie and Lois gave him a silent warning. In order for him to feel comfortable, she had conceded that he could be the one to ask Betty to keep their secret. But she had done her best to impress upon him that he had better be polite about it.

Before he could even get a single word out, Betty appraised him from head to toe and crossed her arms.

"Well, you're as handsome as you look on the screen, I'll give you that," she announced in her light Scottish burr. She leveled a finger in his face. "But I'm telling you right now, that doesn't mean shite if you do so much as one wee thing to hurt this lass."

"Uh, well, yeah, I—" Nick stammered.

Betty's face broke into a wide smile. "And don't you worry. I know how high your stakes are, and no one's ever going to hear it from me that this marriage of yours is as fake as the sets you act in front of."

Lois attempted to hide her snort behind her hand.

"I never thought—" he began.

"Of course you did. Not that I blame you. But you should know better. Hell, if I was going to blab to the rags about what it's like working for Lois, she'd hardly still have that bollocks reputation, now would she?" Betty shook her head and gestured to Lois. "Wouldn't hurt a fly, that one. Can't understand for the life of me why nobody sees it." She marched right up in front of Nick's face. "We good?"

"Yes. Very good."

"Good." She picked up her bag and moved for the door before turning back to him. "And you better pick up after yourself. I'm here for the big stuff, not to do everything for you. I'm not your mother."

With that, she flounced out of the kitchen, and Lois couldn't hold her laughter in any longer.

Nick watched the door for a moment before finding his voice. "She's a force of nature, isn't she?"

"Indeed she is."

He sighed. "Go ahead and say it."

"I wouldn't dream of it."

"Yes, you would. It's killing you to keep it in."

"It really is, but I'm not heartless." She patted him on the shoulder. "She said more than enough, so I won't pile on."

"Thanks. I think."

Nick and Betty got along beautifully from then on.

The doorbell roused Lois from her memory, and she headed for the door. She opened it to find Frannie Haynes, her regular manicurist—and incidentally, Betty's daughter—standing there with her large case.

"Hi, Frannie, come on in."

"Hey, Lois." She took in the empty living room. "I'm not too early, am I?"

"No, you're perfect. Nate's running behind, but she'll be here soon."

"Great." She put her case on the card table Lois had set up for her. She looked around and added in a whisper, "Is he here?"

"Why, Frannie, are you planning to steal my husband?" Lois teased.

Frannie snapped her finger in mock disappointment. "Damn, you figured it out."

Lois made her way over as Frannie began to unpack her supplies. "Need any help?"

Frannie cocked her head to the side. "Do you really think you'll ever get a different answer to that question?"

"Probably not, but it's not going to stop me from asking. You should know that by now."

"I do. As always, thanks for asking. But no." She pointed to the chair. "Sit."

Lois raised her hands in surrender and did as she was told, just as Nick bounded down the stairs.

"Oh, hello." He took in Frannie and everything she was setting out. "Are you getting a manicure?"

"I am. Nick, this is Frannie. Frannie, Nick."

He strode over and shook Frannie's hand. "Nice to meet you."

"Likewise." Frannie turned to Lois and wiggled her eyebrows.

"Watch it," Lois warned her with a wink.

Nick barely noticed. He was busy taking in the table. "So you make house calls? I had no idea that was done."

"I do," Frannie replied with pride. "Our salon is the only one in town that does." She eyed him appreciatively. "We do men's nails, too."

Nick looked down at his hand, oblivious to Frannie's tone. "Good to know."

Frannie looked from Nick to Lois and back again. "Huh."

"What?" Lois asked, suspicious of her expression.

"Oh, nothing."

Lois changed the subject. "Aren't you supposed to be at the studio today, Nick?"

"Yeah, I'm due in about half an hour. I was just about to head out."

He looked at Frannie and hesitated, remembering that she was a relative outsider. He started to stoop toward Lois.

Frannie spoke without looking up from her case. "Don't worry, you don't have to kiss her goodbye on my account. I know it's all phony."

Nick froze mid-crouch. "I..." He straightened and looked at Lois. "Really?"

Lois stared right back. "Relax. I trust her. She's Betty's daughter, an ace manicurist, and my friend. And before you start in, Betty didn't tell her. I did." She paused for dramatic effect. "Because I trust her."

"Aw, thanks, Lois." Frannie turned her smile to Nick. "She's right, you know. My manicure table is like a confessional. I take it all to the grave."

Nick eyed her skeptically. "Forgive me; it's not that I don't want to trust you." He glanced at Lois. "Or that I don't trust *your* judgment. But is that really how this works? You mean to tell me that talk of our...situation...won't come with every 'Jungle Red' request?"

Frannie rolled her eyes in disgust. "God, not that again. I swear, is that movie *ever* going to stop giving us a bad name?" She pointed a finger at Nick's chest. "When I say my table's a confessional, I mean it, you understand? Take that 'Jungle Red' nonsense right out of here."

"Point taken." Nick stage-whispered to Lois, "Just how many Scottish ladies do you have lined up to put me in my place?"

Lois winked. "You better get out of here before you find out."

"Done." He inclined his head toward Frannie. "It's been a pleasure."

Frannie smiled. "Indeed it has."

Nick opened the door and startled. Nate stood there, hand reaching for the doorbell.

"Oh, hello, Nate."

"Nicky. What's knittin', kitten?"

Lois greeted her from the living room. "Come on in, Nate."

Nick gestured her in with a sweep of his hand. "Right this way."

He hovered on the verge of saying something else, but Lois recognized the look that crossed his face as he thought better of it. Unable to resist, she called after him.

"You were about to say her coven awaits, weren't you?"

She meant it mostly as a joke, but at his sudden and furious blush, she cackled at how right she'd been.

"Okay, that's my cue. I really need to get out of here before I embarrass myself beyond repair." Nick waved one last time. "Have a lovely afternoon, ladies."

"Goodbye, Nick."

"Ooh, what did I miss?" Nate pulled an extra chair up to the table.

"Nick put his foot in it, but I really can't blame him," Frannie replied as she started on Lois's nails. "I probably came on a little strong."

"Testing him to see if he's good enough for our Lois? I've been trying to do the same thing."

Lois looked back and forth between her friends. "While I appreciate the sentiment, he doesn't need to be good enough for me. This marriage isn't real, remember?"

"Maybe not, but you are living under the same roof. And he does have a drug arrest under his belt. It's our solemn duty to keep an eye out for you." Nate looked to Frannie for backup.

Frannie nodded. "Absolutely. And especially since it's fake, I have to ask." She paused in her filing and leaned in eagerly. "What's he really like? Is he the bad boy they're making him out to be, or just some poor soul who's paying for his mistake?"

Lois stared her down. "My god, do you actually want him for yourself?"

Frannie waved her hand dismissively. "Of course not. You know I have far too much to worry about without adding a man to the mix. No, this is purely a fact-finding mission. After all, you said this was temporary. When you throw him back onto the market, ladies will want to know if he's worth pursuing. I want to be armed with knowledge if they come to me."

That stupid jealousy floated up again. Lois promptly stuffed it down and focused elsewhere.

"Aren't you the one who *just* complained to Nick about 'Jungle Red' and your bad rep? And here you are, ready to gossip?"

"First of all, it's not like I'm going to spread anything around to just anybody. I can discern the gossips from those in real pursuit of the truth." She stopped shaping Lois's nails and gave her a fierce expression. "Second—and most importantly—this is not gossip anyway. It's information-gathering to assess the potential jackassery of attractive men, which is an important public service for our half of the population. I do my part in that service, whenever I can."

"That is true," Nate chimed in. "You know how seriously I take my code of fitting room secrecy. I'm a vault. But when it comes to male jackassery, I'll warn my fellow sisters every time." She winked. "We are a coven, after all. You said so yourself."

Lois laughed heartily at that. "Those are fair points. And as a fellow sister, thank you both for your service."

Frannie barely paused a moment before leaning in again. "So? Nick?"

Lois sighed, unsure quite what to say. She finally settled on the simple truth. "No jackassery. I still have no idea what happened with the dope, but...there's certainly a lot more to him than I think most people realize."

She looked up in time to catch Nate and Frannie exchanging a knowing look.

"What is that about?"

"Nothing, absolutely nothing," Nate said.

"Nothing, my ass." If her hands weren't currently occupied, she would have crossed her arms over her chest. "Whatever you're thinking, just stop. You asked, I answered. That's all there is to it."

"Okay then."

"I, for one, am glad to hear it." Frannie continued her buffing as she brought it back to Nick's virtues. "So many of the best-looking ones are such colossal bawbags."

Nate stopped her. "Bawbags? That's…a *great* one."

Frannie shrugged. "What can I say? I grew up in Scotland. Creative insults are one of our strong suits." She began to soak Lois's hand, and smiled to herself.

"Aw. I just remembered Nick gazing adoringly at Lois," Frannie continued. "It was really rather precious."

"Oh, really?"

"It was not precious," Lois protested. "And he was not adoring me. Don't be ridiculous."

Was he?

Ignoring her completely, Frannie continued speaking to Nate. "I tried flirting just to see what he'd do, and I don't think he even noticed." She turned an assessing eye on Lois. "Are you sure your marriage is fake?"

"What? Of course it is!"

The memory of Nick's nearness that first night of their marriage flashed, and Lois's cheeks burned.

This marriage has to stay fake. It has to.

"You know, for someone who has no interest in Nick, you're awfully defensive." Frannie grinned at her.

Lois breathed through her nose and tried her hardest to not rise to their bait. Again.

"Look, you wanted to gather information, and I think we've established that Nick is not a jerk. But the very last thing I need is to be linked to a man indefinitely. I assure you, this is purely a little image rehabilitation, and I will be cutting ties long before said image becomes all about my marriage rather than my career. Now, can we please move on? Surely the two of you have something interesting to talk about?"

"Not really." Nate held up her hand before Lois could jump in. "But we will take pity on you anyway."

"Thank you." Lois turned to Frannie. "How's Lucy?"

Her friend's face softened at the mention of her daughter. "She's good. I tell you, that girl has more energy than I can keep up with. She's such a handful sometimes."

"But a handful you'd do anything for, no?"

"You bet I would. I *do*." A shadow crossed her face as she looked down at her manicure equipment.

Lois slipped her hand out from under Frannie's and gently switched their positions. "Fran? What is it?"

"It's nothing really." But when her friend looked up, her eyes projected an astounding mixture of sadness and fire. "It just gets me sometimes, you know? I mean, do you ever wish you could…I don't know…shoot fire out of your hands or something? To shut them all up, make them take us more seriously?"

"God, you have no idea."

At the same time, Nate chimed in with a quiet but resounding, "Hell yeah."

The three of them had been meeting at either Lois's or Nate's house for some time, but it never felt like Frannie was simply offering a service they paid for. They had formed a fast and easy friendship. Though they usually didn't get into too much deep, personal detail, Lois had always felt an unspoken kinship with the woman. She was beginning to realize at least part of the reason why.

Frannie gave a rueful chuckle before continuing. "I started out as a bookkeeper and accountant, did I ever tell you that? Before the war. That's why I came to America in the first place. I always had a head for numbers." She paused, thoughtful. "Numbers just always make sense, you know, no matter what."

She raised her head with a half-smile. "Anyway, I came here for business school. That's where I met Marty, Lucy's father. When he enlisted and I finished school, I went to work. I was damn good too. But then the war ended. And suddenly, it didn't matter how good I was. I was no longer needed."

"They let you go?"

"They did. My job needed to go to the boys returning from war. I tried to argue that there'd be room for me too, but they wouldn't hear of it. Said I should understand the sacrifices they'd made and give up my job happily." Frannie shook her head bitterly and got up, pacing the room. "As if I didn't make sacrifices too? I lost my husband. My child will never know her father, all because of this war. I don't begrudge anyone who fought, but to say that my sacrifices are somehow less..."

"Just because they're different," Nate finished for her.

Frannie nodded.

"And I'm assuming you tried to find accounting work elsewhere after that?" Lois asked, suspecting the answer.

Frannie's mouth twisted in a grimace. "So many places. Do you know what one old gasbag actually had the nerve to tell me? That if I really wanted to provide for my daughter, I should just marry again and let a husband provide for us."

Nate made a noise of disgust. "He didn't."

"He did. Mum had known Lorraine for an age, and she knew I had a steady hand with polish. So when I'd exhausted the prospects, Lorraine and Enzo hired me on, and here I am." She lifted her head. "And it's not that I'm not grateful, or that I don't enjoy what I do. It's just..."

Lois met her eyes, and understanding flowed between them. "It's not your passion."

"No, it's not." She sat back down. "But it keeps a roof over my daughter's head. And friends at my side."

Lois took her hand, and Nate followed suit with Frannie's other.

"And we're not going anywhere."

Frannie smiled and squeezed their hands before releasing them. "Let's get these nails finished, eh? I've still got this one to do"—she gestured at Nate—"and you know what a mess her hands always are."

"It's an occupational hazard," Nate countered with feigned insult.

Frannie twisted the cap off the nail polish bottle. "Speaking of your occupation, seen anyone good-looking in their knickers lately?"

As the three of them laughed and filled the remainder of their afternoon with lighter subjects, Lois's mind lingered on everything they'd talked about. It came from endless angles, the injustice of it all. That unfairness had been burning in her, keeping her moving forward all these years. And she couldn't stop now. She was close to actually getting somewhere.

Again she reminded herself to keep her eyes on the prize, and not the man currently occupying the bedroom down the hall.

No matter how preciously adoring he was.

Chapter Twelve

Nick paced around his dressing room at the studio, pausing occasionally to rearrange the various personal items scattered around it—his old Army dog tags, a battered copy of *Pygmalion*, framed photos of his sister's kids, and him with Max on the day he opened the bakery. He felt restless today, much more than usual. In anticipation of meeting his lawyer and his publicity agent later that afternoon, he had trouble quieting his nerves.

The swing in his favor steadily continued in the weeks since marrying Lois. The fervor in the press may have died down somewhat, but the interest hadn't extinguished completely. They were still newlyweds after all, and every time they ventured out to a well-traveled hotspot, the gossips drooled over them.

Holiday for Teacups—No, wait. That's not it. Teacups in July, *right* —was proceeding at a good clip as well. The more laughs they generated on set, the more confident Nick felt about how the film would be received upon release. As atrocious as the script read, little doubt remained that he and Lois had improved it signifi- cantly enough to get noticed.

Despite it all, having this meeting stood as a reminder of what he'd done, of just how much he'd risked in order to get here. And how he hadn't made it out of the woods and where he wanted to be just yet.

So much he wanted to accomplish, if only given the chance.

This film was only the beginning, but it *was* a beginning. All he had to do was keep the momentum going.

He had the day off from shooting today, and planned to spend the morning relaxing at the house while Lois was at work. He didn't last long. He tried a book, a radio play, a jaunt around the backyard. He went back inside and wandered from room to room. When Betty arrived to clean, he had the sense to grab his hat and head into the studio—for what, he didn't quite know. But the last thing he wanted was to get in Betty's way and drive her crazy.

And so he found himself in his dressing room. The scenery had changed, but he remained bored out of his mind, which in turn led his mind to wander. And the nerves set in again.

He felt like walking, but didn't want to meander aimlessly around the studio—that was a surefire way to get stuck talking to people who were only interested in entertaining themselves with his scandals.

Nick looked at his watch. Still an hour until his meeting.

A thought occurred to him, and his mood brightened considerably.

Lois would be close to finishing her photoshoot. Maybe he

could catch her as it wound down, walk her back to her dressing room. For appearance's sake, of course.

It had nothing to do with his desire to see her.

Nothing whatsoever.

He strode out of his dressing room and started toward the stage where she worked, his steps lighter now that they had a purpose. His head felt clear, his lungs less constricted. He tried not to dwell on the reason why.

Oh, why the hell not?

The fact was, he looked forward to seeing Lois. Why pretend otherwise? He liked spending time with her, tremendously. He felt more himself around her. Even when he fought his attraction to her, kept her at a gentlemanly arm's length, it still felt better than not having her around at all.

If he was being perfectly honest, he couldn't remember when —or even if—he'd ever felt this way around someone.

As he neared the soundstage, Nick tucked the admission away for the moment. Just because he'd acknowledged it, he didn't have to examine it too closely yet, did he? Especially when he was about to be face-to-face with her.

He entered to find a huge Halloween-themed setup, even though it was still a couple months away. In front of a generic sky backdrop stood a fence and hay bales of various sizes. Pumpkins and stuffed bats and black cats resided among them, and there was even a raven sitting on one of the fenceposts.

Nick's eyes barely registered all of this before they were drawn to Lois, perched on one of the hay bales. Her costume immediately reminded him of the black dress that had caused such a huge commotion on Rita Hayworth in *Gilda* the year before. Only this one cut off above Lois's knees. The short dress, dark sheer stockings, and black heels all worked together to show off her long legs. A tall witch hat completed the picture.

And there went Nick's breath. Again.

Lois caught sight of him. Surprised but smiling, she waved a black-gloved hand at him.

The photographer turned from his camera. "Oh, hello, Mr. Bradley. Just a couple more shots, and then she's all yours." He winked conspiratorially.

Behind him, Lois's lip curled and she rolled her eyes. By the time the photographer faced her again, she had schooled her face back into a placidly seductive smile. Nick laughed, admiring her restraint.

He had always thought the photos the studio arranged for its female stars were asinine, especially these holiday-themed ones. The cheesecake shots were a staple of Hollywood publicity, and they'd certainly gone over well with the boys overseas during the war. But he'd always felt a little resentful on behalf of the women he worked with. They inevitably wore the most ridiculous—and skimpy—costumes, while the worst things Nick had had to don over the years were a Santa suit and a shiny cowboy outfit.

Not that he really had any right to talk. He had just been ogling Lois, hadn't he?

True to his word, the photographer wrapped up after a few minutes, and Lois hopped down from her hay bale. She made her way over to where Nick stood against the back wall.

"I wasn't expecting to see you here," she greeted him.

"I found myself in the neighborhood, so I thought I'd drop by and say hello."

"Isn't that nice? Hello."

"Hello."

They smiled at each other for a moment. Before Nick could drown in those sea glass eyes, he pulled his attention upward and voiced a question that had lingered in his mind since he came in.

Gesturing at her hat, he asked, "A little on the nose, isn't it? They could've at least tried to be subtle."

He tired more and more of the way the studio treated her.

Lois didn't look put out in the slightest. "Subtlety doesn't come anywhere near these shoots, but I'm afraid I'm the only one to blame for the costume in this case." She fingered the brim of her hat. "Picked the hat myself."

"Really? But why?"

She shrugged. "They probably would have put me in it anyway, but at least this way I'm getting out ahead of it."

"Controlling your story as much as you can. I get it."

"I thought you might." She considered him for a moment before continuing. "And anyway, it gave Nate the chance to have a little fun."

"Well, please give her my compliments. Rita can eat her heart out."

"Picked up on that, did you?" Lois chuckled. "She'll be happy to hear it. I think Jean Louis must've beaten Nate out for a job once or something, because she took a perverse glee in copying his design." She looked down at her legs. "Or half of it anyway."

Damn it. She had to draw my attention right to them, didn't she?

Nick pulled his gaze away from her lower half to find Lois giving him a wry grin.

He swallowed and changed the subject quickly. "Are you headed back to your dressing room? Want some company on the walk back?"

"I am, and I'd love some. Thanks."

He offered her his arm. She took off her hat and linked her arm in his as they left the soundstage.

"And thanks for being so ready to defend my honor back there. With, you know…" She held up the hat as she trailed off.

"Aw, it was nothing." He felt suddenly, inexplicably shy, and hoped she didn't notice.

"Well thanks, just the same."

They fell into a companionable silence as they walked. They attracted a bit of attention, but luckily no one stopped to talk to them. A few waved or smiled, and a pair of young chorus girls mooned dreamily at them, but most minded their own business. Nick was glad.

After a few minutes had passed, Lois spoke quietly. "Can I ask you something?"

"Of course."

"You okay?"

The simple question startled Nick. He should've been used to it by now, but it still amazed him every time she picked up on his moods so uncannily.

"Is it that obvious?"

"Not too much. But we have been living under the same roof long enough now that I can pick up a few things. I didn't expect to see you at the studio today, and then you turn up at my photo-shoot. As good as I look right now, I doubt you just wanted to be seen with me."

Nick breathed a quiet laugh. "That is true." He paused. "I'm meeting with my lawyer and my publicist in a little bit."

"Ah. I see." She brought her left hand to join her right where it rested on his arm. "Are you expecting more trouble? I thought I'd heard that the studio got your charges dropped. Did it not work?"

"No, it worked, they did." Nick took a breath. "Everything's been going pretty well, actually. Better than I expected. It's just… I don't know. I really don't have reason to worry."

"But you worry anyway."

"I do." He met her eyes. "Silly, huh?"

"Not at all. I feel queasy every time Bartholomew calls me into his office, even when it's nothing."

"But at least you can go in knowing you've never broken the law."

"Doesn't stop an awful lot of people from treating me like I did." She nudged him. "Thanks for assuming my record's clean, by the way."

"Any time. There really should only be one felon per household, after all. But you know, even if you did do something, Nate's not the only one standing by with a shovel."

Lois's eyes widened slightly, and the corners of her mouth lifted in a slight smile. Nick hadn't expected to say that, but as he watched her take in his words, he was glad he had. She had dispelled a lot of his apprehension simply by being there, walking next to him. If he could return at least a fraction of the favor simply by stating the truth, he'd do it every time.

Because it was absolutely the truth.

In a very short time, Lois had come to mean a great deal to him. He adored his warm, loving family, and he had the benefit of a few good friends, Max especially. But none of them worked in the movie business. They supported him, but they would never completely understand what it was like to exist in the studio system. How infuriating and stifling it could be. Coupled with the immense joy and passion it brought, which was what kept him from leaving the profession—and all the crap—behind.

But Lois understood. God knew she had plenty of reason to walk away, and yet here she stayed—in a ridiculous witch costume, no less.

They arrived at Lois's dressing room door and came to a halt together.

"Here we are," Nick said

"Yep. Here we are."

He thought she might be as disappointed as he felt. He hoped so.

Nick slipped his arm out of hers and peeked at his watch. "Almost time for my meeting."

"I'm sure it'll be fine." She smiled at him. "Thank you for the escort."

"My pleasure."

"I was about to wish you luck, but that doesn't seem right." A wicked glint crossed her face as she thought of something. "I'll leave you with this. Fart the alphabet, Nick."

Nick barked with amusement, and several people nearby turned to stare at them.

"Indeed I will. Thanks."

Lois sobered slightly, and she seemed to debate for a moment before speaking. "Listen, Nick, if you need to talk later…you know where I live."

Nick returned her grin. "Careful, I might just take you up on that."

"You should. See you later."

"See ya."

Her hand rested on the door handle, but then she turned back to him. She grazed his cheek with a light kiss, so fast he barely had time to blink, and then she was gone.

He walked to his meeting, ready to face anything.

NICK RETURNED HOME that evening and found Lois in the kitchen, standing in front of the open refrigerator.

"Hey." She closed it and faced him. "How'd the meeting go?"

"Not bad actually." Before she could vocalize her smirk, he added, "Yes, you were right."

"I'm glad."

"Me too." He sank onto a stool at the counter. "They really just wanted to check in, I think. Make sure things were progressing okay."

They'd acted perfectly civil, but it was still a strange meeting. He could tell it would be a long time before they started to trust him again. Not that he could blame them. He had made a mess of their jobs. But uneasiness threaded through him nonetheless.

Lois watched him, seeming to sense his feelings, but she didn't press him. Instead, she turned back to the fridge.

"I was just contemplating dinner when you came in. Any ideas?"

As if animated by her words, his stomach came to life and reminded him that he hadn't eaten lunch.

Getting up to join her, Nick asked, "Did I see a couple steaks in there this morning?"

"You did. Feel like putting those superior skillet talents of yours to use?"

"Absolutely. If you make that sauce you put together a couple weeks ago?"

"Deal."

They got to work. Just as on set, they made a good team. Lois opened a bottle of wine, and he switched on the radio. They got in each other's way more than a few times, but it just made them laugh harder each time it happened.

They were side by side at the stove when Lady M appeared at their feet, looking hopeful.

"Sorry, kitten, this isn't for you," Lois said, shooing her away. "Not yet, anyway."

Nick flipped a steak and leaned against the counter, observing her with the sauce.

"It's too bad you don't have that witch hat right now. Stirring your cauldron, cat at your feet. Imagine the headlines."

Lois grinned over at him. "Prince Charming standing by, ready to be turned into a toad."

"Might not be so bad. I wouldn't have to wear a tie."

"I doubt flies taste as good as steak, though."

"True. Guess I'd have to get the witch to kiss me and break the spell."

Jesus. Where did that come from?

Lois didn't seem to mind, though. She just arched her eyebrow. "Aren't you supposed to find a princess to do that?"

"Not necessarily."

She took him in for a moment, then went back to stirring. As he moved to the counter to finish the salad, he thought he heard her say, under her breath, "Double, double, toil and trouble."

The dinner turned out delicious. They talked and laughed while they ate, sharing studio war stories as they often did.

"So I've gotta ask," Nick ventured. "Some of the stories I've heard over the years…"

"Are too wild not to be at least somewhat true?" The decided lack of venom in her voice encouraged him.

"Well, yeah. But working with you, knowing you…that's, I don't know, just not…you."

Lois shrugged. "I've been told I need to be on my best behavior." At Nick's snort, she smiled. "I suppose it's not me, really. Just another part I play. One of the juiciest, and certainly longest-running, roles I've ever played, if I do say so myself." Her face turned wistful. "But you'd be surprised what an outlet it can be."

"Ah. Now that makes sense."

She shook her head. "I'll never forget my first tantrum. To this day, I still don't remember exactly what the director said that set me off. But I sure do remember that feeling when I let loose."

"That good?"

"So very good." She exhaled. "And I turned in a pretty good performance on-screen. So it seemed only logical to start channeling all that rage into an off-screen role and keep it out of the camera's reach."

"Very logical indeed."

Appreciation flashed in her eyes. "And just like with any part, over the years I've put quite a lot of careful thought into it."

"As one does." He smirked. "You've clearly done it well. No one would ever suspect it's an act."

"Yep, I've become the very best diva Hollywood's ever seen. Elevated being 'difficult' into quite a fine art." She huffed. "You know, even after finally having my contract foisted off to Parkmoor—only to find my reputation still firmly attached, like it was somehow legally bound to it—the diva act ended up as the only way I could retain any power in my career. There's actually a fair bit of control that goes into a tantrum, more than most people realize." Lois held up a finger. "And I do have rules."

He laughed. "Somehow this does not surprise me at all."

"Thank you…I think."

"Well, don't leave me in suspense." He made an impatient gesture. "Let's hear those rules."

Her lips twitched, trying to hide a smile, and Nick watched in fascination as she began to tick them off on her fingers. "For starters, I have found the perfect volume and pitch for yelling, so as not to damage my voice for actual work. When my anger takes on a projectile nature, I never throw anything valuable. I may wave my arms and stamp my feet, but no action may result in the mussing of my carefully styled hair and makeup."

"Even I have trouble with that one." He grinned.

She returned the smile, such a stark contrast with her words. "I've managed a pretty good trade-off between fire and ice"—she lowered her voice to a whisper—"but I'll let you in on a little secret."

Nick leaned forward, mesmerized.

"Since, according to the newsreels, we live in the 'atomic age' now, I've also been working on a nuclear incarnation of my fury." She shrugged again. "But I'm still perfecting the details of that one, so I haven't detonated it on anyone yet."

"Be sure to warn me when you do."

"So you can run for cover?"

"So I can get a front row seat."

Heat shimmered between them for a moment, before Lois blinked, pulling out of it first. Nick tried to contain his disappointment.

"I do have one hard and fast Rule of Being Difficult, though." A strange, sad look twisted across her features, but she covered it quickly with a shake of her head. "Vitally important and never to be broken—I never, ever take it out on the so-called 'little people.' They're the ones who really make the magic happen. And they didn't give me this damn reputation."

"They are the ones who make it possible for us to do this, give us a reason to keep coming in to work every day. So you spare them."

"I have to."

"That does explain it."

"What?"

"How protective all the crew's been since we got married. Like they'll kick my ass if I don't treat you right."

Lois scoffed. "Don't be ridiculous."

She really doesn't see it, does she?

She seemed reluctant to explore that idea, so Nick spared her by changing the subject. "Shall we move on to dessert?"

Lois gave him a small smile. "Sure."

Nick had picked up a handful of Max's pastries a few days before, so they took what remained of them, along with their wine, into the living room.

When they settled on the couch, Lois said, "I really am glad your meeting went well today."

"Thanks." He hadn't wanted to talk much about it earlier, but felt more relaxed, ready now, especially after all she'd just shared. "It was all pretty routine, but underneath I got this sense... I wonder if they'll ever really trust me again."

"You don't think they do?"

"Nah. I made a real hash of everything, you know? I was always one of their easy clients, the one they didn't have to worry about, and now..."

"You're the guy with the dope."

"I'm the guy with the dope." Nick sighed. "Don't get me wrong, they've been fantastic, getting me through all this, but... the way they look at me now. Every time they see me, it's like they're trying to see if my eyes are bloodshot. I half expect my lawyer to whip out a cup next time for me to piss in."

"Give them time. You did shock a lot of people, after all."

"I did."

Lois tucked her legs under her and turned to face him more fully. "Can I ask? Why?"

He'd been waiting for the question since the day they met. When she'd surprised him by *not* asking. At the time, he hadn't any idea exactly what he'd say if she did. How much of the truth he could share, how much she'd believe.

But he knew her now. Trusted her. And she knew him.

So he told her the simple truth.

"I wanted to do comedy."

Lois's face went blank, and she blinked a few times, not hiding her confusion. "I beg your pardon?"

Nick smiled. "I wanted to do comedy. Really, I wanted to be heard."

He searched her face, and only saw curiosity, intrigue. Not judgment.

He set his wine glass down and faced her before continuing. "You know the kind of movies I've always made. When I got to Hollywood, I was the drama guy. I was also the athletic guy. So that's what they gave me, the serious action stuff. And I loved it. I really did. I actually made a living reenacting all the games Max and I played as kids. Can you imagine anything better? I knew I'd eventually want to do other stuff, but I was still new. I had plenty of time to branch out later, might as well do the hero thing while I was still young."

"I hate to break it to you, but you are still pretty young. Unless you smuggled a portrait into the attic that I don't know about."

Nick laughed. "No. What you see is what you get."

"So, what changed?"

He took a breath, but before he could speak, understanding dawned on Lois's face and she answered her own question.

"The war."

"The war," he confirmed, nodding. "It's a funny business we're in. We try to reflect life back to people, and I guess we do, at least in part. But in the end, all we're really doing is playing. No matter how real it seems, that's all it is."

Lois reached out and covered his hand with hers.

"I was pretty lucky, you know." Even though it hadn't all been luck. He knew for a fact that there had been strings pulled behind the scenes on his behalf, to keep him from the worst of it, simply because of who he was. But he'd deliberately—maybe naively— never sought out details. It made him queasy every time he thought of it.

"So many guys had it so much worse," he continued. "Still

have it worse. They'll have it worse the rest of their lives." He swallowed. "But I saw enough."

It was the sounds, really, that stayed with him. They came to him sometimes, out of nowhere, making him shudder.

Lois's fingers stroked his hand lightly. "I worked the Canteen a lot, but I visited the VA hospital a couple times too. I remember one patient I met. God, he was barely more than a teenager. The nurses said he'd been left for dead, but somehow managed to survive. I sat with him for a while, and I'll never forget his hands. They wouldn't stop shaking. He said the only time they did was when his sweetheart held them." She looked up, tears in her eyes. "His dream had been to be a drummer. But he couldn't hold her hands and drumsticks at the same time, so…"

Nick flipped his hand over and laced his fingers with hers. "I know an awful lot of guys like that." He paused. "When I came home and went back to work…they expected me to make war pictures. All these guys who hadn't been there. So focused on the fact that I had, and thought people would want to see me in action. And I don't know. Maybe people did. I tried. Made one." He met her eyes. "But I couldn't do more. I don't want to relive it, over and over. And I really don't think other guys want to keep seeing it either."

"That boy I met certainly wouldn't."

"The war was terrible. We lived through hell. All of us. Everyone here at home lived through a kind of hell, too. Nothing but constant fear for years. We won, but it cost so much. We all need to heal. It might sound silly, but I think at least part of the way we do that is to laugh. If I can give that to people…"

He trailed off. He hadn't shared these thoughts with too many others. Most of the ones he had told didn't get it. So he'd stopped, kept it to himself, until it threatened to explode out of him.

"I assume you told them that." It wasn't a question. She got it.

"You wouldn't believe how much. But they dismissed it every time. I'm thirty-five, and they treated me like a kid, almost. Like they knew the numbers and I didn't, and I should just shut up and not make waves."

Realization broke across her face. "You got caught with the pot on purpose."

He shrugged. "They wouldn't pay attention to waves, so I tried a tsunami."

Lois laughed. "I knew it!"

Her response surprised him. "What?"

"You've been around this town long enough. It never made sense to me that you could be stupid enough to get caught, especially now that I know you." She grinned. "I was right."

"You look pretty smug for someone who ended up as part of the collateral damage of my mess."

"The damage remains to be seen, and you know it. Still, it was an awful risk to take. You could've ended up really screwed."

"I suppose I could've. Still could. But I had to try. And it was just a little dope."

Lois made a face.

"Oh come on, you know all that 'reefer madness' stuff is bull. I tried some once when I was younger. I've had worse reactions to booze."

"As true as that may be," Lois countered, "most people don't see it that way. Especially the ones who've never tried the stuff."

"I know. But the bad press was the most essential part of my plan. And I figured as long as it was a small enough amount, they probably wouldn't throw the book at me."

"You had a lot of faith in 'probably.'"

"I had to. If I thought about it too much, I would've lost my nerve."

"And what about the studio?" She narrowed her eyes. "You were counting on them keeping you on but sticking you with a punishment movie, weren't you?"

A stab of guilt flashed through him at the word *punishment*. "I was. I knew I made them too much money for them to fire me outright. I'd never been one of the guys with a rogue image. And I hoped they hadn't listened too closely when I'd asked to do comedy." He lifted a shoulder sheepishly. "They hadn't."

"Thus your desperation to make *Teapots at Dawn* funny."

Nick's raised his eyebrow at that one, and Lois just shrugged with a smirk. He let it go and nodded at her supposition. "Thus my desperation."

She shook her head slowly. "And it's working."

"I hate to even say it out loud, but yeah. I think it is."

Lois gave him a rueful, slightly sad look. "Spoken like a man." She sank into the couch and leaned her head back, groaning. "Jesus Christ, can you imagine if I tried pulling a stunt like that? I'd be out on my ass so fast."

Nick didn't know what to say to that.

She lolled her head in his direction, and her hand came to rest on his knee. "It's nothing personal, you know that, right? I don't begrudge you, really I don't. You've had to deal with your fair share of shit, and you deserve a break." She sighed. "It just washes over me sometimes how much easier the world would treat me if I had a cock."

Nick tried to ignore her hand's proximity to his own offending party.

"Thought you didn't want one."

"I don't. Some justice would be nice, though."

He covered her hand with his. "I hope you get some. You deserve it too."

"Thanks."

They sat like that for a minute, and Nick let himself revel in the details of the moment. The weight of her hand on his leg, how smooth her skin felt as his thumb brushed against hers.

"This is gonna sound obnoxiously selfish, but when I planned all this, I never thought beyond my own consequences. I never counted on anyone else being involved. On *you* being involved."

"I swear, if you apologize again, I—"

"I won't," he cut her off. "I'm just... I'm glad it was you they paired me with."

He didn't know if he was crossing a line, but he meant it. And he wanted to say it.

A slow smile built on Lois's face. She looked down at his lips, and just like that, electricity surrounded them, as it had after their wedding dinner. He watched her throat move as she swallowed.

She lifted her eyes back up to his, and he registered a decision in her eyes.

Right before she leaned in and brought their lips together, obliterating any and all thought.

Chapter Thirteen

She hadn't planned to kiss him. She'd been doing such a great job shoving aside her attraction to him. Pretending not to notice the way his hair always dipped forward to drop a warm brown curtain over the top of his brow, or how wonderfully often he rolled up his sleeves and the light caught the hair that sat atop his perfectly toned forearms. Seriously, what was it about men's forearms? They nailed her every time.

Lois had tried to let her frustration at the system take over, to dwell on what Nick could get away with that she couldn't. But she was tired. And her frustration didn't originate with him. She understood where he was coming from. From the way he'd listened, reacted to her during dinner, he understood her as well.

And it felt good to sit next to him, his warm hand covering hers. His warmer leg under her hand.

So damn good.

Then he'd said what he did, and all her resolve had crumbled. She hadn't even cared. All she wanted to do was kiss him.

So she did.

She could tell she'd surprised him. His lips were completely still against hers. But oh, so warm, and soft. Thankfully it only took him a moment to recover before he parted them and kissed her back hungrily.

She slipped her tongue inside his mouth as soon as his lips opened, tasting the lingering flavor of wine. It wasn't the wine that was making her feel drunk, though. Nick was all the buzz she needed.

They broke apart and looked at each other, a question hovering between them. She could see her answer reflected back to her in his eyes.

Hell, yes, we're doing this.

Their lips found each other again, at once eagerly devouring but in no rush. Their tongues slid slowly together and started a beautiful dance.

Nick's hand found her waist and he pulled her closer, moving his fingers around to the base of her spine. Lois was all too happy to press into him, to ease the desperate ache in her breasts. A futile effort, she knew, but it felt glorious just the same.

She brought her hand up to his jaw, grazing her fingers against the day's worth of stubble there. She continued around to the base of his neck before sliding up. He kept his hair short, but it was just long enough for her fingers to take root.

Nick's lips blazed a trail across her cheek and down her neck. His tongue made a lazy swirl in the hollow between her collarbones, before making his way back up the other side of her neck and coming to land near her ear. He worried her earlobe gently with his teeth, and she couldn't control the low groan that escaped her.

That seemed to trigger yet more hunger in him, and he returned to her mouth with a deep groan of his own.

Lois had no idea how long they stayed that way, nipping and tasting and attempting to inhale one another. Time stopped bothering to exist.

At one point she found herself in Nick's lap, with absolutely no recollection of how or when she'd gotten there. She undid several buttons on his shirt and slipped her hand inside, reveling in the feel of his taut muscles and the tantalizing dusting of hair that covered them. He slid his hand up her ribcage and cupped her breast almost reverently. His thumb grazed her nipple and when she moaned in response he began to knead gently, all the while continuing to tease with his thumb.

The men—and boys—in Lois's dating history ran the full gamut of skill levels when it came to kissing. She'd had her fair share of lousy kissers, and a couple of really good ones. Or so she'd thought.

Nick Bradley put every single one of them to shame.

This was... There really were no words to describe it. Hell, Lois couldn't even remember what words were.

And it was glorious.

Yet more time passed before they finally broke apart, panting and incredibly disheveled. Their eyes locked.

"Hi," Nick whispered.

"Hi."

They smiled as they leaned their foreheads together, staying that way for a bit as their breathing began to slow to normal speed, and reality began to settle itself back around them.

Lois was still sprawled on Nick's lap. As she reluctantly slid off, he ran a hand through his hair. It was sticking up in multiple directions—and quite frankly, it looked much sexier that way.

"I, uh..." he began. "That was..."

"Yeah. Same."

They both laughed quietly.

He looked about as shaken as she felt.

What had just happened? And where the hell did they go from here?

There was no doubt the kiss had been nothing less than phenomenal. Nick had awakened nerve endings Lois didn't even know she had. And by the look of him, she was no slouch either, if she did say so herself.

But then that old bastard reality began creeping back in. With a vengeance. This marriage was supposed to be fake. They were supposed to be acting. She hadn't imposed her rules for herself for no reason, after all. It felt like hours ago now, but they'd just had a whole conversation about the world they inhabited, the system that drove them to extreme lengths in order to achieve what should have been simple career goals.

Where did that kiss, this…whatever it was…between them fit into all that?

As if he had been reading her thoughts, and likely realizing along with her that no easy answer would be found tonight, Nick spoke up. "I, uh…I guess it's been a long day, hasn't it?"

"It has. We should probably…" She gestured toward the stairs.

"Yeah."

They both got up. It wasn't until she stood that Lois realized her legs still felt like Jell-O. She took a deep breath to steady herself.

Ever the gentleman, Nick reached down and picked up their wine glasses. "I'll take care of these before I go up."

"Thanks." She hesitated. "Good night, I guess."

Nick balanced the two glasses in one hand and reached out with the other to skim her cheek, sending a shiver down her whole body.

"Good night, Lois."

He turned and headed to the kitchen, leaving her to stumble her way up the stairs to her bedroom.

THE NEXT MORNING, Lois was still valiantly—albeit unsuccessfully—attempting to quiet the dazed jumble of thoughts swirling around her as she made her way to the Parkmoor wardrobe building.

Nick had had an early call, but their late night had quite obviously hindered his ability to get up with any time to spare before he needed to leave. They had danced awkwardly around each other in the kitchen as he downed his coffee and she made herself breakfast. His rush to get to work had prevented the asking of any unanswerable questions, but it also meant that absolutely nothing was settled between them.

Lois couldn't stop going over it all in her head. She managed—barely—to keep from reliving the memory of the kiss, the feeling of his hands all over her. She'd spent enough time doing that last night. Over and over again.

Today her head was more practical. Infuriatingly messy, but practical. Her thoughts ping-ponged in a constant back and forth about what came next, leaving her nowhere near figuring it out.

She knew what she was supposed to want. Her career goals. Period. They required her sole focus and dedication. She had no room for a relationship, especially with another actor. It was a recipe for disaster, as she'd seen firsthand. Two egos never made a right. And even if the man wasn't a complete jackass, it was inevitable that if someone had to make a career sacrifice—and someone always did—it would be her. She'd never broken her rule, and she shouldn't be about to start now.

But you've never met an actor like Nick.

And there was the other side of the argument. Nick *was* different. Not just from any actor she'd met. From any *man* she'd ever met. He saw her, understood her. Championed her. Put her career needs right alongside his.

The sensation was almost as heady as that kiss had been.

And holy crap, that kiss.

She'd never believed it was possible to have all of it, all at once. That way lay madness. She'd resigned herself to the fact that certain things simply weren't in the cards for her. But then Nick Bradley came along and upended everything. He had her really hopeful for the first time in…maybe ever.

It was scary as hell.

She wanted so much to trust it, to trust him. But she was so used to being burned. She'd almost forgotten how it felt not to be.

Lois made her way down the hallway to Nate's office, hoping her friend wasn't swamped with fittings.

Nate's door stood open, but she wasn't alone, so Lois knocked on the doorjamb and hovered.

"Lois, hi! Come on in; we're just finishing up." Nate waved her in.

She leaned over her desk, showing some sketches to one of the studio's brightest starlets, Ruby Church.

Ruby had spent most of her childhood at Parkmoor, charming the bejeezus out of every man, woman, and fellow child she encountered. Her bright and vivacious nature had kept her working steadily throughout her teen years as well. She mostly made breezy comedies, but last year the studio had taken a chance on putting her in a tearjerker, and Ruby had the dramatic chops to make the risk worth it. To top it all off, she was a newlywed at the tender age of eighteen, having wed her longtime sweetheart and frequent costar Bobby Frasier in a ridiculously lavish ceremony attended by most of Hollywood.

Needless to say, Lois had not been on the guest list.

Ruby turned and flashed a huge smile at Lois.

"Ms. Ashford, I'm so happy you're here," she gushed as she rushed over and took Lois's hand in both of hers. "I've wanted to meet you for ever so long."

"You have?" Lois couldn't contain her surprise.

"Oh, of course. I've seen every one of your pictures. I've always thought it'd be just dreamy to work together." She scrunched her nose. "Not that they'd ever let me." Just as quickly, her face brightened again. "But you know how it is when anyone tells you not to do something. Just makes you want to do it even more." She finished with a wink.

Lois laughed. The girl's mood was downright infectious. "Well, thanks. And you were just brilliant in *Sail Away*."

Ruby brought her hand to her chest, and her eyes gleamed triumphantly. "Thank you so much. Gosh, that means so much coming from you. I really had to fight tooth and nail for that one, but I got it."

Nate strolled over to them. "I was just showing Ruby a few ideas for her next movie."

"Oh, yes, and they're just swell. Thanks ever so, Nate."

"My pleasure, honey."

Ruby looked to Lois again, this time with open curiosity. "Okay, I have to ask. How is it being married to Nick Bradley? He's such a dreamboat. Those eyes, whew! Is it just for the cameras, or do you really get to have all the fun too?"

All Lois could manage in response was a startled sound or two.

Her non-answer didn't faze the young starlet. "Oh, don't worry if it is fake. I won't tell. Mine is too, you know."

"Really? But you and Bobby are so…"

"Adorable? Precious? Meant for each other? That's what everyone says, so we decided to use it to our advantage." Ruby shrugged. "I'm sure you know how it goes. The minute these show up"—she pointed to her chest—"men just start looking at you different. No one ever did anything, of course. Being who I am, they wouldn't dare. But still. I knew the minute I turned eighteen, it wouldn't be long before some gross lech tried something, and I do have a career to focus on, after all. So I decided to take myself off the market. And who better than my very best friend in the world, who I love dearly. And who I knew for a fact would never even want to touch me."

Realizing what she'd just insinuated about Bobby, she flushed. "That is…" Her shoulders slumped. "I'm so sorry; that wasn't mine to say. Please—"

"Don't even give it a second thought," Lois assured her. "It'll never leave this room."

"Never," Nate seconded.

"Thank you." Ruby took Lois's hand. "I always knew I'd like you, Lois." She took a short breath. "Well, I've taken up enough of your time. I should be on my way."

As she reached for her purse and gloves, Ruby continued,

"You and Nick simply must come to dinner with me and Bobby. We'll have the most marvelous double date."

"I'd love to, but are you sure you should be seen with us?"

Ruby swatted the air with her gloves. "Nonsense. What good is star power if you can't use it? Navigating the studio system is like picking your way through a bunch of landmines, especially for those of us not in possession of a cock." This she punctuated with a lewd thrust of her hips and a roll of her eyes. "We women need to stick together."

Lois gave Nate an incredulous smile as Ruby breezed to the door.

"Do ring me, Lois. Toodles!"

And then she was gone, a trail of sunshine left behind in her wake.

"Well, she's quite the adorable force of nature, isn't she?"

Nate laughed and went to straighten her sketches into a neat pile. "Indeed she is. Always a breath of fresh air. And absolutely no filter."

Lois chuckled. "I'll say." She lowered her voice. "So Bobby Frasier, huh? I never would've guessed. I'm sure it's no surprise to you, though."

"No, I knew. I'm glad he's got Ruby. He's got a hell of a road in front of him, especially if he wants to keep acting. He'll need good friends, a safe place where he can be himself."

"Don't we all."

Nate looked up and seemed to see Lois for the first time since she'd walked in. "Wow, you look tired."

Lois made a face at her. "Gee, thanks."

"Oh, please. You'll still be gorgeous when you're a corpse. I'm sure no one else noticed. In all seriousness, though. You're here without a fitting appointment, looking like you haven't slept. What's up?"

What indeed. Where to even begin?

Lois wandered over to Nate's couch and plopped down. "I didn't sleep much."

Nate gave her a sly grin as she followed her over and sat. "Wait a minute. What kept you from sleeping? Or should I ask *who*?"

"Get your mind out of the gutter. It's not like that."

It's a little like that.

"Am I wrong in assuming this has something to do with your illustrious husband, however?"

Lois inhaled deeply and looked sideways at Nate. "It's a safe assumption."

"Okay, then. What's going on? I thought things were good."

"They are. Were. Are." Lois buried her face in her hands. "I don't know."

"Hang on a sec." Nate went to her desk and came back with a bottle of amber-colored liquid and two paper cups.

"Do you always drink on the job?"

"Only when it's absolutely necessary." She poured their drinks and handed Lois a cup. "And you look like it's absolutely necessary. Talk to me."

"Nick and I..." Lois cleared her throat. "We may have kinda, sorta...kissed last night."

"A-ha!" Nate pointed at her. "You said you didn't sleep with him!"

"I didn't sleep with him! Clothes stayed on." Mostly.

"So what are we talking here, a little peck on the cheek, or a full-on smooch fest?"

"Nate. Seriously."

"You know how...absent my husband is. I need to live vicariously. I require details."

"It wasn't a peck on the cheek." At Nate's expectant eyebrow raise, she tried to continue. "It was..." Lois chewed on her lip, and then the words rushed out. "It was a time-stopping, limbs-melting, best-fucking-kiss-of-my-life kind of kiss, okay? And I have no idea what the hell I'm supposed to do now!"

"Damn. Way to go, Nick." She took a drink. "So how exactly did it happen?"

"I'm not even sure. During and after dinner we got to talking. I told him about my Rules—well, most of them anyway—and then we got into Nick's situation. He really opened up, you know. Told me about the whole dope thing. Totally premeditated to get the studio's attention, by the way."

"I *knew* he wasn't stupid."

"That's exactly what I said. Anyway, we were thoroughly connecting. He's been through a lot more than he lets on." Lois took a deep breath, attempting to quell the fireworks that had resumed their bursting in her chest as soon as Nate started prodding her. "And then he told me he was glad he'd gotten partnered up with me."

"Awww."

"I know. I couldn't help it. I kissed him."

Nate swatted Lois's shoulder, impressed. "Nice going, lady."

Lois snorted ruefully. "And then we were off. I honestly can't say how long it went on, but it was...a while." She bit her lip again. "He's *unquestionably* good."

"He must be. I've never seen you like this." She paused expectantly. "So...what happened then? You obviously came up for air at some point, or you wouldn't be sitting here."

"Yeah, we caught our breath and just kinda left things. Said good night. I went to bed, tossed and turned for a while. Tried to relieve some of the pressure by"—she cleared her throat and gestured south—"taking care of myself. Went back to tossing and turning. And here I am."

"Hold it. You took care of yourself? Are you kidding me?"

"Come on. You cannot possibly be judging me for that. With Walter traveling so much, you mean to tell me you don't?"

"Of course I do. I would never judge you for *that*. What I am judging you for is doing it when you had an obscenely good-looking, able-bodied male—*who had just kissed you senseless*—right across the hall. Why in the world wouldn't you let him do it?"

Why hadn't she?

Lois shook her head. "Do you know how complicated that

would've made things? The kiss was bad enough. I needed time to think, figure out what it all means. I wasn't about to sleep with my husband." She heard herself. "And yes, I am aware of the absurdity of what I just said."

They exchanged a glance and laughed.

"Oh, Nate. What am I gonna do?"

Nate leaned her elbow on the back of the couch and propped her head on her hand. "I wish I knew. How was he this morning?"

"I don't really know. He had to be here early, so we completely avoided the subject. Which was fine, actually. I wouldn't have known what to say anyway."

"I've gotta ask, Lo. What would be wrong with taking it further? Yes, I know you have your strict no-fraternizing policy, but he's clearly got talent, or you wouldn't have it this bad. Why not explore a little?"

"A part of me wants to. Truly wants to."

"But?"

"But I keep coming back to the reason I married him in the first place. My career, setting my reputation to rights. I can't ignore that." She met her friend's eyes. "I have been so stuck, for so long. And I'm finally close. *Damn* close."

Lois had trouble vocalizing the rest of it.

What if I let myself have this? What if it's great and then it goes away? Or worse. What if I just end up trading one label, one career trap, for another? What if it makes me resent him and it all goes to hell?

She closed her eyes, and Nate reached over and rubbed her shoulder.

"I get it," Nate said. "You've had good reason to build up some pretty thick walls. One earth-shattering kiss isn't about to topple them."

"Is that supposed to make me feel better?"

"Hell if I know."

Lois opened her eyes for the express purpose of rolling them.

Nate just chuckled. "I know you have to do what you have to do. But don't forget to have a little fun along the way, huh?"

She knew Nate had a point. And fun didn't even begin to describe what kissing Nick had been like. But she didn't know if she'd be able to keep it simple, carefree fun.

That kiss had stirred something deep inside her. If she was being completely honest, it had started stirring long before last night. She had a sneaking suspicion that if she examined it more closely, she'd be able to trace it back to that very first day in Bartholomew's office.

Her brain kept trying to tell her to keep him at arm's length, and last night her body had taken over and drawn him in.

She was starting to get an inkling of which direction her heart leaned, but the questions remained.

She didn't know yet if she had the courage to follow it, repercussions be damned.

Chapter Fourteen

Tinseltown Trappings

*In most other professions, the idea of working with a spouse
would be the stuff of nightmares. But not so for some of our
favorite dolls and dreamboats! It must especially make newlywed
life easier, being able to do things like ride to and from work
together… And when your partner-in-crime is an actual movie
star, can you really blame a gal for lingering in a car, getting up
to all kinds of scandalous antics?*

For the second time in as many days, Nick found himself pacing around his dressing room like some kind of caged animal with energy to spare. Today's energy felt different, though. While he wanted very much to go find Lois again, he wasn't sure it would do anything to alleviate the tension this time.

He was fairly certain it would end with both of them reduced to a pile of ash.

But if it feels anything like it did last night, would that really be such a bad thing?

Nick flopped down on his couch and groaned. For someone who had gotten almost no sleep the night before, he wished exhaustion would catch up with him already. Shouldn't he be tired, dammit?

After Lois had gone upstairs last night, Nick stood in the kitchen for much longer than it had taken to wash the wine glasses. He'd offered to take them in the first place because the thought of going up to his room, listening to the sounds of her getting ready for bed across the hall, was just too much to bear.

He'd want to be in there with her, and there was no way that was a good idea.

Not that it wouldn't feel good.

If that kiss was any indication, it would feel a hell of a lot better than good.

He leapt to his feet and began pacing again. He wasn't an early riser, but he'd actually been grateful for the early call this morning. He'd spent most of the night tossing and turning, unable to turn off his mind—or his cock, for that matter—and finally drifted off for maybe an hour. During which he, of course, dreamt of Lois. He'd woken with barely enough time to spare, which had saved them from having an awkward conversation over breakfast.

He was filming some pretty strenuous physical comedy today, and Nick threw himself into it with more gusto than usual. As wonderful as it was to have somewhere to put his energy, though, the restlessness rushed back in the minute they yelled "cut."

So here he was, pacing again. And no closer to having even a small clue what to do next.

A knock on the door startled him.

"Ready for you on the set, Mr. Bradley," an assistant called out.

Nick could've hugged the man for saving him from thinking himself into more of a corner.

But his mind didn't exactly quiet down on his way back to the set.

A knee-jerk part of him thought he should apologize to Lois—

the part of him that had been conditioned over and over by his mother to always be a gentleman, to keep his promises, treat women with respect. The same part of him that had felt like a cad for almost kissing her on their wedding night.

But he didn't want to apologize for something that had just felt *right*. So very right.

The whole night had felt that way. They'd both really begun to share parts of themselves. Once he got started, it was easy to open up to her, unburden himself. Hell, he didn't even talk that way to Max most of the time, and he was the closest thing to a brother he'd ever had.

"Hello, Mr. Bradley." A passing chorus girl, straight from the turn-of-the-century Moulin Rouge, waved saucily at him.

He waved half-heartedly back as he kept walking. He had a vague recollection of her being one of the same girls who'd mooned at him the other day as he had walked with Lois in her witch finery.

Nick sighed. *Lois.*

Last night, when she'd leaned in and brought them together, some kind of dam burst inside him. He wasn't a rover by any means, but he'd dated his fair share of women, a couple seriously enough, or so he'd thought at the time. But this thing with Lois… He'd never felt anything like he had with his lips on hers.

It was utterly terrifying.

It was utterly exhilarating.

Thus the train wreck his concentration was today.

He arrived back at the soundstage, and the effort of trying to remain still while Jackie touched up his hair nearly killed him. She eyed him warningly several times, but thankfully sensing his mood, refrained from saying anything to scold him. That was something, he supposed.

Everything had changed between him and Lois. There was no getting past it. But nothing had changed around them, which was the problem. So much was on the line. He still had an arrest to come back from, a career trajectory to change. She still needed to repair her reputation. They'd made a very specific arrangement.

Where would it leave them if they changed the terms of that arrangement now?

Of course, he couldn't even come close to answering that question by himself. He knew the obvious solution was to talk to Lois. Until he knew how she felt, it was pointless to even try to come up with the answers.

The problem was, he was a little afraid to find out. What if the two of them weren't on the same page? What if they were? Did he even know what book he was reading?

Way to be dramatic, Bradley.

Nick rolled his eyes at himself, enormously grateful Jackie had finished with him and moved on to one of the extras. He couldn't tell if Lois addled his brain, or if he'd always been this addled and she just threw a spotlight on it.

With impeccable timing, a directing assistant ushered him over, and the minute his feet hit their mark, he let his mind go blank. By the time Hornsby mumbled "Action," Nick's character had blissfully taken over.

When he finally wrapped for the day, Nick hung up his costume and grabbed his things. Having been able to turn his head off for the rest of the afternoon had him feeling at least somewhat ready to see Lois. Continuing to stew in his own thoughts would only serve to make things worse.

He was still unprepared for just how quickly he found her.

Rounding the corner of the building next to the parking lot, he stopped short. There she was, leaning against his car. Waiting for him.

And god, she was beautiful.

She wore a pair of houndstooth trousers that he thought, every time he saw her in them, made her look somehow sophisticated and saucy at the same time. Her navy blue sweater clung invitingly to her curves—the heavenly curves he'd molded his hands to last night. He fought a groan.

She looked up as he approached, giving him a small smile as she removed her sunglasses. He thought he detected a hint of shyness in her expression.

Or maybe he was the one who felt shy?

He had the strangest mix of feelings at the sight of her. Shyness, yes. But at the same time an overwhelming desire to sweep her up in his arms and pick up exactly where they'd left off last night.

Arching over all the chaos of emotion, though, one solitary word flashed through his mind.

Home.

He swallowed hard. He'd have to unpack that one later.

Lois pushed off the car and straightened up. "Hey."

"Hi there. I didn't know you were on the lot today."

She gestured absently. "Yeah, I came to see Nate."

"Oh. Costume fitting?"

"Friend summit." Lois gave a small shrug.

They both opened their mouths to speak, then laughed.

"We do have a bit to talk about, don't we?" Nick asked.

She nodded. "I drove here, but I can come back for my car tomorrow if…"

"Yeah, of course. Let me just…" He moved around to open the passenger-side door. He took off his hat and threw it, along with his jacket and briefcase, in the back before gesturing to her.

As she moved to get in, their shoulders brushed, sending a spark jolting down his arm. Her gaze flew to his, and what he saw there told him she felt it too. She inhaled audibly and slid into the seat.

Nick rounded the car and got behind the wheel, aware of the growing discomfort that minuscule, accidental touch—on top of the sight of her in that sweater—had started in his nether regions. Driving might not be the best idea at the moment.

Embarrassed, he attempted to clear his throat, but it came out more like a growl. Even more embarrassing.

"Sorry, I... Would you mind if we, um, talked here for a bit? It might be...safer that way."

She gave him a quizzical expression before understanding widened her eyes. She pressed her lips together in a clear attempt not to laugh. "Of course. Here's fine. It'll probably be good for our image anyway. People might think we couldn't make it off the lot without making out."

Lois's smile faded and a furious blush overtook her cheeks as she realized what she'd said.

Her words would have been innocent enough just twenty-four hours ago. They probably would have joked about it. Instead, the memories of last night flooded back in vivid technicolor.

Yep. Definitely glad not to be operating a car right now.

"I'm sorry, I don't know what I was thinking." She paused. "Aw, hell, I know exactly what I was thinking. I haven't been able to think of anything else all day."

"Me either," he said on an exhale.

They locked eyes, and two sets of shoulders sagged in relief.

"I am so glad to hear you say that."

Nick shifted in his seat to face her. "I spent the day wanting to talk to you, but I've gotta be honest, I have no idea where to even begin."

"Neither do I. This is crazy. I don't know if I've ever been at such a loss."

She bit her lip, and all Nick wanted to do was reach over and kiss her frown away.

Instead he said, "I do know one thing. Last night was..." He trailed off. He knew what last night was, but all his words suddenly seemed insufficient.

Luckily she saved him from having to find any. "It was. You're...you're a hell of a kisser, Nick."

Now it was his turn to blush. Since when did he blush this much?

"You were pretty damn great yourself, Lois."

She surprised him with a cocky grin. "I know."

A laugh exploded out of Nick.

How did I get so lucky to be here with her?

They sat there for a few minutes, just breathing the same air. Their hands rested a few inches apart on the seat between them. Nick couldn't say who moved first—maybe they moved at the same time—but at some point their hands came together.

Lois looked down at their twined fingers and broke the silence. "I've been back and forth all day in my head. I didn't exactly plan on last night."

"That's for sure." He watched their fingers too.

"And as fantastic as it felt…"

"We're in the middle of so much else."

Lois nodded. "I…um… When I told you about my Rules? There was one I left off the list…"

Understanding socked him in the jaw. "Let me guess. You don't get involved with costars."

"No," she answered quietly, "no one I work with. I suppose that's not so much a rule for being difficult as it is…"

"For your own protection?" He fought the urge to ask her for a list of everyone who'd ever hurt her so he could hunt them down.

She smiled sadly up at him. "It always has been, yeah." She gathered in an enormous breath. "But here I am, wondering if I should chuck that one out the window."

As much as that gratified him, the rational, logical part of Nick knew that they'd be better served by sticking to her rule. That they should curb whatever this was between them. As well as all his plans had been working, they weren't anywhere near finished.

But when he'd made those plans, he hadn't counted on Lois entering the picture.

And now that she was here, he couldn't imagine his plans *not* including her.

He still wasn't sure what the next step was, but he knew enough to see that he didn't want to let her walk out of his life when all this was over. With a start, he realized that as scared as he was to let her in, the prospect of not having her in his life scared him even more. But all of that wouldn't amount to shit if Lois wasn't ready yet. She had her own goals to accomplish. And he wanted her to be as certain as he was.

A thought occurred to him, and he shared it before he could lose his nerve.

"Maybe we shouldn't overthink this. Do we really need to figure it all out right now?"

Lois met his eyes. "What do you mean?"

"I mean, yes, we still have a lot to accomplish with this…partnership. But what we also have is time. Why not use it? I can't explain this—whatever it is—between us any more than you can. But it's not nothing. Is it?"

"No. It's not."

He tried to hold in his sigh of relief.

"So, what exactly are you suggesting?" she asked.

"I'm suggesting we just…don't decide anything." At her raised eyebrow, he continued. "We have a week or so left on this picture, plus a bunch of publicity down the line. Time left on our marriage arrangement. We could just let it sit. See what happens. Or doesn't." He hated to add that last part, but felt he should.

"Huh." He could see her letting the idea sink in. "That's…not bad, actually. We wouldn't be breaking any rules, per se…just… not strictly following them either. I think." One side of her mouth quirked up. "It would be a relief not to think."

"I find thinking gets me in trouble more often than not."

She laughed. "So we let it sit."

"We let it sit. Go slow."

Lois tightened her grip on his hand before letting go. "Let's go home." She glanced down at his lap. "Do you need me to drive?"

He flashed her a wry smirk. "I'll be fine, thanks."

A sense of calm washed over Nick as he started the car and headed for the house. Maybe it was taking the coward's way out to put off making a decision, but Lois had warmed to the idea. And a new addition to his plan had started to formulate that he needed more time to contemplate.

Didn't you just tell Lois we shouldn't overthink this?

He ignored the voice in his head.

He'd have to proceed with caution. He'd always been a pretty slow mover, and it had largely served him well.

A large part of the reason Lois had agreed to their marriage was that it came with an expiration date. She'd seemed relieved when he promised to behave like a gentleman. True, the first move last night had been hers, and for all he knew she worried about taking advantage of him as well, of taking this to a physical level they hadn't agreed to. It was equally possible that the physical was the only level she was interested in. Because of the rules she'd set for herself. Her career was paramount to her, and she didn't want anything to get in the way of that. He didn't want to get in the way of it either. She deserved to have all those bozos who'd kept her down see her for the powerhouse talent she truly was.

No, he definitely needed to take this very slowly. But one thing was starting to become startlingly certain.

Rules or no rules, he wanted to woo his wife.

Chapter Fifteen

Hollywood Happenings

That's a Wrap! Filming has finally finished on the infamous Bradley-Ashford vehicle over at Parkmoor, and we hear there was quite the celebration—an actual celebration!—on set. We're just as surprised as anyone over the lighthearted mood emanating from the soundstage in question. And that's not all—chatter abounds over the picture itself, which might not actually be the stinker everyone expected going in. Looks like Parkmoor might just have a pair of Star Rumplestiltskins on their hands!

As they entered the final week of filming, Lois was simultaneously relieved and concerned about the way she and Nick had left things. Relieved that he felt the same way, and that he'd suggested they simply not make any decisions. Concerned about what would happen when the picture was over, about whether they could, in fact, keep things slow.

Whether *she* could keep things slow.

Sitting in that car, it had taken tremendous effort to keep her hands off him. Despite all her worries about whether it was a good idea to even consider anything more than the platonic relationship they had, her reservations zipped out the window whenever she was near him. She still hadn't decided if that was a good thing or not.

Her attraction to him was powerful. One small kiss—okay, it hadn't exactly been a *small* kiss—had her desperate for more.

Luckily, she had work to throw herself into. Production needs kept them both too busy to focus on much of anything else. Because it was the final push, the pressure mounted to finish on time, and make it count. The last scene they had to film involved a crowded ballroom, and was complicated enough that it would take them three days. But it was a good complicated—she hoped. Lois had come up with the idea for her and Nick's characters to deliver their increasingly manic dialogue while weaving among all the other oblivious revelers, and if they hit it just right, the physical movement would add the extra layer of comedy they needed. She secretly harbored an extreme pride over her vision for the scene.

Filming went by in a blur, and before she knew it, Hornsby yelled—all right, fine, whispered—"cut" and *The Tealeaves Stalk at Midnight* was officially "in the can" as everyone liked to say. Lois shook her head. *Teacups in July*, why was that so damn hard to remember? At any rate, there were still edits and preview screenings and the like before they foisted it upon the general public, but the bulk of the work was done.

They had actually pulled it off.

The mood on the soundstage grew increasingly light. Lois and Nick had arranged a small party for the crew, which everyone seemed to be enjoying thoroughly. She had taken care of the champagne, and cups were being filled to the brim and passed around. Nick called on Max to work his magic, and cast and crew alike devoured dozens of delectable pastries, in addition to a giant sheet cake covered with piped-on icing teacups. Lois may have joked at the wedding about marrying Nick for Max's desserts, but it was turning out to be a delicious matrimonial bonus. He was a wizard with sugar.

Even Bartholomew stopped by the party for a bit, looking obnoxiously smug. As if the whole thing had been his idea.

All right, technically it *had* been his idea for them to work together. But if not for the tweaks the two of them had made, they'd be wrapping production on a tea-laden turkey. It might not be a peacock, either, but they'd made it pretty damn good, if she did say so herself.

Lois stood on the periphery of the soundstage, reflecting. Despite her crappy reputation, she'd made a pretty good number of films. She could say without reservation that she had never enjoyed any of them as much as she had this one. She tapped her cup against her lip. No point in pretending she didn't know exactly why that was.

The reason himself came striding toward her, munching on a twisted pastry.

"Have you tried these?" Nick asked.

"Yeah, what is that filling? It was more than just chocolate."

"This hazelnut paste from Italy. You wouldn't believe the wild and wonderful things Max has been doing with it."

"Think he can get a case of it for us? I'd eat it straight."

Nick's lips split in a wide grin. "I'll see what I can do."

He was down to the last bite, but instead of eating it himself, he held it out to her with a questioning raise of his eyebrow. Lois nodded and made to reach for it, but before she could, he raised his hand toward her mouth.

"Allow me."

Before she could even enjoy the burst of sweetness as the pastry began to melt in her mouth, she felt the feather-light, but very deliberate, brush of Nick's fingertip against her lower lip. He didn't mask the naked hunger—*sweet shit, am I actually better than a dessert?*—in his expression as he watched her eat.

She nearly forgot how to swallow.

He blinked first, and then pointed at her cup. "Any more of that lying around?"

Lois made a desperate grab for the bottle on the table behind her and poured him a cup of his own, grateful for the distraction. There were far too many people around. They didn't have to lay the newlywed act on so heavily here. And she needed to maintain at least a veneer of control.

She lifted her cup. "To *A Midsummer Night's Teacup*."

He snorted as he returned the toast. "That may be your best one yet. May she be as good to us at the box office as she's been to make."

"Amen, brother."

"So, what's up next for you? Gotten your marching orders yet?"

"It doesn't start for a few weeks, but they delivered my next script this morning. I think it's a melodrama, but it didn't feel right to peek before we were finished here. What about you?"

Nick lifted one shoulder casually. "No idea. I suspect they're gonna keep me in purgatory a little longer. At least until the response to this one starts to come in."

Lois could see that his attempt at nonchalance didn't reach his eyes. She looped her hand inside his arm and squeezed gently.

"You worried?"

He gave her a small smile. "Not really. It's nothing I didn't expect. I just don't want to lose momentum, you know?"

Lois looked around the soundstage. The party was winding down as evening approached and people trickled out to go home to their families. She hated to see Nick feeling down. Making a decision, she took their cups and set them on the table.

"Okay, this discussion is getting far too serious. There's plenty of time tomorrow to think about what comes next. Right now, we should still be focused on all this." She made a sweeping gesture, taking in the entire stage. "Look at what we did. I'd say it's pretty fucking huge, especially if you think about where we started. So tonight, we celebrate."

Nick caught her mood quickly and his face lit up. It thrilled her to see.

God, he's gorgeous when he smiles.

"What exactly did you have in mind?" he asked.

"I know just the place. Come on."

AFTER A QUICK STOP home to change, Lois directed Nick to a spot about twenty miles west across Highway 101. There wasn't much around besides some farmland and ranch houses, but Lois knew of a little gem hidden among them.

"Are you sure we're going the right way?"

"Just trust me."

Nick drove another mile or so, and Lois pointed ahead. "It's right up here. Take the next turn off the highway."

He followed her instructions, and R&G's Roadhouse loomed up, its neon sign welcoming visitors.

The car's tires crunched across the gravel as Nick pulled the car to a stop. He leaned forward to squint out the windshield.

"You brought us to a roadhouse?"

"Well, technically you brought us here."

"Cute."

She grinned impishly at him. "It's one of my favorite spots. Come on."

They climbed out of the car.

"You've been here before?"

"Sure, plenty of times." She met him in front of the car and linked her arm through his. "Stop looking so judgmental, will you? I've known the owners since forever. They serve lousy beer, but their taste in music is flawless. And the best part?" She leaned in conspiratorially. "No one ever knows, or cares, who I am here."

That got Nick's attention.

"Yeah?"

"Yeah."

They reached the door, coming face-to-face with a hulking, completely bald man. At first glance, one would think he was casual, without a jacket and with his shirtsleeves rolled up above his elbows. Closer inspection revealed an impeccably knotted necktie and highly polished buckles on his suspenders.

"Evening, Otto."

"Ms. Ashford, a pleasure as always," he rumbled. He took in Nick, examining him from head to toe as if he was a specimen in a lab. "You expect me to let you in here with her?"

Nick's mouth rounded into a near-perfect "o" and he blinked a few times. "Well…um…yes?"

Otto folded his massive arms across his chest. "Why should I? I read about you. You're liable to get this place shut down, and I won't allow that on my watch. How do I know you don't have any of that illegal junk on you right now?"

"I assure you, I don't. It was a one-time thing." Turning apologetic—and faintly haunted—eyes on Lois, he added, "I thought you said there was anonymity here."

"There is." She pivoted to the doorman. "Otto. Come on."

He softened slightly at her voice, but didn't give in. "I don't know, Ms. Ashford. What are you doing, getting mixed up with a guy like him anyway?"

She appreciated his protectiveness, but this was getting ridiculous. Nick deflated more with every passing moment. He looked liable to bolt any minute now, and this was supposed to cheer him up.

She hated to turn it on Otto, but the time had come for the diva to emerge.

Straightening to her full height, Lois put her hands on her hips and stepped up in Otto's face.

"Let me make myself very clear, Otto. This gentleman is my husband, and if there's anyone on this planet I'd want to be *mixed up with*, it's him. He told you it was a one-time thing, and his word is good. You know me. And I trust him. Implicitly. That should be enough for you, should it not?"

She stared Otto down, refusing to let him break eye contact.

"Because if it isn't," she continued, "I'd be perfectly happy to get in the car and take my business further down the road to another establishment. And I'm pretty sure Rosie and Guy wouldn't like that too much."

Otto gulped almost comically. The watchdog's face crumpled into the puppy she knew him to be underneath all that muscle.

"I'm sorry, Ms. Ashford. Didn't mean to presume."

"Thank you, Otto. But I'm not really the one you should be apologizing to."

He turned to Nick, who was watching the whole performance with a somewhat thunderstruck expression.

"Right. No offense, sir. Just a little protective over Ms. Ashford, I guess. She's one of the good ones."

Nick smiled at that. "I heartily agree with you there, Otto. No offense taken."

Otto stepped aside to let them through the doors. "You all have a good time now."

"Thanks, Otto," Lois said.

As she passed him, he leaned to whisper, "So he's a keeper then?"

"Yeah, I think he might just be."

She'd barely admitted the words to herself, but once they escaped her lips, she did rather like saying them.

The roadhouse was pretty crowded for a weeknight, and she followed as Nick led them to a couple of open seats near the corner of the bar.

"Beer okay?" Nick asked.

"Yeah, fine."

He called out to the bartender and ordered for them.

"I'm sorry about that back there. I really didn't expect him to turn on you like that."

"Don't worry about it. I get it. He was just trying to protect the place. And you. Besides, it gave me a chance to finally see the diva in action. I must admit, it was impressive. Seeing you fell a giant with an icy stare and some choice words."

"You scared?"

"Nope."

"Good."

Their beers arrived, and she held his blue eyes, now nearly black, as she sipped.

Where the hell does he get the nerve to be this sexy?

Nick broke the spell a moment later as he took his first taste of the beer, and his face twisted.

"Ugh, you weren't kidding. This beer is lousy."

She chuckled. "Isn't that part of the charm of a roadhouse, though?"

"Fair point. If it tasted good, there'd probably be something wrong."

"Exactly."

"Well then." He raised his glass. "To our movie."

Lois joined him in salute. "To our careers, taking flight."

"To partnership."

"To partnership." She smiled as they clinked their mugs together.

Nick surveyed the room. "Aside from all that business at the door, you were right. I don't think a single head turned toward us as we came in here. I can't remember the last time that happened."

"Nice, isn't it?"

Nick sighed theatrically. "So nice." He leaned his elbow on the bar. "You mentioned Rosie and Guy before. Safe to assume they're the 'R and G' from the sign?"

Lois smiled, remembering the couple's decision to open the place. "Correct. Though those aren't their real names."

"Nicknames or aliases?"

"Nicknames." She paused, considering. "Actually, nicknames of their nicknames." At Nick's confused look, she explained. "I should start with the fact that I met Rosie and Guy in an acting class when I first got to Los Angeles. They were newlyweds, taking classes on a lark to see if they'd be good enough to try to break into the pictures."

"And were they?"

Lois gave him a rueful sigh. "Sadly, they were not. But they were confident enough to recognize that and not be too disappointed. Luckily for them—and us—they also had a dream of running a roadhouse." She raised her arm to take in the room. "And they are much better at it than acting."

"I can see that. So, wait, where do the nicknames come in?"

"Well, their lack of talent did not curb their love of Shakespeare. In class, everyone started calling them Rosencrantz and Guildenstern."

Nick made a low rumble of understanding. "Rosie and Guy."

"Exactly. They initially wanted to use the full versions for this place, but decided against it."

"That's too bad. I think the Bard himself would probably have approved."

Lois laughed. "I think he would have too. But I think what it really came down to was money."

"Money?"

"Two letters are an awful lot cheaper when it comes to neon. And they get questions this way, which I think they relish. Depending on who's doing the asking, they give the long or the short version."

"I wonder which version I'd get."

"Oh, they'd know you could handle the long one. I think they'd like you quite a bit, actually."

Lois could see Nick trying to hide the beam of pleasure that coursed through him.

"Then I hope to meet them someday." The band started a particularly lively number—impressive given that their member count was much smaller than the usual big band orchestras—drawing his attention to the stage. "You were right about their taste in music too."

"Tell me, Nick, do you dance?"

"A little." He looked over his shoulder at the dance floor as it began to fill up. "What, now?"

"Sure. Unless, of course, you're afraid you won't be able to keep up with me." She batted her eyelashes with taunting innocence.

Nick narrowed his eyes and stretched his neck from side to side before getting up and extending his hand.

"Oh, it's you who should be afraid of keeping up, sweetheart."

Lois growled, "Challenge accepted. Look out, Bradley."

Then they were off, right into the middle of the dance floor. Nick more than kept up with her. One number turned into several, as they twirled and jumped around the floor. More than once, he lifted her off her feet and swung her around in time with the music. They were both sweating bullets, and feeling far more drunk off of the dancing—and each other—than the watery beer.

It was quite possibly the most fun Lois had ever had. And judging by the matching glow in Nick's eyes, he was right there with her.

For a few hours, they existed as simply a random couple having fun on a crowded dance floor. No reputations following them, no pretending necessary for any audience. Just Lois and Nick, dancing up a storm.

It was downright magical.

They stayed nearly till closing, and Otto gave them a wink as they passed through the door to leave. Nick put the top down on his Cadillac for the drive home, and they turned the radio up to be heard over the noise of the road rushing by. The breeze felt wonderful on their flushed skin. Neither one of them said much of anything during the trip. There was no need.

It was nearly four in the morning by the time they stumbled through their front door. Lady Macbeth yowled angrily at them from her basket at the foot of the stairs, highly affronted at having been woken up by two such annoying humans.

Fatigue started to catch up with them. Lois's limbs felt heavier with each step as she and Nick trudged up the stairs, still amused by everything and nothing in particular. They stopped and each leaned on their respective bedroom doors, facing each other.

Nick stuck his hands in his pockets. "That was a perfect celebration."

"Told you I knew just the place, didn't I?"

They remained in their places for a moment, before Nick pushed himself up off the door and slowly bridged the gap between them. He rested one hand on the door next to her head. As dark as it was, she could still make out the fire flashing in his eyes. Fire that leapt from him right into her core. She held her breath as he drew closer.

He hovered a fraction of an inch from her, his breath fanning over her lips. He moved ever so slightly back and forth, caressing her without making actual contact, until she was sure she'd melt into a puddle on the spot.

Just when she couldn't take any more, he grazed his tongue along her lower lip. She was frozen to the wall, wanting desperately to wrap her arms around him but unable to resist waiting, anticipating what he'd do next.

He brought the flame closer and began to sip at her slowly, tortuously, all the while keeping one hand on the wall and the other behind his back. Their tongues finally met, dancing in a rhythm that would've gotten them arrested for indecency at the roadhouse.

Too soon, Nick pulled back, and Lois's head followed off the wall like a magnet. He straightened fully and lifted his hand to trace a tender trail down her cheek.

"Good night, Lois."

Before she could protest, he was gone, his bedroom door closed.

Lois slumped back against her own door, unable to do anything but stare.

Damn, he's good.

Her legs felt like lead, but she somehow found her way into

her bedroom. She at least managed the energy to take off her shoes before collapsing onto the bed. She wasn't sure how long she lay there before drifting off.

Nick certainly was taking the "slow" thing seriously. And she had to hand it to him; it was actually a pretty smart move. He'd managed to give her just enough to make her thoroughly secure in the knowledge that she wanted his lips to explore a lot more than just her mouth.

He wants slow, does he? Two can play at that game.

Lois fell asleep focused on ways to get Nick to give in without driving herself crazy in the process, completely forgetting to give her attention to any reservations about being with him in the first place.

Chapter Sixteen

Hollywood Happenings
Spotted poolside at the Beverly Wilshire: that gorgeous husband-and-wife team of Ashford and Bradley, basking in the sunshine… and the buzz building over their newly-finished movie. (And may we just add, what's seriously criminal about these two is what a stunningly attractive couple they make!)

Speaking of Ms. Ashford, did anyone catch the news about her former studio, Neptune Pictures, coming from our buddies over at Variety? Looks like the money's starting to run out…and so are the stars! The lady just might have been smarter than we thought, getting out years ago when she could…

The minute the door settled into its frame, Nick melted against it, all his bones dissolving into jelly. He didn't know what he'd been thinking. He had tapped into every ounce of willpower in him—and even some he didn't know he had—to pull himself away from Lois. And now he was utterly depleted.

As they'd driven home, he couldn't remember the last time

he'd felt so happy. Dancing with her had been a dream. She was fantastic, matching him step for step, and before the first song had even ended, he'd completely let himself go.

When they'd gotten home and faced each other in the hallway, every last detail about her intoxicated him. The faint flush that still painted her cheeks, glowing even in near darkness. The way her raven hair fanned over her shoulders, wild from the perfect combination of the dancing and the wind passing through his convertible. Her body appeared to be languid and buzzing at the same time, mirroring exactly the cacophony coursing through his.

Completely absorbed, he let her gravity pull him toward her. He had been vaguely aware of his head, reminding him to go slow. Not that he really needed the reminder. Her gaze had come to a boil as he crept closer, and instinct told him he was right to draw this out.

Their earlier kiss had been hungry, but now he wanted to take his time, savor it. Savor her.

She deserves to be savored.

He could have stood there until the sun came up, and long into the morning. But then he'd remembered the thought that had come to him the other day. *Woo her.* And so he forced himself to stop. To leave her wanting more.

He hoped it worked. Because he sure as hell wanted more.

So much more.

He finally dragged himself away from the door, and the temptation to go back across the hall and finish what he'd started.

After falling into bed, Nick slept like the dead. It was nearly noon before he made his way downstairs. Lois was making coffee, and from the looks of it, she hadn't been up long herself. He took comfort in that.

"Morning," she greeted him. "Want a cup?"

"Definitely. Thanks."

He watched her, curious, as he grabbed himself a mug and she filled it along with her own. She looked a bit tired from their late night, but seemed otherwise unruffled. That was odd.

He felt like he'd been hit over the head. He'd only had a couple of beers—weak ones at that—yet he had a hell of a hangover. All from her.

She really needs to carry a warning label.

But she didn't look rattled at all. He couldn't believe she remained unaffected by the evening. By that kiss. He'd been watching her closely, had felt her breath catch, seen the prickle of goosebumps on her skin when he'd touched her cheek. So how could she act so unflappable now?

He tried to play it casual as they started their now usual breakfast routine. They fell into their easy pattern, neither one of them mentioning even one thing about the previous night.

Nick would have been frustrated if he hadn't noticed one small, very particular difference in her behavior.

She didn't once look him in the eye.

Not while they made their breakfasts. Not while they sat and ate, and made small talk, passed the morning paper between them. Not when he offered to clean up and she made her way upstairs to finish getting ready for the day.

Lois was one of the most direct people he'd ever met. She'd probably stare down a lion. So for her to be avoiding even the smallest eye contact this morning…

Nick allowed himself a smug grin as he rinsed out his mug. Maybe she wasn't so impervious to him after all.

Onward.

Slowly.

A FEW DAYS LATER, Nick and Lois sat at a poolside table at the Beverly Wilshire Hotel. They had decided to inject a change of scenery into their morning, for a number of reasons. Neither of them was needed at the studio that day. Lois had her new film coming up, but Nick lingered in limbo, and if he stayed in the house one more day, he knew it wouldn't be long before he drove both of them crazy. The speed with which she agreed to going out told him she knew it too.

Despite the slow…whatever it was…building between them, they also couldn't ignore the fact that the primary purpose of their marriage was publicity. Especially now that they had wrapped their picture. So they took advantage of the pleasantly warm day and headed to the pool, where they could eat and lounge without much interruption, but still be seen "out and around" town.

Nick sat in a robe and swim trunks, already prepared to hit the water should the mood hit him later. As he sipped coffee and read *Variety*, he couldn't help sneaking glances at Lois.

She had also changed into a swimsuit when they arrived, but he wasn't sure if he could call her cover-up a robe. Having seen it when it came out of her bag, he had no idea how it worked. What had started as a seemingly plain, large piece of fabric, now crossed and recrossed over her body artfully. It quite frankly defied physics. He was starting to suspect that its contact with a goddess had elevated the fabric to its true calling.

The goddess in question was currently engrossed in her new script. From time to time, she absently munched on the remains of her fruit and cheese plate. A pencil perched haphazardly behind her ear. Watching her all morning, Nick knew exactly when she'd reach up and use it to make a note. He recognized her tell—a little scrunch of her nose, followed by a slight head tilt. Then the pencil was put to work.

She enchanted him thoroughly.

He must've let his appreciation out with a noise, because she looked up from making a note with a little, "Hmm?"

"Oh, nothing." He pretended to focus on the newspaper as she resumed writing.

A little while later, bored with *Variety*, Nick put the paper down and turned to the worn copy of *Pygmalion* he'd brought with him. Lois noticed, and turned curious eyes on him.

"Okay, I've been meaning to ask since you moved in. Why in

the world do you have so many copies of *Pygmalion*? Should I be worried?"

"I wouldn't change you for the world," he replied with a wink. "No, it's actually the very first play I ever did, back in school."

"You never forget your first." She grinned.

"You really don't."

She seemed afraid of the answer, but asked anyway. "Were you Higgins?"

Nick grimaced. "Ick, no." He puffed out his chest. "Freddy."

Lois's face brightened. "You are most definitely a Freddy. And I mean that as a compliment. I've always thought Higgins was an utter ass. Did not deserve Eliza."

"My sentiments exactly." He leaned forward. "So, what about you? Your first?"

A lovely shade of pink graced her cheeks. "Eliza Doolittle, as a matter of fact."

"Oh, really. How very…meant to be."

"Indeed."

They shared a grin.

"Just a sec. I can see why you like it, but that still doesn't explain all the copies. When you were unpacking, I swear I saw at least a dozen."

"Oh, well, I guess you can blame my family." Nick's mouth curved up at the memory. "My mom found this old edition with a great, fancy cover and gave it to me closing night. My sister had already found another version without realizing, so she saved it for a birthday present. They were so unique, I was fascinated. Before I knew it, I started collecting them. Anytime I found one with a great cover, or interesting notes in the margins, I picked it up." He shrugged.

"A little bit of history, to go with your own history. I like it."

He warmed at her approval.

They lapsed into another companionable quiet for a while, before Nick broke it to venture a question that had been on his mind all morning.

"So how's your new script?"

She scanned the area around them dramatically before leaning in to whisper, "I'm afraid to admit it, but it's actually pretty good."

Nick chuckled. "I thought it might be. You've been so absorbed all morning."

"Yeah, it's a real surprise. I mean, it's nothing earth-shattering. Pretty standard melodrama stuff. It's an ensemble too, which means no one really has a terribly big part. But mine's actually good. It's nice to have something I can sink my teeth into."

He leaned back and folded his arms across his chest. "Maybe I'm a good influence after all."

That got a snort. "Oh, yes, by all means, please let my success go to your head."

He shrugged. "If the shoe fits…"

She threw a grape at him, which he promptly popped in his mouth, giving her an exaggerated wink in the process.

Lois rolled her eyes and groaned lightheartedly. "I'm going to read now." She picked up the script and waved her hand at him. "Weren't you going to swim or something?"

He put his hand over his heart, all mock hurt. "Is my lovely wife trying to get rid of me?"

"Yes. Go away." This without looking up.

Nick laughed again and stood up. He'd been sitting too long. A swim would do him good. He shed his robe and twisted at the waist a few times to limber up a bit. He walked to the deeper end of the pool. Rounding the corner, he turned to face the pool and caught sight of the table he'd just left.

And found Lois staring at him.

All-important script forgotten, her eyes traced a path over his body. Even from this distance, he could feel the trail of fire it left on his skin.

Well then.

She remained so focused on his body, she didn't even realize he'd raised his head and caught her looking. A lazy warmth settled in his chest. He leaned over and did a few more exaggerated stretches before diving neatly into the water.

Might as well have a little fun, right?

As he sliced through the pool, Nick had to admit he was glad to have somewhere to divert his energy—and to hide. If he absorbed Lois's blazing scrutiny much longer, his swim trunks weren't going to be able to provide sufficient cover. And this was a family pool, after all.

After completing several laps, he emerged from the water feeling refreshed. He grabbed a towel and headed back to the table, drying off along the way.

Lois had put her pages down, but she was giving such an unusual amount of attention to the cover as he approached that he struggled to keep from laughing.

"Finish your script?" he asked casually.

"I did." She glanced up, and her gaze settled right in the middle of his chest. She cleared her throat. "As a matter of fact, I was just thinking of taking a dip myself."

Nick picked up his robe and put it back on—he wasn't heartless.

And then it was his turn to gape.

There was technically nothing unusual about her suit, but it gobsmacked him anyway. The pale blue one-piece hugged and accentuated all her curves, and showed off those gorgeous long legs. His mouth suddenly resembled a desert.

She turned to say something, but a slow smile overtook her face as she caught his expression. All the fluster of a moment ago vanished, replaced by smug confidence.

He was enraptured.

"Didn't your mother warn you not to let your face freeze like that?" She ruffled his hair as she sauntered past him. "Enjoy the view, Nicky."

He couldn't resist teasing her. "Like you did?"

She turned back and a pair of molten emeralds singed him

slowly from head to toe. "When a view's good, it needs to be appreciated."

Then she was gone, and he'd never been happier to be reduced to a pile of cinders.

After making no secret of watching Lois put Esther Williams to shame, Nick finally turned back to their table, letting her swim in peace. Not that she paid him any attention. He did it more for himself because, well…it was still a family pool. He bunched his robe more securely around his lap as he shifted in his seat.

He had just picked up *Variety* again when a pair of men passing through the pool area caught his attention. Their attire, unlike anyone else around, screamed "executive" and made them stand out. One at least had his jacket off in what Nick suspected was an attempt at blending in, but the other looked like he had a large stick lodged firmly up his ass, despite his show of glad-handing several of the people he passed.

As his eyes lifted to the man's face, Nick recognized him as Arthur Ronson, head of Neptune Pictures—and Lois's old boss. He'd never had cause to actually meet the man, but he'd seen him around town. Ronson was easy to pick out, due in large part to his hair, which had always reminded Nick of an imploding dollop of hot fudge.

The fudge in question was now turned in his direction. Ronson gave him an amiable wave, and looked to be on the verge of coming over to introduce himself, when his more casual companion pulled his attention away and he moved on. They made their way toward the door leading to the lobby, just as Lois emerged from the pool. Nick thought Ronson might pause to say hello to her, but he only spared her the slightest glance as he kept walking.

That was unusual. Lois did have her dark notoriety, but he would have thought Ronson would have shown her at least something more than bland indifference.

For her part, Lois hadn't seen Ronson, and smiled as she returned to their table.

"That's interesting," Nick mused, still baffled by the man's behavior.

As she took off her bathing cap and shook out her hair, Lois asked, "What is?"

"Your old boss was just here, and barely even noticed you."

Her head snapped up, all warmth suddenly absent. "What?"

"Arthur Ronson. Just came through here with some other exec. He was head of Neptune when you were there, wasn't he?"

Lois nodded slowly.

"He was all smiles for me, and I've never even met the guy. Shouldn't he have at least owed you a 'hello?'" Nick was perplexed—and miffed—on her behalf.

She dropped into her chair, her breath coming at a quick pace that had nothing to do with her swim. "Bastard," she muttered, the icy fury in her eyes one he'd never witnessed before.

Wanting to make her feel better in some way, he continued. "He's certainly got some pair, schmoozing in such a public way, given everything *Variety*'s been reporting about the studio."

A new spark lit in her sharp eyes. "What exactly have they been saying?"

He pointed at the paper on the table between them. "According to this, they've got quite a streak going of outspending what the box office is bringing in, and now they're close to losing a couple of big contract players to other studios. The actors are apparently seeing the writing on the wall and jumping ship. And *Variety* doesn't exactly traffic in idle gossip."

"No, they don't. Huh." She leaned back in her chair, looking over her shoulder at the door Ronson had vanished through earlier. Her foot tapped out a rapid rhythm under her chair.

As Lois processed the information, a deep satisfaction seemed to settle over her, though it wasn't a gleeful one. A definite hurt loomed behind it. Nick flashed on the early days of their living together, the way she would always pore over the trade papers during breakfast, scanning for something she never seemed to find. He hadn't realized until now that she'd stopped doing it so often in recent weeks. Seeing her agitation return filled him with his own.

Still unaware of the precise origin of Lois's terrible reputation, now he was pretty confident he could trace it directly back to something—or *someone*—at Neptune. He didn't know how much Ronson had contributed, or if he'd simply turned a blind eye to her distress.

A lightning bolt of anger struck Nick in the chest at the thought.

How *dare* someone hurt this extraordinary woman. He wanted to drive his fist into anyone and everyone who had. Repeatedly.

Lois projected calm, though. She'd gone inward. He didn't want to shatter that calm, especially in such a public place, so he tamped down his rage with an effort.

This wasn't about him.

Quietly, he asked, "Neptune wasn't the best place to work, was it?"

Her eyes flew to his, then immediately shuttered. "It was…a long time ago. A lifetime, really."

Nick nodded. Her evasion of his question spoke volumes, but he didn't press her. Couldn't.

If she wasn't ready to talk about it—whatever it was—he understood that. It had certainly taken him a while to open up to her about his arrest and everything that led up to it.

He hoped she knew she could trust him when she was ready.

Chapter Seventeen

__Hollywood Happenings__
What a night at the Brown Derby! An unexpected—but thoroughly intriguing!—double-date… Hollywood's favorite young firecrackers, Ruby Church & Bobby Frasier, laughed the evening away with their older (though not necessarily wiser) counterparts, Nick Bradley & Lois Ashford. According to everyone in attendance at the hot spot, a good time was had by all! Perhaps the Two Troublemakers are turning the tide after all… In addition to this fun date, it appears Ms. Ashford has been playing quite nicely with others on the set of her new picture…

*P*rep had begun in earnest for her new film, and it already presented a change of pace for Lois. She hadn't been exaggerating when she'd told Nick it was a decent script. She'd had her fair share of good roles over the years—owing to the talent they couldn't take away from her despite her reputation—but she had to admit, this part was one of the meatiest she'd had in ages. Almost enough to make up for all the ones her reputation had cost her.

Even more remarkable, though, was the treatment she was getting—or *not* getting—from everyone. She had trouble putting her finger on it at first, but it finally dawned on her.

All the trepidation, the fear.

It seemed to have gone missing.

Sure, plenty of people still looked at her sideways, or hesitated before coming up to speak to her. She doubted that would ever completely disappear. But it was far less pronounced. In a few cases, she thought she detected a touch of actual, unvarnished respect.

Given her history, it was enough to make her head spin.

Afraid to even think it for fear of jinxing it, it seemed like her alliance with Nick had started to pay off in a real way. Maybe things could change after all.

It was a strange, unexpected sensation, this hope.

But then there was her almost-run-in with Ronson. She still fumed over the gall of him. After everything he'd done, everything about her career—and hell, even her dating life—he was directly responsible for, she made hardly a blip on his radar. Not that she would have wanted to get into it with him, but it still stung. Especially after such a lovely morning of flirting with Nick.

She tried to focus on Nick in his swim trunks, but her mind kept drifting back to that news item about Neptune. It was still nothing more than a rumor, and she had no way to know if the repercussions would fall where she wanted them to. For all she knew, Ronson might actually *be* a cockroach—capable of coming out of a nuclear blast unscathed.

But hope simmered at the back of her mind, waiting, tempting her despite everything.

She'd surprised herself with how badly she wanted to tell Nick when he'd asked about Neptune. She sensed his curiosity, and she could hardly blame him. But what had really captivated her was what else she had seen in his gaze. A fire, barely contained, but held in check nonetheless. It was as if he was ready to charge into battle. On her behalf.

But she'd deflected. Because the Beverly Wilshire pool had hardly been the place to have that discussion, especially with Asshole Ronson so close.

That's not the only reason, though, is it?

No, she supposed it wasn't. She'd balked because deep down, a part of her remained scared.

She knew it was silly. Her story would be safe with Nick. *She* was safe with Nick. This extraordinary man who'd come into her life as a studio-wielded weapon and had turned out to be the best ally she never knew she could expect. Who was ready for battle at the slightest hint of wrong done to her.

Who looked at her like she was a goddess, and kissed her like he wanted to devour her.

He'd trusted her with his story, shared his hidden depths with her. And he hadn't pressed her when he sensed she wasn't ready to share her own. He was letting her do this on her terms.

But that tiny, fearful part of her wouldn't quit. The *what if.*

What if he judged? What if he didn't think it was that bad?

What if he thinks I'm really difficult after all?

It was ridiculous. This was Nick. He wasn't an ass. He wasn't like anyone else she'd met, certainly not in this town. He had her back.

No matter how much she tried to pretend otherwise, though, nearly ten years of conditioning, of being ostracized, hadn't exactly had no effect. Trusting anyone but herself didn't come easy to her. She'd almost forgotten how.

Until the day Nick walked in. And she started to remember.

She wanted more than anything to keep remembering.

NOT LONG AFTER her film started shooting, Lois and Nick returned home after a pleasant, if somewhat exhausting, evening —a double-date with Ruby Church and Bobby Frasier. They were both wary when Ruby followed up on her invite. As much as the tide seemed to be turning in their favor, they didn't want to bring any negativity down on the young couple. No matter how much Lois tried to demur, though, Ruby wouldn't hear of it. In the end, her infectious enthusiasm won out.

Lois had to admit, as young as Ruby was, it felt extraordinarily nice to have someone powerful in her corner for a change.

She settled onto the couch to remove her heels, and Nick sank down next to her.

"That was fun," Lois said.

"It was. I'm glad you and Ruby hit it off that day." He took a breath as if he wanted to say more, but then bit his lower lip instead.

"What is it?"

"Oh, nothing. Just…"

Lois tilted her head, waiting.

He caught her eye, and the words exhaled out of him in a rush. "My *god*, they're young."

Lois threw her head back and laughed. "I spent the whole night thinking the exact same thing!"

"Thank you! I was afraid it was just me. I mean, don't get me wrong, they're delightful people."

"But they are still teenagers. Old enough to be married, but…"

"Teenagers."

They looked at each other and laughed.

Lois leaned back on the couch and rubbed her aching foot. "Nothing like spending time with the under-twenty set to make thirty feel old."

"And I've got five years on you, grandma." He gestured to her foot. "Here, let me."

Lois couldn't resist the offer, and swung her leg up. He settled it in his lap, and his hands began to work nothing short of magic. A small groan escaped her.

"Heels are not for the faint of heart, are they?" he asked, amused.

"Indeed they are not. Thanks."

He nodded. "So do you think we had that much obnoxious energy when we were teens?"

"I'm sure you did. You've got a pretty obnoxious amount of energy now."

Nick lightly ran his finger across the bottom of her foot, making her squirm. "You think you're funny, don't you?" He cocked his head to one side, assessing her as he resumed the massage. "What were you like back then? Did you drive your parents crazy?"

"I wasn't so bad. I did drive my brother and sister crazy, though."

His brows rose, intrigued. "Oh, really?"

"I'm the baby, you see." She heard a rumble of understanding echo in his chest. "And they're older by several years. I was…a bit of a surprise."

"A welcome one, I hope?"

Lois smiled. "Very welcome. Much to my siblings' dismay. Let's just say, I tended to get away with a lot."

Nick shook his head. "They were clearly amateurs. Should've figured out how to rig the system."

"Why do I get the feeling you speak from experience?"

He shot her a wicked grin. "I've got two years on my sister, but I very rarely got in trouble. The secret's in the provoking. Start the trouble when mom and dad aren't looking. Then when they turn around to see her retaliating, stand there with an angelic, highly put-upon face." He demonstrated. "Works every time."

"So you've always been a little devil."

"More fun that way."

"That is certainly true."

Nick began on her other foot, and they lapsed into a comfortable silence.

After a while, he turned his head toward her. "You said you grew up near San Francisco, right? I feel bad for never asking, but did you want to invite your family to the wedding? It wouldn't have been a big trip."

"I did mention it to them, but it seemed silly for them to come down for something that was…"

"Not real."

"Yeah. What about you?"

"Same. My dad passed away a few years ago, and my mom lives with my sister and her family, helps out with the kids and stuff. They always have a lot going on, so I didn't need them to come."

"Do they know? About us, being for publicity and all?"

"Sure, I told them. My mom was actually a little disappointed. You'd think she'd have her hands full, but her desire for more grandkids apparently knows no bounds." He paused. "And yours? The knowing, I mean. Not the grandchildren."

Lois gave a soft laugh. "Yes. To the knowing. They've thankfully left me alone about the kid thing. With my brother and sister they've got a few already, and they understand how important my career is to me." She looked up at him. "They weren't too thrilled with you at first, but I talked them down."

Nick's eyes went wide. "Me? I'm a great catch!"

Lois smirked. "You know, once you get past the whole dope arrest thing."

"Well, yeah. But who's counting that?" He shot her a nervous look. "And they're really okay with me now?"

"They are. I assured them that you are a perfect gentleman in every other regard."

"Thanks." Nick's hands slowed on her foot. "Do they…" He hesitated, and she could see the debate going on behind his eyes, before he gave in and asked. "Doesn't it bother them? What everyone says about you?"

Lois inhaled deeply. "It does. Always has." A lump formed in her throat as a memory came to her. "My father wanted to come down here and start taking names, throw a few punches. I'm sure he would've been a sight to see."

"What stopped him?"

"My mother. Before she retired a couple of years ago, she had a career, in a field where women weren't too welcome, and she fought tooth and nail for it. She knows that it means more when you fight your own battles, recognized that I wanted to fight mine. Reminded him that I could."

"How'd he take it?"

"Not too well. Just because his little girl could didn't mean she should, in his eyes. But he did understand. It was part of what made him fall in love with my mother in the first place."

"Lois, I still don't understand. What happened?"

"How did I get my terrible reputation in the first place, you mean?"

"It doesn't make sense. Not to me, anyway."

He reached over and smoothed a stray hair off her temple, letting his finger drift down her cheek. She closed her eyes and leaned in to the caress, the tiny show of tenderness filling her with warmth. And courage.

Lois slid her leg off his lap and tucked it under her, straightening her spine. She filled her lungs and began.

"As you might have guessed, it started at Neptune. Those first couple of weeks were like a dream come true. I screen tested, they signed me, and my whole future was wide open. And then I got called into a meeting with the big boss." Acid rode a wave of disgust into her mouth. "Ronson. I couldn't believe my luck. I thought I must have really made an impression. He talked about my prospects, told me how thrilled they were to have signed someone with my talent. Finished the meeting by asking me to drinks."

Nick's nostrils flared, slight but unmistakable. "I assume it wasn't a business meeting he was proposing?"

"It was not. It was also not a meeting that would have included his wife."

With a clenched jaw, he asked, "How old were you?"

"Twenty. Young. Impressionable." Her mouth twisted in a wry grimace. "Or so he thought. Was pretty surprised when I turned him down, though he covered it quick. Told me there were no hard feelings and sent me on my way."

"That wasn't the end of it."

"Of course not. A few weeks went by, and I started getting acclimated to the studio. But I hadn't received any roles yet. I thought it was a little strange, but chalked it up to being new. Maybe that was just the way it was done. Then I got another meeting. They had a movie they were ready to put me in. And he asked again about drinks. I got the vague impression that the movie was somehow tied to my answer."

A low growl emanated from Nick.

"My immediate thought was disgust. Anger. I don't know how, but I held it in check. The optimist in me—who does exist, believe it or not, or at least did at the time—thought maybe it was a test. Plenty of studios have morality clauses; maybe he was just making sure I was up to snuff. So I said no. Again. When he didn't press the issue, I thought maybe I'd been right. I got my script, went into wardrobe fittings, was all ready to start."

Anger flared, hot and sudden. It started at the tips of her ears and worked its way across her whole body in a flash. Nick must have seen it, because he reached over and took her hand.

"When I got to the set that first day, I got the...*worst* looks. Like I was poison. Like I had no right to be there. I couldn't understand it. The director treated me with such disdain. I tried to ignore it, acted my heart out in my first scenes. When we took a break later, I overheard a couple of other actresses talking about me." Lois closed her eyes over the hurt, surprised by how much it still stung. "Asking who did I think I was, what right did I have to make so many demands, to be so..."

"Difficult." He finished her thought on a whisper.

She nodded. "I didn't get the chance to make any friends, have any control over the impression I wanted to make. It was all taken from me, before I could even get started."

"Didn't they see that wasn't who you were?"

"They might have if they'd bothered to look. But their minds had already been made up for them. It's how this business works, most of the time. You know that."

"But you were so young."

"I was. That's why I didn't storm into his office and confront him, no matter how much I wanted to. I knew he was responsible, but what difference would it have made? He tried to change my mind a couple times, offer me a way out, promise me that it could all change if I just went out with him once. But there was no guarantee that would really be the case. And there was no way I wanted success on those terms."

"Wasn't there anyone you could have gone to?"

She couldn't help the snort of disbelief that escaped her. "Nick. I was brand new to Hollywood and he ran a studio. Do you honestly think anyone would have believed it if I had? And even if they did, you know what they would have told me. I can practically hear it now. It's just drinks, just one time. I should say yes and be grateful, or move aside for the dozens of other girls who'd be happy to take my place."

Lois shook her head.

"I wasn't going to put myself through that. I knew I was right, and I refused to let anyone call it into question. So I swallowed the anger." She inhaled sharply. "And I had so much anger. It didn't take long for it to be too much. I told you a bit about what happened the first time I lost it on set. It should have been a disaster. But it…freed me somehow. If I had the reputation, I might as well reap the benefits, right?" She sighed and met his eyes. "And so here I am."

Nick swallowed audibly before asking in a low rumble, "Did he ever lay a hand you?"

"No." She was eternally grateful for that. "No, he kept all his weapons verbal."

Not that those weapons hadn't caused plenty of damage, nonetheless.

Nick was silent for a long minute, his only movement the rise and fall of his chest, at a rapidly increasing pace. Lois watched him carefully.

Telling him her story had been harder than she expected. Not because of his reaction, but because of her own. She hadn't voiced her experience to all that many people, and certainly not in many years. She would have thought enough time had gone by to dull her emotions, so her body's visceral response to the memories shook her.

But now that she was finished, she felt lighter somehow. Very much like when she let her anger fly that first time. Letting herself feel everything again, not hiding from it, unburdened her. She could already feel the freedom in it.

Nick was another story. He finally pushed himself off the couch like a rocket and began stalking back and forth in front of the fireplace, the anger vibrating around him almost visible.

"Nick?"

He stopped and brought his gaze to hers. His blue eyes, usually so bright and full of mischief, were now almost black, incandescent with a fury she'd never seen in him.

"Lois—" He pressed his lips together with such force they were nearly invisible. He filled his lungs before attempting to start again. "I—"

She wanted to get up and go to him, but she recognized the signs of an impending explosion and had the sense to stay on the couch.

Nick scraped his hand through his hair. "I don't even know where to start," he growled. He turned anguished eyes on her, and the explosion came. "How the hell could anyone do that to you? How *dare* they? How dare *he*? I could just..." His fists clenched. "And you..."

"Me?"

"All this time, you've had to live with this, deal with this. Have people like me come in and get used against you." He reached his arm out, as if he wanted to touch her. "You, with all your talent and your passion... God, you're *luminous*."

She blushed at that.

"And then that—" His lips scrunched together again, before curling into a sneer. "That...that *talking pile of pig shit!* He comes in and tries to take advantage, and then has the balls to ruin everything for you. I want to fucking ruin him. He's lucky I didn't know that day at the pool. I would've..."

As Lois watched him stand there trying to catch his breath, seething on her behalf, an extraordinary peace washed over her.

Followed immediately by an absurd impulse to laugh.

Out of all the wonderful things he'd just said, her mind had decided to seize on one phrase in particular and was now stubbornly refusing to let go. She felt the mirth bubbling low in her chest. The more she tried to hold it back, the more powerful the spasms grew, and a tiny snort escaped through her nose. She glued her lips together and covered them with her hand, but it was no use.

It started as a low moan and then exploded into a full giggle.

Nick started, then turned narrowed eyes on her.

"Are you...*laughing?*"

"No!" Another giggle. "Maybe."

"I'm sorry, do you find my anger funny?"

"Of course not! Nick, I would never. It's just..." *Here it comes again.* "Oh god. I can't help it. You called him a...a...talking pile of pig shit." She dissolved again.

Nick was still deadly serious. "Because he *is* a talking pile of pig shit."

"I know! That's exactly what he is! Don't you see?"

"No!" He remained incredulous.

"I never thought of it before, until you said it, and now it's all I can see. He really, actually does look *exactly* like a pile of pig shit!" She glanced at Nick through the tears starting to pool, and finally saw some humor creeping into his expression. "That toupee he wears? The color and the curl? It's..."

His eyes widened and the corners of his mouth began to twitch. "Pig shit."

"Yes!"

She reined in her laughter long enough to catch and hold his eyes. She could see his chest start to vibrate, and then they both burst. At one point, she actually snorted, loudly, which really broke Nick. He sank back down on the couch next to her.

Just when she thought she was regaining control, Nick nearly doubled over.

"Oh god, I just got the most ridiculous picture in my head," he wheezed. "A little cartoon pile of crap, with eyes and a mouth, talking." He made a talking puppet motion with his hand.

"You should pitch it to the Warners. He could have his own series of shorts where he follows Porky Pig around…"

"Talking!" they both exclaimed.

Nick affected the animated pig's accent. "That's shit, folks!"

The two of them collapsed against each other and howled. It took them a while to finally come down.

Lois spread her hand over her abdomen and groaned. "My stomach hurts."

"Mine too." Nick paused, remembering something. "So that's a toupee?"

"Oh sure. From a distance, you wouldn't know. But up close, it's… Well, you can definitely tell."

"That's…surprisingly satisfying to know."

"It really is oddly comforting. You have no idea how many times I've wanted to walk up to him in a crowded room and just fling it right off."

"I'd pay good money to see that."

They shared small smiles, before Nick's face turned serious.

"What can I do? Because I want to do something. Hell, what I really want to do is march right up and pummel the crap out of him."

"As much as I appreciate it, please don't." She reached over and cupped his cheek for a brief moment. "You've been working so hard to fix everything, and I think the last thing you need is another arrest under your belt. Somehow, I don't think they'd be so forgiving this time."

"Probably not." He sighed. "Tell me there's something I can do."

"I think you already have."

"How do you figure?"

"You know, I've lived with this for a long time. And I thought I'd felt it all. Anger, frustration, hurt, tears, resignation. But tonight was the very first time I've ever been able to laugh about him." She took a long, refreshing breath. "And it felt *good*. Unbelievably good." She nudged his arm. "Looks like there's something to your theory that we need laughter to heal."

He chuckled.

Lois rubbed the back of her neck, suddenly feeling drained. "I think I'm gonna turn in now."

"Okay."

She stood and experienced a wave of tenderness when she looked down at Nick. Taking his face in her hands, she bent to leave a lingering kiss on his cheek.

"Thank you, Nick," she whispered against his skin. "For the laughter. For everything."

A COUPLE OF HOURS LATER, Lois lay in bed, staring at the ceiling. As exhausted as she'd been when she left Nick downstairs, sleep remained stubbornly elusive. Her mind kept going over their conversation. Not her story—she'd relived that more than enough —but rather his reaction to it. And her reaction to him.

She marveled at the emotion that had coursed through her as she watched him. She had been right about his readiness to do battle on her behalf, but she had underestimated just how fired up he would be. Seeing that fury collected in his eyes was something she wasn't used to.

It had been so long since she'd had an ally. A partner. A *champion*.

Yes, she had an incredibly supportive family. She hadn't exaggerated her father's reaction. But it had come from afar. All of their conversations about her situation occurred over the phone. She hadn't been able to see the fire that no doubt pulsed in both her parents.

Here, really only Nate knew the extent of her history, but she'd known it for a long time, and was no stranger to the way the system worked for women. She'd been fierce, but resigned. She, too, knew how little could really be done.

But Nick's reaction felt different. It worked its way deep into the core of her, lifted her spirits in a way nothing had in an extraordinarily long time.

And she'd had no idea how desperately she needed to draw amusement out of her circumstances. With that one little well-earned and perfectly timed insult, it was as if Nick had cracked her chest wide open, allowing air to rush in to spaces that had been deprived for far too long.

Her chest wasn't the only thing cracking open. Her heart lurked dangerously close to the edge as well.

Lois could still taste the skin of his cheek, feel the prickle of his day's worth of stubble teasing her lips.

What exactly are we waiting for?

She was having trouble finding the answer. She'd been keeping him at bay, willing to go slow while she let herself worry about what it would mean to let him in. She supposed a part of her feared losing herself in the process. She'd spent so much time fighting to be heard, to be seen the way she wanted to be seen. Clinging to the need to protect herself.

She was so very tired of protecting herself.

Especially with this man, who had seen her from day one. Who had called her luminous.

She wanted to see what that flame in his eyes would look like if fueled by desire instead of anger. If it was anything like she felt when she touched him, she suspected it would be quite the wildfire.

Heaving a sigh, she turned to glance at the clock on her nightstand. Two a.m. Probably too late to do anything about it anyway. She'd heard Nick come upstairs not long after she did. Surely he was fast asleep by now.

Lois had just turned onto her side, willing sleep to come, when she heard him.

Light footsteps in the hallway. She sat up, straining to hear more. The sound of the bathroom door closing, followed by a rush of water as he turned on the shower.

Anticipation shivered over her skin, and she made a decision. She swung out of bed before she could lose her nerve.

LOIS RESTED her hand on the bathroom door for a moment. She lifted it and knocked, hoping she was forceful enough to be heard over the water.

Nothing. She thought she might have to knock again—or give up—when Nick called out, "Come in." It almost sounded like a question.

Here goes.

She entered the bathroom and closed the door behind her. She wasn't sure why, since it was just the two of them in the house, but it somehow felt right, more intimate.

His back still faced the door and her. The frosted glass of the shower door hid all but his head and shoulders from her. She watched the muscles of his back rise and fall as he took a breath, before turning slowly to face her. His eyes found hers immediately. Concern was uppermost in his expression, but something else hovered behind it.

That fire.

He was holding it in check. Barely.

His voice was all bass gravel when he spoke. "Lois. What are you doing here? Is everything all right?"

"I couldn't sleep either. I heard you come in here, and…" She toyed with the sash of her robe. She blinked, then held nothing back from her expression. "May I join you?"

The only part of him that moved was his Adam's apple.

And then, a slight, jerky nod of his head, his eyes never leaving hers.

Lois pulled at the sash and dropped the robe to the floor.

His eyes darkened as he took her in. The Adam's apple made another fierce bob, and he extended his arm to open the shower door, almost too slowly.

Her eyes charted their own course down his body, following the cascade of water down long, beautifully carved muscles. She finally saw what those damn swim trunks had hidden, and it was worth the wait. He clearly liked what he saw as well.

She made her way closer and stepped over the rim to join him. He closed the door, securing them in a cocoon of steam.

Lois raised her hand and placed it carefully on his chest, her fingers skimming over the wet hair clinging there. She took a gulp of air.

"Will you do me a favor, Nick?"

The concern rushed back, and he looked almost afraid to move. "Anything."

"Please don't be a gentleman tonight."

Chapter Eighteen

Her words unleashed him. Lois watched in fascination as his last reservations went up in smoke and he let his expression go completely hungry, feral.

She was right there with him.

They came together in a blinding flash. The minute their mouths found each other, they let out twin moans of relief. Their laughter mingled in a ghost of breath, before desperate desire took over.

Lois raked her hand through his hair as he turned her under the shower spray. His hands swept over her faster than the water, as if he was trying to touch every inch of her at once. She explored the planes of his back, the glorious strength of him. She arrested her journey when she reached his backside, reveling in what she found there.

She had never realized just how lovely an ass could be.

"Guess all that dancing we did paid off."

"If this is what it does to you, we can dance every damn night," he growled.

Her laugh gave way to a groan as his tongue traced a blazing path down her throat. He let his mouth play for a moment where her neck met her shoulder, before continuing on to her breast. His hand slid up to caress the underside while his lips settled over her nipple, working gently at first. When his tongue entered the picture, she let her head fall back. Water pelted her face, while she gripped his shoulders as hard as she could.

"My god, Lois. What you do to me."

He rose up and captured her mouth in a lush, searing kiss before returning to give her other breast equal attention.

He was slowly robbing her of all coherent thought. It was all she could do to stay upright as sensation pooled deep and rich in her core.

"Nick," she drawled.

Her voice drew a deep rumble from his chest. He straightened again, and she pulled his head down to meet hers. As they claimed each other's mouths, Lois slid her hand between them. She traced each of the ripples of his stomach, then continued lower. All it took was a light graze of his cock to set off a moan she felt in her own chest. She laughed into his mouth and increased the pressure of her hand.

After only a few minutes, Nick grasped her wrist and pulled her hand away.

She gave him a smirk. "What's the matter? Too much for you?"

Lois didn't know how it was possible, but his gaze turned even more wicked. "Honey, I'm just getting started."

He spun her around again and pressed her back against the shower wall. Before she could even marvel at how he'd managed to keep them from slipping, those lips were working their magic again. He started with her forehead, planting feather-light kisses across her eyes and the bridge of her nose. He let his tongue make a lazy sweep of her mouth before continuing on, down her neck and between her breasts. When he didn't linger there, a disgruntled sigh escaped her.

Nick raised his head and gave her the slowest, most tempting smile she'd ever seen. His hands settled firmly on her hips, never taking his eyes from hers until his knees came to rest on the floor of the shower.

Her breath hitched when his lips found her stomach and resumed their path. His tongue flicked her navel and she let out a surprised giggle. She could feel him smile against her skin, and then he was on the move again.

He planted a kiss on the inside of each of her thighs, just below the spot where they joined her hips. She breathed his name again, pleading.

And then he found his target. He started with a few light kisses, enough to drive her mad. His palm followed the line of her leg down to her knee, lifting it to his shoulder. She should have been unsteady, but he returned both hands to her hips and gripped her tightly, keeping her safe.

He met her eyes one more time, and she saw reverence join the heat and desire in his.

"You're a goddess, Lois." He left another kiss at the center of her, and she nearly came undone from that alone. "And you deserve to be worshipped as one."

And worship he did.

Already enough on fire, she thought for sure it would be over far too soon, but Nick was masterful. He sucked and licked and teased until she danced on the razor's edge, only to pull back at the last second and slow to a glacial pace. Her nails dug into his scalp and a strangled sound came from somewhere in her throat. His laugh reverberated through her and practically did her in.

He repeated the process several times, driving her to the brink before snatching her right back. He seemed to sense when she couldn't take any more, because he finally held nothing back, driving harder and faster, making a thorough feast of her.

She finally exploded in his grasp, coming apart more completely than she ever had. His arms circled her waist and held tight, still keeping her safe.

Her safety was becoming his specialty.

Thinking was near impossible, but one thing did manage to

float through her mind. Nick wasn't her first; she'd been with a few other men over the years. But not one of them had made her feel the way she did at that moment. Safe. Alive. *Worshipped.*

It was overwhelming.

Lois slumped against the wall and closed her eyes, breathless.

Nick placed one last, tiny kiss at her core and set her leg down before standing. She felt his finger run a caress down her cheek.

"I think my bones have disappeared."

He chuckled softly. "So it would seem."

She opened her eyes to find his lovely blue ones staring back at her.

As risky as it was to her stability, she managed to pull one hand from the wall and glide it up his chest, unable to resist touching him.

"You look awfully smug."

"Are you saying I don't have reason to?"

She sighed. "Oh, no. I'll definitely give you this one. You should be very proud of yourself."

He leaned in and whispered against her lips, "Thought so."

She huffed a laugh and dove deeper for a long, languid kiss.

"I suppose we should get out of here before we get all pruny." He took her hand and rubbed her fingers.

"You're probably right." She raised their joined fingers and kissed the back of his hand. "I think there's another, drier room down the hall we can relocate to."

Another slow kiss.

"Is there now?"

"Mm-hmm."

Without letting her go completely, Nick reached one arm behind him and turned the shower off.

He grazed his cheek against hers and whispered in her ear. "Shall we?"

THEY MADE a half-hearted attempt to dry off before wrapping each other in towels and stumbling into the hall. They would have crossed the short distance to the bedroom much faster had they not stopped for necessary kissing breaks every few feet. When they reached Lois's doorway, Nick leaned against the door frame, taking her in.

He couldn't believe they were here.

Nick had come up to bed nursing quite the storm in his mind. Lois's experience infuriated him, and he still wanted to put his fist through Ronson's face. Or at least a wall.

But her laughter had grounded him. It hardly seemed like anything to him, but it clearly meant so much to her that he'd helped her find that humor. Her small kiss of thanks had warmed him to the core.

He'd gotten into bed, hoping sleep would arrange his thoughts into some manageable sense. Instead, he'd remained awake and fitful. He had an overwhelming desire to knock on her door, take her in his arms, and simply hold her until the sun came up. But she likely needed the sleep more than he did, and it wouldn't have been right to wake her.

So he'd found himself in the shower. He'd started with cold water, hoping to shock his system into a restart, before switching to warm on the heels of worry that the cold would leave him even more awake.

And then she'd knocked, and nothing else mattered.

He'd initially been afraid to give in, a stupid, stubborn part of him clinging to his plan to take things slow. The minute she'd asked him to abandon being a gentleman, slow didn't stand a chance. He owed it to her to give her what she wanted, didn't he?

What he wanted was to worship her. When she'd cried out, bursting apart in his arms, he'd never felt so full, so happy.

Now he watched her for a moment, her skin still flushed and glowing. She took a few steps before realizing he wasn't following.

She swept hungry eyes along his whole body, before her

breath caught. She bit her lower lip, already swollen from his kisses, and a small, private smile spread over her.

"What is it?"

Her cheeks turned a deeper shade of pink. "Nothing, really. Just a bit of déjà vu, I guess. That day in Nate's closet, when we first talked about getting married and were figuring out where we'd live?"

"I remember."

She shook her head and let out a breath of a laugh. "I thought of what it would be like to live with you. And right in the middle of trying to decide if it was even a good idea, the most unbelievably vivid picture popped into my head." She raised her eyes to his. "You. Fresh from the shower, wrapped in a towel."

"Really," he drawled, coming off the wall, drawn to her like a magnet.

"And here we are."

"Here we are." He brushed a wet lock of hair behind her shoulder and let the backs of his fingers trail across her skin, leaving a rash of goosebumps in their wake. He lowered his voice to a whisper. "Any other visions I can help you with?"

She drew her tongue slowly across her lips, and the mere sight of it made him instantly harder, as if that was even possible.

"I might be able to think of a thing or two."

Lois came up slightly on her toes and brought their lips together, while her hands moved to free the towel from his hips. Her firm, possessive grip on his ass nearly drove him over the edge.

He pulled her close and backed her toward the bed, the plush terry that still covered her biting into his skin. He normally loved the feel of these towels, but this one was excruciating to him now. It had to go.

He pulled it loose, and drew her back in for a deep kiss. He wasn't nearly finished when she broke away. Before he could protest, Lois sank down to the bed and scooted herself back. Her eyes blazed an impossibly vivid emerald, glowing with invitation.

It was the most seductive thing he'd ever seen, and he propelled forward with a growl. As he settled his weight around her and took her mouth hungrily, her leg came up and slid over his hip. He grazed his teeth down her neck, and she pressed her hips up against his aching cock.

He'd never wanted anyone so much in his life.

Nick brought one hand up to cup her breast, reveling in the fullness of it against his palm. He traced the other hand up her neck and cradled her jaw, pausing to look at her.

"Christ, Lois. I want you so much."

She smiled languidly and arched up into his touch. "I want you."

He leaned in for another kiss. Their tongues were enjoying a delectable slow dance when a terrible thought hit him.

"Shit."

Lois's eyelids flew open. "What?"

"We can't... I don't..."

She stiffened beneath him and pierced him with a narrow stare. "Are you serious? Are you going to pull that gentleman crap on me again? I told you—"

"God, no!" he cut her off. "I want this, Lois. I want you." He pressed his hips down against her core, letting the evidence speak for itself. She groaned into the contact. "So much it hurts."

But what stopped him now was something they'd never needed to talk about, and the last thing he wanted was to put her at risk.

Lois raised questioning eyes to him, and he hung his head.

"I don't have anything with me. You know...of the rubber variety?"

Relief washed over Lois's face and she laughed, planting a soft kiss on his shoulder. "It's all right."

"No. It's not. If I had any across the hall, I'd be back with them already, but..."

"Oh. So you really don't have any."

"No." He bit his lip. "When I moved in here, I had every intention of sticking to—what did you call it?—'that gentleman crap.'"

Her eyes softened and her hand came up to cup his cheek. "I'm sorry I called it crap. I really have liked it. You know, until my patience ran out tonight."

She brought his head down to hers, and he let himself get lost in the taste of her.

Until the throbbing began again in earnest and he broke away with a groan.

"Relax. I've got something of my own." Lois gave him a quick peck and looked down, almost shyly. "Put it in before I joined you in the bathroom."

He blinked in stunned silence before finding his voice. "Wait a minute. *You* had something this whole time?"

She nodded. "A lady needs to be prepared." A wicked gleam overtook her last remaining shyness. "Please don't tell me you thought you married a virgin."

"No, of course not." He realized immediately how that sounded. "Not that I think you get around; I just figured you had…" At her smirk, he relaxed. "I really hadn't given it much thought at all, actually." He paused. "Did you…need any help? I mean, it's…there already?"

Not that he actually knew what to do with the female version —Lois was the first woman he'd been with who hadn't relied on him to provide. But if she needed assistance, surely he could figure it out.

She laughed. "All done. But thanks."

"You know, you could've told me you had this covered, instead of letting me go on."

"What fun would that have been?" She wrapped her arms more firmly around him. "Besides, you made me forget with that kiss."

"You kissed me, remember?"

She shrugged. "Minor detail."

Their eyes found each other, and everything stilled. Nick

skimmed his palm over the curve of her waist, and her hand came to rest at the center of his chest. He knew she could feel his heart pounding, and wondered if hers was doing the same.

Unable to wait any longer, he pulled her mouth to his. They swallowed each other's moans as their bodies pressed closer. He adjusted his hips, bringing the tip of him to graze her center. He felt her shiver in anticipation.

"Lois, I…"

Her fingers gripped the hair at the nape of his neck. "Do it."

He drove inside her in one swift motion, and deep groans of satisfaction escaped both of them simultaneously. Nick began to set a slow rhythm, savoring the feel of her warmth around him. His teeth found her neck and nipped, as her hands traced a lazy path along his back.

"God, Lois, you feel so good."

She found his mouth and moaned her response into it.

Lois spread herself wider and arched up into him, and suddenly their slow pace seemed unbearable. He fit his hands under her and lifted her closer, driving harder. She threw her head back as her hips matched his.

"More, Nick."

That he could do.

He brought one hand up between them and pressed his thumb above the place where they were joined. Her cry reverberated through him and almost made him come right then and there, but he managed to hold on, wanting to take as much time as he could.

Her nails dug into his backside as she urged him deeper, faster. His thumb continued its work, and he could feel she was close.

Even closer than he'd thought. His name exploded from her lips as she contracted around him. That was all it took for him. He roared with his own release. The two of them shook together for a long moment before collapsing in a heap.

He couldn't move, and didn't want to. When he finally opened his eyes, he found hers still closed, dark eyelashes sweeping over her cheeks. He couldn't resist leaning in to place a kiss there.

A slow grin broke out on her face. Her eyes fluttered open and he matched her grin with one of his own.

"Don't let this go to your head, but you're very good at that," she whispered.

He chuckled. "Oh, I think I might have to let that go to my head a little." He barely had enough breath left to get his voice out, but he didn't care. He pressed his lips to her temple. "You're quite talented yourself, you know."

She hummed her appreciation and nestled closer. They shared another kiss, which seemed to last for a blissful eternity.

He never wanted to leave this bed.

They lay there for a while, taking their sweet time exploring each other's bodies with hands and lips, before sleep finally came for them both. At one point near dawn, Nick drifted awake.

The sight of Lois curled against him robbed him of breath.

Her hair fanned out across his arm and on the pillow behind her, still slightly damp from their shower. He watched her hand rise and fall along with his chest.

He'd always enjoyed sex—really, what man didn't—but being with her tonight… He could honestly say he'd never experienced anything like it. Which, when he thought about it, was true of everything about her, right from the first.

He'd never felt so whole in his entire life.

Which was ironic really. Because as he watched her, the realization came to him that his heart was now residing outside his body. It was right here, in his arms, sleeping peacefully.

And he'd be more than happy to keep it that way forever.

Chapter Nineteen

Unfortunately for Lois, work continued on her current film, which required hours spent at the studio instead of remaining in bed all day with Nick. While they had the nights all to themselves, she couldn't get enough of him.

She had never been so content to not get enough sleep.

Every time she sat down in the makeup chair, she wondered if her makeup artist would finally notice the effects of it on her face and chide her, but that day didn't seem to be coming. Maybe it all depended on the reason for the lack of rest.

A few days after that first night together, Nick had insisted on taking Lois out for what he called a "proper" date. He had then surprised her by pulling into a drive-in movie, and sheepishly apologized for its apparent corniness. Lois's heart had responded with a round of cartwheels in her chest.

They spent the first half of the movie critiquing and comparing it—rather unfavorably—to their own. It was entirely possible that it improved greatly in its second half, but Lois and Nick would never know, as they had abandoned watching in favor of other activities, like a pair of eager teenagers.

Their dates continued to end that way more often than not. Unlike the early days of their marriage, they tried to find quieter, more out-of-the-way places when they went out, where they could enjoy each other's company in privacy—and be as nauseatingly affectionate as they liked away from the public eye. The publicity from it surely wouldn't have gone amiss, but now that things had become real, neither one of them wanted anyone joining them in their little haven.

Lois woke one morning, ready to enjoy a welcome day off. Warm sunlight filtered in through the gauzy curtains covering her bedroom window. It really was *their* bedroom now, as Nick hadn't gone back to the guest room. She let the lovely thought fill her along with the deep breath she inhaled. The peaceful feeling fizzled a little when she reached across the bed and found the space beside her empty.

She barely had time to process her lack of Nick when an aromatic wave of coffee, vanilla, and warm sugar wafted toward her and settled like a comforting fog. The next instant, her missing companion appeared in the doorway, holding two steaming mugs and a large plate piled high with what looked—and smelled—like an assortment of Max's best croissants and danishes.

Even more delectable than the breakfast was the man holding it. His hair, still mussed from bed, curled over his forehead rakishly. He wore only a robe, cinched loosely enough that a broad expanse of his golden chest was exposed. Lois wanted nothing more than to nuzzle into the dark curls of hair collected in the small canyon between his pecs.

She swallowed as her mouth watered, and Nick noticed, grinning wolfishly.

"Good morning." A strand of blue in the plaid of his robe matched his eyes uncannily, showing up the spark of desire there that matched her own. Neither one of them ever bothered to mask that desire anymore.

It was no wonder they had such trouble keeping their hands off one another.

"Morning. I was just wondering where you'd disappeared to." She sat up as he approached the bed.

"Since we don't have anywhere to be today, I thought I'd bring breakfast to us for a change."

He handed her a cup, and she took the plate as well while he settled himself next to her. Lois took a sip and sighed into the warmth as it made its way down into her chest.

Nick let out a small growl of his own. "Your first taste of coffee always kills me."

An entirely different warmth spread through Lois's chest. "Does it now?"

He mumbled his assent as he came closer for a lazy kiss.

"You hungry?" Nick asked as he leaned back.

"Always. But I could do with a pastry too." She winked as she grabbed one from the plate. "Gotta keep my strength up, after all."

He laughed, deep and irresistible. Lois bit into the danish and let it dissolve on her tongue. She held it out to him, before he could reach for one of his own.

He kept his eyes fixed on hers as he sank his teeth in, and she could practically feel them on her own skin. A shiver danced across her body.

They lounged in bed for a while, making their way lasciviously through several pastries, even more enjoyable for the fact that they had all the time in the world today to follow up with each other when they finished.

Lois was swallowing a last sip of her coffee when Nick straightened a little.

"Oh, I can't believe I forgot to tell you. Guess who I saw on the lot yesterday?"

"Who?" she asked.

"Rex Tyler."

"You're kidding." Rex Tyler was a popular western actor—and one of Neptune's biggest stars. "What was he doing there?"

"I have no idea. But he was hovering near the production offices when I saw him."

"Interesting. So there might be some truth to that *Variety* bit after all."

"Sure looks like it. I was dying to go up and talk to him, but I didn't want to look like a gossip or a vulture. Or a green-eyed monster."

Chagrin washed over Lois, and she reached out and stroked his hand. "I didn't even think. You're not worried about being replaced, are you? Rex mostly does westerns."

He turned his hand over and brought hers up to his lips. "Nah, I don't care about that. As fun as it is to ride a horse, I haven't made a western in ages, and that's fine with me. I'd much rather they move me away from the action."

"No word yet on what's next?"

"Not yet." He settled their twined hands on his thigh.

Without letting go, Lois rolled onto her side to face him. "Have you given any thought to television?"

Nick cocked his head to one side and his eyebrows shot up. "Television? The thing everybody thinks is a fad?"

"Not everybody. I've heard a fair amount of rumbling that it's not going anywhere. A lot of the radio guys are going there." At his furrowed brow, she added, "An awful lot of the radio guys who do *comedy*."

"Huh." Nick stared into space, considering. "Television."

"Just something to think about."

"It is." Coming out of his reverie, he turned back to Lois. "Do you really think it has a chance of going anywhere? So many of the big studio guys seem to think it's a dead end."

Lois scoffed. "That's because most of the big studio guys have no imagination. I mean, look at what's happening at Neptune. Aside from being a vindictive lech, Ronson also suffers from a tremendous lack of vision. They might have been doing some interesting stuff when I first signed with them, but when was the last time there was any significant buzz out of there?"

"Yeah, I don't think it's coming as much of a surprise that actors are jumping ship."

"Of course not." She scooted higher in bed, enthusiastic. "But none of the studios is much different. Once they get something making money, they milk it for all it's worth. Not that I can blame them; you can't do any of it without money. But it's made them forget how to take risks. Look at you. As much of a star as you've been for them, they wouldn't even consider listening to your ideas because they already had you sorted in your box."

"That's true."

Now it was Nick's turn to roll to face her. He propped up on one elbow and regarded her.

"What about you?"

"Me?"

"Mm-hm." The corners of his mouth twitched up. "What would you do, if they let you out of your pre-determined box? If you could do anything at all, no restrictions, what would it be?"

Oh, what she could do. She'd thought about it plenty. But she'd never told anyone, not even Nate. It wasn't just others' reactions that made her hesitate. It was also the prospect of what might happen if she gave voice to her ideas. It would make them more real, leaving her that much more disappointed when they remained unachievable.

But the way Nick looked at her. Like he was fascinated, excited to hear what she had to say.

Being with him made her want to dream bigger, made her feel like maybe things might not be so impossible after all.

She closed her eyes and took a fortifying breath. "As much as I love acting, and always will…I want to try my hand at directing. Helming a film, shaping it, having a vision and making it come to life. Why should the boys get to have all the fun, you know?"

Lois cracked one eye open at a time and found Nick grinning widely at her.

He didn't seem to be laughing *at* her, but her long-held cynicism had doubt nipping at her heels.

"I suppose some people would find that to be a very silly idea."

Without hesitation, Nick retorted, "Then those people would be a pack of morons. For what it's worth, I think you'd be an absolutely brilliant director."

There it was again, that heady sensation that came from having a champion in her corner.

"You do, huh?"

One side of his mouth twisted up in an "isn't it obvious" expression. "Of course. I've thought so for a while, actually. You practically directed half of *Teacups*. That ballroom scene was all you, and it's going to make the picture." He shook his head and beamed at her. "If you directed a whole film of your own, I'd come to the set every day just to watch *you* in action."

Lois's cheeks warmed as she chuckled. "I'm afraid you might have to wait a long time. I doubt anyone's too eager to put me in charge of a movie."

"If only we had a studio of our own. I'd put you in charge of every one."

"And I'd put you in comedy after comedy."

"I like that plan."

Lois settled back into her pillow, and their hands found each other in the space between them.

"If only." She huffed. "God, can you imagine? Our own studio."

"No one putting us in boxes."

"No one telling us no, for no good reason."

They grew quiet, the idea swirling around them. Lois let herself enjoy it for a moment, lingering in her imagination before it evaporated into a picture that would never come to fruition.

Nick snorted beside her.

"Instead of a lion, our mascot could be a cartoon turd."

A bubble of laughter fizzed in her throat. "Smoking a joint."

That earned a bark of amusement. "Our motto…" He made a sweeping gesture. "For art's sake, look how far we've come."

They both broke up at that, before their laughter settled into a pair of sighs.

"If only," Lois whispered.

Nick looked over at her and seemed to come to a decision before hopping off the bed. She watched him disappear across the hall, only to return a minute later carrying a small velvet pouch. He moved the croissant plate to the nightstand and sat in the center of the bed next to her.

"I had this made a while ago. I was saving it to give you at the premiere, but…" He shrugged and handed it to her. "I feel like you should have it now."

Lois took the weighted little bag, surprise mingling with intrigue. She pulled the drawstring open and upended the contents into her hand. At first glance, one might think it was a locket, but upon closer inspection, that wasn't the case at all.

In her palm sat a little silver film canister, the letter "L" engraved in its center in an elegant, sweeping cursive.

"Nick." She raised suddenly misty eyes to his.

He smiled shyly and whispered, "Look at the back."

She flipped it over to find a director's chair and megaphone embossed on the charm, each one monogrammed with a tiny "L" in a script to match its counterpart on the front.

The mist turned to actual water and threatened to spill over.

"Max found this silversmith when he was looking for a birthday gift for his sister last year," Nick explained softly. "He makes the most interesting, odd stuff. All kinds of jewelry and trinkets. I wanted to get you something to celebrate the movie, but I had no idea what I was looking for. I spotted a plain version of these little film canisters, and asked if he could customize one. He was very obliging." He swallowed. "It's just a silly thing, really."

She brought a hand up to cradle his face. "It's not silly at all. It's…" A tear made its escape and slid down her cheek. "Nick, it's perfect. I love it."

No longer able to hold back, she threw her arms around his neck, but not before she caught the smile beaming across his face. His arms snaked around her and pulled her close, holding tight.

Behind his back, Lois opened her hand and took another peek at the gift.

"I can't believe you already had this." Her voice barely a whisper, but he heard it.

He pressed a kiss to her neck.

She pulled back to look at him. His eyes displayed a little mist now too, which made her smile.

Leaning in to kiss him, she stopped just before making contact. "Thank you, Nick," she breathed against him. He closed the distance and kissed her slow and deep.

Lois's heart overflowed. She couldn't put into words what the little charm meant to her. She had been afraid to share her goal with him, yet all the while he already knew, already believed in her.

She wasn't entirely sure she could put into words what Nick was coming to mean to her, either. So she poured it all into the kiss instead, hoping he understood. Felt it too.

Because she suspected she was falling passionately, magnificently in love with Nick Bradley.

Chapter Twenty

Nick stood in front of the mirror with two tuxedo jackets, weighing his options. Edits were finished, test screenings had been conducted, and the time had finally arrived for the premiere of *A Midsummer Night's Teacup*.

Dammit. Teacups in July, *it's* Teacups in July.

He hoped if he repeated it to himself enough, he wouldn't slip and call it by the wrong name to a reporter that evening. The handful of test audiences who'd seen it had generally liked it, and if he wanted more people to actually shell out money in the coming weeks, he needed people to believe that he liked it too.

Which he did. He was genuinely proud of what he and Lois had accomplished. He couldn't afford to embarrass himself by giving the impression he'd phoned it in, as had been everyone's expectation at the start.

Lois was downstairs taking a phone call. Her dress for the premiere hung on the closet door, pressed and ready for her to step into. She had insisted on applying her own makeup, but accepted the studio's offer to send a hairstylist over earlier in the afternoon. Lois claimed to be lacking in hair skills, which Nick didn't quite understand. He thought her hair always looked beautiful when she did it every day. But he supposed the fancier stuff must be more complicated. Certainly more waves and sprays involved.

He was grateful all he had to do was shave and run a little pomade through his hair.

Soft footsteps in the hall preceded Lois into the bedroom.

"What do you think? White dinner jacket, or black?"

"Summer's been over for a while; is it even a question?"

"Living here, I'm never sure. I mean, if the weather wants to keep giving us summer, do the rules still apply?"

"You do have a point there." Coming up behind him, she slipped her hands onto his waist and rose up on her toes to rest her chin on his shoulder. He leaned into her warmth and let it spread through him.

She considered him in the mirror for a moment before continuing. "The pictures from tonight are still going to be seen where it's most definitely not summer, though. As delectable as you look in dinner whites, I'd still go with the black. It's not as if you're capable of looking anything but handsome either way." Her eyes found his in the mirror and darkened. "I'm gonna spend the whole night wanting to remove whatever jacket you pick."

She landed a quick kiss on his jaw and went back to her dressing table to finish her makeup.

He'd never had so much fun getting ready for a premiere.

Nick tossed the white jacket on the bed and went to hang his black one next to Lois's dress. Picking up his shoes to give them one last shine, he remembered her reason for going downstairs.

"Who was on the phone? Anyone interesting?"

"It was kind of interesting, actually." Lois sat back in her chair. "It was a theatre producer—Bertie Hamilton?"

"Oh, sure." Recognition flared. He'd left Broadway for film before getting the chance to work with Hamilton, but he knew of his work. The man generated hits, quality ones.

"He's getting ready to mount a new play. And he wants me to star."

Her voice remained casual, but he could tell it was forced. She was excited. As well she should be.

Pride burst in his chest. "Lois, that's fantastic!"

She met his eyes in the mirror and grinned, almost shyly. "Yeah, it's…kind of a lot to take in."

"Take it in. Bask in it. You've earned this."

As Nick continued to buff his shoe, he began to take it in himself, faltering for just a second. Broadway meant New York. A whole country between them. He still didn't know when he'd get his next project, which meant he might not be able to go with her. A stab of longing pierced his chest, deflating it a little. Lois had already become a pretty heady addiction for him, much more potent than what he'd been arrested for. Could he say goodbye to her?

Don't be an ass, Nick.

He shook his head. This was ridiculous. It wasn't as if it was permanent. And Lois had absolutely earned this. Deserved this. Success was long overdue for her, and he wanted to see her achieve every height possible. Even if he had to stay in Los Angeles, there existed such things as weekends and air travel.

Lois's voice pulled him out of his head. "He gave me some time to think about it, but I'm not going to take the part."

Surprise jerked Nick's head up. He put the shoe down and came to stand behind her. "Why not?"

"Don't sound so disappointed. You trying to get rid of me?"

"Never." His hands came to rest on her shoulders and he placed a kiss on top of her head. "But, love, at the risk of sounding incredibly presumptuous and self-centered, if this is about us...please don't even think about turning this down. I won't lie, I did just have a flash of panic about living on opposite coasts, but it was stupid. We'll figure it out. You should take this."

Lois smiled at him and covered his hand with her own. "Thank you for saying it, but that's not what this is about." She brought his hand up to her lips. "Not that it wouldn't be excruciating to be apart, because it would. But you're right, we would work it out. I have no doubt about that."

"What's stopping you, then? Do you think Parkmoor won't let you out?"

"No. I'm not entirely sure what I'm in for at my contract meeting next week, but if they renew, I doubt they'd have a problem with this. Plenty of people fit Broadway in between movies."

He gave her a light squeeze in question. He felt her shoulders rise and fall.

"I guess what it comes down to is...I'm a film actress. I do like the stage, but my heart's always going to be in film. It's where I belong. And honestly, the timing of this couldn't be more perfect. I know I've earned this, and now I have concrete proof that someone genuinely recognizes my talent." Her mouth curved up slyly. "It's going to be a nice piece of leverage when I walk into that meeting."

Nick let out a low chuckle. "You're not going to tell them you're turning it down until after you've signed, are you?"

"Nope."

He knelt and wrapped his arms around her, never breaking their gaze in the mirror. "For the record, if you did do the play, I have every confidence you'd be resoundingly brilliant." He kissed her neck. "And I'd be right in the front row, leading the applause."

Lois melted into him. "You're quite the cheerleader, you know that?"

"Not hard to be when it comes to you." He nuzzled closer and began to nip at the base of her ear.

She groaned. "Okay, it kills me to say this, but you need to go back to your shoes."

He answered with a growl and continued toward the collar of her robe.

Lois straightened, attempting to push him away. "If you keep going, we are never going to make it to the premiere." He affected a pout and she laughed ruefully. "You know I want nothing more than to take you to bed and ravage you. And I absolutely would if there wasn't so much riding on tonight." She gestured to her hair. "And if I knew how to fix this if it gets damaged in the ravaging process."

He hated that she was right.

Standing, he asked, "Even though you're turning it down, I can still congratulate you, right?"

"I think that's acceptable."

"Good." Thankful that she hadn't started her lipstick yet, he leaned down and kissed her with everything he had. "Congratulations."

"Thank you," she breathed.

As Nick went back to his shoes, he heard her mutter, "Oh, great. Now I can't tell if I need more blush."

"That's not a problem. Just keep me by your side all night and you won't ever have to reapply." He gave her an exaggerated "rawr," and her low, throaty laugh reverberated deep in his bones.

He didn't think he would ever tire of making her laugh.

THE PREMIERE itself went remarkably well. It was by no means the biggest one either of them had ever attended, but the film still managed an impressive turnout considering everything that had led up to its making. The press presence was larger than Nick had expected, though he really didn't know why he should have doubted it. They always flocked to a spectacle, and he knew a fair number didn't fully believe that he and Lois had behaved themselves enough to make a decent picture.

Their marriage still drew attention as well. Walking the red carpet, they endured question after question about how married life was treating them, and countless requests for "just one more shot" of them being affectionate.

Not that it was a chore to be affectionate. As a matter of fact, Nick found it exceedingly difficult to keep from pulling Lois aside and doing all kinds of inappropriate things.

She was an absolute vision.

He had started to get used to being knocked on his ass whenever she entered a room, but she looked particularly stunning tonight. Her dress had appeared pretty on its hanger, but on her body, it was nothing short of ravishing. The way it clung to her, hugging her curves in all the right places, the strategically placed beading that caught the light and reflected it onto her face. He had thought it was a silvery color, but certain ways she turned, he thought it might actually be a pale green. Or maybe it just reflected the color of her eyes somehow.

Jesus, you've got it bad.

Watching her, he felt like a whole case of champagne had been dumped inside him and the fizzing was never going to end. And he was perfectly fine with that.

The movie had turned out pretty good, if he did say so himself. Not without its flaws, but still entertaining. The audience seemed to like it. Granted, it was always hard to tell with premiere audiences—largely made up of industry people who, while they had discerning tastes, tended to set aside criticism in favor of ass-kissing. They knew where their bread was buttered.

But Nick and Lois were not exactly in a position to do much for them, so their asses didn't warrant the usual kissing. The positive response to the film felt a little more genuine as a result, which heartened him.

After the screening, a select—but still fairly large—group of the assembled made their way to Beverly Hills. Joe Bartholomew had what could only be called an estate, and he'd opened it up for the evening's festivities. A small band played bright music, champagne flowed, and good spirits abounded.

Nick grabbed two flutes off a passing tray and handed one to Lois.

"Think it's too soon to call this one a win?" Nick asked.

Lois's dark red lips curved upward. "I think it might just be safe." She raised her glass. "Cheers, Nick."

He brought his glass to hers with a bright clink. "Cheers, Lois."

They stood for a moment, taking in the throng of people milling around them. Most were focused more on the revels than the two of them, but they fielded a hearty number of congratulatory greetings.

After a little while, Bartholomew found them and boomed his own congratulations.

"I had a hunch about you two, and I must say, I'm very happy it paid off."

Despite Nick's reluctance to give Bartholomew all the credit— he and Lois hadn't exactly sat idly by—he knew the producer was well-intentioned. And it had been Bartholomew's idea for them to get married, for which he'd have Nick's eternal gratitude.

Lois's words echoed some of his thoughts. With a sardonic tilt to her head, she replied, "Wow, way to toot your own horn, Barty. What are we, just the trained monkeys who gave you that payoff?"

"God knows trained monkeys would've been far less expensive." He leaned in conspiratorially. "But also far less talented."

Lois nudged him as she laughed. "Thanks. I think." She turned to Nick. "There was a compliment in there somewhere, right?"

"I think I may have heard one."

Bartholomew groaned. "Of course it was a compliment. Honestly, what am I going to do with you two?" The question sparked something behind his eyes, and he clapped Nick on the shoulder. "Which is an excellent segue, as a matter of fact. Bradley, I've got a picture lined up for you if you're interested."

Lois's brows shot up, and she gave him an expression that clearly said, "See, I told you."

Trying to play it cool, Nick responded lightly. "I might be interested. What've you got?"

"Gene Matthews was in my office the other day. He saw an early cut of *Teacups* and was very impressed. He wants you for his next film. Starts up in a few weeks."

Holy crap.

Matthews was one of the best comedic directors around. His films were smart, witty—and highly successful.

Unsure how he managed it, Nick somehow pushed his voice out. "That sounds great."

"Excellent. I'll tell Matthews, and let's chat in my office in a couple of days." He raised his cocktail at them. "Enjoy the party, you two."

Nick could only stare after him.

Lois laid her hand on the center of his chest and pressed her lips to his cheek. "Nick. This is huge."

Her touch brought him back to earth, and excitement pulsed through him. He snaked an arm around her waist and pulled her close for a kiss, not caring how many people observed them. He only just remembered to be careful not to spill their champagne.

The fizz inside him was overflowing.

"I can't believe it. Gene Matthews."

"Can I amend what I said earlier? I'd say this is most definitely a win."

He took in her bright eyes and her dazzling smile. "*You're* most definitely a win."

A furious flush crept up her neck and into her face. He wanted to find a corner right then and there and start on those inappropriate things. Judging by her expression, she might just beat him to it. They both smirked, reading each other's thoughts.

Nick bent close to her ear. "Back terrace, or some nook down the hall?"

Lois hummed her approval. "It's a little chilly now that the sun's gone, don't you think?"

"I'm sure we can find a way to generate some heat." He gave the outer edge of her ear a gentle lick, and she shivered. "But we can stay inside if you'd rather."

"The prospect of a cozy alcove somewhere is tempting. This house must have—"

Lois froze mid-sentence.

Nick could feel the ice begin to radiate off of her. The muscles beneath his hand tightened, and the rise and fall of her chest picked up at an alarming rate.

"Lois? What is it, love?"

He pulled back. Her face was absolutely still, despite a raging tempest in her eyes. He had never seen her so positively livid. It frightened him. He followed her gaze to where it was fixed over his shoulder.

Understanding jolted through him.

Followed by pure, unadulterated fury.

Arthur Ronson had just arrived. Head of Neptune Pictures, ruiner of Lois's professional reputation. Bastard of epic proportions. With absolutely no reason to be at this party.

And yet there he stood. Jovially slapping Bartholomew on the back. His wife at his side, smiling politely but unable to completely hide her boredom. Despite the rushing that had begun in his ears, Nick could hear Ronson's voice, carrying across the room and over the din of the party. Something about "checking out the competition."

He heard a low growl beside him, and his eyes snapped back to Lois. "Do you want me to go kill him?"

She turned back to him, slightly dazed, as if she'd forgotten his presence next to her. Her face softened a bit. "I'd be over there doing it myself if it wouldn't ruin everything."

"I have no such reservations. Allow me." He'd put his fist through the man's face with glee.

That got a small chuckle out of her. She raised a hand to cup his cheek. "If only it was that simple."

Before he could say anything more, Nate materialized in front of them, holding a set of keys.

"Here, my car's just around the corner. Go."

Nick's anger surged. "This is our party. Why the hell should we be the ones to go?"

"Because that gigantic ass sure as shit won't." She tried to focus on Nick, but her gaze kept flitting to Lois, all concern for her friend. "Besides, it's probably safer if you two get out of here now."

Alarm rocked through him as he looked back to Ronson. "He wouldn't dare pull something, would he?" He'd appeared impassive that day at the pool, but now that Lois finally stood to achieve some success, who knew what he was capable of.

Nate snorted. "Not him, honey, you."

"What?"

"I can see your faces. Every method of homicide you're considering is clear as day."

He opened his mouth to protest, but Nate cut him off.

"Believe me, I'd be right there with that shovel, even use it to get in a blow or two myself." She sighed. "But I've watched you both work your butts off to get here, and the last thing you need right now is to add murder to your rap sheet, however justified it may be."

Lois seethed quietly at his side, clearly making an effort to focus on the conversation instead of the daggers shooting out of her eyes. She heaved a defeated breath. "We can't just go. Nick said it: it's our party. We'd be missed."

Nate waved a dismissive hand. "Oh, please. It'll be fine. You two haven't exactly been subtle with your canoodling tonight.

Most of the room is expecting you to disappear somewhere for a quickie at some point."

A flash of pink appeared on each of Lois's cheeks, and Nick was sure he sported a matching pair.

He shook it off quickly. "We had a driver tonight; I'll see if I can find him."

Lois gripped his hand tightly.

Nate registered it, but didn't comment. "Cars are wedged in everywhere on the property. It'll take him forever." She reached for his other hand and pressed her keys into his palm. "Take mine. It's on the street. You can bring it back to me tomorrow."

"But how will you get home?" Lois asked.

"Don't worry about me. I've always been an industrious gal." She winked.

Nick's chest flooded with warmth at the way Nate was taking care of everything. At the way she was trusting him with her best friend.

"How do we know you won't kill him yourself?"

She rolled her eyes theatrically. "They call it plausible deniability, Nick. I'm trying to look out for you here."

Was she ever.

Nick looked to Lois. She met his eyes and answered the question in them with a small nod.

Lois squeezed her friend's arm. "Thanks, Nate."

"Go on. Get out of here, before the bastard spots you and tries to offer his congratulations." The venom in her voice could've felled Ronson from across the room. Nick wished it was possible.

He exchanged a last look with Nate, hoping it conveyed the depth of his gratitude, and then he and Lois left their own party.

They didn't let go of one another's hands until they reached the car.

Chapter Twenty-One

Hollywood Happenings

*Well, folks, the rumors were indeed true… Teacups in July is
not a bad little comedy! We won't lie, it wasn't the best thing
we've ever seen, but its two leads — and their chemistry! — made
it quite the romp. And they couldn't have been more delightful on
the Red Carpet. Though it was slightly unusual to hear both of
them mistake the name of their own picture… But can we really
blame them, given how clearly smitten they are with each other?
We have it on good authority that they ducked out of their own
celebration early, presumably to moon over each other somewhere
more private…*

They'd been driving for nearly an hour, and while her
pulse had calmed considerably, Lois was still seething.
As soon as they'd gotten to the car, Nick had started the engine
and turned to her.

"Home?" he'd asked.

She put her hand on his forearm, needing the feel of him to
ground her. "Do you mind if we just drive for a bit?"

He'd looked relieved, and pulled out without another word. He moved his arm to the seat in between them and twined their hands together. After navigating them toward the ocean, he turned and continued north.

Miles of coast later, their hands were still joined, and neither of them had yet to speak.

The further they drove, the more her tension receded. She could feel it ebbing slowly out of Nick as well.

She inhaled deeply, comforted by the air flowing in the open windows and the faint rush of the waves on their left. She closed her eyes and leaned her head back against the seat.

Words finally escaped out of her. "How *dare* he show up tonight?"

Nick's grip tightened in comfort. "Why do you think he did it?"

Lois had been wondering the same thing. "I honestly don't know. Part of me wouldn't be surprised if he doesn't even remember what he did to me. He's that much of a prick." She opened her eyes and rolled her head toward Nick. "But I keep thinking it probably has to do with the trouble his studio's in."

"I thought I heard him say something about the competition."

"He's like a vulture. He smelled success from one of his former players and wants everyone to know he spotted me first."

"After making your life a living hell."

"Like I said. Prick."

"At least it's an indication that word of you being a success is getting around?"

"I suppose." It did give her a degree of satisfaction to think Ronson could be in trouble instead of her for a change.

A few minutes passed, then Nick asked, "Do you think his wife knows what a pig she's married to?"

"I've always wondered about that. She's still with him, though, so she's either clueless or doesn't care." She stared out the window. "So many times over the years, I've been tempted to tell her."

"What's stopped you?"

"I'm not sure exactly. I'd want to know if it was me, but maybe she wouldn't. She might not believe it anyway, so it never seemed worth the risk."

Quiet settled over them again, and Lois continued to watch the darkened coastline pass by as they drove.

Nick brought her hand up and brushed his lips across her fingers in a light caress. "You okay?"

"Yeah. You know, that day at the Beverly Wilshire was the closest I've come to seeing him in an age, and I've always had all these plans for what I'd do if we ever did cross paths again. God, I never expected it would be tonight. I'm not afraid of him; I never have been. But I had finally started to let it go a little. Then there he was tonight, and…" She grunted her frustration. "I'm just so *mad*. Tonight was ours! We truly had a reason to celebrate, for the first time in I don't know how long. I'm so damn tired of it not being fair."

Nick was thoughtful for a moment. She noticed a small pull-off spot up ahead. He must have seen it too, because he took advantage of the quiet road and crossed the highway to park there.

He got out and came around to open her door. "Come on," he beckoned.

Lois followed him out, curious. "What are we doing?"

He led her to the edge of the turnout, facing the pounding waves. He smiled at her as he cocked his head toward the water. "Let's scream."

A startled laugh bubbled up her throat. "Scream?"

His grin widened. "Sure. Let off some steam. The bastard might not be here, but the ocean can take it in his place."

Lois considered him. It sounded like a ridiculous idea. But a very tempting one. She shrugged.

"Oh, what the hell? Why not?"

He kept hold of her hand and turned to face the sea. Lois followed suit.

"So…is there a method here?"

"Nope. On three, we just…let it all out."

"Okay then."

Nick counted, and then they both yelled at the top of their lungs. It felt astoundingly liberating.

They were lucky there was no one on the road. They might have been picked up for disturbing the peace.

To Lois's great surprise, her own peace was restored. Releasing her fury into the void left her feeling almost lightheaded, in the best possible way. Her breath was coming fast and excited, and she looked over to find Nick in the same state.

He cocked an eyebrow at her. "Better?"

She couldn't help the grin that broke over her face. "Much better, actually. You?"

His teeth flashed silver in the moonlight. "Definitely." He looked back to the car, almost disappointed. "I suppose we should head back?"

A wild exhilaration rose in Lois's chest. "Or we could keep driving?"

Nick's face lit in answer. "Or we could keep driving."

They returned to the car and he pulled out, continuing up the coast. They drove for what must have been another hour. They still didn't say much, but the tension had evaporated, leaving behind only their usual ease. The ease that had settled between them from day one.

The ease Lois had come to cherish.

Before they knew it, they were nearly to Santa Barbara, but neither one of them cared. The highway moved inland slightly and crisscrossed a set of train tracks. A collection of blue-roofed buildings was just visible through a collection of trees, and Nick made a small noise of recognition.

"Wait, I know this place. I was here once, years ago." He glanced at her. "Want to stop for a bit?"

His excitement was infectious. "Sure, I'm game."

Nick pulled onto a side road, marked with a sign directing

them to the cozy little resort. They came upon a large main building, flanked by a charming collection of smaller cabins, all whitewashed wood and the blue roofs they'd seen from the road. Lois spotted a swimming pool nestled between the cabins, empty at this late hour.

Nick parked the car, and came over to take her hand when they both got out. He scanned the property before finding what he sought.

Gesturing with his head, he pulled her along. "Come on."

They wove between a couple of the buildings to find a tiny train depot. Lois couldn't contain a wondrous laugh.

"The train runs right through?"

Nick grinned, looking like a little boy. "Yep. Fun, isn't it?"

"It is."

Christ, he's perfection.

He continued to lead her over the tracks and across the depot. She heard the ocean before she could see it. Encountering one more building, they passed through a spot in the middle of the ground floor left open for pedestrian traffic, and emerged on the other side onto a small boardwalk. The waves crashed onto the sand of the small beach in front of them.

It was an utterly enchanting place.

Nick sighed. "It's just as I remembered it. Pretty great, huh?"

"It's wonderful."

They turned to each other wordlessly, mouths finding each other in an instant. She reveled in the way everything else vanished when her lips touched his, their tongues twining in hungry exploration.

They broke apart and Nick searched her face.

"Want to stay here tonight?"

She gave a breathless laugh. "That sounds perfect."

"I'll go see if they have anything available."

"Don't be long."

He growled his approval and gave her a quick kiss. He pulled off his jacket and wrapped it around her shoulders, and, seemingly unable to resist, brushed his lips across hers one more time. Then he was gone the way they'd come.

Lois wandered to lean on the boardwalk railing, watching the tide, marveling at the beauty they'd managed to make out of the night. The moon was nearly full, limning the world in silver. Cool, salty air whispered across her skin. She burrowed into Nick's jacket, letting his warm, spicy musk envelop her.

He returned before long, coming to the railing next to her, his shoulder a solid, inviting pressure against her own.

As if honoring the magic of the night around them, he kept his voice quiet and deep. "We're in luck. Got a cabin facing the water. I think it's just down that way."

"Hmm." Contentment had overtaken her power of speech. She leaned in and rested her head on Nick's shoulder.

His arm came around her and pulled her close, his lips coming to rest on the crown of her head.

They had a room waiting, but neither of them felt the need to move. She didn't know how long they stood there, before Nick broke the silence with a reverent whisper.

"I love you, Lois."

Her heart was suddenly aglow like a burning coal. Its warmth radiated out and through her entire body, burrowing deep into the marrow of her bones. It was simultaneously the most alive and at peace she had ever felt.

He had completely stilled, as if holding his breath.

The words seemed inadequate, but she supposed they would have to do.

"I love you too, Nick."

She could feel his body melt back to life. His hand came up to cradle her jaw as he turned to face her. She looked up into the blue of his eyes, alight with passion. The moonlight brought the planes of his face into stark relief, setting sparks in the stubble scattered across the angles of his jaw. He'd opened his bowtie and undone the top two buttons of his shirt, allowing a tiny tease of chest hair to peek out.

He'd always been handsome, but tonight he was magnificent. Partly due to the moonlight.

But largely because he was *hers*.

He closed the remaining distance between them and kissed her, long and lush. They drank each other in, unleashed by those simple, glorious words.

Nick released her mouth and pressed his forehead to hers with a deep exhale.

"Lois, I…" He took another gulp of air, and she could feel him steadying himself. "There's something I need to say, and…I don't want you to say anything, not yet, just think about…"

She traced her finger across his temple, and down to his jaw. "What is it, Nick?"

He brought his head up to meet her eyes. "I know when we went into this that we agreed it would just be for a year." Lois's heart began to race as he continued. "But I…I want you to know. I feel like my life really, finally started the day you walked into it. You've walked right off with my heart. And I know there's a lot that's still up in the air, so don't answer yet, just think about it, but…just know that I'd very much like this—us—to not be temporary."

As she looked at Nick, so earnest, so very beautiful, Lois's heart threatened to beat right out of her chest. Their time together had been full of passion, laughter, more happiness than she had ever expected. But she hadn't let herself think too far ahead. Had been afraid to. But now that she'd finally admitted to him—and to herself—that she loved him, and knew that he felt the same, she let the hope take root. To plan for a future that included Nick.

There was still a part of her that felt afraid, but she didn't want to examine it now. Not when he was standing in front of her, his heart on his sleeve. His heart hers.

He'd asked her not to give him an answer yet, and she took the out he offered. For now.

But she was coming to know, deep within her, what she wanted. To dream of its possibility. She wanted it all.

And tonight, she wanted nothing but him.

THEY MADE their way to the little cabin. It was cozy, just one open room and a bathroom. Two soft chairs sat in front of a huge window that overlooked the ocean. A mirrored dressing table stood in one corner. One large, inviting bed occupied the center of the room.

Nick moved to the window, trailing his hand along her arm and letting it linger as he passed her. As he let the night breezes in, Lois shrugged off his jacket and set it on a chair. She perched on the other chair to take off her shoes, but before she got even one buckle undone, Nick knelt in front of her, stilling her hands.

"Let me."

He made quick work of the buckles, but took his time sliding the shoes themselves off, pressing his fingers into the arch of each foot. She sank back into the chair with a moan. Appreciation hummed in his throat as his rakish gaze met hers. Setting her foot on his knee, his hands slipped under the hem of her skirt and slid slowly up her leg. He didn't take his eyes from hers as he found the clips holding her stocking up and freed the nylon from its moorings. He removed it with a long, gliding caress and placed a kiss on her ankle before repeating the process on the other leg.

Suddenly impatient, Lois took his face in her hands and kissed him. He rose up on his knees and pressed her back into the chair, hands roving over her thighs and hips before settling on her waist. She caught his bottom lip in her teeth and felt his groan in her own chest. She smiled against his lips and felt his own curve up in response.

She went to work on the buttons of his shirt as they kissed. She pushed it off his shoulders, and ran her palms across the glorious expanse of hair covering his chest as he pulled his arms out of the sleeves.

He stood, chuckling at her pout over the loss of contact.

Reaching for her hands, he pulled her to her feet and drew her close for another head-spinning kiss. She felt his hands find the zipper at her back and slide it down. He eased the fabric over her shoulders, and as she stepped back to let the gown collapse in a pool at her feet, his eyes blazed over her body. When they finally returned to her face, they reflected the ravenous hunger in her.

She leveled him with a seductive smile as she took his hand and walked backwards, to the bed. He let her lead him, but his posture was all prowl, ready to pounce at any moment.

We'll see about that.

She turned so that his back was to the bed and pushed him to sit. His surprise quickly gave way and he licked his lip ravenously. It was all she could do not to jump him. But she was having too much fun drawing out his reaction.

She held his eyes as she reached behind her to the hooks of her longline bra. With every small flick as she released a hook, Nick's throat worked convulsively. When the last hook came undone, she slowly peeled the undergarment away and dropped it to the floor.

Nick took in her freed breasts hungrily, but he grimaced in consternation when his gaze traveled just below them. She didn't have to look to know that the bra's boning had likely left its usual red marks across her abdomen. She was used to the pressure by now.

He clearly wasn't. He pulled her in to him and began planting feathery kisses on each of the bones' indentations. Her breath caught at the tenderness of the gesture. He massaged her stomach and waist gently as he trailed his mouth upward, finding the hollow between her breasts. She let her head fall back and groaned her pleasure at his touch.

His mouth drifted to one side, and he took the tip of her breast into his mouth. He was slow and gentle at first, but it didn't take long for desire to overtake them both. He nipped and teased until she threaded her fingers roughly in his hair, pulling him closer. As his tongue began to work its magic, she felt like she'd never be able to pull him close enough. He stopped, but mercifully only long enough to give her other breast equal devotion.

She was already close to a climax and he hadn't even touched her below the waist yet. She bent to take his mouth, pulling a growl from deep within him. She managed to tear herself away—barely—and stepped back. Nick looked ready to follow her, until she hooked her thumbs inside the waist of her tap pants. He leaned back with a grunt of anticipation.

She had him, and let a smug smile spread over her face. She could see a hint of amusement register behind his eyes.

Lois took her time sliding the silky fabric over her hips and down her legs. She straightened and stood there for a long moment, letting him drink her in. As an actor, she was just vain enough to know she was attractive. But the way Nick looked at her, like he was seeing not just the outside, but all the way into her core—and he wanted all of it.

She'd never felt so beautiful.

As if unable to refrain from touching her, he took hold of her waist and brought her close. He dipped his head to rest his cheek against her stomach, after placing a light kiss there. He remained, simply holding her, despite the fierce hunger that still raged through both of them.

He breathed her name against her skin, the sensation of it raising every hair on her body.

He released her, and slid up the bed, reclining on his elbows in invitation. She crawled over him and settled in, their tongues gliding over one another. Nick ran his hands up and down her back, finally coming to a stop on her ass to knead gently. She moaned into his mouth and brought her hands to his waistband. She could feel the hard length of him straining to get out. She was more than happy to oblige it.

She had barely opened his fly when his hand darted down to dig in his pocket.

"Wait a sec." His hand emerged with a small envelope, and Lois threw back her head in laughter.

Which ground their hips together, causing them both to emit impatient groans.

She laughed again. "Didn't think we'd make it through the party, did you?"

He gave a tiny shrug as his cheeks went suspiciously pink. "It never hurts to be prepared."

She leaned in to whisper close to his ear. "Mine's in my evening bag."

It was Nick's turn to throw his head back. The motion, combined with her position, grazed his chest across hers. The coarse curls teased the already sensitive skin of her breasts and she drew a ragged breath.

Their eyes snapped to each other, and the laughter vanished, replaced by pure, unfiltered desire.

Need.

Nick freed himself from his pants in a flash, while Lois took the envelope and opened it. She trailed one finger along the length of him, eliciting a deep moan, then slid the rubber on. She straddled him as he guided her hips. She sank down, and when he was fully inside her, they both cried out in blessed relief.

He opened his eyes to meet her gaze. They began a languid rhythm, never breaking eye contact.

They'd made quite a lot of love at this point. Tried a million positions, learned each other's bodies thoroughly, knew each other's sweet spots. They were unbelievably compatible. Could wring exquisite pleasure from each other.

But this felt different.

So much more *exquisite.*

It was slower, deeper, all-encompassing.

Declaring their love had freed them somehow. They were completely unguarded, nothing but emotion flowing between them. She finally understood what people meant when they said they could see right into someone's soul. She was diving into Nick's, and he into hers. It was an extraordinarily powerful feeling.

He brought himself up to sitting and wrapped one strong arm around her back, as if he couldn't get close enough. Neither could she. His other hand came between them and massaged her clit with deliberate, dreamy pressure, the sensation drawing a whimper from her.

Their movements intensified, but they kept their pace almost painfully slow, unable to rush.

Lois's pulse quickened as she felt her release building, and she dug her nails into his shoulder. He shook underneath her, close to climax himself. She moaned his name as she held on, wanting to hold back the tide as long as possible. He clenched his jaw, and she could see him trying to do the same.

Just as the wave was about to overtake her, she watched a surge of overwhelming tenderness pass through his eyes—and it detonated her.

"Oh god, Nick, I love you."

She barely registered his own breathless "I love you" as she shattered apart in his arms. Lois clung to his neck as he followed her over the edge, a shudder ripping through his body.

They held tight to each other as their muscles relaxed and they returned to earth. When they could, they slowly sank back onto the bed together, wrecked and utterly satisfied.

Chapter Twenty-Two

A Comedy Surprise

Parkmoor's latest is, if not a smash, at least an amiable jaunt into screwball territory. While the script is less than stellar, with a few glaring plot holes that simply can't be ignored, its two stars are the real revelation. Nick Bradley and Lois Ashford have managed to pull the film—and likely their careers—back from the brink of disaster. This reviewer is actually looking forward to seeing what they each do next. Here's hoping there's more comedy in both of their futures.

Nick woke late the next morning to the sound of the Pacific crashing on the shore just outside the window. He spooned around a still-sleeping Lois, his body spent, his muscles heavy on bones he wasn't entirely sure existed anymore.

He'd never slept better in his life.

Lois's head was tucked against his chest, and he bent forward to brush his cheek against her hair. She always smelled faintly of vanilla, and he couldn't get enough. He wanted desperately to kiss her, to have a glimpse of the eyes that so mesmerized him.

Those eyes had been so full of love last night. He was awestruck by the intensity of his love for her, still more by the fact that she returned that love.

As much as he wanted to, he didn't have the heart to wake her. She felt so peaceful in his arms. So he stayed as he was, tightening his hold, and savored the moment. He counted the handful of tiny freckles on her shoulder and arm. Watched as the breeze from the window fluttered a few wisps of her hair. Loved her.

Lois finally stirred. He felt her deep inhale in his own chest. Her arm slid out from under his and came to rest on top. As she wove their fingers together, she hugged his arm closer. He bent to nuzzle her neck, chuckling softly when she purred.

"Good morning," he whispered.

"Mmmm… It is a good morning."

She stretched her legs against his before snuggling closer.

"How'd you sleep?"

Lois sighed. "Beautifully. You?"

"Same."

She finally turned her head to look over her shoulder at him. He couldn't resist a kiss. What he had intended to be a quick peck turned into a lazy expedition into each other's mouths. She tasted so damn good.

They broke apart, smiling.

"Hi."

"Hi yourself," Nick replied.

Lois turned fully in his arms, nestling their fronts together. He brushed the hair back off her temple as her hand came to rest on his ass.

"What time is it?" Lois asked.

"No idea. But I very much doubt it's anywhere close to early."

Lois snickered, before burrowing her face into his chest. "I suppose we'll have to go back at some point, won't we?"

He made a noise of disgust at the thought, but knew she was right. "I guess so." A new thought occurred to him. "Think we could get away with staying at least one more night?"

She raised her head to look at him, considering. "I don't see why not. I wrapped my part of the picture a few days ago. And I left plenty of food in Lady M's bowl since we were going to be out late; besides, Betty can refill it if it gets too low." She frowned. "Though Barty did say he wanted to see you."

Hope sparked in his chest. "But not for a couple days. He has to talk to Matthews first." He let a grin light his face.

She caught his excitement. "So we don't really have to leave until tomorrow morning."

"And we never did take a honeymoon, you know."

"That's true. Oh…" She widened her eyes in mock dismay. "But we don't have anything to wear but our clothes from last night. Whatever shall we do?"

He made a show of grimacing. "That is a quandary. I hate to say it, but…we might just have to stay in bed."

She gasped. "Do you think we'll get bored?"

Nick didn't respond, only gave her his most roguish stare. He watched her lips curve in seductive anticipation; then he pounced with a growl. She squealed in delight, and when it dissolved into throaty laughter, he couldn't help joining in.

They did not get bored.

THEY PASSED the day in a blissful cocoon, but late in the afternoon, Lois remembered that it was Nate's car they'd driven here. Nick had completely forgotten too, and agreed they should step out of their reverie to give her a quick phone call. After everything she'd done to help them, they owed her at least that.

Lois wrapped his tuxedo shirt around her while she picked up the phone on the room's desk, and it was all he could do not to jump up and pull her back to bed. He settled for watching her explain to Nate where they had absconded to with her car.

At one point, Lois turned away from him, but not before he observed the flush creeping into her cheeks.

He hoped it was about him.

She hung up and faced him again. "Aside from some teasing, Nate's fine with everything. She said if it were up to her, we could keep the car and stay away as long as we want."

"How nice of her. What on earth would she have to tease you about, though?" Nick asked as he got out of bed and made his way over to her, stark naked.

Lois drew in a sharp breath as her eyes raked over him in blazing appreciation. "Oh, not much. Just the usual."

"The usual, eh? Do tell." He drew a lazy finger down her cheek.

She arched her eyebrow. "I'd much rather show."

He groaned as she pulled him in for a kiss and did just that, propelling them both back to bed. It was a very long time before they came up for air again.

Sadly, the next morning dawned, and despite their reluctance, they checked out relatively early.

Nate might not have cared about the car, but she had given Lois the message that Bartholomew had been looking for them, and would be expecting to see Nick the next day.

So there they were, heading back to reality.

They felt a little silly preparing to leave the hotel in bright, early morning daylight dressed in rumpled evening wear. But Nate came to their rescue yet again. She had cryptically told Lois to check the car's trunk when they were ready to leave. Sure enough, when they took her advice, it paid off.

"She's a costume designer," Lois said. "And a disgustingly prepared one. I should've known she'd be hauling around a whole trunkful of clothes."

They were disappointed to discover a fair amount of period costumes on the top of the pile, but once they rooted a little deeper, they managed to find a couple of decent current outfits. Maybe not anything either of them would normally wear, but they fit. And at least they were appropriate for daytime.

After a quick stop home to freshen up and change into their

own clothes, Nick and Lois headed to the studio. At the gate, the guard on duty affirmed what Nate had told them. Bartholomew had left a message summoning Nick to his office as soon as he arrived.

"Must be good news," Lois assured him cheerfully.

"I hope so."

She pressed a good luck kiss to his cheek and left to return Nate's car keys to her.

Nick made his way to the producer's office, feeling lighter than he had in ages. The prospect of working with Gene Matthews filled him with nervous exhilaration. He tried to keep his insecurity at bay. With his and Lois's film, he'd proven he could do comedy. To himself, but also clearly to the acclaimed director.

He inhaled sharply.

A highly acclaimed comedy director wanted him. He was finally getting the chance he'd wanted for so long.

And then there was Lois.

His skin heated at the memory of the last couple of days. He didn't think he'd ever get enough of her. She ignited his passion in a way no one ever had, but he was just as happy to simply hold her close, feel her tucked against him. The sound of her laughter warmed him to the core. The way she believed in him meant the world to him, but he also loved how unafraid she was to call him on his shit.

He loved her. And it thrilled him.

When he'd put his plan in motion all those months ago, he'd known all the risks. Been ready to face what came. But he'd never in a million years expected to not only be paired with Lois, but to fall in such crazy, all-consuming love with her.

Nick smiled to himself as he approached the office's reception area and greeted Jenny. She ushered him into Bartholomew's office. The older man looked at him in surprise.

"Lois isn't with you?"

"No. Were you expecting her? Your message made it sound like it was just me you wanted to see."

"Well technically, yes. We have a lot to talk about. But I was rather hoping she'd be here. I've got something to show the two of you."

"She is on the lot. Should be over with Nate Reynolds."

Bartholomew's eyes brightened. "Excellent. Jenny," he bellowed.

His secretary peered around the doorframe, looking resigned.

"Call over to wardrobe and see if you can find Lois Ashford. I'd like to see her too."

"You got it, Mr. B."

When she disappeared again, Bartholomew waved Nick into a chair. "You ducked out early the other night."

Nick shifted uncomfortably. They'd done their best to let go of Ronson's appearance at the party, but a touch of anger still lingered. He couldn't let Bartholomew know why they'd left. It was none of his business, and Nick was in too good a mood. Besides, even if he had wanted to—which he didn't—it wasn't his story tell.

So all he said was, "We did."

Bartholomew gave him a brief, knowing glance and then waved it off. "No matter. Nothing too exciting anyway. Just the same old boring shop talk." He leaned forward, elbows on his desk, all seriousness. "Good things are ahead for you, Bradley. I talked to Matthews yesterday, and we're ready to put you to work. You are ready to work, aren't you?"

"Of course, sir. I'm very much looking forward to working with Mr. Matthews. It's a wonderful opportunity."

"I'm glad to hear it." He settled back in his chair, the smile returning to his face. He looked to the door.

Nick wasn't sure if he was expected to say something.

Before he could decide, Bartholomew continued, seemingly impatient. "I did want to wait until your wife got here, but I suppose it couldn't hurt to start sharing these with you."

He picked up a stack of newspapers and tossed them on Nick's side of the desk. Nick could see that they'd all been folded to specific pages on the inside.

"The reviews have started coming in for *Teacups in July*. I think you'll be pleased."

Nick glanced up, intrigued, before taking the top paper from the stack. Not the most effusive review he'd ever read, but it was largely positive, especially regarding his and Lois's performances. The next one was of a similar nature. Relief coursed through his veins.

And promptly turned into cold lead when he read the third.

***

LOIS WAS SURPRISED to get the call at Nate's office. She'd just been enduring yet more ribbing from her friend about how nauseatingly satisfied she looked. She played along and pretended to be annoyed, but she knew Nate could see right through her.

And she was indeed satisfied.

She couldn't suppress her grin as she walked to Bartholomew's office. It was the first time she'd ever looked forward to what awaited her upon being summoned.

It had been unexpected, to be sure. Nick was the one with a new project on the horizon. Owing to the ensemble nature of her film, she had completed all of her scenes in the first round of shooting, and relatively quickly. She'd still have sound correction and publicity down the line, but she was essentially on a break. And with her contract renewal negotiations not until the following week, she doubted they'd be offering her a new film just yet.

She figured it must have something to do with *A Midsummer* —she cut herself off mid-thought. *Teacups in July*. She really needed to stop joking about that. Nick had been worried they'd joked too much and were going to slip up, and indeed they both had. Just because the premiere was over didn't mean the interviews would stop, and they couldn't afford to let it keep happening.

She said hello to Jenny, who waved her in.

"Morning, Barty. I thought you just needed Nick today."

"Lois, come on in. I do, mostly, but I wanted to share a bit of good news with you too."

She spotted a bunch of newspapers scattered on the desk.

Ah, the reviews must be in. Barty's cheerfulness bodes well.

Lois looked to Nick for confirmation, but he hadn't looked up from the paper in his hand. Come to think of it, he looked rather frozen to his chair. That was odd.

Bartholomew waved his hand at the stack as she approached. "Word is spreading about your little film."

"Is it, now?"

She picked up an article and scanned it. Pretty good. They weren't too impressed with the script, but that wasn't exactly a shocker. The review praised their acting, though, and Lois enjoyed a surge of well-earned pride.

But Nick's silence brought her up short. No, not silence precisely. If she wasn't mistaken, she could hear him breathing. She looked down at his profile. His jaw was clenched, and his grip had started to wrinkle the page in his hand.

"Nick? What's up, is that one not so good?"

"Of course not," Bartholomew chimed in. "They're all fantastic."

Nick raised his eyes to hers, and she was taken aback by the storm in them. He looked downright anguished. Angry. And almost nervous.

He handed her the paper without a word.

She started to read. It began innocently enough. Partway through, she realized this one wasn't simply a review of the film.

The most pleasant surprise to come out of this little comedy might just be the magic it's made for its two stars. Nick Bradley's been in desperate need of a turnaround after that unfortunate incident earlier this year, and it looks like he's found it. He seems to have traded in his funny business for being just plain funny on-screen, and we couldn't be more pleased for him. And he's having an extraordinary effect on his new bride as well. Rumor has it she was a perfect angel on set—a welcome change from her usual. Appears Nick was just dabbling in being a bad boy, and his newly restored halo is rubbing off. This paper very much approves of the couple's good fortune. Might we even go so far as to suggest another project for the emerging dream couple? That Shakespeare classic The Taming of the Shrew *is just ripe for a new adaptation, don't you think?*

Ice shot through Lois's entire body. She stared at the newspaper, unable to move. She was vaguely aware of her breath growing shallower.

On its surface, it read as an innocuous piece. Full of excitement and gushing praise.

And backhanded compliments.

Particularly aimed at her.

Silence hung over the room like a lead balloon. Somewhere in the back of her mind, she supposed Bartholomew probably expected her to say something. He'd have to wait.

Nick understood.

That's why he'd acted so strangely. Why he'd kept his head down.

She might have found reassurance in his anguish on her behalf, if she could feel anything at all.

This. This was it. Exactly what she'd given voice to that day in the accessory room, when she and Nick had agreed to the publicity marriage. The reason why the marriage shouldn't have been a good idea. Not for her.

The reason she had blithely ignored when she dared make the mistake of...

Having hope.

How could she have been so stupid?

"Lois?"

Nick's desperate whisper threatened at the edges of the haze filling her mind. She closed her eyes against the wave of pain that assaulted her senses.

"Ms. Ashford, what is it?" Bartholomew huffed. "You two are having the strangest reaction. What's got you so spooked?"

She opened her eyes to see him pick up the paper. She hadn't realized she'd let go of it.

"Oh, this one," he continued. "I thought this was one of the best. Really highlighted the redemption angle."

Nick made a strangled sound beside her. She was still having trouble looking at him.

Bartholomew rooted through the stack, searching for something. "You know, this wasn't the only one that mentioned *Taming of the Shrew*. Who knows, maybe there's something to it. Could be a good follow up for you two, eh?"

"Bartholomew." Nick's voice could have cut glass.

The producer's head snapped up. "What? The idea's not half-bad. The Bard's sure to at least deliver you a better script, right?"

Nick's stare was positively venomous.

Bartholomew finally seemed to sense the mood in the room, looking between the two of them. His gaze landed on Lois, projecting what he probably thought was solicitude.

"You're not offended by this whole 'shrew' business, are you?" He waved his hand. "It doesn't mean anything. This is a win. Exactly the win we were hoping for."

He didn't get it. He probably never would.

If any situation called for the nuclear fury in her arsenal, this was it. But she couldn't summon the energy.

Lois felt numb. Hollow.

She finally looked at Nick. He was staring at her with such concern. Such *love*.

She felt a small crack start to form in her heart.

Suddenly the room was entirely too small, too suffocating.

Pulling just enough air into her lungs to speak, she said, "I have to go. I need to…" Her brain hiccupped, unable to come up with an excuse, so she didn't bother finishing. "You two have a lot to discuss anyway, so I'm just going to…"

She started toward the door.

"Lois, wait."

Nick grabbed her hand. The touch startled her, but she didn't pull away. She let herself take the briefest hint of comfort before slipping out of his grasp.

"I'll see you later, Nick." Her voice sounded flat, even to her own ears.

"Let me come with you."

"No. Stay. You have things you need to do… And so do I."

She dared a look, and saw the flash of fear in his eyes.

Feeling plenty of her own fear—along with an excruciating sadness—she fled the room.

Chapter Twenty-Three

It killed Nick not to follow her. He wanted nothing more than to take her in his arms, make everything better. But she'd told him not to come, seemed to need to be alone. So he'd stayed.

And given Bartholomew an earful.

That, at least, he could do. Maybe it wasn't the wisest choice, but he didn't care. Someone needed to call him out on what an insensitive boob he'd been. This wasn't a win for Lois. Anyone who knew her the slightest bit should've been able to see how hurtful that article would be. And to have the balls to suggest that they should even *think* about that adaptation?

It made Nick's blood boil.

Bartholomew, to his credit, listened and looked chagrined. But it wasn't nearly enough to take away the pain he'd seen in Lois's eyes.

The producer tried to assure Nick that she'd be fine, and insisted that he stay to finish their meeting. Nick didn't agree, but wasn't exactly in a position to argue.

They talked film details for a while, Nick barely listening. To his surprise, Bartholomew had already invited Gene Matthews to join them toward the end of the meeting. Nick risked slipping into the reception area before he arrived to call over to wardrobe in an attempt to find Lois, with no luck. He went back in and tried harder to pay attention. He couldn't afford to alienate Matthews, especially since the director had requested him specifically.

After what felt like an interminable morning, Nick was finally free to go. He rushed straight to Nate's office, but she maintained that she hadn't seen Lois since she'd dropped off the car keys that morning. He might have thought Nate was covering for her friend, except for the genuine surprise—and then anger—that crossed her features when he told her about the newspapers. It worried him immensely that Lois hadn't sought out her best friend.

Where the hell was she?

After calling the house and getting no answer, Nick searched around the lot. No sign of her. He checked in with Nate once more, before calling for a car. He figured he might as well head home. She'd have to return there eventually, and he'd be waiting when she did.

He opened the door to find Lois waiting for him.

A tidal wave of relief engulfed him at the sight of her.

"Lois, thank god. I've been looking everywhere for you." The words rushed out of him. "When Bartholomew finally let me go, I went to Nate, I called here, I walked around the studio…"

He trailed off, taking in the room. It was relatively dark, the late afternoon sun making a feeble attempt to get past the mostly-closed curtains. Lois sat on the couch, a half-empty wineglass in her hand, Lady M curled protectively by her side. She was disconcertingly still.

"I've been here," she said quietly.

"I thought I might find you in Nate's office." Her words struck him. "Wait, you've been here the whole time? I called…"

"Yeah, I heard the phone. Sorry. I just…I was thinking. Deciding some things."

She still hadn't met his eyes.

Nick started forward, but only came as far as the armchair. He wanted to go all the way to her, but something in her manner stopped him from completing the distance.

"Lois, I am so sorry. I hadn't finished reading when Bartholomew called you in. I had no idea what you were walking into." He raked his hand through his hair. "I'm so furious. How dare they? And Bartholomew! I unloaded hell on him, believe me. I think he got the message."

He was breathing heavily, but Lois remained deadly calm. He fought the urge to keep talking to fill up the silence. He wanted her to say something, anything.

"I've decided to take the job on Broadway."

Okay, maybe not anything.

"I thought you weren't interested."

"I wasn't. But...now I think it's for the best. I called Bertie Hamilton this afternoon."

"Oh."

It was the last thing he had expected her to say. But maybe it was for the best. It would give everyone a chance to see her do something new and exciting, show off her talents. He hated that they'd have to reside on opposite coasts for a while, but he'd meant what he said to her the other day. They would make the best of it somehow.

"I..." Nick croaked. He cleared his throat and tried again. "I think it'll be great, then. You'll be able to use it as leverage, too, when you come back to the studio. Make them think twice before trying to push you into anything dicey."

"I won't be coming back to the studio, Nick. I'm not going to renew my contract with Parkmoor."

Nick was thunderstruck once again.

"I don't understand. I thought you said your heart was in film."

"It was. But get your heart broken enough and...you start to realize maybe it's just time to walk away."

"But all the effort you've put in, everything we did these last few months to turn things around... It was working."

"For you."

The sharp words were punctuated by the dull thud of her wineglass on the table, reverberating around the room.

She finally looked at him, and he saw the hot, barely contained fury in her gaze.

He wanted desperately to calm that fury, heal her pain.

"I know how horrible the implications in that article were, but we can fix this, I know we can."

She huffed a bitter laugh. "It's too late for that."

"It's never too late. Look at what we've done already, we—"

"You were *fucking arrested*, Nick! ON PURPOSE!"

Her words hit him like a slap as she exploded to her feet.

"You intentionally committed a crime, and now they want to throw you a goddamn parade!" She sucked in a sharp breath. "All because you reined me in, put the village witch in her place. Thank god you came along to save the day." She spat the words, disgusted.

"Lois, I—"

"I turned down a date. With a gross, married man. I did the right thing! And I have been paying for it for ten *fucking* years!" She let out an anguished cry, full of all her fury and frustration. "All that work. All the things we did together on that film. I actually let myself—"

She cut herself off with a choked sob. Nick longed to hear the end of the sentence.

Lois's breath shuddered in her chest. "You actually broke the law, Nick. But you're a man. So you get a halo—they *actually* used the word *halo*—and all I am is the shrew you tamed." She pressed her lips together in a pained grimace. "No matter what I do, I will always be the shrew."

Nick had no idea what to say. He knew she was right, and his heart broke for her.

He watched as she closed her eyes and inhaled deeply. She exhaled slowly, seeming to let go as she did. She opened her eyes to him.

"So I need to go where I'm not the shrew. Where I'm not…difficult."

Nick nodded. "A fresh start. Where they see *you*."

Appreciation flashed through her eyes, along with something else, there and gone.

He continued, his mind already making plans. "I won't be able to join you right away, with this new movie, but I'll see what I can do with weekends, maybe…"

He trailed off at the look in her eyes.

That something else he'd seen before. He knew what it was now.

Dread and panic settled around him. He felt sick to his stomach. The words were barely a whisper, but he managed to get them out anyway.

"You don't want me to come with you. At all. *Ever*."

She didn't answer, but the tears shining in her eyes, the unguarded, crushing sadness he saw there, said plenty.

Pain rocketed through him, stealing his breath.

He gripped the chair in front of him for support. "Lois, please," he rasped. "It doesn't have to be this way."

Her lip trembled slightly, and he watched her throat work before she could speak. "I'm sorry, Nick. I'm so sorry. But when we agreed to this, part of that agreement was that if it wasn't redemption for both of us…"

Anger flashed, surprising him. He rounded the chair and closed the distance between them, unable to keep the desperation from his voice.

"No. Ending it was not the only option we discussed that day. And even if it had been, that was *before*…" He gestured between them. "Before this, before us. We're an *us* now, Lois. Aren't we?"

She closed her eyes, and a tear spilled down her cheek. He brushed it away with his thumb, her exhale hot against his wrist.

"What about all those things we said the other night? I love you, Lois. And I know you meant it when you told me you love me."

Lois's eyes flew open, fierce. "I did mean it. I do love you, Nick. I love you so much."

Her unspoken "but" hovered in the air between them.

Nick slowly lowered his hand. "I told you not to answer right away about…" He couldn't manage to get the word "forever" out. He swallowed, his own tears threatening. "This is your answer, isn't it?"

"Please understand, Nick. *Please.* I have to do this. And I have to do it on my own." She turned and walked a few steps away from him. "If I'm ever going to feel passionate about what I do, if my work is ever going to mean anything, it has to be *mine.*"

At the sound of his ragged inhale, she faced him again. He could see the sorrow in her eyes, before they blazed.

"Don't you see? My entire career has been determined for me, beyond my control. I thought I was finally breaking free, but…" Her teeth dug into her lower lip. "I just traded one label for another. The godawful truth of this town is that I am always going to be defined by the men in my life. It's all they're ever going to see."

"It's not what I see."

Heartbreaking tenderness flooded her expression. "I know. And you have no idea how much that means to me."

"But it's not enough," he whispered.

She gave an infinitesimal shake of her head.

The weight of it crushed him.

The absolute hell of it all was that he understood. With perfect clarity. She'd been trying to live her passion, her dreams, for a decade, and instead of seeing her talent rewarded, she'd been systematically pushed down, kept on the margins. He'd experienced his own version of feeling trapped by the studio, but it was nothing compared to what she'd had to endure. Was still enduring, when they should have been rising up together.

All the promise, all the hope he'd felt since Lois had come into his life was draining from him. And there wasn't a damn thing he could do to stop it.

His tears were coming freely now, and he didn't even have the energy to wipe them away.

"I wish things were different. But they're not. And I..." She lowered her head for a moment. "I just can't do it anymore. I need a victory. A real victory. A victory that's mine alone. On *my* terms."

She reached out and then stopped herself, cupping the air instead of his cheek.

Closer. Please come closer.

His center of gravity pulled him toward her, trying to close the gulf, but before he could, she retreated.

Her voice was nothing but a painful rasp. "I'm so sorry, Nick."

And then he was alone. She disappeared up the stairs in a flash.

He sank into the chair, and let the grief overtake him.

Chapter Twenty-Four

Hollywood Happenings
Shocking news out of Parkmoor Studios! On the heels of her
successful comedy, reforming diva Lois Ashford is leaving the
studio—and Hollywood! From what we can gather, the decision
came from the actress herself, and execs are not happy with her
timing. It seems the lady has been lured away to the bright lights
of Broadway, moving east to try her hand at treading the boards.
We have no idea what this means for her fairy-tale romance,
either—we sure hope she's not leaving her handsome hubby
behind with a broken heart!

Two days later, Nick found himself outside of Nate's office. That first evening, after Lois fled upstairs, he had sat in the chair, in the dark, for most of the night. Unable to bring himself to move. He couldn't remember actually getting up, but sometime near dawn he realized he was hovering in the bathroom doorway. He had wanted to shower, to see if that might wash away some of the pain and bring him some clarity, but all he found was a fresh wave of pain. One look at the shower stall and he flashed back to the night when she'd joined him there, finally brought them together.

He'd stumbled to the guest bedroom, unoccupied since that night, and collapsed on the bed. Not long after that, he'd heard Lois stirring across the hall, and nearly fell to pieces all over again.

No longer able to stand it, he'd thrown a few of his things in a small bag and left. He'd been hiding out, imposing on Max's hospitality ever since.

He wasn't exactly wallowing. Instead, he frantically tried to come up with something—*anything*—he could do to make things better. He knew part of it was selfishness, pain at the thought of living without her. But he was also desperate to take away her pain. He had no doubt she could do it on her own—but he didn't want her to have to. He wanted to share her burden.

And so he had come to seek out Nate.

Her office door stood open, and she sat at her drafting table, making notes on some sketches. At his knock, she looked up, eyes widening at his appearance.

Oh, great. Do I really look that bad?

"Geez, you look like shit on toast."

"Thanks awfully," he retorted drily.

Nate's face softened as she came toward him. "You know I didn't mean it that way, hon. Come in."

She closed her door and gestured him to the couch, taking a detour to her desk drawer. She held up a bottle of something strong-looking in invitation. Nick managed a pathetic nod, and she poured him a cup as she settled next to him.

"You've talked to her?" he asked.

"I have."

"How is she?"

"Not great. In a lot of pain, but…"

"Determined."

Nate smiled sadly. "Very. I'd ask how you're doing, but I can see the answer pretty clearly."

"It's really that bad, huh?"

She gave a soft chuckle. "Maybe not to everyone, but I do know you. And I speak the language of appearances."

He leaned back in his seat. "I wish I could make it all go away. I wish I could make it better for her."

"I know. For what it's worth, I think she probably does too."

He let his desperation show. "What do I do, Nate?"

She turned sympathetic eyes to him. "I hate to say it, but I think you already know the answer to that. It's why you're here, talking to me."

He hated that she was right.

Nate was thoughtful for a moment before continuing. "She's been fighting this war for a long time, Nick. Long before she met you. She was tired when you came along, but...these last few months, I've seen something different in her. She's actually been hopeful. Happy." She inhaled sharply. "This last blow came when she wasn't expecting it. Took a direct hit at that happiness. She's reeling. And she has to do what she can to survive. To thrive again."

It wasn't anything he didn't already know, hadn't been telling himself for two days. But hearing it out loud, from someone else who cared deeply for Lois, made him feel a bit less alone, less panicked.

"I have to let her go."

Nate made a soft sound of agreement.

His fear still bubbled under the surface, threatening to pull him down again. Having Nate there, knowing she'd understand, he let himself give voice to that fear.

"I know she has to do this; I know it's her only way forward." His breath scratched his throat. "But I'm so scared, Nate. I don't want to lose her. What if she doesn't come back?" This last was nothing but a whisper.

Nate took his hand in both of hers and held tight. "She loves you, Nick. There is not a single doubt in my mind about that. I know how impossible this all feels right now, but you need to trust that. You need to trust *her*."

He nodded. That he could do. He always had.

"You two are nausea-inducingly right for each other." Nate smirked. "Besides, I've gotten far too used to coming up with clever reefer puns to hurl your way. It's one of the highlights of my day, and I do not want to give it up."

Nick was relieved to know he could still laugh, if only for a second.

"Thanks, Nate."

"Come here, you." She pulled him into a welcome hug.

There was no way this was going to be easy. He knew it was going to be downright awful.

But he loved Lois Ashford with all of his heart.

And if she needed him to love her from afar, then that's what he would do for her.

LOIS SAT at her kitchen table, tapping one dark red fingernail against a blank sheet of stationery. This was one of the few remaining tasks she'd set for herself before leaving for New York, but she struggled in getting started.

Her trunks were packed. Betty had come by earlier that morning and offered to not only keep an eye on the house, but to cover any furniture that might need it while she was away. Lois had hesitated, unsure of Nick's plans. They hadn't spoken since that dreadful night, but she didn't want to turn him out of the house. It had become theirs. But she didn't know if they'd see each other before she left. Didn't know if she'd be able to face him and still say goodbye.

Focus on what you need to do.

She shook her head and stared at the blank page. Nearly everything was done, wrapped up in advance of her departure.

Her mind wandered again, this time to her last meeting at the studio.

When she'd marched into her contract meeting and announced she wouldn't be returning, Bartholomew had gone from shocked to apoplectic to groveling in rapid succession. He'd fallen over himself in apologizing for his remarks about the articles, and she appreciated how genuine he seemed.

But no amount of sincerity was enough to change her mind. He knew it, too. They'd parted ways as amicably as possible considering the circumstances, and that was that. Her tenure as a contract player at Parkmoor Studios was over.

The doorbell startled her back to the present. She rose to answer it, curious. She was expecting Nate, but not for another couple of hours.

Lois opened the door, and her heart lodged in her throat.

Actually, her heart stood in front of her.

"Nick." She was incapable of any kind of volume. "Hi."

He looked…*wonderful.*

Certainly not perfect. His hair was shaggier than usual, and the dark circles under his eyes sent an icy shard of guilt through her chest. It killed her to not see the spark of amusement that usually hovered behind his every expression.

But after a few days without him, he was the most wonderful sight she'd ever seen.

It was all she could do not to throw her arms around him. She knew that would only make things worse for both of them, though, so she kept her arms pinned to her sides.

She didn't know if it was wishful thinking, but she thought she detected a similar struggle deep in the blue of his eyes.

Nick gave her a tiny, tentative smile. "Hi. Is it okay if I come in for a minute?"

"Of course." She stepped back to let him pass before closing the door, careful not to let her arm brush his.

He hovered in the entryway, seemingly nervous.

"You didn't have to ring the doorbell, you know. It's… This is still your house too."

Nick sucked in a breath. "I didn't want to barge in. I didn't know…" He trailed off, staring at her like he was parched in a desert and couldn't be sure if she was a mirage.

She suspected her own face projected the same yearning.

He cleared his throat, collecting himself. "That's actually part of the reason I'm here." He fished in his pocket and produced a set of keys. "I thought I should bring these back to you."

She felt the early stirrings of tears begin.

Dammit. Do not cry right now.

"Nick, please don't feel you have to leave, just because I am. You should stay."

"No. I…I wouldn't want to be here without you. It wouldn't feel right."

She desperately wanted someone to remove the elephant that was now sitting on her chest.

A thought occurred to her and she seized on it. "But wait. Your things are still here." She'd carefully avoided them as she packed.

Nick's face went almost comically blank before deflating. "Shit. I forgot."

Lois would have laughed at how adorable he looked if it all wasn't so tragic.

She threw him a lifeline. "Betty's still going to be coming in from time to time. You can take your time, leave the keys when…" She struggled to push the rest of the words out. "When you're ready."

"Yeah, okay. Sure." He put the keys back in his pocket, then glanced at his other hand, seeming to remember what it held.

Lois noticed the small ivory envelope for the first time. She'd been so focused on his face, she hadn't taken much of anything else in.

"I, um," he began, "I wanted to give you this."

He extended the envelope toward her, and she took it. She ran her fingers over her name, written in his bold, scrawling script.

"You don't have to read it now." Her eyes found his, and he smiled sheepishly. "As a matter of fact, it's better if you don't. Wait until you get to..."—he swallowed convulsively—"to New York."

"Nick..." She had no idea what to say. A million thoughts pushed and shoved at each other, trying to get out, but none of them was able to survive the riot and prevail.

Nick took her in for a long while. His lower lip shook almost imperceptibly, then stilled. His chest grew as he filled his lungs and took two steps toward her.

His hand twitched, and she thought he might reach for her, but he maintained control.

She wasn't sure if she was grateful or gutted.

Definitely both.

He swallowed, and she watched as he opened the floodgates and let love surge into his eyes. She swore she felt the ground move beneath her.

"Lois." His voice was full of that surge as well. "I know you are going to do the most extraordinary things on Broadway. The people of New York don't know how truly lucky they are."

The tears were about to begin in earnest, but before she could try to stop them, Nick closed the distance between them. He brought his lips to hers in an unbearably soft caress, shattering her heart in the process.

He held the kiss for a long—*not nearly long enough*—moment, and then his forehead came to rest on hers. His exhale teased against her skin.

"Goodbye, Lois."

"Goodbye, Nick."

And then he was gone.

He let himself out, and her back melted into the door. She pressed his letter to her chest and felt silent tears bathe her face. She couldn't have stopped them if she tried.

So she let them come, mourning the loss of Nick's warm, beautiful presence in her life.

And then she straightened, wiping her cheeks with the back of her hand.

Her heart might be in tatters, but she still had work to do. She returned to the kitchen and picked up her pen.

She had an important letter of her own to write, one last—long overdue—act of defiance before she left this town and started to piece together a fresh start.

Chapter Twenty-Five

A Ravishing Revelation

Bertie Hamilton has done it again, weaving his unique brand of magic at the 44th Street Theater. Playwright Colin Canfield once more serves up a charming mix of wit and emotion, but this time his words are elevated to glorious new heights when coming from the mouth of star Lois Ashford, in her Broadway debut. This critic is usually wary of Hollywood types attempting the rigors of the stage, but Ms. Ashford so far exceeded my expectations, I hardly know where to begin. Her luminous presence is a welcome addition to our little community, and I am sure I am not alone in hoping we can keep her here on this coast in perpetuity.

Three Months Later

Lois exited the stage to another round of thunderous applause. The curtain call complete, she wove her way through stagehands beginning their reset and her fellow actors congratulating each other, and her, on their latest successful performance. As she neared her dressing room, she rode the wave of exhilaration she felt every night upon finishing the play. It was truly remarkable to get such instant, gratifying feedback from the audience. And no two crowds were the same, each group bringing a fresh dynamic to the words she and the rest of the company repeated night after night. It was so very different from film.

And yet.

As much as she was loving Broadway, Lois did miss moviemaking. She supposed that was a good sign, that she'd feel refreshed and ready if and when she decided to go back to it.

She certainly would be able to go back with her head held high. Her gamble was paying off in a big way. The play was a huge success, selling out nearly every show. Critics and audiences alike loved her performance, and she reveled in going to work every day with a group of people who treated her with respect. She had made a large number of friends, whom she hoped to work with again, and keep in touch with when they parted ways.

They were nearing the end of their scheduled run already, and Bertie Hamilton had begun to float the idea of extending the show, or at the very least lining up another play with her in it. As flattered, and tempted, as she was, Lois hadn't given him an answer yet.

Throughout rehearsals and the early part of the run, she had put off thinking too far ahead. Now that a conclusion was in sight —and unassailed success was hers—she knew she had some decisions to make. She just wasn't sure what exactly she wanted her next steps to be.

Lois changed out of her costume and into a robe. She sat at her dressing table, looking forward to removing her heavy stage makeup and letting her face breathe. She caught sight of the small card taped to her mirror and reached up to touch it.

On opening night, she had walked into her dressing room to find a cheerful explosion of purple and yellow pansies, with an unsigned card.

Not that it needed a signature.

The card had only three words written on it, words that immediately identified its sender. And gave her a burst of unexpected and welcome laughter.

Fart the alphabet.

It still made her smile every night.

Plenty of people had passed through her dressing room—dressers, actors, acquaintances in attendance offering congratulations—and the card repeatedly garnered quizzical stares and even the occasional question about its meaning. But she always let the question remain unanswered. It was their private joke.

Her hand came to the necklace nestled against her chest. The little engraved film canister. She had looped it onto a long chain, long enough to remain hidden under her costume. But it was always there, resting on her heart.

God, I miss him so much.

She closed her eyes as the intense rush of longing filled her.

Lois had hoped it might get easier as the weeks passed, but of course it hadn't. She was fairly competent at getting through most tasks, holding normal conversations. It was easiest when she was on stage—the glorious benefit of being able to pretend to be someone else for two solid hours.

But then she'd be going about her business, doing something seemingly innocuous, and the smallest thing would remind her of him, take her back to something he'd said, remind her of the laughter in his eyes. The feel of his arms around her, his lips on her skin.

One of these days, hugging herself in wasn't going to be enough, and she'd actually, finally explode in a million pieces. It was inevitable.

She let her breath out in a long groan and turned back to her reflection. She'd only just picked up the cold cream when a knock sounded at her door.

"Come in."

The door cracked and Jimmy poked his head in. The young assistant stage manager was bright, earnest, and incredibly hard working. Lois had no doubt he'd go far and would deserve every bit of his success.

"Sorry to bother you, Lois, but there's a visitor who'd like to congratulate you. I can ask her to wait if you'd like?"

"No, that's all right, Jimmy. Please send her in."

Lois had had a number of well-wishers stop in over the last several weeks, often people she'd worked with but had not expected to see much of again. It always made for a pleasant surprise when they took the time to offer their support.

"Good evening, Lois."

The expectant smile died on her lips when she saw her guest.

Catherine Ronson.

Wife of Arthur Ronson.

"I hope you don't mind, but I was in the audience tonight and wanted to see you. May I come in for a moment?"

She must have seen Lois dart a glance behind her, because she added, "You can rest assured I'm alone this evening."

Lois snapped her eyes back to the woman and stood, gesturing her in. "Please."

Catherine closed the door behind her. "The reviews weren't exaggerating. You were remarkable on that stage tonight. Congratulations."

"Thank you." For a minute, all Lois could do was stare. Her mind reeled. And an awkward silence brewed. "Forgive me, I just wasn't expecting to see you here, after…"

"Yes, I imagine I must be a bit of a shock." She gave her a disconcertingly direct look. "As was your letter."

Lois gulped. She wasn't sure what to expect from this woman —was it ever possible to predict the precise reaction to finding out one's spouse was a philandering, vindictive bastard?

Catherine continued. "I suppose I really shouldn't have been that shocked. Arthur's always been…" Her face scrunched momentarily in disgust, and she waved it away. "But I turned a blind eye to far too much. And for that, I would like to offer you my sincerest apologies."

That was a refreshing reaction.

"I appreciate that."

The other woman nodded. "I might as well come right out with it. Apologies are not all I am here to offer you."

Uh-oh.

If she was here with hush money or some other nefarious crap, she could just turn right around and shove it.

"I've decided to sell Neptune Pictures. And I'm here to offer the sale to you."

WHAT?

Never in a million years would she have predicted that one.

Lois felt her jaw go slack, powerless to close it. She wasn't even sure if she was blinking. She was inordinately grateful she hadn't moved from the spot where she'd risen, as the chair hit her completely unawares when her behind landed back on it.

To her credit, Catherine Ronson didn't push, or continue speaking at all, just let Lois take it all in.

As if that was even a possibility.

"Can..." A frog lodged in Lois's throat, and she had to clear it forcefully to evict him. "Can you even *do* that?"

Catherine's lips spread in a sly smile. She motioned questioningly to the armchair across the tiny room. On Lois's jerky nod, she sat.

"I'm glad you asked. You see, my late father was a smart man. Far smarter than I ever gave him credit for. When he retired, he left day-to-day control of the studio to Arthur. Which made perfect sense, as I'd never really had much interest in the movies. I was perfectly happy traveling and working with the family's charitable foundation." Her face hardened. "I see now that I should have kept a much closer eye on my husband. But I suspect my father recognized more of his nature than I did. Which is most beneficial now."

"I'm still not sure I understand."

"Before he died, my father hired the very best lawyers and made an ironclad, unassailable provision regarding his beloved studio. Arthur may run it, but the ownership of it is in my name. And mine alone. The way my father arranged it, there isn't a community property law in the world that could take it from me. But I believe the time has come for me to part with it on my own terms."

Lois let the words sink in. But she still couldn't quite make sense of it all.

"A while back, there were some rumors in *Variety*. Is this what that was about? Your planning to sell?"

Catherine chuckled. "Oh, no. Almost no one in Hollywood has any idea what my father set up. As a matter of fact, I suspect even Arthur doesn't know. Bless his lecherous little heart." She shook her head. "No, those rumors are actually what started me thinking. And then your letter sealed it." She leveled that direct stare at Lois again. "I won't sugarcoat it. Neptune doesn't have the best standing anymore. Too much spending on the wrong things, not enough truly big hits of late. And a studio head who seems incapable of taking risks, moving with the times."

Lois's mind was emerging from its shock and finally regaining proper function.

"With all due respect..." *Might as well just say it.* "Why me? What makes you think I'm even remotely qualified to do this, let alone that I'd have the financial means to"—she pulled a face to match her incredulity—"purchase a studio?"

The older woman sat back and crossed her arms. "Don't sell yourself short, Ms. Ashford. You'll find I'm willing to accept a more than generously low selling price. Due in large part to my husband's behavior toward you. You were undoubtedly passed over for many a higher-paying film through no fault of your own. Think of the discount I'm offering as long overdue back pay. Compensation for emotional distress."

Lois was dumbfounded. An offer like this was...well, it was downright unheard of.

She expected to wake from this dream any minute now.

But Catherine Ronson wasn't finished.

"As for your capabilities, I'm not worried on that front either. As I said, Arthur hasn't been living up to my father's dreams for

Neptune, not by a long shot. If the studio has any hope of continuing instead of running steadily into the ground, there needs to be some fresh blood driving it forward. And according to your husband, you have some ideas that might be just the ticket."

Nick? What does he have to do with this?

Catherine kept talking. "I ran into him last week, purely by chance. Come to think of it, is he still your husband?" Before she could answer, Catherine waved the thought away. "No matter. We had a very interesting conversation. I complimented you on the rave reviews I'd been hearing, and he got the most fascinating look on his face. He's very proud of you, you know. But he was also suppressing quite the fury. I think he wanted to give me what-for on your behalf. But he doesn't know you wrote me, does he?"

Despite the tempest kicking up inside her, Lois managed a "no."

"I could tell there were things he thought he couldn't say. But what he did say was rather remarkable. He told me you were full of talent and brilliance, that it was a crime that more people didn't take the time to see it. He said you had ideas that would set Hollywood ablaze if only you were given the chance."

Warmth filled Lois's chest and tears pricked at her eyes. He was still her biggest cheerleader.

Catherine smiled at what Lois must have been unable to keep from her face. "I realize he's smitten enough to be more than a little biased, but it wasn't just that. I saw more than a kernel of truth in what he said. I can see it in you now. You have ideas. And I want to hear them."

She did have ideas. She'd tried to set them aside, but they were all still there. Itching to get out. And this woman actually wanted to take them seriously.

Lois squared her shoulders and looked Catherine in the eye. The woman smiled.

"Mm-hm. I can see it indeed. And you know, even if you aren't successful, I'm sure you'll at least try. I'd rather see the studio make an effort and fail than take no chances at all. Plus, the thought of his pinched little face when I hand over all he holds dear to the woman he tried to ruin... Oh, revenge will be sweet indeed." She sat up and folded her hands in her lap, all business again. "So. I know what a monumental heap I've dumped on you this evening. Take a week or so. Think it all over. Look at your financials. If you want this, come back to me with what you think is a fair price, as well as a proposal with some of your ideas. We'll go from there."

Catherine rose to her feet, and Lois followed suit.

"I assume you'll need to consult at least a few people about this—business managers, advisors and the like. But I have one request. I am trusting in your confidence. Make sure you can absolutely trust in theirs. If this is to work, we'll need the utmost discretion until everything is finalized. My bastard husband can have no inkling, no chance to fight this until it's too late."

"Of course. I understand completely."

"Excellent." She extended her hand. "I'll be in touch. Good night, Ms. Ashford."

Lois shook her hand. "Good night, Mrs. Ronson."

She sat at her dressing table for a long time after Catherine left, absently listening to the sounds of the theater being put to bed for the night. She felt dazed, shaky, unsure if she was really awake.

And, for the first time in weeks, she started to feel an emotion she was hesitant to acknowledge, for fear of it slipping through her fingers yet again.

Hope.

SHE RETURNED to her apartment late that night, grateful for theatre hours that dictated she wouldn't need to be up early the next day—and for the time difference that meant Nate would still be up.

When she finished recounting her visit from Catherine, Lois

heard nothing but stunned silence from the other end of the phone. As much as she wanted to give Nate the chance to absorb everything, her impatience won out.

"Nate? You still there?"

Her friend heaved a sigh. "Just once, could we have a normal, simple conversation? You know, where you don't drop some huge thing that surprises the crap out of me? Is that too much to ask?"

"Believe me, I'd like nothing more than to bore you to tears."

Nate laughed. "I doubt that's ever gonna happen. So, Catherine Ronson's the one with all the cards, huh? I didn't see that coming."

"Me either."

"Do you have any idea what you're going to do?"

"I don't. It's...so unbelievably tempting. But it's awfully risky."

"Everything worth doing is. Can you run it all by your lawyer? Think you can trust him?"

"I found Don through my brother; they've known each other for years," Lois replied. "If there's anyone I can trust, both with discretion and giving me a straight answer, it's him. I'm planning to call him first thing tomorrow. I do need to find someone to give me a sense of whether I can really do this financially, though."

"Didn't Simon Lord offer to stay on as your accountant even though you left the studio?"

"He did, which was lovely of him. But that's just it. He's with Parkmoor, and that's where his loyalties are. And rightly so." She snorted. "Plus, you know how he is. He'd probably pat my arm and tell me I shouldn't worry my pretty head with something like owning a studio."

Nate groaned. "You're right. I can just hear him—'Now, you just leave that to the menfolk, dearie.'"

They shared a laugh before Lois continued. "Someone good with numbers, who can keep a secret, and won't treat me like a little girl..."

The prospects looked pretty bleak, until it came to Lois. Nate must have had the same thought, because they spoke simultaneously.

"*Frannie.*"

"Of course," Lois said. "She'd be just right. And I'd much rather give her my business than some crusty old fart. Think she'd do it?"

"Are you kidding? I'm sure she'd jump at the chance. Manicures are hardly her passion."

Lois was confident, but then doubt—stemming from years of experience—crept in.

"Am I crazy to think this is even possible? Even if it's all legit, and I can swing it money-wise, and Catherine accepts my offer..." She sighed. "Is anyone even going to want to work for me? I mean, yes, this play has absolutely been a fresh start. It was the right thing to do. I've already gotten some good offers, both here in New York and from other studios. I don't feel like so much of a leper anymore. But casting me as an actor versus working under my direction, having me as a boss... They're very different things. My reputation has been solid for a long time. As much as I want it to, it's not going to magically disappear overnight. Especially if I'm in position of power. That I'm taking from a man."

Nate was quiet for a moment. "I'm not going to lie. There are definitely going to be a fair number of jackasses who will outright refuse to work with you. You know that. But that's their problem. And who the hell would want to work with them anyway?" She huffed. "I wish I could look you in the eye right now, because you need to understand this, Lois. Don't sell yourself short. I think you'll have a lot more support than you realize."

"I don't know—"

"I do," Nate interrupted, brooking no argument. "Let the executives and gossip mongers believe whatever they want to. There are an awful lot of us who know better. I don't need to remind you that we're the ones who really make things happen every day. And we see everything. There's no way we'd be friends if you were all they say about you, and I'm sure as hell not the only one who's paying attention. Come on, how many actual bastards—or *shrews*—have a code of ethics? You've never unloaded on anyone who didn't deserve it. And you're doing yourself a great disservice if you think that's gone unnoticed, hon."

Lois swallowed against the lump in her throat. She hadn't even realized she was crying until a tear slid down her cheek.

All these years, she'd been so caught up in her bubble, isolated in her anger. And as important as her code of ethics was to her, she had never counted on too many people noticing it. She didn't do it to get noticed. She did it simply because it was the right thing to do.

But apparently, she should have been paying more attention.

"Thanks, Nate."

"No thanks necessary. It's just the truth." Lois could hear the smile in her friend's voice. "You know, if you need some proof, I can put a few feelers out there. Test the waters." She kept going before Lois could protest. "And don't worry—no one will have any idea why. You know me. I'm a vault. And I'm very good at bringing others into the vault with me. Even when they don't know why."

Lois laughed. "I'm not entirely sure what that means, or if I even want to. But I do trust you."

"Good." She hesitated. "I hate to risk ruining this lovely moment, but I feel like I should ask. Are you going to talk to Nick?"

Lois pulled in a deep lungful of air. She'd been debating the same question herself.

"I don't know. Part of me wants to." She could practically feel Nate's skeptical look through the phone lines. "Okay, a *huge* part of me wants to. We actually talked about what we'd do if we were ever in charge of things. It started to feel like *our* dream, not just mine. And he said what he did to Catherine, which made a lot of this possible."

"So what's stopping you?"

"Everything I've been fighting against, all this time, it all came from one thing. From *Ronson*. And I finally have the chance to do something about it, something real, tangible. This is my chance to vanquish my demon, slay my dragon. Get my white whale."

"He does put the *dick* in Moby Dick."

Lois chuckled. "Indeed he does. And I know Nick would be all in, ready to stand by my side and be my knight in shining armor. It's rather a beautiful idea."

"But you need to be your own knight."

"I do. In this especially, I really do. At least until it all goes down."

"I get it." Nate paused. "As much as I could talk all night, it's getting late. And I can't even imagine how tired you must be."

"Yeah, I'm still running on fumes, but I do feel the shutdown coming. Thanks for everything, Nate."

"Anytime, anywhere. You know it. Listen, Lo, before I get off, can I just say one more thing?"

"Of course."

"However this plays out, I really do hope you get to have it all. Including Nick. You're astoundingly great all on your own, but the two of you kick a tremendous amount of ass together too."

We do, don't we?

"If you ever decide to give up design, you'd make a hell of a good advice columnist, you know that? Good night, Nate."

"Good night, sweetie."

SEVERAL DAYS LATER, as Lois finished her second-to-last week of her Broadway run, she also completed preparations for her meeting with Catherine Ronson. Frannie had been an enormous help, giving her a realistic—but not impossible—projection of how much she would be able to risk with the studio's purchase. In a bit of serendipitous timing, Don, her lawyer, had business already scheduled in New York, and would accompany her to the meeting. In all their discussions, he'd been cautious but optimistic, and never once tried to dissuade her. His only objections were on her behalf, trying to preemptively ward off any obstacles to her getting an ironclad deal.

Nate had, of course, come through as well. Lois had kept her expectations low. As touched as she was by Nate's faith in her, her pessimism ran deep, hard to completely shake. So she was more than a little taken aback when Nate assured her that she did indeed have—as she put it—an "army" of quiet supporters.

Her proposals and projections were ready. It was the theatre's dark night, so she could turn in early and shore up her rest ahead of the meeting—provided she could turn off her head long enough to let sleep in.

Lois stood at the window in her bedroom, looking out at the lights of the city. As had become her habit, she fingered the little charm around her neck, wishing she could have Nick's arms around her as well.

She knew she was doing the right thing, that she needed to fight her own battle, but it didn't stop her from missing him spectacularly.

And there was another reason for not telling Nick yet that she hadn't admitted to Nate. A small part of her was scared. Enough time had passed, and their separation so painful, that she couldn't help but wonder what would be left of what they'd shared. She knew how powerful their love felt to her, but what if it couldn't truly be enough? When the mess that her reputation always seemed to cause had crept in, it had hurt more than she could have imagined. And she'd run from it. She didn't want it to be a battle they always had to fight.

Lady Macbeth appeared at her feet. Her gray eyes fixed on the pendant. It was probably the irresistible lure of a shiny object, but Lois swore she saw sadness in them as they widened. Her suspicions strengthened when the cat leaned in to rub against her leg, her purr equal parts imploring and comforting.

Lois leaned down to scratch Lady M's ears. "I miss him too, Lady."

As she straightened, her finger caught on a rough edge of the pendant. She supposed she must be holding it at a different angle than usual, because she had no idea how she'd never felt the bump before. She turned it to the light, and spotted what looked like a tiny hinge, almost unnoticeable among the detailing. If there was a hinge, then her very first impression must have been correct after all. She experimented around the edges a little, and sure enough, the little film canister popped open to reveal an inscription inside.

To my very favorite director, read one side. And on the other…
With all my love, Nick.

Tears immediately sprang to Lois's eyes. She wondered why he hadn't told her to open it when he gave it to her. He'd been so shy about it. She marveled—*again*—at how much he understood of her, without her having to say a single word.

Even when he's not here, he's encouraging me to follow my dreams.

She shook her head and grinned. If she couldn't have his arms around her, she at least had his words.

Lois started. *His words.* She had more of them.

She went to the drawer in her nightstand. There was Nick's letter, the one he'd given her the day before she left, still unopened.

Sitting on the bed, she held it for a moment. She had never been able to bring herself to read it. He'd asked her to wait until she got to New York, but even then, she couldn't do it. If the littlest reminders nearly did her in, she had been afraid of what a full set of his words would do to her. And she had a job to do.

But now she couldn't find the fear. She only wanted to let his words in, do what his arms were too far away to do.

It was time.

She opened the letter and began to read.

My dearest Lois,

I wanted to say all this in person, but I honestly wasn't sure I'd be able to get it all out. I probably would have just wrapped my arms around you and held on tight, refusing to let go. And that would have made fools of both of us. So I'm turning to the page instead. This way I can say everything I want you to know.

And there's so much I want you to know. I hope you can feel all the love I want to pour into these words. All the love I have in my heart for you. You are my heart.

It's a strange feeling, knowing one's heart is all the way across the country. And I won't lie—I will miss you more than I'm even sure I can stand. I wanted very much to beg you to stay. But that wouldn't have been right. And so all I can offer you is my best wishes. And all my love. Always.

And I do offer you all of it, my love. You are going to take Broadway by storm, just like you take everything by storm. I may never recover from the way you took me.

I hope that New York is every single thing you hope for, and much more. You deserve every happiness, every success. You deserve for the world to see you for the extraordinary, talented, warm, passionate, astoundingly dazzling woman that you are.

That's the way I see you.

I realize that neither one of us can know what the future holds. But I do know this. I love you, Lois Ashford. And I always will. I meant what I said that night on the beach. I want us, for real, for good. I understand that might not fit in with your plans, and I will accept that because I will always want what's best for you. But I want you to know that when—if —you return, I will be right here, waiting, if you want me. You are worth waiting for.

So farewell, my heart. Safe travels. Break a leg. Merde. And all of that theatre luck. Not that you need it. You make your own. And you've brought it to me as well.

My heart is yours.

Always,

Nick

Lois closed her eyes. She could taste the salt on her lips, but she didn't bother to dry her face. She wanted to feel it all. Her hands were steady as she ran her fingers across the page, across Nick's beautiful words. She was calmer than she had been in weeks. Her heart expanded to fill her chest, fuller than she ever thought possible.

No, that wasn't quite right. Her heart wasn't actually in her chest. It was on the opposite coast.

Lois settled back in the bed, feeling more ready than ever to face tomorrow's meeting, to fix her past.

To start creating her future.

Chapter Twenty-Six

Hollywood Happenings
*Dearest reader, have we got a whopper to bring you tomorrow!
We've been sworn to temporary secrecy, but you can rest assured
we will bring you all the juicy little details just as soon as we
can! We'll leave you with this tiny morsel… A certain struggling
studio is about to find itself under new leadership. And you will
never—ever!—believe who it is. Oh, to be a fly on the wall in
those executive offices!*

*L*ois hovered in the reception area of the studio chief's
office at Neptune Pictures, lit with a warm glow from the
late afternoon sun. Catherine Ronson and her lawyer had
gone in first, and she waited to be called in, listening to the
increasingly raised voices coming from inside. The office manager,
Mrs. Yang, kept eyeing her warily. She was new in the years since
Lois had left the studio, and Lois wondered if her reputation
preceded her as usual, or if the woman was just responding to the
general unease filling the suite of rooms.

As she waited, Lois smoothed her jacket, smiling. Nate had

whipped up the suit for her as a gift, and it was some of her finest work. A straight black skirt skimmed mid-calf, topped with a deep emerald-green jacket that flared slightly below the waist. The jacket's neckline had a creative, swirling cut-out pattern that made a bold statement.

"Every dragon-slayer needs an appropriate suit of armor," Nate had said. "And yours should scream confidence and power."

It indeed provided a lovely boost of confidence, but that wasn't what had touched Lois the most about it. The suit jacket had interesting textured black buttons. When Lois had held them up for closer inspection, her heart had caught in her throat.

The buttons were little black film canisters. An exact match to…

"I may have gone to Nick's jeweler friend and gotten him to share his mold with me," Nate had said, with an almost defensively shy shrug. "I thought the suit needed it."

Lois had hugged her tight. She would never find enough words to express how lucky she was to have Nate's friendship in her life.

Her fingers now found the buttons' match, on a shorter chain this time for all the world to see.

She heard Ronson muttering in anger through the ajar door, and then Catherine's clear, firm tone.

"It's done, Arthur. The studio has a new owner. You're out."

"And just who the hell did you sell to?"

That's my cue.

Lois pushed open the door and sauntered in, ready.

She wished she could have a photo of Arthur Ronson's face to forever commemorate the occasion.

He stood behind the desk, eyes like saucers and jaw slacking comically. Lois simply stood there, waiting.

When he finally sputtered back to life, he turned to Catherine incredulously. "Are you kidding me with this?"

Catherine remained cool as a cucumber. "I am not. Meet the

new owner of Neptune Pictures. Lois Ashford. I believe you two are acquainted, are you not?"

"This is preposterous. She's—"

He cut himself off upon seeing Lois's face. She had to admit, she was a little disappointed. She'd been daring him with her eyes to say it, but he didn't rise to the bait.

Ronson turned to the lawyer, clearly expecting help from the other male in the room. "This cannot be possible. Tell them."

The lawyer remained calm as well, which only seemed to infuriate Ronson further, especially as his words sunk in. "I'm afraid it's more than possible, Mr. Ronson. As we've said, Mrs. Ronson's late father left a very clear legal trail."

"And his daughter has picked it up," Catherine interjected. "The studio was mine to sell, and I have done exactly that. The sale is complete. And there is absolutely nothing you can do to interfere."

He rounded the desk and came toward Lois. "And what exactly do you think you know about running a studio? You're just an actress." His disgust was palpable.

But hers was incandescent.

"See, that's the funny thing about being a pariah. When you're on the sidelines, without too many people to talk to, you have plenty of time to spend watching. Observing. Seeing everything, down to the smallest detail. You learn an awful lot about how things get done." She crossed her arms and let one corner of her mouth tilt up in a smirk. "I'd wager it's a hell of a lot more than you learn sitting in an office, up in an ivory tower all day."

His face was almost purple now. "How *dare* you? You think you're so clever. But you'll never be taken seriously. I'll ruin you. I'll—"

"What?" Lois interrupted, all mock innocence. "Tell everyone how impossible I am to work with, what a shrew I am?"

Ronson's eyes narrowed. "I've done it before."

"Yes. You have." She spread her hands wide. "And yet here I

am. With ownership of your studio. Guess it didn't work as well as you thought it did."

As he stared at her with shock, Lois raised her arm and, with a flick of her fingers, beckoned to the two guards Catherine had brought with them from the booth at the gate.

"Gentlemen, please escort Mr. Ronson out," Lois requested. "I wouldn't want him to be late for his meeting."

"Meeting?" Ronson managed, as the guards flanked him.

"Yes," Catherine answered. "My divorce attorneys are waiting. You'll find they have quite a lot to say."

His eyes went wide. At the slightest touch from the guards, he began to struggle. "You can't do this to me! I won't stand for it! Let me go, dammit!"

Lois clucked her tongue. "I'd be careful if I were you, Ronson. You wouldn't want to get a reputation for being…*difficult*."

That stunned him into momentary silence, long enough for the guards to escort him out, followed by Catherine's lawyer. He paused at the door, but Catherine waved him ahead.

"Go on, Jonathan. I'll be along in a minute."

Once they were alone, the older woman turned to Lois. "Well, I must admit, that went better than I expected."

"I think you're in for one hell of a fight from him."

"I'm sure you're right. Good thing I'm prepared for everything." She smiled as she took Lois's hands. "I am deeply sorry for what was done to you, my dear. I hope I've done enough to rectify what I wish I'd bothered to see in the first place."

"Thank you for saying that." Lois looked around the room. "And you have done quite a bit, you know."

Catherine laughed. "Well. We'll see when you officially start tomorrow. Good luck to you. I feel very good about leaving my father's legacy in your hands. I'll see you at the transition meeting in the morning."

And with that, Catherine swept out the door to rid herself of an asshole.

Lois leaned back on against the desk, letting it all sink in.

I really did it.

Mrs. Yang appeared in the doorway.

"It was impossible not to eavesdrop," she said, still wary. "Is it true, then? Ronson's out. And you're the new owner."

"Yes." Lois sensed the woman was a large part of the reason anything got done at all around here, and she wanted to make a good impression. "Mrs. Yang, I know this is going to be quite a transition, and you are under no obligation to stay. But I would very much like you to. I'm looking forward to working together. If you decide to remain, that is."

Mrs. Yang assessed her for a moment, then nodded. "Thank you. I'll stay." She squared her shoulders. "Now, what's this I hear about a transition meeting?"

Lois smiled. "Right. I'd like to schedule a meeting tomorrow morning at eleven, for all the executives, department heads, and the like, to announce the transition. As you heard, Mrs. Ronson will be there as well to try to smooth any ruffled feathers, of which I'm sure there will be many. Do you think you'd be able to help me arrange it?"

Mrs. Yang pulled out a notebook and began writing. "Absolutely. Leave all the details to me. I'll send out a memo, reserve an auditorium." She looked up. "I can be here as early as you need me tomorrow. Assuming you'll have plenty to go over before we get started?"

The woman's eagerness and efficiency instantly put Lois at ease. "That's wonderful, thank you. I'm sure…eight-thirty will be plenty early."

"Got it."

"Oh, and if it's all right with you, I'd like to have you sit down with the accounting and business manager I'm bringing in. She'll have a lot of plans and figures to go over, and I imagine no one knows this studio better than you do?"

The office manager's eyebrows lifted slightly at Lois's use of "she," but otherwise she didn't bat an eye. Her chest did inflate, however, at the compliment to her role in the studio's running.

"I'll make her transition as smooth as possible, Ms. Ashford. Anything else you need before I get started on all this?"

Lois was about to dismiss her, but her eyes lit on some hideous sculpture near the door. She took in the rest of the office for the first time, and felt her lip start to curl in disgust.

"Just one more thing. Do you think we can get a decorator in here as early as tomorrow afternoon?"

"I'm sure that can be arranged." She came to stand behind Lois's shoulder, as she muttered. "Little shit's taste always was in his ass."

A startled laugh exploded out of Lois, and she turned to look at Mrs. Yang, whose eyes widened. She seemed on the verge of apologizing.

Oh, that will never do.

Lois held up her hand before the woman could speak. "Do not even think of apologizing, Mrs. Yang. We are in complete and total agreement."

They nodded to each other and looked around the room once again.

Lois smirked. "You know, I think this—"

Mrs. Yang groaned. "Oh, no. Please tell me you're not going to quote *Casablanca* at me."

Lois laughed again. "As a matter of fact, I was not. I was simply going to say that this is all going to work out quite well."

"All right then." She started to leave, but turned around as she got to the door. "By the way, you may call me Anna."

"Okay. But only if you call me Lois."

"Deal."

Lois ran her hand across the edge of the desk. She knew she still had quite a challenge ahead of her, but with Anna Yang on her side, she felt much more confident. And her chest swelled with pride at the memory of what had just happened with Ronson. She didn't think she'd ever forget the electric jolt of throwing the bastard out of his office—now *her* office.

There was only one thing still missing.

She crossed to the doorway. "Anna, will you be all right handling things on your own right now? There's someone I need to go see."

Anna waved her off. "Of course. There's not really much for you to do until the morning anyhow. Go."

So Lois left her new studio in excellent hands and went to see to her heart.

LOIS STOOD outside Mom's Bakery, trying to calm her nerves. She didn't know what she'd find, or if Nick was even there at all, but it was her best hope of finding him. She pushed the door open and marched in, instantly and pleasantly enveloped by the heavenly scents of vanilla and sugar.

"He's right. That smell is magic, every single time," she mumbled to herself.

She heard a low chuckle from behind the counter. "Is it, now?"

Max's eyes were warm with laughter as he turned, but they widened—and promptly cooled—when they lit on her.

"Hi, Max."

"Lois. You're back."

"I am." She attempted a smile, but was fairly certain it probably came out more like a grimace. "I hate to bother you, but…I'm looking for Nick. I thought maybe I might find him here?"

Max folded his arms across his chest and considered her for what felt like an eternity. Just when Lois was positive he wasn't going to say another word, he spoke.

"You back for good?" His tone held anger, to be sure, but she thought she heard something else behind it. Anticipation? Encouragement? *Was it possible?*

"Yes. I'm here to stay."

He nodded slowly and chewed on his lip.

"I ever tell you I've got a back patio?" He examined one of his fingers, brushing flour off of it. "I mean, it's not very big or anything, but I've fixed it up. It's nice. Quiet. Most people don't even know it's there."

Lois raised her eyebrows. She had no idea what Max's pride in his patio had to do with anything, but she wasn't exactly in a position to argue with him. She was trying to find a way to bring them back to the subject of Nick without offending him when he continued.

"Nick knows it's there."

Max raised his eyes to her deliberately, and her heart picked up its pace. She took a step closer and met his gaze expectantly.

With a quick flick of his head over his shoulder, he gestured her to a small hallway off the kitchen.

"Play your cards right, and I *might* save you a piece of cheese-cake," he grumbled.

"Max." She planted a quick kiss on his cheek. "You're my hero."

"Yeah, yeah. Go." He pointed a stern finger in her face. "Do not make me regret this."

"That I can promise."

She flew down the hall, but slowed as she approached the screen door. Her breath caught in her throat when she saw him.

True to Max's word, the patio was small, with a little bench and one small table and chairs. A lattice-work trellis provided some shade, making dappled patterns on the patio's only inhabitant.

And what a magnificent inhabitant he was.

Nick sat at the table, feet propped on the opposite chair, reading a book. The remains of a pastry sat on a plate in front of him. Lois smiled at Nick's insatiable sweet tooth.

She opened the screen door and stepped out. He looked up casually, likely expecting to see Max. When he didn't, his eyes flew wide and the book thunked onto the table. He seemed momentarily paralyzed.

"Lois." His voice came out in a deep rasp.

"Hello, Nick."

Recovering himself, he swung his legs down and stood. "You're here. How did you…"

It took all her strength not to fling her arms around him. But she wasn't sure if she should. If she could. So she stayed rooted in place.

"I…I thought you might be here. I was going to go to Parkmoor, but Nate told me…"

Nick's hand came up to rub the back of his neck. "Yeah. When it was time, after I wrapped the picture with Matthews, I…I didn't renew either. Thought I'd take my chances as a free agent."

"Why?"

"I know, it probably sounds crazy given all I pulled." He shrugged. "But after everything, it just…didn't feel right to be there anymore." He finally met her eyes. "Not without you."

Her tenderness for him almost overwhelmed her. As did a terribly timed urge to laugh.

"I'm sorry; it's not funny. It's only… That makes things so much easier. I hope."

Genuine confusion flooded Nick's handsome face. "Easier?"

"I think so." She couldn't hold back a groan. "Oh, there is so much to tell you. I don't even know where to begin." She looked up at him, focusing on the gold flecks in his vibrant blue eyes to steady herself. "I guess I should start with the big news. It'll be in all the papers tomorrow, I'm sure. But I wanted to tell you before that. Arthur Ronson's out at Neptune."

"What? How?"

"Turns out ownership of the studio was ultimately in his wife's name. And she sold it right out from under him."

He laughed heartily. "Well, I'll be damned. Good for her. I'm sure he's not going quietly, though."

"He most definitely is not. Luckily, he doesn't have a leg to stand on." She smirked. "The jackass was most beautifully escorted off his own lot just a little while ago."

"Wait. If this isn't hitting the papers till tomorrow, how do you know all this?"

She drew herself up. "Because I was there. I'm the one Catherine Ronson sold the studio to."

Nick's jaw went slack, and he wore an expression of pure shock. He tried to speak several times, to no avail. Lois sympathized. She'd been right there, and still had moments when she didn't entirely believe it had really happened.

He finally found his voice. "So…you own a studio now? And not just any studio. Arthur Ronson's studio?"

"Yep."

Nick huffed a breath of laughter. "Lois, that's…" He raised pride-filled eyes to her. "That's incredible." He shook his head. "Sorry, it's gonna take a bit for it to really sink in. Can I ask… how? What made Catherine Ronson sell to you, of all people? Not that you're not great for it, it's just…"

"I know. To be honest, I'm still pretty shocked myself. It's a bit of a long story—which I will tell you later—but in a nutshell, I wrote her a letter before I left for New York. Telling her everything."

"Wow."

"Yeah. It felt like it was finally time, you know? Anyway, that letter, combined with a chance meeting she had with a certain someone who apparently sang my praises"—she quirked an eyebrow and saw a telltale blush begin on Nick's neck—"led to Catherine turning up in my dressing room one night for a very interesting conversation. And the rest is history."

"I had no idea when I ran into her that she knew. I would have…" His mouth twisted. "Okay, I honestly don't know what I might have done differently if I had."

"Well, whatever you said had her pretty convinced I'd be worth taking a chance on, so…thanks."

His eyes blazed now. "I only spoke the truth."

"Come with me," she blurted. "Partner with me. I was going to try to poach you from Parkmoor, but now I don't have to. I… This is our chance. All those things we talked about doing, the crazy dreams of having our own studio. Let's do them. Together."

Nick didn't mask his surprise. She could tell he was tempted, but hesitation hovered in his gaze too. A wariness she'd put there.

"Lois, what are you saying? Because I'm not sure I could only *work* with…" He trailed off, but continued before she could interject. "And you don't need a partner."

"No. I don't."

He shoved his hands in his pockets, avoiding her eyes.

"But I *want* one," she said. Nick's eyes flew to hers. "Actually, that's not entirely true. I don't want just any partner. I want you, Nick. You're the only partner I'll ever want."

She could see the dawn breaking on his face.

"But…aren't you worried about being taken seriously? About being judged in relation to me?"

Lois took a step closer to him. "Honestly? I am so damn tired of caring what anyone else thinks. I'm through with trying to fit myself into someone else's narrative, fighting when they won't let me in. I'm in charge of my own narrative now. And I have a beautiful opportunity, *finally*, to make some waves. To make them take notice. To tell *my* story, *my* way."

She closed the distance and grasped Nick's hands. "And you are a part of that story, Nick Bradley. A big, important, wonderful part."

"Yeah?" He blinked against the gathering moisture in his eyes.

Lois nodded, feeling her own tears coming. "I needed to get away from this town, to prove to myself that I could, I think. I was so angry, so frustrated that things just never seemed to change. You became my safe harbor, my hope that maybe things could, after all. But then the mess wormed its way into even that. I was furious. At the studio, at the columnists. And at myself, for allowing the hope in. I was so afraid of losing myself in this"—she gestured between them—"in us. And I let that fear push you out of my life."

She took a deep breath. "Going to New York was right, for a lot of reasons. And I don't know that any of what's happened would have if I hadn't gone." She placed a tentative hand on Nick's chest. "But god, I missed you."

Nick closed his eyes as a sound escaped his throat, part gulp and part laugh. He covered her hand with his own. "You have no idea how shitty it's been without you."

Lois laughed as well. "Oh, I think I have some idea." She raised a hand to cup his cheek, and he leaned into her touch, his eyes still closed. "When Catherine came to me with her offer, I was so shocked and excited. It was everything I ever wanted. But it wouldn't be nearly as much fun without you."

He opened his eyes, and Lois could see that familiar, lovely glint of amusement behind them. "I am fun."

She smiled up at him. "You are." She brought her other hand up and framed his face. "You gave me an extraordinary gift, you know. You helped me remember how to hope. How to dream. And in every one of my dreams, you're right there beside me, my love. So."

Lois took a step back and squared her shoulders. She took Nick's hands in her own and extended her leg back in preparation. Before she could go too far, her movements were arrested. She tried again, frustration mounting.

"Shit," she hissed.

Nick looked at her with concern. "Are you all right?"

"I'm fine. I just…" She deflated with a groan. "I had this all planned on the way over here. I was going to turn convention on its ear. Get down on one knee." She bit her lip, venturing to meet his gaze. "But Nate made this stupid skirt too damn tight!"

Nick threw his head back and laughed. It was the best thing Lois had ever heard.

She allowed herself a moment of her own laughter before composing herself.

"I'll just have to do this standing up then." She squeezed Nick's hands. "That beautiful night in Santa Barbara, you asked me a question. I should have answered then, because I sure as hell knew what I wanted. But I didn't, and I am so very sorry that my leaving—and hurting you—had to happen before I could give you that answer."

A tear rolled down her cheek, and she could feel Nick's hand jerk, as if he wanted to brush it away. But she held tighter, refusing to let go.

"I love you, Nick Bradley. With all my heart. You make me laugh. You give me hope. You make me feel safer than I ever thought I could be. And I want you by my side. In everything. Always. So will you do me the great honor of staying married to me? For real?"

Nick's lips broke into a dazzling grin as his own tears made their way down his cheeks. He broke free of her grasp to cup her face.

"Lois Ashford, there is nothing in this world that would make me happier. Yes, my heart. Yes."

Their mouths finally came together. They were soft, slow at first, simply reveling in the taste of each other again. But then all the yearning of the past few months took over, and their kiss turned passionate, hungry. They gripped each other tightly, both of them unsteady on their feet.

They finally broke apart, resting their foreheads together and exhaling twin sighs of relief.

Nick opened his eyes, and Lois noticed his attention catch somewhere on her chest.

"Those buttons. Are they...?"

"They are."

"Nate strikes again?"

Lois nodded, and they both laughed.

It felt so very *right* to be laughing with Nick again.

"You were wonderful in that play, you know," he said softly. "Granted, I might be a little biased, but I've never seen anyone with such a luminous presence on stage."

"Thanks." Her head snapped up. "Wait. Were you...? You saw it?"

The corners of his mouth crept up shyly. "There was no way I was going to miss it. I was there opening night, tucked up in the balcony."

"But…I had no idea. Why didn't you say anything?"

"I didn't think I should. If anyone knew I was there, that would have been the story." He brushed her cheek with his thumb. "And it needed to be your story."

Lois's eyes filled again. "But you were there."

"I had to be."

She kissed him again. Every time she thought her heart couldn't be fuller, Nick found new ways to make it overflow.

Lois hated to break the kiss, but she suddenly remembered what she'd brought with her. She handed him the little package, wrapped in simple brown paper.

"I almost forgot, I brought you something."

Curious, he unwrapped it, eyes softening further when he saw the intricately designed cover. "*Pygmalion*. Lois."

"I was at the Drama Book Shop and spotted it." She shrugged. "Okay, I went there looking especially for it. For you. I thought you should have another for your collection."

"It's my new favorite." He brought his hand up to her face again. "You're my favorite."

"Good. Because you're mine."

Another kiss, and time was suspended once again.

Nick chuckled as he broke this one. "Man, I wish I could've seen Ronson's face."

"Oh, Nick, it was priceless. I can't even begin to tell you."

"I'll bet."

Out of nowhere, the gravity of everything she'd done, and everything that lay ahead of her, came crashing down.

Nick noticed, and peered down to examine her face. "Lois?"

"Oh my god." Her eyes flew to his. "I own a studio, Nick. A fucking *studio*. What have I gotten myself into? Am I crazy?"

He smiled. "Probably."

She rolled her eyes.

"But if anyone can do it, it's you." His smile grew. "It's us."

"It is us." She sighed. "It's going to be tricky."

"Would you really want it to be any other way?"

She snorted. "No."

Nick cocked his head to one side. "The road ahead may be tricky, but I know one thing it won't be. Not for you."

"What's that?"

A slow grin curved his mouth. "Difficult."

She laughed. Oh, how she loved this man. She slid her arms around his neck and pulled him into a tight embrace, ready to begin this new, exciting chapter of their life together. And certain of how right Nick was.

Lois Ashford was through with being difficult.

Epilogue

***The Latest Reviews from Your Friends at Photoplay!**
Lois Ashford & Nick Bradley have finally made another comedy,
their first together under the Phoenix Pictures banner. Ashford is
at last returning to her roots, after a year of fewer-than-expected
growing pains at the helm of her studio. (We hear she, with
Bradley's help, has been really revolutionizing the place over
there, and based on the quality of this—and their other recent
pictures—we believe it! Who'd-a-thunk it?) Their new vehicle is
a welcome breath of fresh air, albeit with one small caveat: You'd
think after over a year of marriage, along with running a studio,
their smoldering chemistry would have dialed down a few
notches, but it hasn't. At all. Their glances alone are enough to
scorch a hole in the screen. You might want to leave the kiddos at
home for this one!*

One Year Later

Lois stood at the window behind her desk, surveying the
lot beyond it. Several productions were in progress in
those buildings, including the studio's first foray into television. It made most of the executives nervous, but Lois felt confi-

dent that it was more than just a fad to be temporarily cashed in on.

She still couldn't quite believe how many of the studio's personnel had stayed on when she took over. Naturally, there had been some exodus—those who objected to Lois in particular, and those who just outright refused to work for a woman. It had been good riddance to them.

But Lois had underestimated just how reviled Arthur Ronson had been, not just by her. A tremendous amount of studio employees at all levels had hated working for him, but kept quiet for fear of losing their jobs or appearing disloyal to the beloved founder who had installed his son-in-law as chief, if not owner.

Enough of them were willing to give Lois a chance, and it was paying off. The studio had become a happier, more productive place.

One of the biggest surprises had been Nate's defection from Parkmoor. Lois still didn't know how she'd finagled her way out of her contract, but it thrilled her to install Nate as the new head of the costume department, and not only because the position had been vacated by one of the "good riddance" bunch.

Frannie had settled in beautifully as well. Lois knew she faced an especially fraught situation, given the male-dominated finance department. But luckily, they all had a good amount of respect—along with a healthy dose of fear—for Anna Yang. And Anna and Frannie had become quite the formidable team.

The studio still had a ways to go in reversing the downward slope that had originated before Lois took over, and in earning the clout afforded to other production houses, but it was certainly on its way.

And now that the dust had finally started to settle, Lois was preparing for her first film as a director. It would begin shooting soon, and she had to admit she was filled with a few nerves—and a lot more excitement.

Lois was still watching her empire when the door burst open and her heart strode into the room, waving a sheaf of paper.

"Have you seen Colin's new script? It's brilliant! Do you think it would be unethical if I used my position to poach the lead role from Mike Griffiths?"

Lois laughed as she rounded the desk and rested her hands on Nick's shoulders. "As much as I hate to burst your bubble, darling, yes. I'm afraid it would be terribly unethical. And that's not the kind of studio we're trying to run here."

He tossed the script on the desk and slipped his arms around her waist. "I know. It's just so good."

She kissed him. As was typical, their lips worked magic together and made them both temporarily forget everything else.

When they broke apart, Nick looked wistfully down at the script again.

Lois stepped back and gave him a playful shove. "And don't think for a minute you can kiss me into changing my mind. You know I'm right."

Nick grinned. "I wouldn't dream of it. I just enjoy kissing you, that's all."

"The feeling is mutual, I'm sure." She gestured to the pages as she half-sat on the edge of the desk. "So it's another winner?"

"Such a winner. All jealousy aside, I'm telling you, that man and his typewriter are the best things you could have imported from New York."

"Well, my Broadway debut wouldn't have been half the success it was without his words. I'm glad he's fitting in at Phoenix."

Lois had changed the studio's name from Neptune to signify the new era, and most everyone had supported the decision enthusiastically. After a flash of inspiration, she'd decided that Phoenix Pictures had a nice ring to it—and felt entirely appropriate. The only protest had come jokingly from Nick, who made an exaggerated show of being highly offended that they'd have to use a bird for their mascot instead of a dope-smoking cartoon turd. But he'd given in, since they were putting the past behind them and looking to the future.

"Colin's revolutionizing the comedy division, that's for sure."

Lois eyed her husband lovingly. "You sure it's just him?"

Nick blushed endearingly before putting on a cocky air and leaning against the desk next to her. "I may have some skills."

"Hey, that reminds me—did you see the reviews of our latest? Definitely an improvement over the last batch."

"Mostly. *Photoplay* was a little insulting."

"Insulting? How?"

"They implied our chemistry was almost indecent, as if they were scandalized." He straightened and pulled Lois close again. "There's nothing whatsoever scandalous about us."

Lois threaded her arms around his neck. "Definitely not. Although they weren't entirely wrong about our chemistry."

Desire darkened his eyes and he let out a low rumble. "We do have a talent for indecency."

She brought her mouth a hairsbreadth from his. "It's one of my very favorite things about us."

He closed the gap and they shared a long, delicious kiss. He brought his lips to her ear, and his warm bass sent a shiver down to her toes.

"How long till Mrs. Yang gets back from lunch?"

Lois ran her nails along the spot where Nick's hair met his neck, delighting in his echoing shiver. "We've got a good, solid half-hour."

Nick let her go to lock the door. She barely had time to lament the cold left in his wake when he turned back to her, his eyes raking over her with a fierce hunger.

"Would you care to be indecent with me?" he growled.

She stalked toward him. "Always."

They stumbled to the couch together, laughing as they crashed down onto it. Nick looked down at her with the most exquisite mixture of tenderness and desire.

"I will never tire of your smile, you know that?" Nick whispered.

Said smile grew wider at that. "What a coincidence. I was just thinking the same thing about you."

"Fancy that."

Lois hummed her approval as she pulled his head down to hers, their desire setting them both ablaze. She had no cares about their reducing each other to ashes.

This was the aptly named Phoenix Pictures, after all.

Acknowledgments

First of all, thank you, dear readers, for picking up this book and taking a chance on me and the fictional version of classic Hollywood I've created. I hope you've enjoyed reading about Lois and Nick and all their friends as much as I've enjoyed having them live rent-free in my head for the last few years.

I most certainly could not have brought this book into the world without the help and support of some very special people. My fellow Sploosh Sisters—Daria Vernon, Amanda Pereira, Genevieve Kersten, and Jillian Graves—are the very best critique group I could have asked for. You all helped me shape this book into its best version, and your cheerleading and affection for my characters warms me no end. And your friendship and support over the strange roller coaster of the last year and a half has meant the world to me.

Thanks to my editor, Michele Chiappetta of Three Point Author Services—you helped me polish my book with a thoughtful eye, and were such a pleasure to work with. Thanks for answering all my many questions, and for assisting me in making sure Lois was a responsible cat owner!

To my cover designer, Daybed Books—thank you for so perfectly bringing Lois and Nick to life and capturing the spirit of this book. You took my vague "it'd be cool if it looked like a classic film poster" and turned it into a stunningly beautiful cover that gives me all the heart-eyes every time I look at it.

Lauren Smith, you have been so generous with your time and advice about self-publishing and all its many ins and outs. You helped make navigating the process a lot less daunting and scary.

I owe a great deal of thanks to The Ripped Bodice bookstore in Los Angeles. Not only did I meet my Sploosh Sisters there, but the very first time I ever showed anyone a piece of this book was at one of their writing workshops. It is also through their many classes and events that I met Jeanne De Vita. Jeanne, I am super grateful for all of your continued support and encouragement, the writing advice and expertise you so generously offer, and for your friendship.

Thank you to Kat from TBQ's Book Palace for your early beta-read of *Difficult* and for your feedback that let me know I was on the right track. Thanks to Rachel Rozdzial for your fantastic beta feedback as well—I'm so glad we exchanged work and I can't wait to see your characters in readers' hands too. And thanks to Heather, Megan, and Tiffany for being so excited to read this book —you were among the first to read it in its entirety, and your encouragement and support meant so much.

I'd also like to send a special shout-out to the Wicked Wallflowers Coven on Facebook. Jenny and Sarah, you've created not only a fantastic podcast, but also one of my favorite places to hang out on social media. And to all of the absolutely lovely people in the Coven—thank you for making me laugh, sharing thirst traps on the regular, and being the best, most supportive cheering section. You've provided exactly the warm virtual hug I've needed on many an occasion.

This is not an ad, but I would be remiss if I didn't thank the 40s Junction channel on Sirius XM for existing, and providing an excellent soundtrack to get me "in the mood" while writing this time period. I also have tremendous gratitude for the late, great Robert Osborne and everyone at Turner Classic Movies for supplying me with endless amounts of classic film trivia that I've been storing in my mind for years, in preparation for the moment when I sat down to write this series—even before I knew that was my plan.

To Kat, Cathy, Julie, and Meg—I will be forever grateful for your friendship, your sisterhood. I love you all, and I am so glad we've been in each other's lives for so long, navigating all the ups and downs together. And to Mady and Amelia—you are my favorite young storytellers, and I cannot wait to see the mark you make on the world. Your belief in my magic humbles me and gives me a boost whenever I need it most.

All of my friends and family who have supported my writing journey with such excitement and encouragement—thank you for your kind words and warm wishes.

To my Dad—I don't even know where to begin to thank you for being, overall, the best dad, and more specifically, the best writing cheerleader. Your excitement over my forging a writing career has meant so, so much to me, as has your support over the details and minutiae of publishing this book. I love talking writing with you, and I absolutely could not have done any of this without you.

And my Mom. I still can't quite believe you're not here with me, and I wish so much you could have gotten to see the finished version of this book. Your encouragement of my artistic pursuits, your example, your *love*, absolutely shaped me into the woman I am today. And so much of my writing I owe to you as well—my deep appreciation of classic films, love stories with happy endings, chest hair, and so much more were imprinted on me from an early age at your side. I love you and I miss you every day.

About the Author

Brianne Gillen is a romance author, costume designer, theatre educator, and life-long storyteller, based in the Los Angeles area. She loves classic films, especially the screwball comedies of the '30s and '40s, and will never turn down the opportunity to browse the treasure troves otherwise known as vintage clothing stores. She is also a voracious reader and firm believer in happily-ever-afters. She has done a bit of playwriting, and in recent years, has contributed her opinions to a few online publications centering on the art and craft of costume design. *Difficult* is her debut romance novel.

www.briannegillen.com

twitter.com/BooksbyBrianne
instagram.com/booksbybrianne

Coming Soon...Stay Tuned for Nate's Story!

SINGLE INDEMNITY, BOOK 2 OF THE PHOENIX PICTURES
SERIES

For news, updates, & sneak peeks,

sign up for Brianne's newsletter:

Subscribe at www.briannegillen.com

www.ingramcontent.com/pod-product-compliance
Lightning Source LLC
Chambersburg PA
CBHW031622100726

47898CB00006B/1908